Table of Contents

Part 3

I dedicate this book to two of my favorite people.

My sweet daughter, Charlotte and
My wonderful sister, Susan

In memory of my parents, Bill and Sanjean Oakley
and
My funny, loving Casey

Prologue

"Kristy! Kristy, help me! You have to save me, please!" Kristy Garrison wakes up to the desperate calling of her name. In a sleepy daze, she asks her husband, Robby, if he heard a voice calling her. Kristy is a heavy sleeper and it takes her a few extra minutes to wake up and comprehend what is happening. Her firefighter husband only needs six hours sleep so he gets up first in the morning to be with their almost five-year-old son, Logan. She is amazed at the energy Robby has in the morning when she can't function without a cup of coffee and a shower.

Kristy, help me! I need your help!" Robby doesn't answer so Kristy rolls over to ask him again. Panic sets in when she realizes her husband's side of the bed is empty, "Help me!" She hears the voice but louder this time. There is no doubt in her mind the voice is Robby's. She leans over to her bedside table and finds her glasses. With the darkness and her shaky hands, she barely gets them on her face.

She yells, "Robby! Robby is that you? Where are you?"

"Kristy, I'm here and I can't hold on for much longer!"

Kristy begins to panic. Her husband is in trouble and she doesn't know where he is. With the room pitch black, she feels her way down to the end of the bed and reaches the door to their bedroom with a thud, "Kristy are you there! Please help me!"

She grabs the doorknob and clumsily turns it. Kristy yells as she opens the door into the hall, "Robby, I'm coming!"

In the hall, she doesn't know which way to go. Kristy stops to listen for his voice but all she hears is her own pounding heart and quick shallow breath. Feeling frustrated, tears roll down her cheeks. Kristy finds the hall light and flips the light switch. Still darkness. Franticly flipping the light switch up and down, she hopes it will eventually turn on. Kristy calls out for Robby. He responds by calling her name. It comes from behind her in their bedroom.

She runs back into their room and instead of total darkness, it is eerily lit up by an orange glow coming from outside the bedroom windows. Kristy sees flames surrounding the whole room.

"Kristy, help me!" She could tell his voice is getting weaker but now knows he is calling from outside on the bedroom balcony. She runs to the balcony door as the room fills up with smoke.

Coughing, she tries to yell over the roar of the fire, "I'm coming sweetheart. I'm almost there!" She opens the door and has to cover her face from the extreme heat. Flames are shooting up all around the balcony. Finding it hard to see, she yells, "Where are you Robby?"

"I'm over here. The railing!" His voice comes from the left. Through the dense smoke, she sees two strong, sooty hands clinging to the railing. She runs over and grabs onto Robby's wrists. Looking over the railing, Kristy sees his dirty frightened face looking up at her. She can't hear what he is saying but can tell he is pleading with her to help him.

Trying to pull him up, Kristy feels him slipping from her grasp. Robby closes his eyes and shakes his head as if telling her it is no use. She tries with all of her might to hang on to him and not let go. She can feel the sweat forming between their hands. In slow motion, Robby begins to slip away from her. He opens his beautiful aqua-blue eyes and she sees tears streaming down his blackened cheeks. He mouths the words, "I love you and Logan so much." Still grabbing for his hands, she watches in horror as he disappears into the flames.

With fresh tears filling her eyes, Kristy lets out a chilling scream. She cries out, "I'm so sorry darling. I'm sorry I couldn't save you. Robby, please forgive me," sobbing, she leans against the railing and covers her face with her hands. She mumbles "Robby" repeatedly.

Part 1

I decided, very early on, just to accept life unconditionally;
I never expected it to do anything special for me, yet I seemed to
accomplish far more than I had ever hoped.
Most of the time it just happened to me without my ever seeking it.

—Audrey Hepburn

Chapter 1

Kristy's wet eyes flew open and she gasped. She looked around and confusion set in. With her heart racing, she wiped sweat and tears off her face. She looked towards the balcony and realized there was no fire. She lay back against her pillow and rolled to her right side. She buried her face into her pillow and started sobbing uncontrollably. She was having that horrible reoccurring nightmare. This time it felt very real.

Her grief counsellor told her she was having this particular nightmare because she felt responsible for her husband's accident. It happened only five short months ago but her guilt was getting stronger.

On the night of the accident, Robby should have been home babysitting Logan. She had plans to go out with her friends, Becky and Mary-Sue but Kristy could feel a cold setting in so she decided to stay home. Robby had heard that a huge barn fire was burning outside of Guthrie and since she was staying home, he thought he should go out to help. Kristy was fine with it since Logan was already in bed and she was heading to bed too. She didn't let him kiss her on the lips because she didn't want him to catch her cold. Robby kissed his wife on the forehead and said. "I love you. I hope you feel better when I see you in the morning." That was the last conversation she had with her husband. She felt so much guilt and couldn't stop thinking, *what if I had gone out.* Robby would have stayed home to look after Logan instead of going to that fire.

Sitting up and clutching her pillow, she yelled through her sobs, "What did I do wrong? Why am I being punished with this nightmare?" Pausing, she felt a trickle of sweat roll down her side. Kristy cried out loud, "Why am I sweating like a pig?"

Lying back down on her pillow, she closed her eyes and took a few deep breaths and fanned herself with a book until she finally stopped crying. Calming down, Kristy realized her whole body was wringing wet with sweat. She also noticed the room was too quiet. "Oh great! That damned air conditioner has shut off again." She let out another suppressed yell and started to choke on the hot, thick, July air.

Unable to take the pressure any more, Kristy leaned down on the side of the bed and grabbed the first thing she found. She picked it up and threw it at the air conditioner. She waited for the loud thud but only heard the squeak of Logan's toy penguin. She became enraged and jumped out of bed to hunt for something else. She found her sneaker, which satisfied her. Running over to the air conditioning unit installed in her bedroom wall she started hitting it. Between hits, she yelled, "Why do you have to stop working all the time?" She hit it from the left, "Why is everything in the house and my life falling apart?" She hit it from the right, "Why is my husband laying in a nursing home unable to put his arms around me?" The hits became slower but her crying got harder, "I don't know how I can go on. I am not strong enough to take care of Logan, Robby and everything," Kristy leaned up against the wall and slid down it so she was sitting on the floor. She hugged her knees and sobbed into them. She begged, "Please God, please help me. Please give me the strength to get through this for my little boy," softly crying, Kristy repeated, "Please help me?" Over and over again.

Suddenly, a loud clank sounded next to her and the air conditioner turned on. She turned to the whirring noise coming out of the wall in disbelief. Finding this funny, she started to laugh and cry at the same time. She got up and stood in front of the cool air. She looked up to the ceiling and said, "Thank you God. This is a start."

Kristy stood in front of the air conditioner with her arms spread out to her side. Between the Oklahoma summer heat, her nightmare and the adrenaline flowing through her, it took about five minutes before she cooled down.

Kristy sat down on her bed with a clearer head. She realized that she needed those mini-meltdowns to help her release from the stress she was under. Squinting at the clock on her bedside table, she saw that it was only 5:30 in the morning. It was too late to go back to sleep since she was getting up at 6:00 anyway.

She grabbed her glasses and put them on. The darkness was lessening with the dawn of the morning. She lay back on her bed exhausted and closed her eyes. She pictured her handsome husband Robby on the first day she met him.

Holding tightly to her mother's hand, five-year-old Kristy was walking towards the big doors of Central Elementary School for her first day of kindergarten. As they got closer, she held on to the back of her mother's skirt trying to hide from what was about to come. Her brother Cliff, who was four years older than her, told her the many horrible things that happened at school. He also told her, Miss Hughes, her kindergarten teacher was mean and had black eyes like a witch. He also told her, "Not too many kids know that she has worms in her ears and spiders in her hair." There was no way Kristy was going to get near her.

Her family had just moved to Guthrie, Oklahoma the year before from Mountain Home, Arkansas. Guthrie is north of Oklahoma City with a population of about 13,000 people. Her father had been hired as the Green's Keeper at the Golf and Country Club. Later, he would become the Club Manager, a position he held for many years.

Darren Baker was tall with dark blonde, curly hair, blue eyes and a deep dimple on his right cheek. He grew up in and around Barnsdall, Oklahoma where Darren's father worked for an oil company in the little community of Wolco, not far from Barnsdall. After graduating from Barnsdall High School, Darren moved to Tulsa to become a landscape architect. Golf was his passion and his dream was to design golf courses one day. Being a poor student, he found it hard to buy clubs and pay the green fees to golf. Not to be defeated, he got a job at the nicest golf club in the city. He would get up every day before dawn and mow miles of greens, tees and fairways. Darren would be finished by 9:00 and would take a quick shower at the club. Since he didn't own a car, he would ride his bike to University and usually made it into class two steps before his professor. Darren would be finished his classes by 3:30 so he would ride back to the golf club to golf as many holes as he could before it got too dark. Darren Baker was a very good golfer and on the weekends, he would make a lot of money caddying for the rich members.

It was while he was working at the golf and country club that he noticed a beautiful, long legged tennis pro named Anne Taradale. Anne was half Choctaw Indian with a dark complexion, high cheekbones, beautiful hazel brown eyes and long dark, silky hair usually pulled back into a ponytail or braid. Darren wasn't the only male to notice Anne. She had many suitors; members and other employees, who would usually show up to watch her play or teach tennis. Some of these guys had fancy cars and could take her out on fabulous dates. Deciding he had no chance, Darren decided to stop flirting with Anne. To get over her, he just ignored her. What Darren didn't know, Anne had developed a little crush on him. She found him very funny and charming, and that dimple made her weak in the knees when he smiled. She was a little hurt when he stopped talking to her. She wasn't used to men ignoring her. Anne decided that she wasn't going to give up on him and started pursuing him. Darren, even though he tried to convince her he wasn't good enough for her, gave in. The result was a little family of golfers and tennis players.

Kristy's older brother, Clifford, was fair like his father and Kristy was the spitting image of her beautiful Choctaw mother. Her father was very concerned with the male attention that he knew was coming when Kristy got older.

Cliff was quite rebellious and fought with his parents when he was a teenager. He was in trouble with the police for minor things like public drunkenness, smoking pot behind the Masonic Lodge and drag racing through the center of town. He loved to golf and thought that he was on his way to becoming a golf pro. He refused to go to college and didn't think he needed to make other plans for his future. In his mind, he was going to turn pro and travel the world making millions. Of course, he wasn't disciplined enough and would not take advice from anyone. He could never qualify for even the state golf tournaments because he refused to be coached. Cliff was convinced that he didn't qualify because of the crappy golf clubs he had. He became furious with his parents when they wouldn't loan him the money to buy new, expensive ones.

Cliff had broken off all contact with his family and moved to Las Vegas. He got a job at one of the resorts as an assistant manager in the golf pro shop and married a waitress from one of the resort's restaurants. Their marriage lasted only seven months. Cliff was caught cheating on his wife with the many women that came to Vegas on holiday. He would find rich, lonely or single woman and con them into thinking he was a golf pro. For a hefty price, he would give women golf lessons and would usually end up in their hotel room.

Darren, and especially Anne, were heart broken when he disappeared. They knew that he was on a destructive life path but would have to learn his lessons the hard way. Cliff only wanted money, not advice from his parents.

Kristy really didn't miss her brother. He had tormented and fought with her for most of her life. He was very mean to her so there was no love lost when he left.

Tragedy struck Kristy when she was a newlywed. Her parents were driving back from Anadarko when a speeding drunk driver lost control of his pick-up truck. He swerved into their lane and hit them head on.

Kristy was the sole beneficiary to her parent's will. She inherited the house she grew up in and everything in it. It was hard, at first, living in their house surrounded by their things. She and Robby barely had a bed in their tiny apartment so it turned out to be a blessing for them. Kristy eventually saw the house as having wonderful memories of her parents and after Logan was born, she shared many of them with him.

Kristy's memory of her first day of kindergarten was so vivid. She smiled to herself when she recalled seeing another five-year-old clinging to his mother. Oddly, this made her feel better. The blonde little boy was crying his eyes out and she couldn't help staring at him. His watering, aqua-blue eyes mesmerized her. They reminded her of the ocean where they had been that summer.

The little boy who was smaller than she was, felt very uncomfortable and embarrassed by her staring. He looked at Kristy and stuck out his tongue at her. She found this to be very rude and very mean. She turned away from him and marched right into the school. She knew right then and there that this rude, crybaby boy would never, ever be her friend.

Coming back to present day, Kristy thanked God her son Logan had inherited those gorgeous aqua-blue eyes. People would stop Kristy and comment on what a beautiful boy he was. He not only inherited his Dad's eyes but he inherited Kristy's dark hair and complexion. The combination was unusual and stunning.

Chapter 2

Kristy had just finished her second cup of coffee when she heard a little voice coming from upstairs. She was grateful she could calm herself down before Logan got up. Kristy promised herself that whatever happened, she would never show fear and unhappiness in front of her son. He had gone through so much when his father, his hero, had been fighting a barn fire and the upper loft he was on collapsed. Robby had lost his balance and fallen backwards through the floor. His head smashed on the cement floor. Even with all his safety equipment on, the impact was devastating. The doctors weren't sure if Robby was going to make it through the night because he suffered severe trauma to his head and neck. By some miracle, and Robby's stubbornness, he pulled through but was in a coma for two months. When he came out of his coma, he remained in a persistent vegetative state and required constant care in a nursing home in Guthrie. To Kristy's heartache, he would never come home.

Kristy Baker and Robby Garrison had known each other from kindergarten and true to her promise; she tried not to have anything to do with him. They had had a rocky relationship all through elementary school. Robby loved to bug Kristy because he could always get a reaction from her. She usually gave her opinion of him loud and clear and so he started calling her 'Big Priss'. She was never afraid of him or the other boys and would stand up to them or cunningly let Robby's mom know what they were up to.

They lived across the alley from one another on the "Egg". The Egg was a block of houses in the shape of an oval with an alley running down the middle. Every time Kristy went out to play, Robby was outside too. Walking to and from school with her best friends, Becky Berry and Mary-Sue James, Robby and his "gang" of annoying friends would walk either in front teasing the girls or behind them throwing things and laughing. At school, they couldn't get away from each other. The school was small so they were in the same classes all the way through elementary school. The worst part was, their parents were very good friends. The two enemies were forced to go over to each other's houses for barbeques or dinners. Robby had a sister, Peggy, who was two years older and thought Kristy's older brother, Cliff, was a jerk. She and Kristy would hang out together and let their pesky brothers entertain themselves.

On a late August morning, just before sixth grade, Kristy noticed a moving van in the alley behind the Garrison's house. She saw her mother talking to Mrs. Garrison next to the truck. Kristy ran out and without thinking, interrupted the ladies in the middle of their conversation.

"What's going on? Why are those men putting your stuff on the truck?" she practically yelled at her.

Mrs. Garrison looked at Kristy and smiled, "Honey, we're moving to Dallas so I can look after my sick parents. Mr. Garrison was able to transfer there and he must start work next week. We weren't expecting to leave so soon, but it is probably for the best that we do."

Stunned, Kristy turned and ran back into her house and up to her room. Once she closed the door behind her, she let out a huge sob. She must have cried for five minutes. When she calmed down, her mind was just whirling with confusion. She should be elated that her nemesis, Robby Garrison, was moving. But why was she so sad about it?

Later, at the Country Club pool, Kristy told the news to her friends and they reacted the same way as Kristy. They were all upset so none of them really wanted to swim.

Things didn't change that much in Guthrie and they liked it that way. Secretly they had liked the attention Robby and his friends gave them, even though it wasn't very nice.

After a bit of an adjustment, life went on for Kristy and her friends. With Robby not there, the boys had no interest in fighting with the girls. As a matter of fact, they pretty much ignored the girls.

Kristy made the honor roll every semester through junior high, was on the school's tennis team, volunteered at the hospital every Thursday afternoon and loved going into Oklahoma City on Saturdays to catch the latest movie or go shopping. During summer vacation, Kristy and every kid in Guthrie, hung out every day at the country club. Things were changing between the boys and girls. The opposite sex was looking better and better.

Just when Kristy thought she had forgotten Robby Garrison, he moved back into her life the summer before their sophomore year. It was a sunny June morning when Kristy, Becky and Mary-Sue had just finished a golf lesson at the country club. They were hot and sticky and couldn't wait to get into the pool before they had to go to work at the new two-screen-movie theater that had just opened. Becky and Mary-Sue were walking in front of Kristy complaining about how hot it was on the golf course when they suddenly stopped dead in their tracks. Kristy ran right into the back of them causing her to drop the lemonade she had just bought.

Bending down to try to scoop up the ice scattered on the pool deck, Kristy said, "Oh great guys. Next time, please give me a warning before you decide to stop like that. Look at the mess."

Kristy then heard a deep voice say, "Well, Baker, it looks like you haven't changed a bit. You're still a big klutz."

The hair on Kristy's neck stood on end and a big shiver ran down her back. She looked up and saw a tall, tanned lifeguard with sun-bleached hair. It wasn't until he took off his sunglasses that she recognized the incredible aqua-blue eyes of Robby Garrison. So many things were going through her head that she had a very hard time getting her words out. "I, um, well, what, um, doing?"

"Well, well, this is a first. I didn't think I would see the day that bossy Kristy Baker would be at a loss for words." Robby laughed.

Becky and Mary-Sue were no help either. They just stood there with their mouths wide open. Finally, Becky reached down and helped Kristy to her feet.

Walking past Kristy, Robby said, "Well, I guess I had better find you a mop. This little mess of yours could be a potential hazard."

Kristy let out the breath she was holding and looked at her friends. Mary-Sue said, "Oh my God. Robby Garrison is back in Guthrie."

Becky piped in, "He is soooo cute. He was such a scrawny, annoying pest, when we knew him before."

Kristy swatted Becky on the shoulder; upset she could say that about Robby. All the horrible things that Robby had done to them played back in her mind like a bad movie. She said, "I can't believe that the first time I see him in what, three years, I have lemonade all over me. I always gave him ammunition for teasing me," looking towards the lifeguard office, she saw him coming back holding a wet mop, "Shhh, here he comes."

Kristy took a calming breath and gave Robby a sarcastic smile. He held out the mop and said, "Here you go Baker. You better hurry, it's starting to dry which will leave a nice sticky mess."

Kristy, turned red from embarrassment then anger, said through her teeth, "Since when do the club members have to clean up? I am sure that my father, you know, the General Manager of the club, would be very upset if he saw one of the members mopping the pool deck. You work here so it's your job," feeling very proud of her come back, Kristy locked arms with Becky and Mary-Sue and said to Robby with a smirk, "See ya pool boy."

The three girls didn't look back to see Robby's reaction. They could feel him glaring at the back of their heads. Becky looked at Kristy and said, "I can't believe you just said that to him."

Mary-Sue added, "He is going to make your life miserable this summer. It is already like it was before he moved to Dallas. You guys couldn't get along then and it looks like you won't now. We are going back to war I think."

Kristy replied, "Oh come on you guys. He started it by embarrassing me and I was letting him know that he can't treat me like he used to. He had his chance to be nice and helpful but he was an immature jerk. Now, I am boiling to death. Can we go swimming and please no more lectures?"

All three jumped into the pool. Kristy could see that Robby was just finishing cleaning up her mess. She was satisfied that she treated Robbie justifiably. Her friends were swooning over how good-looking he was and that spoiled her self-praise. "He has grown so tall and his eyes are so gorgeous," Becky said looking over her shoulder at him.

Kristy said out loud to her friends, "Anyone can look good with a tan." Becky and Mary-Sue both rolled their eyes and dove under the water. In Kristy's mind, Robby was the same mean boy that lived across the alley from her so many years ago.

Chapter 3

Mary-Sue's prediction of Robby making Kristy's life miserable came true. The week after their first encounter was horrible. Kristy wanted to stop going to the country club all together but that was impossible. Kristy taught tennis to four, five and six-year-olds four mornings a week. After classes, she would see Robby in the staff lounge, or at the snack bar. They would just glare at each other making the atmosphere and any one in it very uncomfortable. Kristy's family would eat dinner at the club at least once a week. If they saw Robby there, he would be very polite and friendly to her parents. To make things worse, he would joke around with her brother Cliff, who always took Robby's side.

The Garrisons had moved back to their old house, across the alley on the Egg. She tried to avoid Robby as much as possible. Kristy would always look out her upstairs window and scan the area around the block to make sure he wasn't in the proximity. She would run out of the house, get on her bike and ride as fast as she could until she was on the next block.

Unfortunately, at the club it seemed every time Kristy turned around, Robby was there. When they saw each other he never spoke to her, but held her gaze long enough to transmit his hatred for her. The more Kristy thought about what she said to him at the pool, the more she regretted saying it.

People around the club noticed their dislike for one another and it was the talk of the club. When people asked Kristy about it, she told them that Robby was a bully and he wanted to make her look bad. Most people defended Robby saying he's such a great guy but Kristy knew the real Robby.

After tennis lessons one morning, Holly, the other tennis instructor asked Kristy what really happened between her and Robby. Kristy didn't say anything and Holly said, "Well, Robby told me what happened and I think you took this too far."

Very curious but playing it cool Kristy asked, "What did he say about me?"

"Not anything as bad as what you have said about him. Since when did you become such a snob? You make it sound like you're a prima-donna and he is just a low life scum bag." Holly put her tennis racket in her locker.

Kristy, not believing what she just heard, said, "He is a low life scum bag. You weren't living here before he moved to Dallas. He was such a bully and was very mean to everyone. I don't think he's changed a bit. Before he moved, the boys and girls at school fought all the time, and when he moved, everyone got along just fine. What do think of that?"

Holly replied, "You're right, I wasn't here before so I don't really know what he was like then. I do know that he is quite a nice guy now. Why don't you just grow up and give him the benefit of the doubt."

Shocked and hurt, Kristy responded, "How do you know he is a nice guy? He has only been back a week and a half. Underneath that tanned body of his is the devil."

Holly laughed, "Robby was right, you have gone back to sixth grade. He said that you are acting like a 'Big Priss' just like you did before. You should really get to know him again. He is quite a nice guy and he is very funny. As a matter of fact, I am playing tennis with him tonight."

Hearing the words 'Big Priss' made Kristy's blood boil. Feeling abandoned by her friend Kristy got up and stormed out of the locker room. She could faintly hear Holly calling her name, but she wasn't going to stop. *Why did Robby have to come back?* She thought. Her life was good and uncomplicated and now (to a 15-year-old) it couldn't get any worse.

As Kristy ran by the clubhouse crying, she heard footsteps getting louder behind her. She kept on going thinking Holly was following her. She felt a hand grab her elbow. When she turned around, she realized that it wasn't Holly holding on to her but Robby Garrison. Instead of the usual scowl on his face, she saw concern. Panting, he said, "Kristy, are you OK? What's wrong? Are you hurt?"

His behavior confused Kristy. Her face turned crimson and she became very angry towards Robby. She was embarrassed that he had seen her like that and was still hurting from her conversation with Holly. She yanked her elbow out of Robby's hand, and screamed at him, "Why do you care. You have always hated me and now you are stealing all my friends. Is that your plan?"

Robby was stunned. He stammered, "Wha-what are you talking about."

Kristy continued, "People think I'm a snob now thanks to you. I don't need your fake sympathy," Kristy turned quickly and ran before Robby could say anything more.

The three friends reunited that afternoon as their shift, at the movie theater, started.

"He said what?" Becky questioned her not believing what she just heard. "Well, maybe this means he is coming around. He could actually be a nice guy."

Mary-Sue jumped in, "He is a lifeguard you know. Lifeguards have to be compassionate because they want to help people and save lives."

Mortified that her best friends could even consider, let alone say such things, Kristy said, "Oh no. I am sure that it was some kind of act probably to impress Holly. She was bragging about playing tennis with him tonight."

While pouring the popcorn into the popcorn maker, Mary-Sue said, "Why do you care if he plays tennis with Holly? Be grateful she is keeping him entertained and out of your way."

Becky, opened a big box with Milk Duds, rolled her eyes and pointed out, "Can't he do anything around this town without offending you?"

"Becky!" pleaded Kristy, "Don't you see what he is doing? He has come back to Guthrie to ruin my life."

"Oh, I see. He has carried a grudge all these years and has been plotting your demise until he moved back. I'm sure you think that he got the job at the country club just to execute his plan," Mary-Sue said sarcastically. Both Mary-Sue and Becky were getting tired of Kristy's drama queen act.

Not catching Mary-Sue's sarcasm, Kristy said, "You're right. I bet he did get a job at the club just to start rumors about me. How could my dad have hired him? I know. He manipulated his way into a job just like he manipulates everyone else."

Becky stopped putting the candy on the shelf and looked with disgust at Kristy, "Kristy. Come on. Why do you think this is all about you? He probably didn't give you a single thought while he was living in Dallas."

Shaking her head in agreement, Mary-Sue said, "You have to stop this. It is driving you crazy and you are driving us crazy. Maybe Holly is right. You're acting childish and very stuck-up. Just forget about what happened all those years ago and get on with your life. You are going to ruin all of our summers if you don't stop obsessing about this."

Feeling unsupported and hurt by her friends' words, Kristy sadly said, "I'd better go open the ticket booth. It looks like there is a line outside already."

As Kristy walked off, Becky looked at Mary-Sue and asked, "Do you think we were too hard on her? She looks awfully hurt."

Shaking her head, Mary-Sue replied, "No. I know what we said did hurt her feelings, but we should have done this a week ago. I've never seen her like this. For some reason, she is so threatened by him."

With movie viewers coming into the theatre, the two girls dropped the subject and concentrated on doing their jobs.

Chapter 4

After Kristy got off work, she didn't bother to stick around to wait for her friends. Her ego had been bashed pretty badly and she really wasn't in the mood to hear how 'wonderful Robby is and how horrible she was'. She had to rush home anyway because her family was going to the club for dinner with someone important. She really didn't listen to all the details when her mom told her about it.

Kristy got home and took a quick shower to get the popcorn smell off her. Her brother, Cliff, always teased her that the smell wasn't from popcorn but from her smelly feet.

"Kristy, hurry up! Your father has to be at the club in 15 minutes to meet Mr. Young and his family!" yelled her mother from the bottom of the stairs.

Putting in her last earring, Kristy came running down the stairs looking refreshed and very beautiful. She was wearing a white, sleeveless, cotton dress with a pink belt around her tiny waist. It accentuated her incredible tan, brown eyes and long dark curled hair. She didn't usually wear a lot of make-up since it just melted off in the heat and humidity of Oklahoma but tonight she decided to put on a little blush, mascara and lip-gloss.

She saw her brother wearing a pink and yellow golf shirt, beige pants and tan shoes. She snorted at him, "Don't you look preppy. I didn't recognize you without that smelly, ratty cap you always wear. Don't you sleep in it?"

Cliff ran his fingers through his hair showing a prominent tan line just above his eyebrows. He wished he had it on now and was on his way to play golf instead of going to this dinner with his family.

He loved his OU cap and has worn it every day for the last three years. His dad brought it home for him when he went to a "Golf Course Management Conference" in Norman. It was his good-luck charm and the Sooners football team has been his favorite team since he was 10 years old. His mom and dad took him to a football game in the early fall for a belated birthday present. Instead of being the bright crimson color of Oklahoma University, the cap was a faded red with the stitching of the OU symbol almost gone.

"Hooonk, Hooonk!" came a desperate call from the driveway.

Kristy's mom came running down the hall smoothing out her skirt. "Your father has been honking the car for the past five minutes. I'm about to shove that horn down his throat."

Looking at the clock, Kristy said, "What's his problem? He told us to be ready to leave at 6:00 and it is now only 5:56. Besides, it takes only five minutes to drive to the club."

"I think he is a little nervous about this dinner tonight. Mr. Young is from the bank in Edmond and he will hopefully give the club the loan needed for the new expansion." Looking sincerely at her children, "That will benefit us all."

Pushing her kids out the door, she pleaded, "Please be on your best behavior. That means no fighting or sarcasm," looking specifically at Cliff, "Don't even walk or sit close to each other. It would be too much of a temptation to fight."

Rolling her eyes, Kristy asked, "What if we are bored or the Young's are total jerks?"

"Yeah. If that's the case, I'm going to the bathroom and may never come back," Cliff said as he tried to swat Kristy in the back of the head.

Knowing her son well, Anne caught his arm and with a wicked stare, showed both he and Kristy she meant business.

They got in the car and Mr. Baker turned around and said, "Mr. Young is bringing his wife and three kids to dinner. By the sounds of it, the kids are all extremely smart, mature and athletic. I expect you two ruffians to be on your best behavior and be good hosts to the kids."

Both Kristy and Cliff mumbled "great" under their breath. Kristy thought to herself, *this is going to be a horrible end to a horrible day.*

Harry, the club's best waiter, just finished laying down the last plate for the entrees. Kristy was about to dig into her favorite dish, Fettuccine Alfredo with shrimp when her mom put her hand on her arm and whispered, "Do you know Kristy, Jocelyn is going to Germany in the fall with her German class." Kristy gave her mom and Jocelyn a half smile. "I wish you could speak a second language. Wouldn't it be nice to speak another language fluently?"

Kristy just put her head down and filled her mouth with pasta. If she heard her mom say, 'do you know' one more time, she was going to throw her plate of food at her. Instead, she excused herself to go to the bathroom. As she started to walk away from the table, she could hear footsteps behind her. She was surprised when she turned to see Cliff following her. Rolling his eyes, he said, "Can you believe that Young family? How can they all be so perfect? They do archery, oil paint, play every school sport, are smart and speak five million languages."

Kristy responded with a smirk, "I know. They are all so good-looking, tall, smart and oh yeah, they never fight with each other, or so mom told me. That is just not normal."

"Does that make us normal?" he chuckled.

The Young's had two sons, Mitchell and Gregory. Mitchell was 20 years old and graduating early from University in philosophy. He was trying to decide where he wanted to go to get his Masters. Gregory, 16, attended a swanky private school in Oklahoma City and was the youngest captain the school has ever had for basketball. His father announced proudly, "he was already being scouted by Universities to play bas- ketball for them." Jocelyn, the youngest and only daughter is 15 and apparently speaks perfect German and French.

The boys are very blonde like their mother and Jocelyn had long perfect strawberry blonde hair like Mr. Young. Mrs. Young is tall and slender and suspiciously does not have a wrinkle on her face. Kristy didn't really trust her because she smiled too much. She learned that from watching Soap Operas.

When Kristy got back to her seat, Gregory, who was sitting next to her, got up and held her chair for her. She was a bit stunned but gave him a quick "thank you" and a smile. Just as Gregory sat down, something caught Kristy's eye just over his shoulder. Standing outside on the path looking directly at her was Robby Garrison. Right next to him, with her arm in his, was Holly in her skimpy pale green tennis dress. She was chatting to him incessantly but it didn't look like he was paying any attention to what she was saying.

Time to get some revenge, thought Kristy. She turned to Gregory and opened her eyes nice and wide. Putting her hand on his arm she cooed to him "Thank you again for holding out my chair. You don't find many gentlemen around anymore." Gregory responded with a big perfect smile after Kristy flashed him her best flirty one.

Across the table, she heard her brother mumble, "I think I'm going to puke."

Robby had just come out of the locker room when he heard, "There you are handsome. Are you ready for a little lesson in love?" Robby gave her a puzzled look. "I mean a tennis lesson." Holly corrected herself while blushing.

Robby looked up to the sky. "It looks like we are going to get some rain tonight. Hopefully, we can get some tennis in before it starts."

Holly giggled and put her arm through his said, "Well, if it does start to rain, we can go and get something to eat. We should actually do that anyway, after we finish playing that is." It was obvious she was trying to weasel a date out of him.

Unfortunately for Holly, Robby stopped listening to her. He had just turned towards the clubhouse and in the restaurant window he saw Kristy being offered a seat from a very tall, good-looking, blonde guy. He stopped in his tracks with Holly still talking. He felt a real pang in his chest when he saw Kristy put her hand on his arm and then blondie giving her a big toothy smile. Robby, a little confused, mumbled to himself, "Who is this guy? I'm pretty sure he isn't a member here."

"Robby, hey Robby, I'm over here." Holly whispered in his ear. "You didn't answer my question about getting something to eat after we finish our game."

"Huh, what?" Robby brought his focus back to Holly, "Oh yeah. We can do whatever," as he turned and started walking with Holly in tow, he said, "Come on. We had better get on court," he couldn't help but turn around and take one more jealous glance at Kristy and her date.

After dinner, Mr. Baker looked at his kids and said, "Mr. Young and I have some business to take care of. Why don't the two of you give the Young kids a tour of the club?" Cliff and Kristy knew that was a command not a suggestion.

"Ok," they both said in unison.

Just as the parents walked out of sight, Jocelyn's perfect posture relaxed and in a rude voice said, "I'm so bored," pulling out her cell phone, she asked, "Is there some private place that I can call my boyfriend?" A little shocked by the transformation, Kristy pointed to the small lounge off the main lobby. With that, Jocelyn walked away without even a "thanks".

"Hey Cliff. I noticed some hot babes heading for the pool. Let's ditch these two and see about getting some action," Mitchell motioned towards the outdoor pool.

With a relieved smile on his face, Cliff shook his head and said, "Let's go Dude. I knew you weren't really a nerdy ass."

After being abandoned by the others, Gregory looked at Kristy and said, "Well, I am a nerdy ass and would really like that tour. Are you up for it?"

Why not, thought Kristy. Smiling she said, "Why don't we start with the tennis courts. I actually teach tennis to little guys. Do you play?" Before Gregory could respond, Kristy answered her own question, "Yeah, of course you do."

When they got close to the tennis courts, Kristy could hear Holly squealing and laughing. She heard her say, "Oh Robby. You're soooo bad. Stop pretending to be such a lousy player. I know you're better than this."

"I'm not pretending. I am really this awful," Robby replied.

Gregory and Kristy turned the corner and saw the six outdoor tennis courts were filled with all levels of tennis players. Holly and Robby were on the first court, the one closest to the path. Before Kristy could direct Gregory in a different direction, she heard, "Kristy. Hey Kristy." She turned and saw Holly waving and running over to them with Robby right behind her.

Damn. She thought to herself. *I only wanted them to see me with Gregory, not actually talk to us.*

They stopped and waited for them to come over. Holly quickly opened the gate and looked directly at Gregory. She said smiling, "Hi Kristy. Who do we have here?"

"Well Holly," Kristy replied with the same fake smile Holly had on her face, "We have Gregory."

Ignoring her sarcasm, Holly stuck out her hand to Gregory and smiled. In an over exaggerated Oklahoman drawl, she said, "Well hi Gregory. It's nice to meet someone new around here," looking him up and down, she continued, "And you are so tall and blonde."

Gregory blushed and before he could respond, Robby came bounding up and reached out to shake Gregory's hand, "Hi. I'm Robby Garrison. I'm Kristy's neighbor."

Under her breath, Kristy said, "The devil neighbor." Robby was the only one to hear her so he shot her a nasty look. Changing the subject, Kristy asked, "How is your tennis game going? Is Holly kicking your butt Robby?"

"Well," pulling Holly closer to him he said, "As a matter of fact she is and it feels so good."

"Oh, stop being such a beast Robby," Holly responded basking in his attention.

"Yeah Robby. Don't be such a beast," snared Kristy.

Holly, realizing that Robby's attention had shifted from her to Kristy, asked loudly, "Gregory, do you play tennis?"

Gregory shook his head yes and said, "I usually get out a few times a week when I'm at school."

"Well then. We should play doubles. Robby and me against you and Kristy. What do you think of that?" Holly asked.

Remembering what she had heard just a few minutes ago, Kristy smirked, "What a great idea Holly. We should totally play doubles."

Robby knew he was a bad player so he said, "I'm not sure I have the time to get out and play any time soon."

"That's okay Robby," said Gregory, "I don't have time either. The day after tomorrow, I'm heading to Springfield, Missouri for a two-week basketball camp."

"Basketball? I play too. What school do you play for?" asked Robby.

"I play for Midwestern Prep," answered Gregory.

"No way." Robby paused then shook his finger at him. "I thought I recognized you. You're a center and I think the assistant captain. I play point guard."

"Yeah, but I'm the captain this year. How do you know?" Gregory asked.

"I played for Adams High School in Dallas last year. We played you guys in the finals of the Southern Oklahoma tournament last year." Robby said pretending to shoot a basket.

"Get out," Gregory paused for a second, "Of course. I remember you now. You were MVP of the tournament. Boy, that was such a close game. I couldn't believe you scored from center to win the game. That was beautiful man."

"Yeah, it was, wasn't it?" Robby said gloating and looked at Kristy.

Kristy just shook her head and mumbled, "Really?" She thought. *My life is over. Why does he always come out the big hero?*

Looking at Gregory, she said, "Well, we better go. We have a tour to finish and I know your parents want to drive back to Edmond by nine o'clock," facing Robby and Holly she said sarcastically, "See you later you cute little lovebirds."

Ignoring her, Robby stuck out his hand and said, "Hey Greg. Have fun at basketball camp. Maybe we will meet up again and play some one-on-one."

"That would be cool. See you later," Gregory said returning his handshake. Walking away from the tennis courts, Gregory turned to Kristy said, "What a small world. He is such a great guy and to think he is your neighbor."

Wincing, Kristy said turning her head away, "Yeah great guy. I'm so lucky."

Chapter 5

The next four days was wonderful for Kristy. Robby wasn't around for reasons she didn't care to find out. She was happier and her friends noticed that she was back to her old self.

On the fifth day, Kristy woke up with a sense of dread. She lay in bed and could hear laughing and shouting, mixed in with the bouncing of a basketball. She knew immediately who was responsible for waking her up. It was the two people in the world who liked to torment and annoy her the most, Cliff and Robby.

Kristy rolled over and put her feet on the floor. She sat on the edge of her bed trying to convince herself that she needed to get up and get to the club. She had a tennis class in an hour teaching the cutest and funniest four year olds. Smiling she stood up thinking about the lesson she was about to teach.

Dressed for tennis, Kristy was sitting at the kitchen table listening to the Oklahoma City morning news. She was eating a piece of perfectly browned toast and peanut butter. This was her breakfast every morning accompanied by a piece of fruit and a large glass of milk.

The newscaster was talking about the thunderstorms that were rolling across the state. He reassured everyone that Oklahoma City and area would not be affected by the storms. However, travelling south of the city would not be advisable. There was a possibility of tornado activity down there.

Kristy was happy they weren't going to have rain. When bad weather happened, she turned from a tennis instructor to a babysitter. The parents usually planned to take some kind of workout class during their kid's lesson. Kristy would have to entertain the kids until their parents showed up to get them. She begged her father to buy a TV and DVD player for those particular days. All she had to do was pop in a movie and the kids would be occupied and more importantly, quiet. Her father thought this was a good idea, but of course it hadn't happened yet.

Kristy was about to bite into her fresh juicy peach, when the back-screen door crashed open. Just as she turned around, she heard, "Hey ugly. It's about time you got your ass out of bed," Cliff intentionally bumped her as he walks by to get two glasses of water.

From behind him, she heard someone chuckling. Standing there with a big smile on his obnoxious face was Robby Garrison. Passing a glass of water to him, Cliff said, "Here you go. Cheers. To being the best basketball players on the Egg." Looking at Kristy, he continued, "Maybe you could be good too if you weren't so lazy and stayed in bed all morning."

Robby didn't say anything but gave Kristy an infuriating smirk. Blood boiling, Kristy threw the peach she was holding hoping to hit both with it. Instead, she connected with Cliff's water glass sitting on the counter. With a loud crash, water and glass sprayed everywhere. She heard laughing and "klutz" coming from Cliff's mouth.

Robby, pointing at the mess, said, "You better clean that up."

Biting her bottom lip, she watched them run out of the back door. When the door slammed, she let out an agonizing yell. She could feel this was not going to be a good day.

All was forgotten when she got to work. There, waiting for her were four adorable tennis players. All their faces lit up as they waved and called Kristy's name. She felt like a rock star with these little guys. Her first hour class had four kids, two little girls, Faith and Abby wearing matching colorful neon tennis skirts. Jeremy had red hair and freckles so she nicknamed him Boris Becker. The other little boy was her favorite. Josh had blue eyes and brown curly hair. The mop-topped boy was so funny and loved to play tennis.

They all ran onto the court waving good-bye to their moms. The ladies left quickly because they had a yoga class in five minutes.

Kristy usually had the kids do a 10-minute warm up but because it was hot and muggy, she decided five minutes would be enough. She didn't want them to get over heated and run out of energy too quickly. After about 15 minutes of working on drills, they felt the wind start to blow from the south. This made the drills a little challenging so Kristy decided to start some fun tennis games. As they started the second game, Josh pointed up to the sky behind Kristy and yelled, "Wow! Do you see that?"

Kristy turned and saw a funnel cloud about four miles away coming right towards them. Kristy yelled to everyone on the tennis courts, "Tornado! Everyone run and get under cover."

She dropped her tennis racket and had the kids do the same. "Let's go guys. You need to run as fast as you can to the clubhouse."

Just as they exited the tennis courts, rain and hail, the size of golf balls started falling. Faith got hit on her back and started to cry. The kids were scared with the black sky and all the lightening flashing around them. Kristy looked around for somewhere closer for them to go. She heard a voice yelling her name from behind them. Through the rain and hail, she saw Robby waving at them to follow him. As they started running in his direction, Robby met them and grabbed two of the kids and picked them up. Kristy picked up Faith and grabbed Josh's hand. Over his shoulder, Robby yelled, "We can take cover in the lifeguard office."

The lifeguard office was only 30 feet away and was built with sturdy cement blocks. They all ran through the door and could hear the hail and rain pounding on the tin roof. Everyone was soaking wet so Robby started handing out towels that were sitting on the shelf closest to him. Trying to stop her mind from panicking, Kristy yelled at Robby asking, "Is it safe in here? What about this window?"

There was only one window in the office and it was a large one. It looked out over the pool so the lifeguard in the office had a full view of the pool area. There were usually three lifeguards on duty. Two of the lifeguards watched the swimmers in the pool and one stayed in the office answering phones and doing paperwork. They rotated positions every half hour.

"Right. That will be a problem." Scanning the room for a safe place, Robby continued, "I know. We can all hide in the cupboards and I will tie the doors closed so they can't blow open."

Everyone ran to the low cupboards that were on three of the four walls. There was a counter on top of the cupboards used as a desk. They opened the cupboard doors and pulled everything out to clear off the shelves. Robby yelled over the deafening sound coming from outside, "Everyone lay down inside with your towel over your head. Make sure you stay there no matter what. You got that?" the kids and Kristy all shook their heads, "I will tie the cupboard doors shut so you won't be able to get out even if you wanted to." He handed the kids more towels. They obeyed him and crawled onto the top shelf of the first two cupboards furthest from the window.

Kristy yelled over the hail pounding on the roof, "What are you going to tie the doors with?"

Robby looked around and saw five rescue tubes with long straps hanging on the wall next to the door. He grabbed a couple and with

Kristy's help, slipped a strap through the door handles on the first cupboard. Robby quickly tied a bowline knot and pulled hard on it to make sure it was strong and tight. Kristy had the other strap already through the second cupboard handles. Robby again tied a bowline knot and prayed they would hold. They could hear the tornado coming closer. The deck chairs by the pool were being picked up and thrown around the pool area. Robby knew that it would be a matter of time before one would fly through the glass window. He grabbed Kristy and pushed her into one of the cupboards. He started to close the cupboard door when Kristy stopped him and yelled, "What about you? You have to get in too."

Pushing Kristy's hand away, Robby yelled back, "Don't worry. This really isn't the time to argue with me," He quickly shut the door and began to tie the cupboard closed. Just as he finished, a deck chair flew through the glass window shattering it. The wind picked up the glass shards and they swirled inside the office hitting Robby on his left side. He practically dove into the last cupboard and tried to shut the doors. The wind tore off one of the doors. Making sure he was on his right side, Robby slid through the cupboard to where Kristy was. Luckily, the cupboard had a long continuous shelf without partitions. Kristy was startled and when she realized it was Robby, she started to slide forward until she was up next to Faith. She pulled the crying girl right up next to her. She prayed the other kids were all right and the cup- board doors would stay put.

The knots Robby tied held as the cupboard doors rattled violently. They could hear things slamming against the desk and the walls. Robby felt blood dripping from all up and down his left side but did not feel any pain. He knew from his first-aid training that when adrenaline runs through you, it is basically a painkiller. He just closed his eyes and hoped that it would be over soon.

The chaos of the tornado lasted only a few minutes but it seemed like forever to everyone in the cupboard. The unbelievably loud roar of the tornado, hail and objects crashing into the lifeguard office seemed to go on forever. It finally passed leaving part of the country club demolished.

Silence took over from the deafening roar of the tornado. Robby was the first to realize that it was gone and felt it was safe to get out of the cupboards. He yelled, "Is everyone ok? Kristy?"

She answered back, "Faith and I are fine," she called out the other three kids' names.

They each responded with a whimpering "yeah."

"Everyone stay where you are and I will crawl out to untie the knots." Robby said as he started to slide out, the way he came in, leaving a trail of blood behind him.

As Robby was untying the knots, Kristy reassured all the kids that it was all over and that everyone was so brave. As the cupboard doors started to open, the tennis players came out a little dazed. They were all squinting from the sunlight pouring in through the missing roof. They surveyed the surreal scene. All the furniture was gone. Wet paper was plastered on the walls or floating in two inches of water that had flooded the floor of the office. Computers and equipment were missing or just smashed to pieces.

Kristy shook her head at the scene but then turned her attention to the kids. She checked each one over to make sure they weren't hurt in any way. Faith just had a big bruise on her back from the hail that had hit her as they were running in from the tennis courts. Other than that, they were a little shaken up but were physically fine. She turned to Robby and saw that he was very pale and leaning against the desk clutching his left side. The water around his feet was turning red. She ran over to him and saw about 20 glass shards sticking out from his arms, side and legs. Blood was dripping from each wound. Kristy caught him just as he started to topple over. He looked like he was close to passing out. She tried to get him over to the desk to lie down but he was too heavy. Kristy threw his right arm over her shoulder and carefully walked him over trying not to disturb the glass protruding from his left side. Once he was lying down on the desk, Kristy yelled for the kids to gather up any dry towels they could find and to watch for any pieces of glass floating in the water. Josh remembered the towels in the cupboard. He carefully splashed his way to the cupboard followed by the other kids. They grabbed as many towels as they could and holding them over their heads, they took them to Kristy. She gave them a big smile and took the towels to Robby. She made a pillow for his head and very carefully covered most of his shaking body. She could tell that he was going into shock.

Robby started to feel the pain from all his penetrating wounds. The loss of blood made his stomach woozy and his head was fuzzy. Kristy grabbed his face and made him look at her, "Robby. Robby, stay with me! What do I have to do to help you?" Robby started to sit up but began to sway so he quickly lay back down. Kristy reached down and grabbed water with her left hand as she held Robby with her right. She splashed the cool water on Robby's face. He started to snap out of his haze. She grabbed his face again, "Robby. What do you need me to do to help you? Do you want me to take the glass out and stop the bleeding?"

"No!" panicked Robby, "These are too deep. The glass is actually stopping me from bleeding to death. Why don't you go out and find some help. I will be fine for now."

"Are you sure?" Kristy asked. Robby gave her a weak nod. She turned to the four children, "Okay. Kids, listen to me very carefully. Robby is very badly hurt so I need to go out and find someone to help him," they looked at Robby with concern on their faces, "I need you to stay here. Why don't all of you get up on the desk and I want you to tell Robby stories to keep him awake. Whatever you do, do not touch any of the glass that is sticking in him. I will be back as quickly as I can. Okay?" they all nodded their heads and she could see that some of them were about to cry, "Abby, why don't you tell Robby about the new kitten you got yesterday."

As Kristy ran out of the office, she could hear Abby's little voice, "His name is Pinecone cause he looks like one."

Outside the office, Kristy was so determined to find help, she didn't see the destruction of the tornado. Behind her, she heard sirens. She turned and saw fire trucks, ambulances and police cars driving quickly through the country club gates. She started to sprint in their direction waving her arms. A firefighter noticed her and jumped from the truck before it stopped. He was followed by more firefighters. Kristy yelled, "Help me. Robby is hurt and bleeding!" When they met up with her, they turned and ran to the office. Two paramedics pushing a stretcher and carrying large first-aid bags followed. It took them a little longer to maneuver the stretcher around all the debris lying on the ground.

"Robby. Robby wake up," Faith was patting his face when they walked in.

The firefighter said, "I'm John. How many people are hurt?"

Josh piped up, "Only Robby is hurt. He and Kristy saved us from the tomato."

John saw the almost unconscious boy lying on the desk and ran over to him. He looked at the kids and said, "You have all been very brave. See these guys behind me?" They all nodded their heads yes, "They are going to take you out to an ambulance to make sure you are not hurt. Then, hopefully, they will find your parents, okay?"

"What about Robby and Kristy?" Abby whined.

Kristy walked over and gathered all four up into her arms. She gave them a big hug and said, "I am so proud of all of you. You were all so brave and you took very good care of Robby. I am going to stay here with Robby and you can go with these big firefighters. Everything will be fine and I bet your moms will be looking for you. They will be very worried about you so you need to give them hugs and tell them you are okay. I will see you all as soon as I can."

They returned Kristy's hug and turned to let the firefighters pick them up. Josh gave a little wave as they walked out the door. She heard him say, "Boy. I guess we won't be playing tennis anymore."

Kristy turned her attention to Robby. The ambulance attendants had quickly assessed his obvious injuries. He asked, "Do you know if he has any other injuries?"

"I don't think so. He has lost a lot of blood though. Are you going to take him to the hospital or the Emergency Shelter at the Masonic Lodge?" Kristy responded. She added, "If it's still there."

John responded, "That part of town is fine. He must go to the hospital. You see, he has been injured by flying glass and there will be pieces that we won't be able to see. The hospital will take an x-ray to see where all the glass pieces are. It looks like he will also need a few stitches'

They had Robby on a stretcher with an oxygen mask over his mouth. He was jarred awake by the movement of the stretcher. He looked around and found Kristy's concerned face. He smiled under the mask. He lifted it off his face with his good hand and said weakly, "I think you are actually worried about me Baker"

Walking beside him, she said, "Why would I be worried about you," she smiled back at him, "Remember, I don't like you."

He put his mask back on and grabbed her hand to give it a squeeze. She could faintly hear him say through his mask, "Oh yeah. We don't like each other. You are a big priss and I'm a menace."

Kristy squeezed his hand back and for the first time, she didn't mind being called a big priss.

Chapter 6

Robby was propped up in his hospital bed staring at his sleeping roommate. He was only allowed to lie on his right side, which was feeling a little numb. To keep his mind off the numbness, he watched as his 60 something roommate Kevin or was it Evan, start a low rumbling snore. With each breath, Robby could see and hear the snoring decibel increase. He counted the snores to see how many this guy could do before waking himself up. It was unbelievable to Robby that someone could snore so loudly (even the nurses could hear him from their station) and not wake himself up. He watched this whole scenario start repeatedly until finally a nurse came in with good news, "You have a visitor. Why don't I help you into a wheelchair and get your intravenous set up so you can have a visit away from Griz here," her head motioned to Evan.

Just as he sat up, his right side tingled as the blood rushed back to it. He was also very stiff and sore, "Who is here?" asked Robby, who was very anxious to get out of his room.

Just as he finished asking, a familiar face peered around the corner, "Hey." Kristy said shyly, "Is it okay to visit now?"

Sitting up straighter in his wheelchair, Robby smiled and said, "Yeah, of course it's okay. It's better than okay. I am surprised to see you here."

"Well, you did save our lives, "blushing, she continued, "I can't thank you enough. You came out of nowhere just at the right time when I needed help the most," looking down at her feet, she humbly said, "I really do appreciate everything you did for me, I mean, us. You were really great. I just feel bad that you got hurt."

Leaning back in his wheelchair and closing his eyes, Robby smiled and said, "Wow. I guess it was worth getting splattered by glass just to hear you thank me. I even think there was a compliment in there too."

Kristy smiled back and said, "You should enjoy it now because I can't imagine I will ever give you another compliment again."

"Why don't we look at this as a new start for us. You know, forget about all the fights and nasty words we said to each other," sticking out his hand towards Kristy, he said, "Truce?"

She took his hand and gave it a shake while saying, "Truce."

Robby and Kristy held on to each other's hand a little longer than normal. They looked into each other's eyes and both felt a special connection. They would always share that horrible summer day. They were suddenly interrupted by a loud snore coming from Robby's roommate.

Robby cleared his throat and slowly took his hand away from Kristy's, "Let's get out of here. I am almost deaf from his snoring."

Kristy laughed and stepped around the wheelchair to push it, "Where should we go?"

"Why don't we go down to the lounge? It's just down at the end of the hall." Robby said pointing.

"Um, no!" shouted Kristy, "I saw a big group of people going in there when I came up. I know. I'm pretty hungry. Why don't we go to the cafeteria? My treat?"

A little startled and confused by Kristy's reaction, Robby said, "Yeah, sure. That'd be great since I really didn't eat any of my tasty lunch," he made a sour face, "I could really go for some iced-tea and apple pie. How does that sound?"

"Sounds good. Hold on," Kristy started pushing Robby at a very fast speed towards the elevator.

"Was there any one killed?" Robby asked as he put a forkful of pie in his mouth.

"No, luckily. No one expected the storm to head north. It travelled so fast that it was hard to track. They said that it was only an F2 but it still wrecked a lot of stuff. The funnel cloud started southeast of here and just out of the blue, turned north. A few farms and the country club got the worst of it. Let's see, at the club, the golf course is ripped up. Only fairways and greens of holes 18, 16, 5, 2 and 1 got it. The aerobic studios, squash courts and pro shop were left untouched." making a sad face, Kristy looked away, "The tennis courts were demolished and my favorite racket is probably in another county."

"Oh man. Sorry to hear that," Robby said sympathetically, "Tell me that the pool isn't as bad as I think it is. There was so much stuff flying around that I can't imagine that anything was saved."

With a sigh, Kristy said, "Well, the tornado sucked all of the water out of the pool. The diving boards were ripped right out of the concrete and pool furniture was found in the restaurant and on the golf course. Tennis balls were everywhere too. It's weird to see the trees in the tornado's path that had leaves ripped off them. There were trees practically right next to them untouched. It's crazy if you ask me."

"The restaurant?" Robby had a feeling what was coming.

"Yep. Every window on that side of the club was totally demolished. The restaurant is pretty much gone," shaking her head, Kristy said, "Dad thinks it will take at least two or three months to clean and repair everything. They will have to rebuild the restaurant so no more Fettuccine Alfredo for a while."

"That's too bad, "Robby said with sympathetic eyes. Changing the subject, "What about town? Did the tornado hit anything there? "

Letting out her breathe, Kristy perked up, "Nothing, thank goodness."

"So, the water tower was left alone?" Robby
asked. "Yeah," Kristy said looking at him
strangely.

"Awesome. I have been looking forward to painting it for Halloween. Ever since I was a kid I have pictured myself climbing up that ladder and writing 'Baldy Mike' on it," Robby gave Kristy a sly smile.

"Wait. My friends and I are going to paint it this year. We have been planning it for a while. Everyone in the class liked our idea and agreed we could paint it. We got a picture of Principal Mike and Becky is going to do a caricature of him in royal blue and white. She is such a good artist, "Kristy said.

The kids at Guthrie High School have painted "Baldy Mike" on the city's water tower since the 1940's. Baldy Mike was the high school principal at the time and was very popular with the kids. He thought it was hilarious and the tradition had continued ever since.

It was planned that a few kids from the sophomore class would go up on October 24th and paint it on the tower. It was usually voted on at the end of the freshmen year. The police and fire department (a lot of whom participated in this tradition) would supervise to make sure the kids don't get hurt. Every safety precaution would be taken up on the tower. The whole sophomore class would come and have a Halloween party under the tower while a few would go up and paint. It would stay up there for a week. After Halloween, a few more sophomores would go back and repaint over the words, to get it to its original state.

Robby asked, "Since when do we vote on it. It sounds pretty formal and not at all sneaky?"

"Since three years ago. There were too many kids up there and no one was using any kind of safety harness. A couple of the guys started shoving each other and one was pushed over the side. Luckily, the other guy grabbed him and pulled him back up. The police came and made everyone come down. That year, "Bald" was written up there. There was a big town meeting because the police and mayor wanted it to stop but the majority of the people wanted to keep the tradition. This was the compromise. Actually, it is a lot more fun this way," Kristy gave a little shrug.

"Wait. So, I can't go up and paint Baldy Mike on the water tower?" Robby was disappointed, "I have been waiting a long time to get up there."

"You can be on the re-painting committee," Kristy suggested, "That way you still get to stand up on the water tower."

"Yeah. I guess," Robby said finishing his iced-tea.

Kristy started to get up, "Well. I had better get you back. You look a little tired."

"No. That's um, all right. You don't have to leave. I feel fine," Robby gently objected.

Kristy put her hand up, "Really. I have a lot of things to do this afternoon. The movie theater is going to open again tomorrow and we expect to be pretty busy. Without the pool, golf course and tennis courts, people will be looking for something else to do."

Kristy pulled Robby's wheelchair out from under the table and pushed him up to his floor in silence. Smiling, she passed right by his room.

"Hey. You just missed my room," he said pointing behind him.

"Oh, I forgot to tell you. There are some others here to see you," Kristy smirked.

As they got nearer to the lounge, Robby could see balloons and a cake. He looked around the room, but no one was there. He gave her a quizzical look. Then it happened, "Surprise!" Four little bodies and a few big ones, including his parents, jumped out from behind the couches and the door. Robby jumped from shock almost tearing the intravenous out of his arm.

Josh, Faith, Jeremy and Abby all started to giggle. They were very proud of themselves for surprising Robby. Robby's aqua-blue eyes lit up when he saw the kids. He gave Kristy a scowling look but she knew he was joking.

"We got you Robby," chuckled Jeremy, jumping up and down.

"Boy did you ever. What is all this?" Robby asked.

The two little girls said in unison, "This is a thank-you-for-saving-us party!"

"Yeah," piped in Josh, "The cake has a picture of a tomato on it."

"Tomato?" thought Robby, "Why a tomato?" He wheeled himself over to the table and saw that it was a picture of a tornado. "That is the coolest cake ever guys! Wow! This should be a, we-all-survived-the-tomato-and-were-all-very-brave-about-it party."

The kids liked that idea and thought it was time to dig into the cake. The kid's moms rushed to the table to cut the cake. More patients started coming into the lounge, curious to see what the ruckus was.

"But Robby gets the biggest piece," Jeremy pointed out.

"Actually, I think Kristy should get the biggest piece. She helped to save all of you and she saved me," he said offering his slice of cake, "Can you eat some cake after that apple pie?"

Kristy smiled and said, "Of course I can. Why don't we share that piece? I get the side with the funnel cloud," she sat down next to Robby and laughed, "Ha Ha. We got you good Mr. Garrison."

Sitting at the kitchen table, Kristy started to chuckle and thought herself. *We still call a tornado a tomato, thanks to Josh. I wonder what ever*

happened to him? I think he turned out to be a pretty good tennis player. He should be about 15 now. Shaking her head. *Wow, time goes by so fast.*

"Mom!" Logan called out again.

Kristy came out of her daydream to see her son standing there in his underwear. "Didn't you wear pajamas to bed last night?" she asked him.

"It was too hot." he answered wiping the sweat off his forehead, "I would have slept naked but Daddy always said that you should wear something to bed because if a firefighter has to rescue you, it would be very embarrassing for both of you if you were naked."

"That's good advice. You can sleep in my room tonight. The air conditioner may be working," Kristy said remembering her morning.

"Can we sleep outside in sleeping bags like we used to do with Daddy?" asked a hopeful boy.

"Don't you remember how we woke up with chigger bites all over our bodies?" Kristy asked pulling Logan in for a hug, "Since tomorrow is my day off, why don't we make a fort in the screened porch. We can make it after I get home from work."

Logan's aqua-blue eyes lit up just like his dad's when he was excited about something. Kristy was happy to see so many of Robby's mannerisms in their son. It helped her cope with his absence.

Logan started to talk about what they would need for the "coolest fort in the world."

This is the best way to start my day. Kristy thought. She just sat and laughed at her son and all his wild ideas.

Chapter 7

"And we put the big blanket over the ladders to make the tent, then mom blew up the air mattresses we used when we went to that lake. Remember Dad?" Logan asked the silent Robby. Kristy loved how he talked to Robby the same way he did before the accident. Logan was so excited about the fort he and his mom built on the screened porch that he couldn't wait until after dinner to tell his dad. Logan continued, "Mom said we might be able to sleep out there for this many nights." He held up three fingers to his dad.

"Okay buddy," Kristy said, "why don't you run on and visit with Ozzie Becks while I get your dad cleaned up. I bet he has dominoes set out just waiting for you." Ozzie Becks was an 86-year-old resident in the same nursing home Robby was in. Ozzie didn't have any family so he loved it when Logan came to visit. Ozzie taught Logan how to play dominoes and they usually had some pretty good games together.

Kristy and Logan went to the nursing home every day, usually after dinner, to visit Robby. Logan would tell his dad about his day and after, he would visit with Ozzie and some of the other residents. Kristy would then wash, shave, massage and do the exercises the physiotherapist recommended for Robby. She loved this alone time with him. Like Logan,

Kristy would talk to Robby like he had just gotten home from work. She would tell him about her day, what was happening in Logan's life, tell him all the gossip of Guthrie and the sports scores from his favorite teams.

Kristy always used the same soap, shampoo and shaving cream that Robby had used every day of their marriage. She loved that he smelled the same even in this sterile hospital room. Today, she ran her fingers lightly over all the scars on his left side from the wounds so many years ago. Having just thought about the tornado this morning, the scars were more meaningful today. It was Kristy's ritual to give Robby a long, tender kiss on his lips after he was cleaned and shaved. All she would have to do is close her eyes and her old Robby was back with her. Even though he didn't kiss back, she still had the familiar feel and smell of her husband. If she had a particularly tough day, she would lie down next to him and put her head on his shoulder. It was a little hard in his small hospital bed but it was wonderful therapy for her.

While Kristy was finishing up on the last leg exercise, Logan came running in with Ozzie walking behind him with his walker. Ozzie laughed and said in a thick Oklahoma drawl, "That boy of yours is as smart as a whip. He beat me five games to three in dominoes." looking at Robby, he asked, "How's our boy doing here?"

Kristy laughed, "He's doing great today. He isn't as stiff as he was yesterday. Do you know Ozzie, Robby was an all-state swimming champion in high school? He was a fantastic basketball player too. He was teaching Logan how to shoot a basketball just before his accident."

Robby turned his face towards them. Ozzie saw Robby's face clearly and said, "Now I see where Logan here got those blue eyes. No wonder you fell in love with this one, "he smiled at Kristy, "Listen, dinner is being served. How about it if Logan came in and joined me? I did bet my dessert that he couldn't beat me in dominoes. Now I owe him one. You can come and join us too if you would like?"

"Thanks Ozzie," Kristy put her hand on his arm, "You two go and start and I will come in after I finish with Robby. I still want to massage his feet and calves"

As Kristy was massaging Robby's feet, she remembered how she used to do this before a swim meet and after a basketball game. Robby had problems with calf cramps during and after his sports.

"Don't be such a baby. Here, just eat it." A 16-year-old Kristy demanded, pushing a piece of banana towards Robby. "The doctor said that you are low in potassium. That is one reason you get those cramps in your calves."

"Get that away from me," Robby turned his head away with a look of disgust, "You know I can't stand bananas. I don't like the smell, taste and especially the texture of them."

Robby and Kristy had been dating for the past four months. Their truce turned into a friendship and then into love. The two became best friends and were inseparable.

Popping the banana into her mouth, Kristy said, "Out of this list of top ten foods with the highest levels of potassium, you have only agreed to baked potatoes."

"As long as it has the works on it. I really only like potatoes if they are French and fried," Robby pointed out.

"Are you sure? Let's go through this list again. White beans," Kristy said reading off the list in a book on food nutrition she found in the library.

"That is a maybe if they are in chili or something. I couldn't eat them by themselves." he said scrunching up his nose.

"Ok. Spinach. Not the canned stuff but the fresh leaves. I can make a really nice salad for you," a hopeful Kristy said.

"Um. No thanks," Robby said squashing her hopes.

"Baked potatoes are the next one and that is a yes. Ok. Dried pair- cots?" she said looking at her list.

"I don't like non-dried ones so why would I eat a dried one?" Robby cringed.

Laughing because Kristy knew the answer to the next one, said, "Ha, Ha. Prunes or raisins?"

"Really?" Robby winced.

"Had to ask. Okay, um the next one is acorn squash," looking up she saw Robby shake his head no.

"Plain yogurt?"

"Yuck."

"Fish like salmon?"

Robby held his nose.

"Avocados or mushrooms?"

"I'd rather eat bananas."

Closing the book, Kristy said, "Well, Chili with white beans and a baked potato with the works it is. You are such a pain. I've never met a pickier eater"

"I eat a lot of different food," Robby said defending himself.

"Yeah. Pizza, hamburgers, fried chicken. Nothing healthy," Kristy pointed out, "When was the last time you ate something that wasn't processed?"

"I don't even know what that means," changing the subject Robby said, "Remember, the doctor also said that I need to have my calves and feet massaged to keep all those muscles loose. I think you volunteered for that, didn't you?"

"You can rub your own calves. I said I would rub and stretch out your feet and Achilles tendon. I think you should give me foot massages in return," Kristy said with a smirk.

Robby's first reaction was to object but then it occurred to him that it was only fair. Not letting her know that he agreed, he asked, "Why do you need a foot massage? You aren't doing anything athletic since the golf course and tennis courts are still being repaired?"

Thinking about it, Kristy said, "True, but I really like my feet rubbed."

This made Robby smile. He pulled her into his arms and kissed the top of her head, "Why couldn't there be potassium in an ice cream sundae?"

"There is if you have a banana split with nuts," Kristy said pointing out the obvious.

"Done. My treat. I will get a banana split, minus the banana and double the nuts," Robby stood up and helped Kristy to her feet. Kristy pushed up on her toes and gave Robby a sweet, tender kiss. He pulled her in closer to him and happily reciprocated the sentiment.

Kristy felt the foot she was holding twitch. This brought her out of her daydream. She looked lovingly at her still husband and said out loud to him. "It was so hard to get you to eat healthy. If only you knew how I would puree veggies into spaghetti and pizza sauce. You couldn't even taste it. I even put mashed up bananas and apple sauce in chocolate cake." She laughed and kissed his big toe.

Part 2

I accept life unconditionally.
Most people ask for happiness on condition.
Happiness can only be felt if you don't set any condition.

—Arthur Rubinstein

Chapter 8

"Owww," groaned Kristy. She tried to roll over but realized she had rolled off the air mattress and was lying on the hard floor. She was wedged between her air mattress and Logan's. "No wonder I'm sore," she lifted herself up onto her air mattress and lay there with her eyes closed. She could hear Mr. Flint running the lawn mower three houses away. This reminded Kristy that she should get up and mow her yard before it got too hot. These days that was by 10:00 in the morning.

She looked over at her sleeping son. Kristy was grateful that Logan wanted to sleep in the screened back porch. The nights had been unbearable with the heat and her air conditioner wasn't working. The screened porch was cooler with the slight breeze blowing through it. She did have to talk Logan into taking the blankets down. "You can't have a fort without walls, Mom," he whined.

"But honey. It is way too hot for the walls. Instead, let's pretend we are sleeping out under the stars like we used to do with daddy," she said looking at the sad little boy. Kristy added, "I know. To make it feel real, why don't we draw and color some stars to put up on the ceiling."

Logan's eyes lit up, "Yeah! Can I make a moon?"

Ruffling his hair, Kristy said, "Of course you can. You do the moon and I will start on the stars."

As Kristy was looking at the homemade stars and moon when she heard footsteps on the back steps. She sat up and saw her father-in-law coming up to the door of the porch, "Dad?" She asked surprised.

Not expecting to hear a voice, Robby's father, Bobby Garrison jumped back and caught himself before he fell backwards. Kristy got up quickly and rushed to the door to open it, "Are you okay?" She asked holding the door open.

"Oh, my dear," the startled man said, "I wasn't expecting to see you back here."

Kristy motioned him into the kitchen so they wouldn't wake up Logan. When they got there, she explained to him why they were sleeping out on the back porch.

Bobby said, "I remember how you, Cliff and your parents used to do that when you were about his age."

"Really?" She said, grateful her in-laws were around to tell her stories from her childhood. Getting serious, Kristy asked, "What are you doing here at," she stopped to look at the clock on the wall, "7:00 in the morning?"

"Well, I'm just getting home from the hospital," looking tired he continued, "You see, the last step on the front porch crumbled and Mom took quite a fall. She ended up breaking both her ankles and her fibula bone right under her left knee."

"Oh no," Kristy said with concern for her 65-year-old mother-in-law, "When did this happen?"

"Around dinner time last night. I ran over to see if you could help but you weren't there," he said.

"Logan and I were at the nursing home. He was so excited to tell his dad something so we went over early," Kristy said sounding apologetic, "How is she doing?"

Shaking his head, Bobby said, "Not good. They had to rush her by ambulance into Oklahoma City where they did emergency surgery on her. It will be many weeks before she can put any weight what so ever on her legs."

Stunned, Kristy asked, "What can I do? When can she have visitors?" "It will be a few days before she is settled and hopefully the pain will be controlled. Then you and Logan should drive in to see her. I just came back to pack up a few things for the both of us," exhausted, Bobby rubbed his eyes. He continued, "I am thankful Peggy lives in Oklahoma City, so I will stay with her."

Kristy gave Bobby a hug and whispered in his ear, "Don't worry about things here. Logan and I will take care of the lawn and flowers. Logan can take in the mail and I will water the inside plants," coming out of the hug, she said, "Please call me and let me know her progress. If she feels up to it, please have her call me. I would feel so much better if I talked to her directly. Maybe Logan can cheer her up."

"Of course. I will probably drive back once or twice a week to visit Robby and see my only grandson," he said with a smile. Then getting serious again he said, "You know, this will leave you in a pickle." Kristy didn't understand until he continued, "There will be no one to look after Logan when you are at work."

Kristy could feel panic start to rise inside her. Not wanting to lay any more burden on her father-in-law, she said, "Don't worry about that. I have a back-up plan," smiling, she continued, "Now, you just worry about Mom and yourself. Give a big kiss to Peggy and the girls and let me know if I can do anything. Okay?"

Walking to the back door, he stopped and gave Logan a gentle kiss on the forehead. Bobby then walked back over to Kristy and gave her a kiss on the forehead too, "I don't know what I would do without my loving family."

She waved goodbye and shut the door. The panic she was holding in started to rush back. Kristy ran off the porch into the kitchen. She shut the door hoping not to wake Logan, "I don't have it under control, "she yelled at no one. Pacing back and forth from the kitchen to the living room, Kristy tried to decide what she was going to do about childcare for Logan when she went back to work the next day.

Before Robby's accident, Kristy stayed home with Logan during the day and went to school for nursing, three nights a week. Kristy was on the slow track to becoming a nurse, which was fine because her family was more important. She had two maybe three more years before she finished the RNA program.

Robby had to do two night shifts a week at the firehouse so he made sure he worked on the nights Kristy was at home. This worked well for the first four years of Logan's life until Robby's accident.

After Robby's accident, Kristy quit school completely. She was in such despair and it became apparent that she had to find a full-time job. Robby's medical bills ate up all his insurance so there was nothing left over for Kristy and Logan to live on. Luckily, the mortgage for her parent's house was paid off many years ago. They had a savings account but that was for household emergencies only. Money went into Logan's education fund but that couldn't be touched until Logan went to college.

Kristy couldn't find a job close to home in the medical field. There weren't very many jobs at all. Even though she had no experience as a waitress, Kristy was able to convince the owner of the I-35 Diner to hire her. The I-35 Diner was a very busy diner right on the I-35 highway just north of Guthrie. Kristy was great at the cleaning up part but was terrible at the serving part. She would get orders mixed up and could only carry two plates at a time. She tried three but dropped one plate on the floor in front of the customer. Luckily, her boss, Carl Rogers (distant cousin to Roy), was a very patient and generous man. He knew what a hard time Kristy was going through so he never got mad when she messed up. He made sure that she always worked with his best waitress, Roxanne. Kristy learned a lot from just watching her and Roxy would always answer the hundreds of questions that Kristy had. Their patience paid off because after three months, Kristy was one of the best servers at the "I-35" (as it was known by people from all over) and her tips went way up. It was a popular stop by truckers as well as those travelling by car or bus.

Once Kristy got the job at the I-35, she just had to figure out what to do with Logan. Missing her son badly, Vicki Garrison, Robby's Mom, offered to look after Logan when Kristy was at work. Logan loved going over to Grammy and Poppy's house five days a week. His Poppy would come home and have lunch with them and then they would go outside and shoot basketballs into the modified hoop Robby had made for Logan. Bobby had taught his son to shoot a basketball and wanted to pick up where Robby left off. They usually shot baskets for 15 minutes. Bobby would go back to work at an insurance company in Edmond. Logan would go back inside and have a Freezy Ice Pop to cool down and his grandmother would then have a fun activity for him to do.

Kristy was so grateful for her in-laws and she loved them as much as her own parents. They have only shown her love, kindness and support since her parents' death and now Robby's accident. Logan was in good, loving hands and they refused to take any money from her. She made up for it by bringing pies and cakes left over from the diner. Kristy also cleaned their house on her day off because Vicki had arthritis in her shoulders and hands so it was very hard for her to clean. They thought the tradeoff was fair and it worked out for all of them.

Kristy continued to pace. Talking to herself out loud, she said, "Ok. Who do I know that can look after Logan?" After a pause, the only name she could come up with was, "Ozzie Becks. No. How can I ask an 86-year-old to look after a four-year-old? Besides, he can only play dominoes with Logan an hour at a time," tears started to roll down her cheeks. Becky was out of town, "Mary-Sue!" she yelled out loud. Shaking her head, she thought. *No, she has a house full of family in from Denver.* Kristy bit down on her knuckle and thought of everyone she knew. *Maybe*

Margaret-Ruth could look after him? Wait, I think I heard that little Gerry had the chicken pox.

Her thoughts were interrupted when she heard Logan yell from the porch, "Mommy! Where is Poppy going with two suitcases?"

Great. Now I have a bigger problem. She shook her head. *How am I going to explain to Logan that his beloved Grammy is in an Oklahoma City hospital with broken ankles? He gets so scared when he hears someone is in the hospital. He thinks they are going to end up like his dad.*

Chapter 9

"I don't know what I can do Carl." Kristy was crying to her boss on the phone. "I have no one to look after Logan," she paused to listen to Carl then continued, "I understand that you don't have anyone to cover my shift because everyone is on vacation. Maybe you need to hire Logan to help at the I-35," Kristy held her breath while Carl talked. She responded, "Really?" She continued with great relief, "I will bring a lot of things for him to do. I promise that he will behave and stay out of everyone's way. I think you should put him to work washing dishes or something," listening to Carl she let out her breath and smiled, "Okay. Today only I promise. That will give me more time to work something out. I love you Carl. Thank you so much!"

Hanging up the phone, she yelled, "Logan! You have to hurry and get dressed," running up the stairs, "You are going to work with Mommy today."

Logan wasn't quite sure he heard his mom correctly, "What? I get to go to your work?"

"Yes Honey. So, you must be quick as a whip to get ready," squatting down to his height she said very seriously, "It is for today only and you must be on your best behavior. Mommy has to work and look after her customers. I can't always be there to talk or play with you. Do you understand?" He nodded his head, "You have to be a very big boy and play quietly with your toys or sit and color. It is very important you stay out of everyone's way because they may drop a plate or something hot on you. Okay?"

"Okay Mommy. Do you think I can have ice cream?" His eyes lit up.

Kissing his head, Kristy said, "If you're good, you can have anything you like."

"Wow. I better get dressed. Can I bring Bumper?" He asked holding up his stuffed polar bear.

"Yup. Let's pack a fun bag of things for you to play with. You are going to be at the diner for eight hours so it will have to be big," she replied.

Logan was sitting on a stool on the inside of the counter sorting the clean knives, fork and spoons into silverware holder. Roxy came by and said, "Hey buddy. You're doing a really great job! You have been such a big help today."

Logan smiled at her proudly. He liked doing things like this and was actually having fun. Carl promised him a whole dollar for helping today.

"By the time you finish your job, lunch will be ready," Kristy said putting some dirty dishes into a bin beside Logan, "Let me see. You wanted chicken fingers and fries, chocolate milk and veggies and dip, right?"

Logan pointed at his mom, "You wanted me to have the veggies."

Kristy kissed his cheek, "And you better eat all of them."

"Then I can have ice cream?" He asked.

Laughing she said, "That's the deal," looking at her watch she said, "Ok. In 15 minutes the bus from Kansas will be arriving and I hear it's full today. It will get very busy in here so you need to stay put and eat your lunch."

"Can I color?" He asked pulling out his crayons.

"Great idea!" picking up the silverware, she said, "Thanks for the help." Looking over at the kitchen she said, "I see your lunch. Climb back up on to your stool and I will get it for you."

Logan was eating a chicken finger with his left hand while he colored with his right. He looked up and saw a big bus unloading a lot of people. He noticed a little boy walking in with his mother. They stopped at the door to search for a seat. The little boy looked really sad. The boy's mom pointed to the last two seats at the end of the counter close to where Logan was sitting. He heard the women say while helping her son up onto the stool, "We have to stay here for about 40 minutes, okay?"

"Momma, I'm hungry," the little boy whispered to his mother.

Pulling two dollars and some change out of her pocket, she said, "Here, I think I can buy you some soup," she started weeping, "I'm sorry Boo. I spent most of our money on bus tickets. We have to save some for a place to stay tonight. "

The mother and son didn't realize two aqua-blue eyes were watching them intently. Logan got down off his stool, stood on his tiptoes and picked up his plate of food. He put it in front of the little boy and asked his mother. "Can I share my chicken fingers with your little boy?"

Startled, the mother stammered, "N-n-no. It's fine. We're fine."

Logan could see the little boy looking at the food. He went over and dragged the stool that he was sitting on over to where the mother and son were sitting. He climbed up and pushed the plate to him, "My mom said I had to eat all of this before I can get some ice cream. My tummy is getting full and I want to leave room for ice cream," pointing to the other boy, he continued, "If he eats the rest, then I'll get ice cream and I will even give him some."

The little boy looked up at his mother pleading with her with his big brown eyes, "Okay sweetie. Go ahead and have some," she looked at Logan and said, "You are a very sweet little boy. Thank you for sharing with Milo."

Climbing off the stool, Logan ran over and got his crayons and coloring book and ran back. After he climbed up on the stool, he opened the coloring book and said, "See. I colored this picture and this picture," flipping the pages he continued, "Superman is my favorite superhero. My name is Logan and that's my mom," he said pointing to Kristy.

Not looking up but putting a french fry into his mouth, Milo said quietly, "Spiderman's mine."

Flipping the pages quickly, Logan found a picture of Spiderman, "Here he is. Do you want to color him?"

Kristy looked up to check on Logan. She saw he had moved his stool over and was waving his coloring book around and chatting non-stop to a lady and her son. Kristy ran over and began to lightly scold Logan. "Logan! You are not to move from your little corner," looking apologetically at the lady said, "I'm so sorry. I hope he isn't bothering you?

Not looking directly at Kristy, the lady said, "No, um, really it's fine. He has been very nice to us."

Kristy took Logan's hand and walked him and his stool back to the end of the counter, "Now, Honey. You know you weren't supposed to leave here and you are not to bother the customers."

Protesting, Logan said, "But Mom! The little boy was hungry and his mom only had a little bit of monies. He looked so sad and she started to cry. I think I will give her the dollar Carl promised me."

Kristy looked up and took a closer look at the pair. She noticed that the boy was gobbling down Logan's lunch. His mom was looking down at her hands in her lap and Kristy could tell that she was softly crying. Kristy studied the woman a little closer. She wore a scarf covering what looked like dirty blonde hair and she was wearing a long-sleeved jacket. It was a strange outfit to wear in the middle of July in Oklahoma. Kristy poured some ice tea and put a muffin on a plate. She walked over to the woman and placed it in front of her.

The woman looked up a little startled and shook her head, "Oh no. I didn't order that," it was obvious that she was crying and she tried not to make eye contact.

"It's on the house. Again. I'm sorry my son was bothering you," Kristy said with a sympathetic smile.

The woman barely looked up but whispered, "Thank you," Kristy walked away.

Kristy was curious about this woman's behavior. Something wasn't quite right. She poured out a kid's chocolate milk and set it in front of the little boy, "There you go tiger. Here's something to wash down those chicken fingers," he looked up and gave her a big smile.

The woman turned to her son to make sure that he said thank you. When she did, Kristy noticed a cut and bruising on the side of her face. She was covering it with the scarf. The woman then looked up at Kristy and said, "I'm sorry. I don't have very much money but here's a small tip for your kindness."

Kristy put her hand up and said, "Absolutely not. You may need it for your next stop," she then noticed the bruise under her eye, "Where are y'all headed?"

Pointing behind her, the woman said, "I think this bus is going to Dallas"

Before Kristy could say more, she heard "excuse me miss" coming from behind her. She smiled at this woman and turned to help her other customer.

Roxy came up to re-fill an iced tea glass. Kristy leaned in and said, "Rox. Take a look at the lady at the end of the counter," Roxy casually turned to look. Kristy continued, "I think she has been beaten and is trying to cover up. She doesn't have much money and I don't think she knows where she is really going."

Roxy studied her for a minute and said, "She's been abused all right. I know all the signs from when my sister used to get hit. The scarf, the long sleeves, she's hiding her bruises. I bet she just grabbed her kid and got on the first bus out of town."

Kristy felt a huge knot in her stomach. All of Kristy's troubles paled compared to this poor woman's. She couldn't even imagine being in her shoes. An idea came to Kristy and she knew what she had to do. She walked up to this woman and put her hand on the woman's hand that rested on the counter. The woman looked up and Kristy said looking her directly in her eyes, "Don't get back on the bus."

"P-pardon me?" The woman asked a little startled.

"I understand what is going on. The scarf, you're wearing long sleeves in summer. Don't get back on the bus," Kristy said.

The woman pulled her hand out from under Kristy's, "What are you talking about?" She became very defensive, "I'm, I'm allergic to the sun so please mind your own business."

"No, you're not Momma," a little voice said beside her, "You don't want to show the owies from when Daddy pushed you out of the trailer." She was mortified that her son had told a perfect stranger what had happened, "That's enough Milo," grabbing his hand, "we better get back on the bus."

Kristy ran after her and Logan, who had been watching the whole thing, followed, "Please. Please stop," Kristy shouted. She ran around her and stood in front of her, "I know it's not my business but I really do want to help you."

"We are not a pity case," the woman said trying to get around Kristy.

"Then tell me," Kristy challenged her, "where are you going? What are you going to do for money when you get there? How are you and your precious son going to live?"

The woman slumped her shoulders and started to cry, "I don't know. I really don't know."

Kristy reached over and took the woman in her arms. She could feel her trembling and crying. Kristy just held her tightly and whispered in her ear, "I've got a plan. Please come back into the diner and let me tell it to you. You don't need to get back on that bus."

The woman sniffled and pointed to the bus. She said, "Our stuff. We have a tan suitcase. It's held together with duct-tape."

Still holding on to the woman, Kristy yelled, "Hey bus driver! These two are staying here. Can she get her suitcase out from the luggage hold?"

While they waited for the suitcase, Kristy looked over at Logan. He was holding the other boy's hand. Logan caught Kristy's eye and whispered to her. "He was scared Mommy," Kristy smiled and gave him a wink.

Chapter 10

Kristy still had her arm around the woman when they went back into the diner. Logan was walking with Milo holding his hand. Kristy set down the suitcase behind the counter and yelled to Carl, "Hey Carl. I'm taking lunch now okay?" Luckily, the diner was almost empty after everyone left to get back on the bus. She pointed over to a booth over by the window.

"Just help Roxy and Maureen clean up the dishes from that last group. Then you can have lunch," he yelled back from the kitchen.

She quickly got her section cleaned up and walked out of the kitchen with two turkey sandwiches, two salads, two iced teas and two ice cream sundaes on a tray. Kristy gave the boys the ice cream and set the other food down in front of the woman and asked, "I hope you like turkey? By the way, my name is Kristy," she said smiling at the woman, "What's yours?"

Thinking that Kristy was the nicest person she has ever met, she returned her smile, "Thank you Kristy for the food and the kindness. My name is Laura or some people call me Laurie."

Looking at her, Kristy said, "No. You're definitely a Laura. Now, why don't you take off that coat and scarf. I am sweating just looking at you."

Laura was relieved but still embarrassed by her bruises. Luckily, the boys were too engrossed in their ice cream to really see how badly Laura was hurt. After they had finished eating, Logan asked, "Mommy? Can Milo and me go over to the counter and play with my toys? I want to show him my cars. Okay?"

"It's Milo and I and that sounds like a good idea," Kristy replied, "Make sure that you two are quiet and please don't bother Carl, Roxy or Maureen."

"Wow, they are getting along so well. How old is Milo?" asked Kristy.

"He is four but will be five on September 4th," Laura said taking a big gulp of iced tea.

"You're kidding?" Kristy laughed, "What a coincidence. Logan turns five on August 26th. That makes them," counting on her fingers, "nine days apart," she continued, "Where are y'all coming from?"

"Um. Park City, Kansas," looking around, she asked, "Where are we by the way? Milo and I fell asleep on the bus and I have no idea where we stopped."

"We are just north of Guthrie, Oklahoma. Have you ever been here before?" asked Kristy.

"Not Guthrie or even Oklahoma City. I've been to Tulsa to visit my favorite aunt." Laura smiled thinking of her.

"Why don't you go there? I'm sure she could help you," Kristy pointed out.

"Oh no. That will be the first place he'll look for us. I don't want him to hurt Aunt Melba. She is pretty old and frail," Laura said very concerned.

Roxy came over and sat down next to Kristy. Looking at Laura, she said, "Okay darling. What's your story here?" Roxy pointed to the bruises on her arm.

"Aren't you direct. Can't she finish her lunch?" Kristy said laughing at her friend.

"Sorry, but I only have 10 minutes before I have to go. I have an appointment with my chiropractor. A person can't have boobs this big and not have back problems," Roxy said pushing her breasts up to make her point.

The trio started laughing, "Laura. May I introduce you to the very voluptuous, Roxanne Winters," looking at Roxy, Kristy continued, "Roxy, this is my new friend, Laura," Laura smiled shyly.

"I have to tell ya that you ain't foolin anyone with this disguise. I know all the signs. My little sister used to get beaten by her scum ball husband. She tried to hide it too, but it was pretty obvious," before Laura could say anything, Roxy continued, "I assume it was your husband or boyfriend that did this to you?"

"My husband, Jason," Laura whispered, "But really, it was mostly my fault. I shouldn't have burnt the rice. I can be such an idiot sometimes."

Now it was Kristy's turn to be direct, "You got beaten up like this for burning rice? What would happen if you burnt the meat?"

Laura looked away and tried to hold back her tears. Kristy saw how sensitive the subject was and she said while taking Laura's hand, "I'm sorry Laura. You didn't do anything wrong. I burn food all the time. I get teased about what a bad cook I am but never have I been hit for it."

Roxy, who was sitting next to Kristy, was about to burst, "No way should anyone lay a hand on you like that. I suppose he called you all sorts of names and constantly put you down?" Laura nodded her head. Roxy asked, "How long have y'all been married?"

Laura replied, "We have been married for 4 years but have been together for 5. We were high school sweethearts and then I got pregnant. My daddy made us get married."

"Has he been hitting you all this time?" Kristy asked.

"No. He was real nice at first. He was the varsity quarterback of our high school team and was a big deal in Wichita. We had just moved there from Topeka when daddy got a job as a mechanic at the Ford dealership," Laura said.

Kristy interrupted, "Hey Roxy, you better get going or you'll miss your appointment."

"Oh, I'll be late. This is getting real interesting," Roxy said waving her hand at Kristy, "Besides, I usually have to wait 15 or 20 minutes for him. Now go on Honey."

With a smile, Laura continued, "Well, I was a lot prettier back then and since I was new to the school, a lot of boys paid attention to me. Jason was the big hero so when he showed interest, all the others stopped. I was really flattered that he asked me out. He was cute and built and was a lot of fun to be with."

"When did all that stop?" Asked Roxy.

Kristy interrupted, "Don't answer until I get back. I better go check on the boys," a few minutes later she sat back down, "Okay. Back to your story."

"After high school, Jason was scouted by Wichita State University. A week before his try out, he was at his house drinking with some guys from the team. I was working at the Pizza & Sub shop and he said he would pick me up after work. When he didn't show, I phoned him. He didn't like it when I reminded him of his offer. I didn't have any other way home. He showed up mad and drunk, I was afraid to say anything. That was really the first time he really got angry with me and was yelling a blue streak at me. He started to swerve all over the road so I decided to put my seat belt on. He was insulted that I did that and while he was trying to take it off, he ran off the road and hit a tree. He broke his throwing arm in two places and got a concussion.

"Where you hurt?" Kristy interrupted.

"No," Laura gave her a slight smile, "I had my seatbelt on. Well, he couldn't go to football tryouts, so he lost any chance of making any team. His football career was over and in his mind, it was my fault. He almost hit me then, but stopped just before he did."

"How did you react when he was going to hit you?" asked Roxy.

"I really thought he was going to hit me so I put my hands over my head and ducked. He really scared me so I broke up with him," answered Laura.

"See my sister's husband used to pretend to hit her just to see her cower and cringe. He felt powerful and thought he had control over her. One time she didn't cower and stood up to him. He lost his power so that's when he started hitting her for real. That bastard," Roxy said seething at the thought, "Why did you get back with him?"

"About a month after that, I found out I was pregnant. Daddy wasn't going to have a whore for a daughter so he forced Jason and me to get married. Daddy is a bit of a bully too. It was horrible. Jason was so humiliated that his hero status was taken away from him and that he was no longer a big deal. We moved to a lousy trailer just outside Park City where he worked stocking shelves at a grocery store at night. I worked as a receptionist at the real estate office until I had Milo. About that time, Jason lost his job. He would go drinking with a buddy and then go to work drunk. He really resented me for his 'shit-hole' life. Everything bad that had happened to him was because of me."

"Really? You don't believe that do you?" Roxy asked. Laura shrugged her shoulders. Roxy continued, "He was probably a crappy quarterback anyway and wouldn't have made it on the team. It was his drinking that ruined his life and yours."

"He did start to drink a lot. I didn't mind at first because he would be gone for days. I loved being alone with my baby," Laura smiled at the memory. The smiled disappeared, "Then he decided that I needed to go back to work and he would look after the baby. We would fight all the time because I would come home and he would be passed out on the couch with the baby crying. I had no idea if he had even fed or changed him while I was gone. I was ready to leave then but the sweet Jason would come out and he would beg me to stay. He promised to change and like an idiot, I believed him."

Both Roxy and Kristy rolled their eyes and Roxy said, "I wish I could get it through everyone's head that men don't change. Once an asshole, always an asshole."

"You're right Roxy," Laura said, "He would be nice for maybe two weeks. Then he would go back to drinking up our rent and food money. I started complaining and that's when the hitting started. I would go to work with make-up covering the bruises," touching the fresh bruises on the right side of her face, she said, "His favorite was to back hand me with his left hand or pull my head back by my hair and knee me in the stomach."

Roxy shook her head, "My brother-in-law never touched my sister's face because he didn't want the bruises to show. He would pick her up and throw her into things. He loved to see her crumple like a doll. He would do it over and over again. There were times when she was hurt so bad; he would have to take her to the hospital. He would tell them she tripped down stairs or got hit by a car. She had internal bleeding a couple of times. The jerk would take her to different hospitals so they wouldn't recognize her and put two and two together. Sometimes he would drive two hours with her bleeding and in a lot of pain," Roxy was furious at the memory.

Roxy held up her phone and took a picture of Laura. Roxy said, "Okay honey. Turn to the side. I want to make sure to get a good picture of that nasty head wound. You never know when you may need evidence in court."

Kristy put her face into her hands and cried, "I can't believe there are men out there that could do something like that to their wives. My husband was always looking out for Logan and me. He went out of his way to make sure we never got hurt. Never ever did he call me a name or even think about striking me."

"Oh Lordy! I had better get going," Roxy said taking off her apron, "Laura, honey. I'm glad you decided to stay. We will continue this conversation another time."

"I'd really like that. Thank you, Roxy," Laura waved as Roxy headed towards the door.

"Oh yeah. How about I give you a makeover this weekend? That mousy blonde hair just doesn't do you justice with your bone structure," Roxy pushed her way out the door.

Kristy was wiping her eyes and started to chuckle, "I think that's a great idea."

Shaking her head Laura said, "I don't really need a home color. My hair almost fell out when I tried it one time."

"Oh, don't worry. Roxy is a professional. She was a hairdresser and make-up artist for 14 years before her salon closed. She couldn't get another job doing hair so she thought she would become a waitress," Kristy said imitating Roxy by pushing up her boobs, "With her personality and the fact she is a damn good waitress, she found she was making more money doing this. She gets a lot of tips. There are people who will wait just to sit at one of her tables even though there are open seats in other sections."

"What makes her so good?" Laura asked.

"She is feisty as you have seen. She flirts right back when the guys flirt with her and she is tough," laughing, Kristy continued, "Oh yeah. She can talk anyone into ordering something they don't even want. Carl treats her like a goddess and pays her very well. I want to be just like her," after a pause she said, "as a waitress that is."

Laura said, "Maybe some of her feistiness will rub off on me."

The two little boys came over and climbed up into the booth. They were all excited about something. Milo hugged his Mom and said, "Momma! I really like it here." He was holding a very well loved and dirty stuffed animal.

Laura hugged him back and watched as Kristy came back from seating the three people who came in. She sat down across from her, "I only have a few minutes so I will quickly let you know what my idea is," Kristy said, "To make a long story short Laura, my husband was in an accident fighting a barn fire. He is now in a permanent vegetative state in a nursing home. Logan and I live in this big four-bedroom house all by ourselves. Logan's grandmother babysat him while I went to work. Unfortunately, she broke both her ankles a couple of days ago and there is no one to look after him. Day care is too expensive and out of the question," Kristy took a breath, "So because we have lots of room and Logan needs someone to look after him, I thought that maybe you and Milo can move in with us and instead of paying rent, you look after Logan for me."

Laura was a little stunned. She sat there for a minute letting everything that Kristy said sink in, "I don't know what to say. You don't know us and you want us to live with you?"

Kristy replied, "I know we just met, but I can see that you are a loving mother and you are in as much trouble as I am. We could really help each other out. Besides, look at how well our boys get along," they looked over at the two coloring together.

"They do get along great," Laura said, "I don't think it's a coincidence that they are almost exactly the same age. What about school?

"Whoa," Kristy put her hands up, "Let's get you settled. First things first. You need a place to live and I need a babysitter. We will work the rest out later."

Kristy got up to seat more people who just walked in. Laura got up too, "Kristy. Thank you so much for everything. Only a few short hours ago, I felt my life was falling apart. I was feeling so hopeless," giving Kristy a hug, Laura said, "You have literally saved us. I hope I can pay you back somehow."

Kristy smiled at Laura, "I think it was fate that you showed up here today. When Roxy gets back, I can punch out. I will take you to your new home and we will start the next chapter of our lives together."

Chapter 11

"**S**o that is the main floor, we have no basement so I will show you upstairs now," Kristy said to her new housemate. She picked up the beat-up suitcase and said, "Follow me," when they got to the top of the stairs, Kristy stopped and pointed to the right, "In there is my bedroom and bathroom. You and Milo will have to share a bathroom with Logan. His bedroom is across from the bathroom, right here," she said stopping in front of a door. Pointing to the end of the hall, she continued, "And those two rooms can be yours and Milos."

"Oh, Milo and I can share, we don't need to take up any more room," Laura said not wanting to take advantage of Kristy's generosity.

Before Kristy could object she was interrupted by laughter. Two little boys ran out of Logan's room, "Mommy, can Milo sleep in my bottom bunk? Please, pleeeeaase?

Milo joined in, "Please? I've never slept in a bunk bed before."

Looking at Laura, Kristy asked, "What do you think? I don't know if these two can go to sleep and not be tempted to stay up all night and play?"

Laura added, "I know that this will be the messiest room in the house if these two are roommates."

The two little boys held up their hands like they were praying. In unison, they said, "We'll go to sleep!" Logan added, "and we will clean up the room every night before we go to bed."

Looking surprised, Kristy said, "That will be a first," looking at Laura, she gave her a wink, "Well. Hmm Laura. What do you think?"

Trying to look stern at the boys, she replied, "Let's see. Do you guys promise to go to bed when we ask, and make sure all of your toys and clothes are picked up before you get into bed?"

Trying to contain their excitement, the two boys grabbed each other's hand and yelled, "We promise!"

Laura and Kristy laughed and said, "Okay."

"Yay!" the boys cheered.

"Why don't you get yourselves settled in and I will start on dinner," Kristy said.

"Maybe I should start dinner," Laura laughed at Kristy, "Didn't you say you were a bad cook?"

"I can make a wicked batch of banana pancakes," Kristy said looking at the boys.

"Pancakes?" Milo was surprised, "You have pancakes for dinner?"

"Yup. All the time," Logan said pushing him into their room, "I want to show you my toys. You can play with them any time you want."

Over dinner, Kristy told Laura about Robby and his accident. She also explained to her how she and Logan go over after dinner every night to see him.

"Can I stay home with Milo tonight?" Logan asked.

"Not tonight sweetie. Your dad and Ozzie Becks will be expecting you. We will tell them that you may be staying home with Laura and Milo sometimes," Kristy responded.

Laura looked at her with a quizzical look. Kristy explained, "Ozzie Becks is an older man at the nursing home. He and Logan play dominoes every night. I know I told you that Robby was in a vegetative state but I still think, in my heart, he can hear us. Robby will turn his head towards Logan when he is talking to him and will twitch a certain way when I touch him."

"Maybe Milo and Laura can come and meet him," Logan said. Turning to Milo he continued, "I will have to teach you dominoes so the both of us can play with Ozzie Becks. I can't wait to tell Ozzie, Mommy!"

"Why don't you two go to the hospital now and Milo and I will clean up here. It is only fair after you made us the best banana pancakes I've ever tasted," Laura said clearing the table.

Standing up and giving Laura a hug, Kristy whispered into her ear, "Thank you. I feel things are calmer and the atmosphere in the house is happy again."

Hugging Kristy back, Laura said, "I know what you mean. The boys are so excited to have each other. They seem like brothers all ready," pulling back from the hug, Laura continued, "I've never been in such a calm house. My dad was always grumpy and a bully. Then of course there was Jason," she didn't have to say anymore because Kristy knew what she meant.

Holding up her arms, Kristy said, "This big 'ol house has seen its share of sadness with my parents dying and Robby's accident, but it has mostly felt a lot of love and happiness. It's about time it felt that again and with you two here, I think it will."

Chapter 12

The next few evenings, Kristy helped Laura and Milo settle in. They were both in need of clothes since Laura packed quickly leaving almost everything they owned in the trailer. Laura had only five minutes to pack and she decided to take pictures and important childhood mementos. Luckily, she had them all hidden behind the washer where Jason would never find them. She learned early on in their marriage that if something was important to her, Jason would destroy it in front of her. It was his way of punishing her for ruining his life.

"Here it is!" Kristy yelled to Laura from the hall. Walking into Laura's room carrying a big blue bag, Kristy continued, a little out of breath, "I remembered that I packed these old clothes up but never found the time to take them to the Charity Clothing Drive at the Masonic Lodge. This bag just got thrown in the garage with a lot of other stuff," opening the bag up, Kristy pulled out a pair of boy's jeans, "What do you think, these should fit Milo?"

Laura checked the size and smiled, "These are perfect. Are you sure they don't fit Logan anymore?"

"Logan is two sizes bigger than Milo. He hasn't worn these since last year," Kristy said filling Laura's arms up with more and more clothes, "I think there was a reason I forgot to take these to the Charity Drive. I was to save them for you. I swear, God does work in mysterious ways."

Agreeing, Laura said, "I guess we were meant for our lives to cross. These are wonderful clothes. Milo will be so happy. I don't think he had half as many clothes at home as there is in here. We just couldn't afford much."

"Some of these are hand-me-downs from friends. We just pass them around after another baby was born. Logan would always get a lot of new clothes for his birthday from his grandparents and Auntie Peggy. She only has girls so it is fun for her to shop for little boys," Kristy said, "Now, here are some clothes that belonged to me. After Robby's accident, I lost a lot of weight just from the stress of it all. I bought smaller clothes at the Charity Clothing Drive but when I started working at the I-35, I gained all the weight back and a little more so these are too small for me. Go figure, huh? Since you are about an inch shorter and 2 or 3 sizes smaller than me, I think these should fit," she said holding a dress up to Laura.

Laura took the dress and tears started to fall down her cheek, "I haven't had clothes this nice since I was a kid when my Aunt Melba, you know the one in Tulsa, took me shopping when I went there for a visit," sitting on the bed still holding the dress, Laura continued quietly as Kristy sat down on the bed next to her, "I remember Daddy got so mad when he saw the new clothes. He picked them up and threw them away saying that we didn't need her charity. Momma would argue with him that Aunt Melba was only buying me presents. Daddy thought it was Aunt Melba's way of flaunting her money and making him look bad. My momma married for love not money. Daddy turned out mean and his way was the only way," Laura gave a little chuckle, "Momma told me one time that she didn't love him anymore and that she should have married for money. I didn't get to visit Aunt Melba again after that. I think it's been about 10 years since I've seen her. I would write to her and she would write me back but she would send it to my grand-momma, her sister, who would mail it to me. Daddy would return anything that Auntie would send to momma and me."

Kristy had been taking clothes out of the bag and folded them while Laura was telling her story. Kristy pointed out, "Your dad sounds a lot like Jason. Did he ever hit you or your mom?"

"No," Laura answered, "He had anger problems and would yell a lot. He would also throw things. I don't remember ever getting a hug or kiss from him."

"What about your Mom?" Kristy asked, "Did you ever get love and affection from her?"

Laura picked up a picture of her and her mother off the bed stand. Her mother was holding a very young Milo. She gave Kristy a big dreamy smile, "My momma loved me so much. She was always hugging and kissing me. She would let me crawl up onto her lap and we would snuggle and talk. I remember her stroking my hair and oh how she smelled so good. She worked in a bakery so she would come home smelling like bread and cookies," Laura paused, "I don't know how to describe it, but she smelled soft."

"I know exactly what that smells like," Kristy laughed, "That's how I would describe my mother and grandmother. Maybe it's a women thing. I wonder if our boys will think that when they are older. Why didn't she leave your dad if she stopped loving him?"

"I really don't know why," Laura said as her smile disappeared, "She was a very strong woman. She would always stand up to Daddy and they seem to argue all the time but Daddy was very stubborn. He would keep going until he got his way. Her parents lived in Montana and we saw them only about once a year. I loved going to their ranch with all the animals. I always felt that this was the way a family should live. I never wanted to leave."

"I guess you have never known what a loving, functional family feels like?" Kristy said, "You have always lived in a very male dominated home with a lot of aggression."

"Yeah, you're right. That sucks," Laura replied. She continued, "I remember seeing pictures of Momma when she was a teenager. She was blonde and so pretty. I looked a lot like her when I was that age. We had the same long blonde hair and brown eyes. She was only 48 when she died but looked 68 because of her hard life."

"She died?" Kristy said sounding a little surprised and sad.

"She had an aneurysm but I think she died of a broken heart. She didn't want me to marry Jason but Daddy put his foot down and insisted. She saw what kind of man Jason was and didn't want me to have the same life she had. After Jason and I moved away, she only saw her grandson once after that when she and Daddy came for a visit. Daddy didn't want to but she insisted and for once got her way. They came for only a day and a half. Just before they were about to leave, she said to me that she wanted to come and get Milo and me and that all of us would move to Montana or maybe Tulsa. We needed to get away from our husbands. Daddy and Jason both heard her say that and all hell broke loose. Jason told them to get the hell out and never come back and Daddy started yelling at Momma to get into the car and told Jason he was a worthless piece of shit. Momma and I just clung to each other and cried. They had to pry us apart and Jason pulled me into the trailer and, of course, woke up the baby. He was crying and I could hear Momma calling my name with Daddy yelling and swearing at her. That was the last time I saw or heard from her. Three weeks later, she passed away. I'm sure she willed herself to die since she didn't think she would see us again. I think that Milo and I were her only reason for living."

"Where you able to go to the funeral?" Kristy asked with tears in her eyes.

"Believe it or not, I did. Jason's parents told him that he had to drive us to Wichita for the funeral," Laura looked down at her hands. Her voice got quiet and she continued, "That was the last time I saw Daddy."

"Has he died too?" Kristy interrupted.

"I don't think so. I really don't know and I really don't care," Laura took a deep breath and said with anger in her voice. "I hope he dies a very lonely, bitter man. He bullied everyone and now he is paying for it. I never want to see him again."

Two pairs of feet came running down the hall into Laura's room. Logan yelled, "Mom, Laura. Come see what Milo and I made with my blocks."

"Yeah! It's so cool. Close your eyes," Milo said and grabbed onto his mother's hand. Logan did the same and lead Kristy down the hall.

"Okay, open your eyes!" they said together.

Kristy and Laura opened their eyes. "Oh my," Kristy said a little surprized at what she was looking at. They had made a roadway for their cars taking up every inch of their bedroom floor.

Chapter 13

Krusty was putting the last spoonful of Laura's homemade peach cobbler in her mouth. She then turned the spoon over to lick out any morsels hiding in the spoon. "Miss Laura. That was the best peach cobbler I've ever tasted," she said.

"Remember my momma worked in a bakery and she taught me a lot about baking," Laura replied setting her spoon down, "We loved to cook and bake together."

Picking up her dishes and the boys', Laura said, "You two better get going. You don't want to be late seeing Robby tonight."

Kristy took her plate to the sink then turned and took Laura's away from her. While setting the dishes in the sink she said to her, "These can wait until later. I think it's about time that you two come and meet Robby."

Looking a little pale, Laura stammered, "I-I don't think we should."

"Why not?" Kristy asked.

"I'm a little scared. I've never seen a vegetable before," Laura frowned.

"He's not a vegetable but in a permanent vegetative state," Kristy corrected her, "It will be a little shocking at first. I'll make you a deal,"

Laura looked at her curiously, "Stay for 10 minutes and if you are feeling uncomfortable, you can wait in the main lobby or even better, play dominoes with Ozzie Becks and the boys."

"Can we take Ozzie some peach cobbler?" Logan asked.

"Great idea honey. Ozzie will love it!" Kristy said to her thoughtful son. Kristy looked at Laura, "Well, what do you say?"

"Okay. I'll bring that self-help book you gave me to read," touching the side of her head, she continued, "It's hard to read about spousal abuse when the bruises are still there."

"I can barely see them and that cut above your eye has almost healed," Kristy said gently pushing back Laura's hair.

"Remember what we were saying about Logan's dad," Kristy said to Milo as they walked down the hall to Robby's room.

"Yeah. He can't talk or walk but he can hear us," Milo replied.

They got to his room and walked through the opened door. Laura slowed down and stayed just inside the door entrance. Milo and Logan ran over to Robby's bed, "Dad. This is Milo. He's the boy I've been telling you about," Logan said. Robby turned his head toward Logan's voice.

Kristy whispered to Laura, "Robby always does that when Logan talks to him. He does it sometimes with me but always with Logan," Kristy walked over and gave Robby a tender kiss on his forehead.

Laura noticed that Robby was very handsome. His head had a dent on the left side where Kristy said his skull was crushed. His sandy blonde hair was brushed to cover it. She took a few steps closer and gasped a little bit. Kristy noticed and asked, "What's wrong? Is this too much for you to handle?"

"Oh. I see where Logan gets those incredible blue eyes." She paused surveying Robby's condition, "It's actually not as bad as I thought," she did notice that although the eyes were breathtaking, they didn't focus on anything. He was missing the spark she saw in Logan's eyes, "Why is he holding rolled up wash cloths?" Laura asked seeing Robby's long fingers wrapped around them.

"That's so his fingers don't ball up into a fist and stay that way," Kristy took Laura's hand and walked closer to Robby, "Robby darling, this is Laura my living angel," Laura blushed at her kind words. Kristy picked up Robby's right hand and took the washcloth out. She uncurled his fingers and put Laura's right hand in it and they shook. Laura could still feel calluses on his hands probably from his job as a firefighter. Kristy continued, "And Laura, this is the love of my life Robby." Something occurred to Kristy. Looking at Laura, she said, "You know. You have been here five days and I still don't know your last name. Isn't that crazy?"

"I know what it is," Logan interrupted, "It's Dixon with an x not an s. Laura told me. I told her my last name is Garrison spelled, G-a-r-r-i-s-o-n."

"He is a pretty smart kid. He is helping me teach Milo the alphabet and numbers," Laura said to Kristy, "He has a lot of great toys for that."

"I give most of the credit to his grandmother. She kept him entertained by teaching him the alphabet song. Once he could say the letters she started teaching him how to identify them. Then he learned to spell his name. I think she was going to work on the letter sounds next," Kristy said remembering that her mother-in-law was in the hospital, "That reminds me. Logan and I are going to Oklahoma City to visit his grandmother on my next day off. Would you and Milo like to come? We can do a little shopping and maybe see a movie."

"I've never seen a movie in a movie theater!" Milo squealed.

"I can't say no now," Laura said laughing at her son, "It sounds like fun but I don't have any money."

"Please don't worry about that. It will be my treat. You've been doing so much around the house for me and I should really pay you for looking after Logan," Kristy pointed out.

"Mommy. Can me and Milo take Ozzie his cobbler now?" Logan asked.

"Sure. It's Milo and I and make sure you introduce Milo to Ozzie properly first," Looking at Milo she asked, "Are you ready to play dominoes with three people now? You are doing so well just playing with Logan."

Milo glowed in Kristy's praise. "I am. I just have to remember to wait my turn. That will be the hard part."

Logan kissed his dad on the cheek, "See you in a bit Dad."

Milo decided he needed to do the same. He kissed Robby's cheek and said, "I'm going to play dominoes with Ozzie Becks. See ya."

Kristy saw Robby's eyes blink rapidly when they all started to laugh at Milo's sweet gesture.

Kristy was in the middle of shaving Robby when Logan and Milo came back with Ozzie Becks shuffling behind with his walker. Ozzie said, "I just had to come and meet the person responsible for the best peach cobbler I've ever tasted. I've tasted a lot in my day and they can't hold a candle to what I just ate."

Not use to such praise, Laura smiled shyly and said, "Thank you Ozzie."

Kristy wiped her hands and came over to do the introductions. Kristy was explaining to Ozzie how Laura came to live with them when Laura looked up to see the two little boys playing with the shaving cream on Robby's face. Mortified, Laura yelled, "Boys! Please stop. You really shouldn't be doing that to poor Robby."

Kristy and Ozzie started to laugh when they saw the funny designs on Robby's face. Kristy said, "It's fine Laura. Robby used to let Logan draw things in his shaving cream all the time before the accident."

"He did?" Laura was shocked. She knew Jason would yell at Milo for trying to do that.

Kristy continued, "I had forgotten that he did that with Logan until now. He would sit Logan on the counter by the sink and let Logan put the shaving cream on his face. Logan would draw something like a snowman on Robby's face. They usually had it everywhere by the time they finished and I would pretend to be mad. Really, it was so funny."

"It smells like Daddy," Logan said showing her a glob of shaving cream on the end of his finger.

"Milo," Ozzie said pointing to the little boy, "I like that name." Milo smiled at him.

"It's from that movie 'Milo and Otis,'" said Laura. "It was the only movie I saw as a child. My Aunt Melba took me to it."

Smiling, Ozzie continued, "I've only known one other Milo and it was right here in Guthrie."

"Really?" Milo said wide-eyed.

"Yep. Milo was the name of our principal at my high school way back in the 1930's," he said tweaking Milo's nose.

Kristy interrupted, "I thought his name was Mike like in Baldy Mike," she turned to Laura and quickly explained the Halloween tradition that was still going on.

"Mike was short for Milo. I guess there's not a lot of people alive today that know that Baldy Mike's real name was Milo," Ozzie said.

"Well, we'll make sure that this piece of news will be passed on, won't we Logan," Kristy said. He nodded back at his mom. Then she asked, "By the way Ozzie. What is your real name? I'm sure Ozzie is short for something like Oswald."

"Myron," Ozzie said answering Kristy's question.

"Huh?" everyone said in unison.

"That's right. My real name is Myron. I know, I know," Ozzie held up his hands, "You are asking yourselves how you get Ozzie out of Myron," they shook their head including the nurse who came in when she overheard the question outside Robby's door, "Well, you don't. For some odd reason my mother named my older brother Myron after her father and named me Myron after my brother. I was born with little hair but I did have peach fuzz on my head. My sister Shirley, who was only 18 months older than me, would rub my head and say 'fuzzy'. Because she was only one year old, it came out 'ozzie'. Since we already had one Myron in the family, they started calling me Ozzie. So, there it is ladies and gentlemen. That is how I got the name Ozzie. Much better than Myron don't ya think?"

"Ozzie Becks suits you just fine," Laura said giving him a wink.

Chapter 14

It was early dusk when Kristy, Laura, Logan and Milo drove into their driveway. They had just arrived home from their day trip to Oklahoma City. When the car turned off, Kristy and Laura both turned around to see two little boys sleeping in the back seat. Milo was using Bumper the Bear as a pillow.

Chuckling quietly, Laura said, "I don't remember doing so much in one day. No wonder they are sleeping," yawning, she continued, "I'm a little pooped myself."

After carrying the two sleeping boys up to their room, Kristy and Laura decided it would be best to let them sleep in just their underwear. They wanted to disturb them as little as possible. Tucking the bed sheet around them, they kissed both boys' heads and snuck out of the room as quietly as possible.

Closing the boy's bedroom door, Kristy whispered to Laura, "Do you want me to make you some coffee?"

"No thanks. Actually, how about herbal tea? I think I will head to bed soon and coffee would just wake me up. I am quite relaxed and feel like a nice cup of that summer blend tea I saw in the cupboard," Laura said stifling another yawn.

"Great idea. I haven't had hot tea in quite a while," Kristy said heading towards the stairs.

Laying her head back on the living room chair, Laura said, "That was such a fun day," looking across at Kristy who was sitting on the couch with one leg tucked under her. She smiled and continued, "Thank you again. That was such a treat for Milo to go to his first movie. It was a little loud for him at first but then he was mesmerized by the movie."

Chuckling, Kristy said, "Did you see how he sat on the end of his seat with his eyes glued to the screen?"

Sitting up to imitate him, Laura laughed, "He just kept shoveling popcorn in his mouth without looking down," sitting back she said, "I really like your in-laws. Robby's parents sure love you and Logan."

"I really love them," Kristy said setting her mug down on the coffee table, "They really embraced me as one of their own after my parents died. They were as devastated as much as I was when Robby had his accident. I don't know what I would have done without them. It's funny how we all dealt with it differently. I just wanted to stay with Robby the whole time and they took comfort with having Logan around. It was like having the young Robby back with them I think."

Shaking her head, Laura admitted, "There were times that I had hoped Jason would end up dead after one of his drinking binges. I used to daydream that the police would come up to the door to tell me. I would fake being sad but I know I would be relieved that he was gone. I would pack everything up into his beat up old pick-up truck and Milo and I would drive down the driveway with that stinkin trailer burning to the ground behind us," getting lost in her daydream, Laura continued, "I hated that trailer. There were so many bad memories in that place. I felt like I was in a prison. Jason would hardly let me leave unless I was with him. I could sometimes drive his truck into town to get groceries or take Milo to the doctor. He usually was hung over and didn't feel like going," looking down at her tea cup, she said, "He started working on a road crew so he made me quit my job to stay home with Milo. The people I was working with started noticing my absences and bruises. He was more concerned people were saying bad things about him than actually hurting me," Laura rolled her eyes.

"Didn't they do anything to help you?" Kristy was stunned.

"No. I think a few wanted to but were afraid of Jason," she answered. Laura continued, "We lived out in the boonies and he would actually lock the gate at the end of the driveway when he left so no one could come out to see me. It was ridiculous really, he made sure I didn't have any friends in Park City."

Kristy was quite shocked to hear the heartless things Laura was saying. She thought to herself that she probably would be the same way if she was abused one way or another in her life like Laura was. Pouring Laura more tea, Kristy asked, "Would you have gone to Montana to be with your grandparents?"

Shaking her head, no, Laura explained, "My grandmomma has ALS, you know, Lou Gehrig's disease. My granddad couldn't take care of her and it was getting really hard to work the ranch. I received a letter from him about six months ago and he said that he was selling the ranch and they were moving into Billings to live in some kind of home where a nurse could look after grandmomma. It sounded like he was going to use the money from the ranch to pay for the home and her medical bills," tearing up, she said, "I don't even know if she is alive. I stopped getting mail when Jason decided to punish me for spending too much money at the grocery store. Milo was sick and I bought some medicine for him. I guess I cut into his drinking money."

"How sad for you. Have you ever been able to say good-bye to anyone in a normal way?" Kristy asked.

"What's normal?" Laura responded.

"I don't know," Kristy said. After thinking for moment, she said, "I guess, being able to hold someone's hand as they died or just saying good-bye and I love you as they left," frustrated that she wasn't getting her point across, Kristy continued, "I think it's so important to have closure when someone is leaving your life. I'm sad I didn't get the chance to have that with my brother but I feel very fortunate that I was able to do that for both my parents."

"They didn't die right away?" Laura asked.

"No. Robby and I were able to get to the hospital before they passed. My mom could talk but had massive internal bleeding. She knew that she was dying. All she wanted to talk about was how she met my dad and when Cliff and I were kids. They were able to bring mom's bed in the same room as dad. Dad was on life support but didn't have any brain activity. He was considered brain dead. They needed Mom's permission to pull the plug." Both Laura and Kristy were crying and Kristy continued, "Mom made us promise that they wouldn't take Dad off life support until after she passed. I held Mom's right hand and she held Dad's right hand with Robby holding Dad's left. We were all connected. About two hours after we got there, Mom kissed Dad's hand and then told Robby and I how much she loved us. She then closed her eyes and peacefully passed away. I asked for Dad to come off life support right away," wiping a tear from her left cheek, she smiled slightly and continued, "I wanted them to be together when they went to heaven. I imagined their souls leaving holding hands," stopping to blow her nose, Kristy finished her story, "It didn't take long for Dad's heart to stop beating. Do you know they were physically still holding hands when he passed? Their love was unconditional to the end."

"Was it hard to watch them die?" Laura asked wiping her tears with her sleeve.

"It's always hard to see a loved one die. I was happy they did it peacefully. We only had five minutes with them. Both had signed an organ donation card and they needed to get them to surgery before it was too late. They were really selfless. It's nice to know a part of my parents still live on and they saved so many people's lives. I think my dad's heart went to a 16-year-old boy so I know it will beat for a long time." Kristy laughed breaking the sadness, "People said he had a big heart."

Chapter 15

Kristy was sitting up in bed on another beautiful Oklahoma summer morning. She had turned off the clunker of an air conditioner and opened the patio door. She could hear the birds and the neighborhood waking up. It was so peaceful and soothing. Her conversation with Laura the night before had been emotional and had left her sad and melancholy.

She looked at the clock on her nightstand. It read 7:12. Kristy thought, *this was much too early to be awake on my last day off.* She reached for her writing pad and pen that she kept in her nightstand drawer. She started writing down everything that needed to be done around the house and at her in-laws. *This should be my honey-do list,* she thought. *Now it is just my to-do list.*

Smiling to herself, she closed her eyes and pictured Robby mowing their lawn and her in-law's lawn. It took him forever because he would be so busy waving and talking to the neighbors. He would always come in the house after mowing the lawn with all kinds of stories and gossip. He thought he should write a column for the Guthrie News Leader about the funny, unusual happenings he had heard.

Just as she was writing down her sixth chore, she heard a shuffling noise coming from the hall. She looked up and she saw the bedroom door move which was about two-thirds closed. Laying down her list and pen, she watched the door closely. Under the door, she saw shadows moving back and forth. Smiling, she waited.

"Shhh, Milo! Walk quieter," Logan complained.

"Shhh, Logan! Talk quieter," she heard Milo say back.

Kristy quietly got up and snuck out of the open patio door. She could look through the window next to the door, into her room. The bedroom door was obviously moving back and forth. She rolled her eyes and thought, *these two need a lesson on spying.*

Suddenly, the door flew open and the boys ran and jumped on Kristy's bed yelling "Wake up!" they started pounding on the bed looking for her.

"Mommy!" Logan called out, "Where are you?"

Kristy came running through the open patio door growling, "I'm right here."

"Ahhhh!" Screamed the two little boys jumping. Milo dove under the covers and Logan fell off the side of the bed.

"Ha, ha. That will teach you to try to scare me," Kristy said jumping on the bed.

Logan stuck his head up beside the bed and started laughing. He crawled back up on the bed and gave his mom a big hug. Both pulled the covers back revealing Milo pretending to be asleep and snoring.

"What is all the ruckus down here?" Laura asked coming into the bedroom, "Well, isn't this quite a scene?" looking at a disheveled bed with three bodies wrestling in it. Laura picked up a pillow that had fallen on the floor. She started swatting at the boys. In no time, every- one had a pillow and a full-scale pillow fight had broken out.

"Can we have a pillow fight tomorrow too?" asked Logan with Milo shaking his head in support. The boys were sitting at the kitchen table eating a bowl of Cheerios and bananas.

Kristy poured two cups of coffee and was walking to the table, "That is a negative. We won't have any pillows left if we did it every day," she said setting a cup in front of Laura and sitting down next to her. She cherished her first sip of coffee every day.

Taking a drink of her coffee, Laura glanced up at the clock. She almost choked when she realized she was going to be late, "Oh my goodness. I have to get to Roxy's," she said standing up.

She was going to take her coffee and put it on the counter when Kristy said, "Just leave it here. It will save me from getting up and getting another cup. Why are you going to Roxy's?"

"Don't you remember?" Laura answered looking for her other shoe, "She said she wanted to do a make-over on me. I have to get there by 8:30 because she needs to leave for the diner by 11:30." Panicking, she said, "It's almost 8:30 now." She was putting on her other shoe hopping on one foot, heading out the door, "Say goodbye to the old pitiful me. The next time you will see me, I will be ..." she paused and posed, "Gorgeous!"

They were all waving and laughing at Laura as she left. Logan asked, "Mommy?" Kristy looked at him, "What are we going to do today?"

Pulling her to-do list out of her pocket, Kristy said, "Let's see what is on the paper. Ummm. Number one is to mow our lawn and Poppy's lawn. Number two is water Grammy's flowers. Then, clean up the screened in porch," she paused and looked at the two making sour faces, "What's with the faces boys?"

"We thought we were going to do fun stuff," Milo said looking at Logan who agreed.

"Let me finish," Kristy said holding up her right hand, "We need to get groceries."

"Awww," the sour faces puckered more.

"We need to get groceries," Kristy repeated, "after we go swimming at the club then home to have a camp-out in the back yard."

"What?" Logan said sitting up.

"That's right. It will take me about 45 minutes for me to mow both lawns. Before I do that, you boys can clean up any toys that I may run over with the lawn mower. Then you can water all of Grammy's flowers. Do you remember how she showed you to do it Logan?"

"Yup," he said, holding in his excitement.

Continuing, Kristy said, "When you finish watering, I should be finished mowing. We will clean up that messy porch so we can sleep in it tonight."

Milo had a hard time believing what he heard, "We can sleep out there tonight?" he pointed to the screened porch.

"It is so much fun Milo!" Logan yelled, "It's just like sleeping outside but without the bugs."

"Wow," was all Milo could say.

"After we finish the porch, I bet we will be hot and sweaty so why don't go to the club and swim for about an hour. We can have lunch and then we have to go get groceries for our campout," Kristy said. Looking at the light brown haired, brown eyed Milo she continued, "And when we get back, your mom will be back looking so beautiful."

"Wait until we tell her about the campout!" Milo said.

"Let's finish breakfast, get dressed and what else?" Kristy asked.

"Brush our teeth," Milo mumbled with a mouthful of cereal.

"What a busy and fun day we have planned. I think we should get hot dogs and marshmallows and roast them over the barbeque," Kristy said to the boys who shook their heads in agreement.

"Can we get popsicles and pop?" Logan asked.

As the boys gobbled their cereal and milk, Kristy finished her second cup of coffee. They made all sorts of plans for their camp out.

Chapter 16

Kristy, Logan and Milo came into the kitchen each carrying two grocery bags. The two boys were debating which Ninja Turtle was cooler when Laura walked into the room. All three stopped in their tracks, "Momma? Is that you?" Asked Milo.

Coming over and kissing her son on the cheek, she said, "You bet it is baby. Do you like it?" Laura asked, turning in a slow circle.

Milo was at a loss for words. He just stood there staring at his newly blonde and beautiful mother. Kristy was the first one to talk, "Laura. What a transformation. You look so young and pretty."

Laughing, Laura said, "Well, I probably look my age then. Remember, I'm only 22 but I looked like I was in my 30's before. Didn't Roxy do an amazing job?"

"She sure did," agreed Kristy setting the groceries on the counter, "What all did she do?"

"Let's see. Obviously, she got rid of my mousy brown hair and gave me blonde highlights. This is almost the same color my hair was before I got pregnant. She gave me a good haircut because it had been years since I've had one. I really like the length. I've never had hair shorter than the middle of my back," Laura said running her fingers through her hair, which was now at her shoulders. She continued, "Roxy said that I needed to get a lot cut off because it was dry and brittle. Stress and bad eating, leads to unhealthy hair and skin," Laura patted her face, "She gave me a mini facial. It was my first facial and it felt so good"

"You do look a lot healthier. Your skin color is nice and pink and the circles under your eyes are almost gone," Kristy noticed.

"That's because Roxy showed me how to cover them and how to apply make-up," Laura felt pleased with her new look, "Remember, since I have been here, I've been sleeping and eating so much better. I've never felt this healthy before," she ran and gave Kristy a hug. She whispered in her ear, "This is all thanks to you. I don't know where we would be right now if you hadn't insisted we stay," standing back and looking Kristy in the eyes, she continued, "I've never known what a happy home felt like until now. I love you like a sister and Logan like my nephew," throwing her arms up in the air she yelled, "I love Roxy, this house, you guys and Guthrie, Oklahoma!"

Milo ran and hugged his Mom around her waist, "I love it here too Momma. Logan is my best friend and Kristy is so much fun, "looking up at her he asked, "Can we get a puppy?"

Kristy put her hands up, "Wait a minute here. Logan's been asking for a puppy for a while. I didn't think I could handle one with every-thing that has happened. It wouldn't be fair to the puppy if we weren't around to take care of it."

Logan interrupted, "There are four of us now Mommy. I think we could all take turns looking after it. Milo and I would play with it and walk it."

"Yeah, we would feed it and give it so much love," Milo finished Logan's sentence.

Kristy looked at Laura, "Do you think they can take on the responsibility?"

Laura looking at the boys said, "We will have to all go and learn how to train the puppy. You will always have to be kind to it and never ever be mean or hurt it."

The boys were shaking their heads in agreement. Logan spoke up first, "We will. I've wanted a dog since I was little."

"We promise that we will take good care of it Momma, Milo said very hopeful.

"I know," Kristy said, "On my next day off, we will go into Oklahoma City to visit Grammy. Maybe, we can stop by the dog shelter and see if there are any puppies that would be a good fit for our little family."

"I like the sound of that," Laura laughed, "I think, boys, that is a yes."

"Yay!" yelled the boys jumping up and down. When they settled down, Logan asked, "What smells so good?"

"Oh Lord. I have two pecan pies in the oven," running over to check on the pies, Laura said, "Thanks for reminding me. Roxy said that she loves pecan pie so I made two. One for us and one for Roxy as a thank you for my make over," pointing to the Tupperware container on the counter, Laura added, "I also made cookies. I think once we get the groceries put away, we should all sit down and have a little snack."

"Great idea," agreed Kristy, "Did I see some sun tea brewing outside?"

"It should be done by now. I'll go get it if you guys want to start putting away the groceries," looking at Milo, she said, "I can't wait to hear about your day."

When Laura got back, Milo said to her, "We are having a camp out on the screened porch Mommy!" He had been bursting to tell her all day, "We are going to roast hot dogs and marshmennows," handing Laura the apples, he said, "This has been the funnest day. We got our chores done and then we went swimming. I jumped in and went all the way under the water. I wasn't even scared."

"Good job buddy. I'll have to take you guys swimming a lot more now," Laura said hugging her son.

"I actually talked to the club manager and you and Milo are now on our membership. It helps that my Dad was the club manager for a very long time there. They have given us a lifetime membership and didn't blink an eye when I asked if you two could go on," Kristy said, "You can go swimming every day if you wanted to."

"How wonderful!" Laura exclaimed, "I've only ever been to one other private club and that was in Tulsa. Aunt Melba and Uncle Jess were members there and the one summer I spent with them, they took me to the club and gave me swimming lessons."

"Well. There is a reason I wanted you to be members. I thought Logan and Milo could take swimming lessons since you are here during the day to take them. I couldn't take Logan before because of work and then everything else started piling up around the house. I felt bad because Robby was teaching Logan to swim before his accident. Robby used to be a life-guard at the club and was a wonderful swimming instructor," Kristy said, feeling a little sad that he wasn't able to finish his lessons with Logan.

"I want to learn to dive from the high board," Milo said pretending he was diving into the water.

"Do you think I could sign up for a yoga class while the boys are swimming? I've always wanted to try it but Jason thought it was stupid and a waste of money." Laura wanted to add, *and drinking beer night after night wasn't?* She kept that to herself since Milo was still in the room.

"Of course. I might join you sometime. It really is a good way to relax and get stronger at the same time," Kristy pointed out.

Testing the cooling pies, Laura asked, "Who wants to take a drive out to the I-35 Diner so I can give Roxy her pie?" Two little hands shot up.

"I think we should all go and have dinner out there," Kristy said.

"What about our hot dogs?" Logan reminded her.

"We can have hot dogs tomorrow. I think we need to celebrate Laura's beautiful new look," Laura blushed at the compliment. Kristy continued, "We can come home and make s'mores for dessert. What do you say?"

"Let's go!" Laura shouted as she carefully picked up her freshly baked pie.

"Laura, that is the best pecan pie I have ever tasted," commented Carl as he ran his finger over his plate to pick up the last of the gooey filling.

"You should taste her peach cobbler and cookies," Kristy paused, "Well, practically everything she has baked is fantastic."

Carl started to cut another piece when Roxy slapped his hand away, "Oh no you don't buster. This is my pie and I kindly let you have one piece."

"Y'all are being very nice," Laura said laughing at Carl's pouting face, "I have another one at home, so I will send a piece in with Kristy tomorrow."

Carl gave her a side hug while everyone sat at the counter laughing. Roxy decided she had better hide the rest of her pie until she got off work so she disappeared into the back.

Kristy looked out the window to check on Milo and Logan. They had gone out to see Boris' new 18-wheeler. They were sitting in the cab pretending to drive it. Boris was one of Kristy's regular customers. He drove up and down the I-35 at least three times a week. Boris always stopped at the diner and ordered his favorite; chicken-fried-steak, mashed potatoes with gravy, corn-on-the cob and two cups of black coffee with apple pie for dessert.

Maureen, the other full-time waitress came over and said, "Gee Laura. Can you make my favorite, sweet potato pie? My grandmother is well known for her sweet potato pie but she is the only one that knows how to make it. I don't think she ever had a recipe for it. As a matter of fact, I don't think I ever saw her cook anything with a recipe."

"I bet she was a great cook, Maureen," Laura said, "My Momma was a great baker and I never saw her use a recipe. She taught me how to bake without recipes," laughing, she continued, "I have had a few disasters but they just help me learn what not to do."

"My grandparents raised me, my four brothers and one sister in Moore, Oklahoma. They also had two or three of my cousins living with them on and off. Grandmother was always cooking up a storm," Maureen said recalling the massive amount of food at the dinner table.

Maureen was a six-foot tall, 25-year-old African-American woman. She and her husband Isaiah Russell moved to Guthrie the year before. The 27-year-old Isaiah was an assistant football coach and health teacher for the Guthrie High School Blue Jays. He was a standout football and track star at Langston University. He met Maureen at Langston where she was a basketball star in her own right. They got married after he graduated and she sacrificed her degree and basketball scholarship to follow him to Guthrie. She was hired to coach the freshman girls' basketball team and decided to take the job at the Diner because of the flexible hours.

"Well, I volunteer to taste anything you make, disaster or not," Carl put his hands on his growing stomach.

"There's a great idea," Maureen said.

"What's a great idea?" Roxy asked as she walked back to the group.

"I think Laura should start an at home bakery and the Diner and other restaurants can buy her baking from her. This way, she can look after the boys and make some money too," Maureen said, thrilled she came up with the idea.

"I don't know. I'm not sure how to run a business. Besides, I've only just starting baking again since I moved in with Kristy. I had to stop because we hardly had any money for groceries. I had to pick and choose what we ate," she continued, "I made sure that Milo got his food first and there wasn't a lot left over for baking," Laura said with a shudder. It was such a horrible time thinking she wouldn't be able to feed your baby.

"Hey, don't worry about that," Maureen patted her hand, "I was a business major before we moved here. I can help you with all of that."

Reaching into her bra, Roxy pulled out a wad of bills. She slapped the bills down in front of Laura and said, "Here you go honey. I will invest in your little home business and this is the first installment. $150 should be enough to buy your groceries. If you need more, I would be happy to help. You can pay me back by doing my Christmas baking for me. And honey, I like a lot."

Kristy clapped her hands, "What a great idea! I've got all the pans and stuff you need for baking."

Carl said, "We do need some new desserts and baking around here. I will be happy to buy them but I want the exclusive rights to them. I don't want my competitors to have access to that great pecan pie."

Laura put her head down on the counter. She was a little overwhelmed at what was happening. When she lifted her head, she rubbed her temples, "I, I'm not sure what to say," looking at everyone, she could see the excitement for Maureen's idea. She put her hands down and smiled, "How can I say no." The little group gave a little cheer and Maureen and Carl gave each other a high five. She continued, "My first priority are the boys. I don't want to be baking all the time and not be able to do things with them. Kristy and I were just talking about taking them to swimming lessons. School is going to be starting soon and there will be a lot to do to get them ready."

Kristy could see that she was a little stressed, "Why don't you take a day or so to think about it over? We can talk about it later to see if things can work out."

"Good idea," Roxy agreed, "You don't have to start big. Just make a few things a day at first then when the boys are in school, you can start making more."

Laura was already feeling relieved and she started to feel their excitement, "Thanks guys. With all your help, I think this might work."

Chapter 17

"You are a useless piece of shit. What makes you think that you can make money baking cakes and crap like that?" Jason said as he discovered his beer bottle was empty, "You are only good for one thing and that's getting me beer. This one's empty so do your job," He tossed his empty bottle at her hitting her on the shoulder as she turned to avoid it.

Just as the bottle hit Laura, she jerked awake. She was breathing hard like she was having a panic attack. She realized it was just a dream but it felt so real. How many times did Jason call her useless? She said out loud, "At least five times a day," she thought for a few seconds then said, "What am I doing? Maybe Jason is right. I will probably screw this business up. Everyone was just being nice and saying they liked my baking."

Laura then noticed the moon and stars on the ceiling. Looking around, she realized she was on the porch not in her room. She started to calm down since Jason was only in her dream and not in the same room. She wondered how he was doing living without her. Laura took a deep breath and shook her head trying to shake him out of it. If she was going to survive, she had to stop thinking about him.

Laura could hear two little voices coming from the kitchen. She yelled out to them, "Good morning boys. Can you tell me what time it is please?"

"We can't tell time," she heard them yell back in unison.

"Oh right," she chuckled. She's made the mistake of asking them to read something when they haven't learned to read yet. Logan knows how to read some words, not sentences. It is easy to forget how young they are when they seem so mature for their age.

Laura started rolling over to get up from the air mattress. A loud groan escaped her mouth when she tried to stand up. She had slept in the same position almost the whole night. Her back was feeling a little sore and stiff.

A couple months ago, Jason came home drunk. He was very angry with Laura because someone at the bar said they saw her buying make-up at the local drugstore. That person made the comment that she probably needed it to cover the fresh bruises on her neck. Jason was so angry, one for being accused of abusing his wife and two that she lied to him about needing money for extra groceries.

He left the bar ready to kill her. He didn't bother to open the trailer door. Instead he just kicked it open. Laura had just put Milo to bed and was cleaning up the kitchen. Jason came in and grabbed her by both her arms. He was yelling and swearing at her for lying to him. Laura couldn't figure out what she had done wrong but any attempt to defend herself fell on deaf ears. It just made Jason angrier. He picked her up and threw her towards the open door. She slammed into the doorframe at a funny angle. When she hit it, she felt a slight pop in the middle of her back. Before Jason could grab her again, Milo came running out of his room and stood in front of his dad crying, "Stop Daddy. You're hurting Momma."

"Get out of the way son. Your mother is a liar and she needs to be punished," he said while trying to push Milo out of the way.

"No Daddy!" Milo pleaded grabbing onto his dazed mother.

Jason saw the fear in his son's eyes. He decided that he didn't need to be judged by his four-year-old son so he picked up his keys and headed for the door. As he walked by Laura, he gave her a kick with his cowboy boot. He pointed at her and through his clenched teeth he said, "Don't ever lie to me again or this boy will grow-up without a mother."

Laura stood up, stretched and rubbed her back to get the soreness out. She stiffly walked into the kitchen to find the boys at the kitchen table making Cheerio towers. Logan's tower had just fallen over and both boys started laughing. Milo's tower was still standing so he stood on his chair and opened his mouth wide. He tried to devour the whole tower. He was able to get two-thirds of the tower in his mouth. He straightened up and Laura and Logan could see that he could hardly chew because his mouth was so full. This started another round of laughter and Milo couldn't keep his mouth closed. Cheerios came spewing out of his mouth all over the table. This had Logan rolling on the floor laughing. Even Laura was holding her stomach because she was laughing hard. She went to the refrigerator and poured two glasses of milk so the boys could wash down the Cheerios that they swallowed. She walked over and grabbed the broom and dustpan and handed it to the boys. She said, "I don't mind you making a mess as long as you clean it up."

With fresh milk moustaches, the boys started cleaning up their breakfast, Laura remembered why she had come into the kitchen in the first place. She looked at the clock and saw that it was 8:00. Kristy had left for work over an hour ago and she estimated that the boys had been awake for at least half an hour. She couldn't believe she slept for that long but she and Kristy had been up until midnight planning for her little venture. Kristy had more confidence that it was going to work than she did.

They decided that Laura should start by making two or three different kinds of pies. Laura loved making pies and Kristy said her piecrust was the best and flakiest she had ever tasted.

Laura thought that she would make pecan pie since everyone seems to love it so much and maybe once in a while add chocolate to it. Also, she thought a caramel apple pie and a cherry crumble pie would be good. If she could get the ingredients, Laura wanted to make huckleberry pie in honor of her grandmother in Montana. She also thought she should stay away from any cream pies until the Oklahoma heat subsided. They would order the groceries through the diner to get a wholesale price on the ingredients. Kristy has all the cooking utensils so she should be set.

She thought she would bake five mornings a week before it got too hot in the kitchen. Laura would send the pies with Kristy when she went to work. They would freeze them there and use them when needed. Knowing her customers, Kristy felt they wouldn't be frozen too long. They had spent at least half an hour trying to come up with a good name. They thought of 'Laura's Likeable Pies'. 'Lovely Laura's Pies'. 'Milo's Mom's Home Baking'. Finally, they decided to simply call it 'Laura's Home Baking'.

Laura knew the boys loved to play first thing in the morning so they would keep themselves busy while she baked. Then they would go for their swimming lessons after lunch. If she had time, Laura thought she might bake muffins or cookies after the boys went to bed.

This was so exciting to her. This will be money that she earned herself and could have control over. Laura knew that with Milo heading to kindergarten, he would need school supplies and clothes. It would be so nice to buy him new, not discounted clothes or hand-me-downs.

Chapter 18

"Hey Carl! Do we have anymore huckleberry pie back there?" Roxy yelled through the door leading into the kitchen.

"Nope. That was the last one. I have one more caramel apple and that's it for the pies," he walked to the door and handed Roxy the last pie, "Hey Kristy. When is Laura going to be making her next delivery?"

Kristy set the dirty dishes she was carrying into the bins. Wiping her hands on her apron, she said, "You mean we are out of pie already? I just brought 10 pies in yesterday. They should have lasted at least three days."

Roxy finished cutting the pie and started to dish out a piece onto a plate, "Well, if she didn't make such darn good pies, they probably would have lasted more than two days. People are now coming in for just pie and coffee since Laura started baking for us."

Rubbing his hands together, Carl said, "Business has picked up about 20% and we have only been selling Laura's Home Baking for two weeks. Word is getting out."

"As Laura's business manager, I think I will recommend that Laura raise the wholesale price of her pies." Maureen said then chuckled at Carl's stunned face, "Supply and demand Carl, supply and demand."

"You wouldn't Maureen," Carl said. He was hoping she wasn't serious.

"I have only made six pies. Two huckleberry, two cherry crumble and two apple." Laura said into the phone amazed that the I-35 Diner was out of pie, "The pecans are still in the oven and won't be ready for another 40 minutes."

She could hear Kristy relay the information to Carl. Kristy came back on the line and said, "Okay. Carl is on his way over to pick up the pies himself. Can you make two more pecan pies after the two in the oven are finished?"

"Actually, no. I am out of ingredients. It would be nice to get a good supply, but we have no room here to store it. I am just stunned that people like them that much," Laura was confused, "Besides, after these come out, the boys and I are having a picnic at the park. Then Logan wants to run through the sprinkler. That's okay, isn't it?"

"Of course, it is. I was just telling him how I used to do it when I was a kid. I think I might join you guys when I get off work. This heat is unbelievable," Kristy said, "Well, I better get going. The diner is getting busier thanks to your baking. Bye!"

As Kristy came out of the garage and headed for the back door, she stopped and watched the two little boys sitting on the back step, eating popsicles. They were wearing their swimming trunks ready to run through the sprinkler. Logan was eating a grape popsicle and Milo was eating an orange. She heard Milo say, "a lick for a lick?" Logan offered his popsicle for Milo to try and at the same time Milo was holding his popsicle for Logan to lick. Kristy loved what she saw so she got her cell phone out and took a picture. After taking the picture, she stood and watched their interaction. She thought, *they are such kindred spirits and their love for each other was so evident. Who would let you take a lick of your popsicle but your absolute best friend?*

It has been three and a half weeks since Laura and Milo came to Guthrie and the boys have not been apart for a minute. As far as she knew, they have never had a fight. The boys seem to know what each other are thinking and always finish each other's sentences. Kristy felt so blessed to have Laura and Milo in their lives. Just a month ago, she was in such despair and now there was so much laughter and activity in her house again. It's amazing to Kristy how fast life can turn from the worst to the best.

"Hey, you two, are there any popsicles left for me?" Kristy asked.

"Mommy!" Logan yelled. Both boys got up and ran over to her and gave her a hug. She could feel something cold on the back of her legs and knew she would have a purple and orange stain on her uniform. She just laughed and enjoyed this wonderful welcome home.

"Kristy!" Laura called out the screen door, "I'm so glad you are home. I really, really have to talk to you."

Kristy was having a hard time reading Laura's demeanor. She was excited about something but couldn't tell if it was a happy or a sad excitement. "Yeah, of course. Boys, why don't you stay out here and finish your popsicles," looking at the melting popsicles running down their arms and down their chests, she continued, "Under no circumstance can the two of you come into the house until you have washed off that sticky mess."

"Yay!" they both shouted.

Kristy walked over and turned up the water running, the boys had finished their snack and were ready to get wet. Kristy barely got out of the way of the water before she entered the house. She saw Laura sitting in the screened porch waiting for her with a shocked expression on her face. Laura said, "Do you want to change before we have our talk?"

"I really would. I'm hot and now sticky and would love to get into some shorts. Is that okay?" Kristy asked knowing how anxious Laura was.

Laura nodded her head yes and said, "I'll get us two iced-teas. Please hurry!"

Ten minutes later, Kristy came into the screened porch, "Sorry for taking a little longer. I really needed to put something on those popsicle stains before they set in," taking the iced-tea from Laura, she continued, "Oh, thanks for this. Now what is it you want to talk to me about?"

"Okay. You know that Carl came to pick up the pies," Laura didn't wait for a response and kept going, "Well, we got to talking and Carl wants to pay me a salary to bake for him exclusively."

"That's great Laura!" Kristy had a lot of questions but decided to let Laura finish.

"As you know, with one oven, I can only bake a little at a time so he wants me to come and do my baking at the diner," Laura said taking a sip of iced tea.

"I'm not sure where. That kitchen is barely big enough for the cooks in there now," Kristy responded.

"Exactly," Laura agreed, "That's why Carl is willing to shut the I-35 Diner for two weeks to do renovations to the kitchen. He figures he can knock out the wall between the kitchen and the storage room and put in a baking area. I would have a prep area, fridge, stove and two ovens!"

Stunned, Kristy said, "Wow. For Carl to shut the diner down and go two weeks without revenue is unbelievable. He made it a 24-hour diner so we could feed the truck drivers whenever they needed. He kind of likes money coming in at all hours. Those drivers make up most our customers and so many drive during the night."

"Carl told me that since I started sending my baking in, business has gone up. He really thinks that the money he loses for that two weeks and the reno costs will pay for themselves in the long run with the added customers," Laura said taking a big breath.

"I think he is right," Kristy agreed, "How will this affect you taking care of the boys?"

"Of course, that was the first thing I asked him," Laura told her, "He said that I could drop them off at school, then come in to bake. I would only have to do it three maybe four days a week."

"But they are finished at noon. Will that be enough time to get your baking done?" Kristy asked.

"No, but when we were at the park for our picnic today, I met a mom whose daughter will be in the boy's kindergarten class. She was saying how she was a nurse but she quit when she had Beth. She was going back part time because they needed a little extra money. She found out that she was pregnant with their second child and the doctor doesn't want her working. Something about problems with her first pregnancy."

"I see where you're going with this," said Kristy, "She could look after the boys in the afternoons so you can stay and bake."

"Yup," said Laura shaking her head vigorously.

"Well, if she can't work, do you think she should look after two very energetic boys?" Kristy said looking out and seeing Milo standing directly over the sprinkler. Logan was laughing and threw a football at him.

Laura shrugged her shoulders and said, "I don't know but I really thought she was hinting that she would babysit the boys if we ever needed. I can talk to her and see if we could work something out."

"I'd be willing to pay her $150 a week for Logan if she picks them up at school and feeds them lunch. I get off at 3:00 so I can pick them up and we can go over and see Robby. I think that would be fair. Hopefully, $300 a week is enough for her. What is her name anyway?" Kristy asked.

"Um, it's Rita Mc something," Laura replied.

"Rita McBain. Her husband is George McBain who is a paramedic at the fire station. I don't know her too well but I do know she is a very good mother. I would feel good leaving Logan with her. Do you want me to talk to her?" Kristy asked.

"No, I'll do it. She gave me her number," Laura smiled, "I'm glad to hear that she is good with kids. I could see how well she took care of Beth."

Kristy set her empty ice tea glass down, "So, it looks like I will have two weeks off before the boys go to school. What do you want to do? We could drive over to Branson and go to Silver Dollar City. Robby and I went there for our honeymoon and thought how much fun it would be to take kids."

"That sounds really fun but I would really like to go to Billings and see about my grandparents. I have a feeling that grandmomma has died. I know granddad will be so heartbroken if that has happened," Laura said feeling sad.

"That sounds great!" Kristy smiled at Laura hoping to cheer her up, "We can drive up and make stops on the way. I have always wanted to see Estes Park and Yellowstone."

"Me too. We drove through Yellowstone one time but Daddy wouldn't stop to see Old Faithful," lowering her voice to sound like her father, Laura continued, "What's the big deal about water shooting up from the ground? I'm driving and I don't want to waste time stopping."

"I think we should go out and tell the boys. I guess we will have to tell them that we have to put the puppy on hold. This trip and you going back to work changes things," Kristy said.

"They are going to be so disappointed," Laura said not looking forward to this conversation. She hoped they wouldn't blame her for it.

Kristy got up and said, "The last one through the sprinkler is a stinky armadillo!"

Chapter 19

"Look boys, we're entering the Oklahoma pan handle!" Kristy shouted to the back of the motorhome. "Only a few more hours until we are home."

"Yay!" came from the back. The loudest cheer coming from Roxy sitting next to Kristy.

Laughing, Kristy said, "You were the one that wanted to come with us."

"Well what else did I have to do other than clean my house for two weeks." Roxy rolled her eyes, "I'm not complaining but those boys have so much energy. They have asked so many questions... and do they ever walk? They have one speed and it is full speed ahead."

Laura came up and put her arms around Roxy's shoulders, "They just don't want to miss anything. They learned and saw so many new things on this trip. They are crazy about their Auntie Roxy. Milo told me that he thinks you are the funniest person ever."

"Oh Lordy," Roxy said fanning herself," I had a blast with them but I think I need a vacation from this vacation to get rested. At least the I-35 won't be open for another three or four days. I think I will sleep for the next 72 hours."

"I know what you are saying," Kristy agreed, "It's going to take that long to clean this motorhome so we can give it back, in respectable condition, to your brother. That was so nice of him to let us use it. We saved so much money on hotels and food. The boys loved the camp grounds with their pools and game rooms."

"It was nice for me to see the old Ranch," Laura said with sadness in her voice, "It was a little out of the way but just seeing it again brought back some of the few happy memories from my childhood."

Roxy took off her seatbelt and got up to give Laura a hug. In Laura's ear, she whispered, "I'm sorry honey about your grandmother. She sounded like a wonderful, strong lady."

"Thanks, Rox," Laura said pulling back from the hug, "I really wasn't surprised that she had passed," Laura was holding back tears, "I was surprised that Granddad was so old and weak. It makes me sad to see him like that. He was such a big, strong man. You'd have to be to work like he did on that ranch. I'm glad Milo got to meet him even though Granddad will probably forget about us. The nurse told me that his, what is it, dem, dem."

"Dementia," Kristy answered from the driver's seat.

"Yeah, his dementia is getting worse," with tears rolling down her cheeks, she continued, "I think that will be the last time I will ever see him. At least I got to say goodbye to him Kristy."

"I'm glad you did sweetie," Kristy said remembering their conversation about losing loved ones.

"I was so happy I was able to get some of her things. Granddad was so nice to let me just go through all her stuff," Laura said wiping her eyes, "That music box is very special to me. I would play it a lot when we'd go visit. I loved watching the ballroom dancers bounce up and down then twirl."

"I'm grateful that you found your grandmother's recipes," Roxy said.

"I didn't think she used any because she always cooked without them. I guess she just knew the recipes by heart," Laura added.

"Maureen will be happy that you found a recipe for sweet potato pie," Kristy laughed.

"That will be the first one I bake," Laura smiled warmly.

"Freddie Mapp, what have you done?" Kristy yelled at the young man painting her front porch as she slammed the driver's side door on the motorhome.

Startled, Freddie turned to Kristy, "What are you doing here? I thought you were going to be home tomorrow."

"We made good time. Now explain what you have done," Kristy said as she walked up to her front porch. Laura and the boys heard her yelling so they came running around the corner to see what happened.

"Oh man! I wanted it to be finished so it could be a surprise," Freddie said blushing. He had the habit of rubbing his blonde brush cut when he was nervous.

"Well, I am surprised," Kristy said giving the tall 20 something man a hug. "When I asked you to house sit, I didn't mean for you to paint it," she paused and continued, "and it looks like fix it too," Kristy smiled up at him.

Freddie was relieved to see the smile. He really thought she was mad at him, "I'm not the type of person to sit around. I love to build and fix things. I noticed a few things that needed fixing, so I did it. "

"There are more than a few things to be fixed. This house has seen bet...." Before Kristy could finish her sentence, two burly men and her best friend, Becky walked out of the house, "What are you guys doing here?" she asked.

Becky ran over and gave Kristy a hug, "Charlie and I saw Freddie fixing your porch and then I remembered you complaining about the faucets in the bathrooms. Charlie called his brother Dave here, who is the best plumber in town, to come and replace them." Charlie Gibbs was Becky's boyfriend of 10 months and a firefighter like Robby. It was Robby who introduced the two.

Grabbing onto Becky to steady herself, Kristy said, "What? Dave, thank you so much. What do I owe you?"

"Are you kidding me? Your husband saved my dog when she fell down that old dried up well. He took such great care in splinting her leg that the vet said it prevented any other damage to her leg. I'm happy to report she is perfect now. I am so grateful to Robby that this is the least I could do for you," Dave said while Kristy walked over to hug him.

Logan came running over to Dave and said, "You're a plumber? Cool. I can't believe you get to crawl around in the sewers and stuff."

"Wow," Milo said looking at Dave like he was his hero.

Laughing, Dave said, "It's not that great guys. It's pretty dirty and smelly most of the time."

"I know!" the boys said at the same time.

Shaking her head Kristy looked at Freddie and said, "Well, let's try out this beautiful porch."

"Um, Kristy. There is more I need to tell you. Why don't you sit down?" Freddie looked a little nervous.

As Kristy and Laura sat on the front porch swing, two little boys came running up with fresh paint on their hands.

"We haven't been home five minutes and you two already need scrubbing," Laura scolded the boys.

"Ha, ha. Don't worry Laura, that paint can come off with soap and water," Freddie laughed.

"Ok Freddie, what else do you need to tell me?" Kristy asked a little nervous.

"Why don't we show her?" Becky pulled out her phone, "I thought you would want to see what has been going onto appreciate everything."

Kristy took the phone and saw the start of a video. She heard Becky's voice say, "Hey Kristy, it's me your long time best friend. This is what's been happening on the Egg while you and your family are gallivanting up to Montana," Kristy gave Becky a look of concern. The video showed Becky walking up to the front porch where Freddie was hammering new floorboards into place, "Freddie! I'm making a video to show Kristy what's been happening. Can you explain what it is you're doing?"

Freddie sat down on the second step still holding his hammer, "Okay Kristy. Don't get mad but I almost fell through the rotting boards on the porch and it gave me the idea to fix them. I also noticed that there are a few things in your house that needed fixing too. So, on my days off, I thought I would repair them. This is what I love to do and I feel bad that I haven't been around to help you since Robby's accident. Robby was the only guy at the fire station to take me under his wing and help me. The other guys just played tricks on me but Robby taught me. I wish I told him how much I appreciated it. Oh yeah. I fixed the front stairs on your in-law's house too. I heard Robby's Mom broke her ankles on it. I'd better get back to work. Damn it's hot out here. See ya," Freddie gave the camera a shy wave.

Kristy was speechless and gave Freddie's hand a squeeze. Becky's voice just came on "Okay folks. That was the very single Freddie Mapp. As you can see, he's tall, handsome, handy and very compassionate. I will probably post this on YouTube so single ladies out there who are interested, can find Freddie at the Guthrie fire station most of the time," Freddie was startled and his face went beet red. Everyone else laughed while Charlie slapped him on the back.

Becky continued, "Well here is another good-looking guy. No, he is not single because he is mine. Hey Charlie, tell Kristy what we have been up to. "

Flashing his gorgeous smile, the dark curly haired, green-eyed Charlie Gibbs said, "Well Kristy. My brother Dave and I have changed all the faucets in the house so no more drips. Well, except for Freddie here," Charlie said as he signaled with his thumb over his shoulder towards Freddie, "Two of the three toilets were ancient so we replaced those too. "

Dave Gibbs came up and put his arm around his brother. With his mouth full of cookie, he said, "And then we raided your freezer. We found all sorts of cookies and cupcakes. So good Laura!" He held up the last bite of cookie before he tossed into his mouth. Dave swallowed and continued. "Seriously. We're so happy to do this. Robby saved my dog and for that I'm eternally grateful. Also, he is a friend of this idiot," he grabbed Charlie's head a put it into a headlock, "Not a lot of people would be brave enough to come close to him."

"Now boys! "Becky yelled at them as Charlie flipped Dave to the ground, "Sorry Kristy. I'll have more for you later. Bye sweetie."

Milo and Logan were laughing at the brothers on the video when something flew out of Milo's nose. Laura pulled a tissue out of her pocket and picked it up. She gave him a dirty look. Laughing even harder Logan let out a big snort. Laura guided the boys off the porch and said, "Oh my goodness Milo and Logan. When you two get the giggles out of you, then you can come back."

There was a pause on the video. Becky came on again but this time she was in the backyard, "I hope you guys are sitting down because this is unbelievable" The camera scanned the backyard and there were five people planting flowers in new flowerbeds. Others were hauling newly trimmed tree branches. "Hey guys! I'm filming what is happening here for Kristy. Ya'll say hi!"

Everyone stopped working and yelled, "Hi Kristy!"

"Is that Boris?" Kristy asked pointing to the fellow carrying the branches.

"Yup," Freddie answered, "He heard what was happening and wanted to help out. He said he could spare an afternoon so he brought a few more of your regular customers with him. They all talked about how you treat them so well. They stop at a lot of restaurants on their driving routes and you are their favorite server," Pointing to a guy on the right side of the screen, he said, "See that guy. He used to be a tree trimmer and said that there were a lot of over grown trees and shrubs that needed trimming."

Rolling her eyes Kristy said, "I know. Robby and I had put cleaning up the yard on our to-do list this summer. Unfortunately, it fell to the bottom of my to-do list," as the camera scanned to the back door, Kristy looked closely at the person walking out, "Is that Maureen?" she asked.

"Hi Kristy, Laura, Roxy and boys. It is real lonely around here without you. Since football practice has started, Isaac and I couldn't go anywhere. I heard what was happening and thought I could help out. I hope you don't mind, but we are giving your house a good spring-cleaning. I know how hard it has been for you to get things done around here so we are here to do it for you. Oh, here is our boss.

Hey Carl, what do you have here?" Maureen asked.

Carl set down what looked like an air conditioner, "Howdy ladies. I heard you complaining about the old air conditioner in your room Kristy. I bought a new, bigger one for the kitchen and staff room so you can have this one. It still works great but is too small for the added baking area. It may smell like fried chicken but eventually that will go away," Carl laughed, "I don't want cranky people working for me so here you go," looking to the back of the yard, Carl yelled, "Boris! Come and give me a hand with this will ya?" Looking back into the camera he said, "Come and see the new diner when you get home. Everything looks great!"

Kristy was shocked by the generosity of everyone, "I can't believe this. How is everyone hearing about this?"

"We better pause the video," Becky said taking the phone out of Kristy's hand, "I have some explaining to do."

Kristy sat back and crossed her arms, "What did you do Becky?"

"I was talking to Mary-Sue, you know your other long time best friend," Becky was stalling a bit.

"I know who she is," Kristy was getting worried.

"Well, since her in-laws came for a visit and decided to stay the rest of the summer, she hasn't been able to have a minute to herself. I told her what Charlie, Dave, Freddie and I were doing and she really wished she could be here to help. Since she couldn't, she came up with the brilliant idea to have her DJ husband talk about it on the radio. Then friends started showing up and strangers started dropping off things like new towels and a shower curtain."

Kristy covered her face with her hands and shook her head, "Becky! I don't want people looking at me like I'm pathetic. Poor Kristy, poor Robby, poor Logan."

"That's just the thing Kristy," Charlie said putting his hand on her shoulder, "No one does. Everyone who has helped here is showing their appreciation for you and Robby. Haven't heard what they are saying? You guys have touched so many lives and you haven't even realized it. "

"That's why I did it," added Dave, "We have had a blast with everyone coming by helping out."

Kristy was amazed, "Really?"

"Really!" The crowd said in unison.

"See look," Becky said as she turned the camera back on, "Here is Mario from the pizza parlor."

"Come and get it!" Mario yelled to everyone, "Lunch is here!"

"Mario! This is wonderful!" said Becky.

"No problem, Bella!" Mario said, "I heard on the radio that this was happening and I wanted to thank Robby and the other fire fighters for saving my restaurant last year when my kitchen caught on fire. As it was, they could put it out quickly before it spread. Robby saved my mamma's pasta maker before it burned to ash. It means a lot to me," he set the pizza down on the patio table. A crowd of people had gathered and started digging in.

"Hey, wait," said Kristy pushing pause, "I don't have a patio table.
Where did it come from and those chairs?"

"The Smith's two blocks over dropped those off," said Freddie, "They got new patio furniture so they said that you could have their old stuff. I was looking at it and it is in great shape. If you don't want it, I'll take it off your hands."

"No, it's okay Freddie," Kristy said chuckling, "I think we'll keep it," letting out a breath she said, "I have a lot of thank-you's to write. I can't believe all of this."

"I think we should have a big barbeque to thank everyone who helped out." said Laura, "The backyard looks beautiful so we could have it there."

"Great idea! I'll do barbeque chicken and ribs with all the fixings," Kristy stood up and put her arm around Laura.

"And I'll bake my grandmother's potato buns and make sweet potato pie!" Laura added.

"I'm in," said Dave

"Me too!" the rest agreed.

"That wouldn't be Big Bad Bill's Barbeque sauce you're going to make, is it?" asked Becky. Kristy nodded. Becky put her arms in the air, "Yes! I haven't had your grandfather's barbeque sauce in ages. Mary- Sue and I always found a way to weasel an invitation for dinner when your parents were making it," turning to Charlie, she said, "This is the best barbeque sauce you will ever taste. What can we do to help?"

"I think you have done enough," Kristy said, "I do need a list of everyone who helped out. Laura and I can do the rest. How about this Saturday?"

Chapter 20

Kristy was standing on the top step of her back deck waiting for Laura and the boys to join her. She smiled as she scanned the crowd of people eating, talking, and laughing. *Thank God for these people*, she thought to herself.

When the others finally got there, Kristy started waving her arms to try to get everyone's attention, "Hello! Hello everyone!" she shouted. A loud whistle came from beside her and everyone stopped talking and turned towards the whistle.

Shocked, Kristy turned and saw Laura taking her fingers out of her mouth. Laura said, "What? My grandpa taught me to whistle to call the horses."

People started walking towards the stairs. Kristy started, "Hi everyone. Laura, the boys and I would like to take this opportunity to thank all of you for everything you have done for us," with tears in her eyes, she continued, "We had quite the welcome home a few days ago. I still can't believe it. I am very humbled by the generosity of everyone. Freddie got the ball rolling by making a few repairs. Then Becky, Charlie and Dave jumped on board. That gave Mary Sue the idea to put it on the radio," she smiled at Mary Sue and her husband Alex, "From what I understand, that's where this project exploded and caused a chain reaction. It shows just how wonderful the people of Guthrie are, especially all of my beloved friends."

Laura interrupted, "Kristy is so right. Milo and I have only been here a short time and have been welcomed into this community. We love it here, don't we Boo?"

Milo let out a "yessss" as he put his arms in the air. Logan copied him and everyone laughed.

"Ok you monkeys," Kristy was laughing too, "As you know, the house was falling into disrepair. Robby and I were waiting until spring and summer to do the repairs ourselves. The list was getting longer on a daily basis. Thanks to ya'll, everything is fixed and then some. I would like to thank those who cleaned the back yard. The flowers are gorgeous. Thanks to the Smiths for this awesome furniture." Looking for Maureen, she said, "Maureen, you and your cleaning crew did such an amazing job with the house. It was a messy job and we appreciate how well you cleaned and organized everything. We will try to keep it that way won't we guys?" Looking down at Logan and Milo.

The boys started giggling and replied, "Yup!"

"To the guys at the Fire Station. Thank you for fixing and painting not only my fence, but my in-laws fence as well," Kristy said pointing to the house across the alley, "You guys are awesome," Kristy found Carl and said, "Boss, you don't know how much it means to me to have an air conditioner that works. I know this one will stay on all night and I'm already sleeping so much better. I usually had to get up and find somewhere else to sleep when the old one clanked off. You're right though. It does give the room a fried chicken smell. Logan found a way to cover the smell by hanging the car air freshener in front. Now I have a nice new car scent in my room," Logan looked up at her proud of his idea, "Last and not least Mario. You went above and beyond bringing food to everyone," Mario blushed, "I understand you are grateful but it's not worth going bankrupt feeding the brutes from the fire station.

Just let me know what I can do for you," spreading her arms out, "And for all of you."

Laura, Milo, Logan and Kristy said together, "Thank you!"

Mario piped up, "I know what you can do. You can give me the recipe for this fantastic barbeque sauce. I might add barbeque chicken to the menu."

"Yeah. I wouldn't mind having the recipe too," Carl said holding up a rib.

"Sorry guys, it's an old family recipe," Kristy laughed, "I swore an oath to my father that I would only pass it onto my children. This way, it will stay pure just like the way my grandfather made it."

"Hey everybody!" Laura yelled, "There is still a lot of food and dessert is Sweet Potato Pie and Mississippi Mud Cake."

As the majority of the people headed towards the food, Rita McBain and her daughter Beth came up to Kristy and Laura, "Hi Kristy. I don't know if you remember me, I'm Rita."

Kristy gave her a big smile and said, "Of course I remember you. You don't know how happy we are that you are willing to watch the boys after kindergarten. You are helping us out so much."

"You are the ones helping me out," Rita replied, "I am so grateful that I can stay home with Beth and still bring money in. As a matter of fact, I will be taking in little Rachel Robinson too."

Shaking her head, Laura said, "That's a great idea. Beth will need a friend to go up against the boys. They are going to be a handful."

"I'm looking forward to it. I have a ton of games and things planned to do with them," Rita said.

"Don't overdo it please. Remember what your doctor said. You need to be careful with this pregnancy," Kristy was concerned.

"My husband reminds me all the time," Rita said patting her stomach. Smiling she said, "Make room on your refrigerator because we are doing a lot of art projects."

"Mommy!" Kristy heard Logan. She turned to find him and when she did he was pointing to the alley. She saw black smoke floating up into air from behind the fence.

She, Laura and a few of the fire fighters ran through the open gate to find a fire burning in her metal garbage can. Beside it were two very guilty looking boys.

"Milo!" Laura shrieked, "What have you done?"

Freddie grabbed the garbage can lid and placed it on the can to smother the fire, "No one touch the metal, it's pretty hot," he said.

"Collin Smith. Get your butt over here now," A very angry Benny Smith said. Seven-year-old Collin knew he was in big trouble so he slowly made his way to his dad.

Milo started crying because he knew his Mom was upset and he burnt the fingertips of his right hand. Laura grabbed his left hand and marched him over to Benny as well. A crowd had gathered to see what the commotion was all about.

Benny said, "Kristy, I'm sorry. Collin thinks that playing with matches is fun," he glared at Collin, "Laura, I'm sorry that he got Milo involved. How are those burns?"

George McBain had come over and looked at the burns, "They aren't too bad but I think I we need to get some ice on them before they get worse."

Laura said to George, "Come with me. I'll show you where the ice is," looking at her crying son, "You are in so much trouble Mister."

Benny looked at Collin, "So are you."

Fire Chief Jarrod Hunter came over to him. Benny shook his head, "This is the third and biggest fire he has set. I don't know what to do with him. I thought I had hidden the matches."

"Those are ours actually. They must have found them on the back porch," said Kristy.

"Why don't you bring him by the fire house and we will educate him about the damage fire can do," suggested Jarrod.

"Thanks Jarrod. We will definitely do that. I'll be in touch," grabbing Collin's arm, Benny said to Kristy, "We will be leaving now. I hope there isn't too much damage to your garbage can. Collin will buy you a new one out of his allowance. Thank you for the wonderful food."

Kristy wanted to say, "Don't worry, it's fine." She decided Collin needed to learn a lesson so she just waved. She would make an example of him to Logan and Milo. Turning to Jarrod, she asked, "Chief. Would it be alright if Milo and Logan join Collin in the fire damage lesson too?"

He thought about it, "Maybe we should have a day when all kids can come to the station and learn about fire destruction and safety. We can do an open house. Great idea Kristy," pointing in Collin's direction he said, "I'm still going to work one-on-one with that one. He may have a little pyro problem so I want to make sure he gets the message. Burning small things can lead to bigger things."

Kristy was just finishing Robby's bi-monthly haircut when Ozzie Becks pushed his walker into Robby's room, "Darlin', that is some of the best food I've had in my life."

Kristy grabbed the washcloth lying beside Robby and walked over to Ozzie. "I'm glad you enjoyed it," wiping the barbeque sauce on his chin, she laughed, "I think a little too much."

"Hey! I was saving that," Ozzie smiled.

"We're just happy that the nursing home was willing to take it. We had a lot left over from our barbeque this afternoon," handing Ozzie a Tupperware container, she lowered her voice, "Laura sent this over just for you. It is the last piece of Sweet Potato Pie."

"Ooowee. Can't wait," looking around the room, he asked, "Where's the rest of the gang?"

They heard the toilet flush and Logan opened the bathroom door wiping water on his hands off onto his pants. Kristy shook her head and sighed, "They do have towels."

"At least he washed them," Ozzie said defending Logan.

Logan ran over to Ozzie and gave him a high five. Ozzie sat down in the only chair in Robby's room. He looked at Logan, "Where's your little buddy?"

Logan crawled up and sat next to Robby on his bed. Making his eyes big he said, "Oh. Milo's in big trouble."

"What did he do?" A curious Ozzie asked.

"He and another kid set fire to the garbage. They snuck matches out of our house and lit it," Logan was very serious.

"I'm very proud that you didn't go with them," Kristy said ruffling his hair.

"I tried stopping them but Collin called me a baby. I tried to tell Milo that it was wrong but he didn't listen," Logan sadly recalled, "I was coming over to tell you when I saw the smoke."

"Was there any damage?" Ozzie asked.

"Are you kidding? We had half the fire station there so that fire was out in no time at all," Kristy chuckled.

"Milo burnt his fingers," Logan added holding up his right hand.

"That hurts a lot," Ozzie said pulling up his right pant leg, "See this scar?" Logan jumped down and carefully touched the burn scar that ran the length of Ozzie's shin, "When I was about nine, my brothers and I were trying to put out a campfire. I thought stompin' on it would do the job, but my pants caught on fire. Daddy picked me up and dunked me in the river right next to our campsite. It put the fire out and probably helped with the blistering. I had third degree burns that were pretty painful. I couldn't go outside to play until it healed because Mother didn't want it to get infected. She put some pretty smelly, home-made ointments on it, but they helped."

"My daddy told me a lot about what fire could do. He said the worse smell is the smell of burning skin and hair," Logan reached up and put his hand on Robby's cheek, "It's because of fire that my daddy is like this."

"Is that why you tried to stop your friends?" Kristy asked hoping to change the subject.

"Collin isn't my friend," looking at Ozzie he explained, "He is a bigger kid that is mean to us little ones. I tried to stop Milo but Collin stepped in front of him. That's when he called me a baby," Logan scowled.

"Well, next time Milo comes for a visit, I'll show him my leg. That will scare him," Ozzie said. He started to stand up and continued, "Come on Logan. Let's go play dominoes. I haven't had a decent game since before you left for Montana. No one around can play like you."

Logan jumped down from Robby's bed and smiled up at Ozzie, "I'll tell you all about our trip. We had so much fun! We saw Old Faithful and a couple of bison just eating by the side of the road. It was so cool!" Kristy heard Logan's non-stop talking as they walked down the hall to the games room.

Chapter 21

"Okay Boo. Momma's going to work now," Laura said kissing her son on the top of his head, "Kristy has a lot of fun things planned for you and Logan while I'm gone."

"When are you gonna be home, Momma?" Milo asked as he ran for one more hug.

"I'm not too sure. I have a lot things to bake," she said taking in the wonderful hug from Milo, "Remember, the I-35 Diner is having a grand re-opening in a couple of days. I need to have a lot of pies and cookies baked for the party."

"Will you have vanilla cupcakes with blue icing?" He asked.

"And dinosaur sprinkles just like you wanted," she replied setting him down and ruffling his hair.

Milo gave his mom a big smile and ran upstairs to tell Logan the good news.

Kristy was looking at yet another 'To-do' list while she was having her second cup of coffee, "Do you think we have everything on the list we need?" She yelled to the boys playing on the back porch.

Logan ran into the kitchen with Milo following behind him. Both were wearing firefighter helmets that Robby had gotten for Logan when he was three. "Do you have red, yellow and black balloons on there?" Logan asked pointing to the paper.

"Yup. See it's right here," Kristy answered showing Logan where it says balloons.

"Do you have a fire truck cake, hot dogs and squirt guns on there?" Milo added.

"Check, check and we'll see," Kristy said making a check mark action, in the air, after the first two items.

"Oh boy," Milo said, "This will be the best birthday party ever! I've never had a real birthday party before."

"Well Sweetie, your mom and I will make sure it is extra special then," Kristy said hugging Milo, "It's pretty convenient that your birthdays are nine days apart. This way we can have one big birthday party for the both of you. We will celebrate, as a family, on your actual birthdays. Logan your birthday is on what day?" Kristy asked.

"In three days on August 26th," Logan said proudly.

Kristy smiled and then looked at Milo, "Do you remember your birthday?"

"It's September," Milo paused to think of the day, "September, um, 4th?"

"Right!" Logan answered. He had been helping Milo learn things like his birthday, how to spell his first and last name, phone number and address. Logan had already learned all of it so he told Milo he would teach him. Logan was very academically advanced for his age where as Milo was behind. Kristy and Laura would find Logan playing teacher and Milo was his student. Kristy thought that this was very ironic considering, they were the same age. Milo was learning quite a lot from this game.

The telephone rang. Kristy got up and answered it, "Hi. Oh wonderful. I will tell the boys. Bye Rita."

She turned and saw two very curious boys looking at her, "That was Rita McBain. She said that Beth will be able to come to your birthday party on the 28th!"

"Yay!" the boys yelled. Logan added, "That makes 10 kids. Six boys and four girls."

"We will have about eight adults as well," counting on her fingers, she said, "There's me, Laura, Grammy, Poppy, Aunt Peggy, Uncle Jack, Freddie and here's a surprise for you," the boys looked at Kristy with anticipation, "Ozzie Becks is going to come too. Freddie will pick him up from the nursing home."

"Whoopee!!" Yelled Milo.

"All right!" Logan added throwing his arms in the air.

"Well, let's get going. We have to pick up party supplies and then get to your last swim lesson," Kristy said grabbing her purse and list, "I also promised Carl that I would pick up the 'Grand Re-opening' sign for that party in two days."

"Oh, it's so nice to have you back home," Kristy said running up to her in-law's car to help Vicki Garrison out. She reached in and got Vicki's cane and handed it to her, "You are doing so well Mom!" Kristy exclaimed watching her mother-in-law carefully walk towards the house.

"I can't do too much or my ankles get very swollen. At least I can get around on my own now," stopping in front of the same steps she broke her ankle on, she said, "I hate steps."

Laughing at his wife, Bobby Garrison said, "Well Honey, at least they are fixed. The reason you broke your ankles is because the last step crumbled when you stepped on it. Freddie Mapp said that all the wood was pretty much rotting away so he replaced all of it."

"What a sweet boy. I will have to crochet him a blanket," rolling her eyes she said, "That is about the only thing I can do these days."

"Grammy!" Vicki turned and saw her grandson and his friend come running towards her, "I have missed you so much," Logan said showing his grandmother a lot of love.

"Hello my sweet boy. I have missed you so much too," turning to Milo, she continued, "Milo, how have you been? I heard you burned your fingers."

Embarrassed by the reminder, he looked down and mumbled, "They're okay," he was very excited to show her the gardens they spent all summer watering, he looked at her and pointed, "Look at your flowers. Logan and I took really good care of them."

"Oh my, they are beautiful," Vicki replied. Looking down on two smiling faces she added, "I've never seen my gardens look so good. Thank you, boys, for doing such a good job. I think you deserve $10 each."

Their eyes widened in disbelief, "$10 whole dollars?" Milo said stunned. "That's a lot isn't it? Wow! Thank you, Logan's Grammy."

"Why don't you just call us Grammy and Poppy like Logan? Okay?" She said. Milo shook his head and gave her a big hug.

"Thank you for picking up the sign," Carl said as he took it from Kristy, "It looks great! People will see it from miles away."

"No problem Carl. The whole town is buzzing about the grand re-opening," Kristy told him.

"I know!" Carl sounded excited, "The ceremony will start at 11:00 in the morning with the mayor and I giving speeches. The open house will start after that until around 8:00 in the evening. I will be cooking all day because I'm expecting all our old and some new customers to come. And," he raised his voice so the man at the counter with strawberry blonde hair could hear him, "of course my favorite banker will be there front and center."

The man heard Carl and walked over to him with his hand outstretched. He had a big smile on his face, "I feel privileged to be involved. I really didn't believe you, Carl, when you said you would get this done in two weeks."

"I had to. I couldn't lose any more days of not being open," turning to Kristy he said, "Peter, I'd like you to meet one of my employees. This is Kristy Garrison." Kristy took his hand in hers and realized she had seen him before. Carl continued, "Kristy, this is Peter Young from the bank in Edson."

"Young!" Kristy startled the man, "I've met you before."

"Really?" Peter said trying to place her face.

"Yes. About 11 or 12 years ago. My dad was Darren Baker, GM of the Country Club," Kristy said noticing Peter make the connection. Carl left them with a wave to go back to the kitchen.

"Of course, Kristy Baker! It's great to see you again. You have grown up since the last time I saw you," he said with a smile. Then getting serious, "I heard about your parents. I'm so sorry that you lost them. They were really wonderful people."

"Thank you. They really were and I miss them every day," changing the subject, Kristy asked, "And how is your family? There was Mitchell, Gregory and Jocelyn, right?"

"Well, where do I start?" He asked shaking his head, "Ummm. Denise and I divorced about seven years ago and I remarried about five years ago to a wonderful, loving woman. Not at all like that plastic, adulteress wife I was married to," Kristy raised her eyebrows to that, remembering how perfect Mrs. Young had seemed. Kristy didn't like how she smiled all the time as if it was the only expression she had.

"Mitch dropped out of the Master's program he was in and plays keyboard in some kind of rock band. He's had a few stints in rehab, but keeps going back to that lifestyle. When we saw you last, unbeknownst to us our youngest Jocelyn was newly pregnant but lost the baby at 12 weeks. She obviously didn't learn her lesson about abstinence or birth control because she became pregnant again 10 months later. All the grandparents insisted that they put the baby up for adoption because there was no way in hell that they could have raised her. They were only 16 at the time and life would have been tough for that sweet baby girl. We placed her with wonderful adoptive parents in Colorado and I'm sure she is doing well," seeing the amazed look on Kristy's face, he finished by saying sarcastically, "I am so proud of my kids."

"Wow," was all Kristy could think to say. Then she continued, "I thought you guys were the perfect American family. I was a little miffed that your children were so smart and accomplished. I felt like such a country bumpkin," she laughed remembering how shiny and put together they were, "What about Gregory? He seemed like a nice guy and was an admitted nerd."

"Yeah Greg was a nerd and a pretty good athlete," Peter agreed, "He was my last hope that at least one of my kids would go onto bigger and better things. He was at Texas A&M on a basketball scholarship when he tore the rotator cuff in his shoulder after a bad fall in practice. He had to have surgery and was out the rest of the season. He just couldn't get his game back after that and they cut him from the team. He went into Theology and is now the pastor of a Baptist church in Hollister. He doesn't have a lot to do with the family, for obvious reasons."

"I'm sorry to hear that. He really was a nice guy," Kristy said. She heard laughter from behind her and saw two boys run out of the kitchen, "Well, Mr. Young."

He held up his hands, "Please call me Peter."

She smiled, "Peter then. It was nice to see you. I had better see what those two are up to. The taller boy is my son Logan and the other boy is his best friend, Milo. They are very curious and adventurous."

"That sounds like a recipe for trouble," Peter laughed.

"Exactly," Kristy smiled, "I will see you again at the opening, I hope?" "I'm not going to miss it. I will introduce you to my new wife," he

said shaking her hand.

Chapter 22

"Well, that was a smashing success," Kristy said putting the last of the birthday presents, for the boys, in the car. She slammed the door and turned around and slumped against it, "I am getting partied out. First the grand-opening, Logan's family birthday party and now the kids' party."

"We still have Milo's family party and I thought I would have a first day of school party," Laura put the trunk down and giggled. She saw the dirty look Kristy gave her.

"Really?" Kristy asked glaring at her.

"Just kidding," laughing and pointing at Kristy, Laura continued, "You should have seen the look on your face," Leaning against the car next to Kristy, she saw Milo and Logan high fiving all the fire fighters just inside the garage at the fire station, "That was so nice of them to let us have the party at the fire station. The kids loved it when they sprayed them with the hose. Even on the lowest setting, those hoses spray a lot of water. I will bake some yummy things for them, as a thank you."

"They are really like family to us. I will make a new batch of Big Bad Bill's Barbeque sauce and bring to them," Kristy started laughing at

Freddie who was running around the garage with both boys over his shoulders.

Laura pointed to Freddie and said, "He is so good with those boys. He would really make the perfect husband for someone."

Kristy looked at her with a smirk on her face, "Nice to hear because I heard through the grape-vine that Freddie has a crush on you."

"Me? You're joking," Laura said denying the rumors.

"Why do you think he comes over so much?" Kristy asked.

"Because he still has repairs to do and I give him baking," Laura answered.

"I'm sure the baking is an enticement, but doing repairs is the excuse to come over," Kristy pointed out.

"He has never said anything to me. As a matter of fact, he hardly ever talks to me," Laura stood up with her arms crossed.

"That's because he is painfully shy. He practically blushes every time he sees you. Shhh. Here he comes and you'll see what I mean," Kristy pointed her chin out to the fire fighter carrying the boys. He stopped just in front of them and bent down to let the boys jump off.

"I have a delivery of two five year olds hyped up on fire truck birth-day cake," Freddie said looking directly at Kristy.

"Thank you so much Freddie," Laura said getting his attention.

The moment he made eye contact with her, his neck and face flushed to a bright pink.

Clearly uncomfortable, he rubbed his blonde brush cut and mumbled, "Yeah, no problem," he turned and yelled over his shoulder, "I'd better get Ozzie back. See y'all later."

Laura looked at Kristy. Kristy smiled and raised her right eyebrow, "Told ya."

"Are you almost ready?" Kristy asked as she walked into Laura's room.

"What do you think? Too much?" Laura twirled to show Kristy her tank top and mini skirt. Laura's blonde hair fell just at her shoulders in beautiful curls and her face was freshly painted with make-up.

"I think you will scare the hell out of Freddie. He thinks this is just a friendly date, remember?" Kristy said sitting down on Laura's bed.

"That's true. My massive hinting didn't get through to him. I finally had to say that I needed a friend to go with me to this movie," she took her skirt off and found some jeans to put on, "If you hadn't stepped in and suggested to him that he should go with me, he would still be avoiding me," Laura decided to put her hair into a less sexy ponytail.

"He hasn't had any experience asking girls on dates," Kristy told her defending poor Freddie.

"I haven't had a date in forever, so I guess we are pretty much in the same boat," Laura wiped her eye shadow off, "It's probably better we take this slowly."

Kristy handed her a hoodie from her closet and said, "The boys and I will leave before Freddie gets here. Can you imagine the drilling those two would give both of you? Wondering why he was here and why they couldn't go to the movie too."

"Thank you. I am nervous enough and I'm sure Freddie doesn't need to be scared away," Laura sprayed on the perfume Roxie had given her. Roxie was tired of it and wanted a new scent, "Did Milo tell me that they are taking their ukuleles to the hospital?"

"Yup. They told Ozzie Becks that they were learning the ukulele in school and so he said that when they learned their first song, they needed to put on a concert for them. Apparently, Ozzie thinks that place needs some livening up. They practiced hard so this will be their reward," Kristy said, walking out the door.

"At least most of the concert goers are deaf!" Laura yelled down the hall.

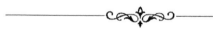

Freddie helped Laura into the passenger side of his truck. Making sure she was fully in, he shut the door and walked around to the driver's side, "Boy, she smells so good," he said quietly to himself, "She is so pretty. I can't believe she wants to be seen with me."

When they got out of the truck, Laura said, "Why don't you buy the tickets and I will go get the snacks."

"Uh, Uh. I can buy the snacks too if you want?" Freddie stammered and held out a $20 bill.

"No, no," Laura held up her hand to show she wasn't going to take the money. "This isn't a date so we can go dutch. So, what do you want?" Letting out a breath, he said, "Yeah sure," he seemed a bit relieved, "I'll just have a large popcorn with butter and a Dr. Pepper."

Kristy was looking at the clock. It read 11:18. "Why am I so worried?" She asked herself, "She's with Freddie Mapp. The sweetest, most responsible guy I know."

Just as she looked back down at her book, she heard a car door slam, then 10 seconds later, another one. She didn't want to be too obvious so she sat at the dining room table, reading.

There was laughter and murmuring voices coming from the front porch. She heard Laura's voice as well as Freddie's. Kristy smiled to herself. She knew that if Laura could get Freddie talking to her without him choking up, it would be easier for him and maybe things will work out.

The front door opened and Laura stood there waiting for Freddie to get back into his truck. She waved and came in. She looked over and saw Kristy, "Oh. You're still up?"

"Of course I am!" she exclaimed, "I couldn't wait until morning to hear how things went tonight."

"Well," Laura paused as she sat down across from Kristy at the table. "He is so sweet and such a gentleman. Laughing she continued, "Quite the opposite of Jason."

"Was he nervous?" Kristy asked.

"Yes, but in such a cute way," Laura smiled, "Once I convinced him this wasn't a date but two friends going out, he calmed right down."

Sitting back in her chair, Kristy said, "Nice but it's after 11:00. The movie ended a couple of hours ago. Where have you guys been?"

Laughing, Laura said, "Ok Mom," Kristy winced knowing she was acting like her mother. Laura put her hand on Kristy's, "Don't sweat it. I would do the same to you if things were reversed." Laura continued, "Freddie was starving so we went to the newly spiffed up I-35. Apparently, he was too nervous to have dinner and popcorn just didn't curb his appetite. Do you know they have the best pecan pie in the state there?" she said as she got up. As Laura headed for the stairs, she said over her shoulder, "Oh yeah. He asked me to go out for dinner to some restaurant in Oklahoma City on Saturday."

She stopped and looked at Kristy. She had her arms in the air. Laura heard her say "Yessss!"

"I assume that means I have a babysitter?" Laura asked and Kristy winked at her.

Chapter 23

"How many lists do you have?" Laura asked Kristy who was sitting at the kitchen table surrounded by little pieces of paper.

Holding up each piece of paper, Kristy said, "Well, I have the Thanksgiving menu, grocery list, chore list, oh, these are the people I have to call to remind them to pick up their turkeys from the school fund-raiser," Kristy held up a two-page list of names.

"Why do you need so many different ones? I think the grocery list is enough," Laura asked.

"I've got too much stuff going on up here," Kristy said pointing to her head, "I don't want to forget anything and this just helps me organize things and with my time management. I have a real problem with that when I have too much on my plate."

"Which seems like that is all the time," Laura laughed handing Kristy a cup of coffee, "What list are you writing now?"

"This is our ever-growing guest list," Kristy handed it to Laura as she sat down at the kitchen table with her.

"Are all these people coming to our Thanksgiving dinner?" Laura said counting the names.

"Yup," Kristy continued, "We have the four of us, Robby's mom and Dad, that's six, his sister Peggy and family so four more, Ozzie, Roxy and"

"My sweet Freddie," Laura said with a dreamy smile. They had been dating for the last two and a half months and were inseparable. Even Milo was crazy about him and really wants him to be his new dad, "What about Maureen and Isaac?"

Shaking her head Kristy said, "They are going home to Moore but Carl said he will come after the big Thanksgiving lunch he is putting on for the truckers." Kristy's eyes flew open, "That reminds me. I said I would take Maureen's shift so she could go to Moore. That means I really can't help you cook. You will have lots of help with the set up and dinner. Both Peggy and my mother-in-law said they would be over to help as much as possible and look after the kids."

"Everything's under control," Laura reassured Kristy, "The pies are already baked and in the freezer. So are the half-cooked dinner rolls. They won't take long to finish baking once they thaw. Vicki is bringing the sweet potatoes and a green bean casserole. Roxy said she will bring a cranberry Jell-O salad and Freddie will be over to help me peel potatoes. While the turkey is cooking, I will make the dressing and cut up some raw veggies since Milo doesn't like green beans. That will just leave the gravy and I'll make that when the turkey comes out" Laura held her hands up, "See? Everything is under control so you can tear up the dinner list."

Ripping the paper in half, Kristy said with a lump in her throat, "Thank you. I can't tell you how wonderful it is to have you here to help. It was going to be a hard Thanksgiving since it's our first one without Robby."

Laura stood up and hugged Kristy's shoulders, "Are you kidding? I haven't had a Thanksgiving dinner since before I had Milo. Jason would go off to some bar and get drunk. I would try to make something special out of frozen chicken. Thanksgiving really wasn't a big deal when I was married to Jason," Just as she finished talking a band of ukuleles came marching into the kitchen.

"Milo and I have written a special Thanksgiving song. Do you want to hear?" asked Logan.

"Yeah!" exclaimed Milo.

"Of course," said Kristy, "You two are getting so good on the ukulele. I hope you will perform for everyone at Thanksgiving dinner?"

Both little faces lit up, "We can sing our new song!" Milo practically yelled.

"We should write some more!" Logan said, "Let's go!"

The boys ran out of the kitchen and Laura yelled after them, "What about your song?"

"I guess we have to wait and hear it with everyone else," Kristy said shrugging her shoulders.

"Now that dinner is over, I'd like to make a toast so everyone please raise your glasses," Bobby Garrison said as he stood up, "To a magnificent meal. Thank you, ladies, for such a wonderful dinner," he patted his stomach. Everyone at the table agreed and said "cheers" to the cooks, "I'd also like to say that I wasn't looking forward to Thanksgiving this year. The Garrison family had such a hard year with Robby's accident and Vicki's ankles. But…" he paused and looked around the table, "as I look at everyone here, I realize how fortunate we are to have such wonderful, supportive family and friends. I think we should go around the table and hear from everyone what they are thankful for. I'll start off. First of all, I'm thankful to still be as much in love with my beautiful bride of 35 years as I have ever been," Vicki gave him a very loving look, "I'm thankful for my amazing daughter, son-in-law and for Kristy, one of the strongest women I know. Your unconditional love for our son is admirable," Kristy blew him a kiss, "I'm thankful for the love and laughter of my grandchildren and I am including you in this Milo," he pointed to him, which made Milo puff up with happiness, "I am thankful for Laura for coming into our lives at the right time. Your presence has helped this family dig out of a very large hole we felt like we were in," Laura became teary eyed and smiled at him, "And finally, I'm thankful for all our wonderful friends who bring joy and laughter to us as well as good carpentry skills," he pointed to Freddie who sat with his arm around Laura.

"Okay Dad, you have practically said everything and left nothing for the rest of us," Peggy said standing up. Everyone laughed and Bobby smiled and sat down, "Like Dad said, I'm thankful for my wonderful family. It just shows how strong we are when we have to face a crisis. I think we have had our fair share of crisis' this year."

"Amen," Vicki Garrison said. She decided she was going to stay seated, "I'm thankful that I have healthy, fast healing bones for an old lady," this made everyone chuckle, "But seriously, I am thankful and very grateful to Peggy and her family for taking such good care of Dad and me while I was in the hospital. And Kristy. Just like Dad said, you are a strong amazing woman," Kristy blushed a little, not sure how to take such praise, "Not too many people would be as loving and dedicated to their spouse if they were in the same situation as you. You take such good care of him and your love really shows."

"Can I say what I'm thankful for?" interrupted Milo.

"Go ahead sweetie," Vicki said.

Milo stood up on his chair and said, "I'm thankful for my Momma, Kristy, my first real best friend Logan, Freddie, Ozzie, Grammy and Poppy and everyone here. I'm also thankful for my teacher, Miss Hughes and for popsicles." With that he sat down.

Laura leaned over and kissed his head, "That was wonderful Boo. Good job."

Milo stood back up and said, "Oh yeah. I'm thankful that my mom doesn't get beat up by my dad anymore."

The room went quiet. Carl decided he needed to break the awkward silence by saying, "I'm thankful for having the wonderful opportunity to live my dream. I've always wanted to own and cook at my own diner. It was hard at first but with such wonderful employees," he pointed to Roxy, Kristy and Laura, "Business has been great and I have been able to expand and renovate. Oh yeah. I'm thankful for Laura's Home Baking. You got me to the next level," he winked at Laura.

"You're welcome Carl," Laura said bowing her head to him, "I'm thankful for my new, wonderful life," she stood up and as she looked at each person she said, "Kristy gave me the help to heal and start to feel good about myself. Roxy gave me an amazing makeover. Carl, you gave me the confidence to believe that I was good enough to make a living at something I love to do. I'm thankful for Logan for being like a brother to my Milo. I'm thankful for all my new wonderful friends," Laura paused, then said, "I'm thankful to be living in Guthrie, Oklahoma," putting her hand on the back of Freddie's head she continued, "Freddie, you have shown me that men can be gentle and loving and still be strong and protective," she bent down and kissed him causing him to blush brightly, "Finally." she took Milo's hand, "I am thankful every day that God brought me you, Milo. You gave me strength to stand up to your dad. You brought me laughter when there wasn't a lot to laugh at and you have shown me what love is really about," Milo reached up and hugged his mom as hard as he could.

"Well, I'm thankful for the Hawaiians," said Ozzie.

"Why Ozzie?" asked Logan.

"Didn't they invent the ukulele? I am looking forward to tonight's entertainment," Ozzie laughed.

"Can we do it now Mom?" Logan asked.

"Why don't you guys get set up in the living room while we clear the dishes. I understand you talked your cousins into dancing while you two play and sing," Kristy said smiling at her nieces, "We can have coffee and Laura's homemade pumpkin and apple pies while we are being entertained."

Bobby said, picking up his plate, "I think I'm going to have some of each. I just can't decide which one I want more," there were a lot of people shaking their heads in agreement.

Kristy leaned against the wall in the dining room watching the action. She thought to herself that Robby would have loved all the noise and laughter going on in the house. He loved Thanksgiving and was always bringing over young guys from the station to join them for turkey dinner.

Laura saw Kristy watching everyone. She could tell she was trying to hold back tears. She walked up to Kristy and took her hand, "Why don't you take some time to yourself while we finish cleaning up."

Kristy couldn't hold the tears back. She hugged Laura and whispered into her ear, "Thanks. I think I will. I really miss Robby right now. He was usually the life of the party at gatherings like this."

"I'll call you when the show is about to start," Laura said pulling back from her. Putting her arm around her shoulders, she guided her to the stairs.

Kristy quietly slipped up to her room and shut the door. She fell on her bed and sobbed into her pillow. It had been a long time since she needed to release her sadness.

Chapter 24

"I can't believe it's two weeks before Christmas," Laura said as she set a large bakery box on the counter at the I-35 Diner, "I still have so much to do. Hey Roxy!" Laura yelled across the diner to her friend, "Here is the last of your Christmas baking. I am now paid in full as to our business agreement."

Roxy came over and lifted the top of the box off, "Darlin', these look so yummy. I don't know if I can wait until I get to my brother's house before I start to eat these." she picked up a chocolate dipped cherry by the stem and dropped it into her mouth, "Mmmm. Won't I impress my brother's snooty wife and her family?"

"Well Rox, I don't think you need baking to impress them," Kristy said setting down a tray of full salt and pepper shakers, "Your charm would impress even the Queen of England."

"You know it honey," Roxy said as she backed into the kitchen with her box of goodies.

Maureen came over to the laughing pair and asked, "Hey Laura? Do you know that guy over in booth five?"

Both Kristy and Laura stopped laughing and casually looked over at the booth. They saw a large unshaven man, wearing a black t-shirt and a dirty jean jacket. He had a ball cap covering his greasy brown hair. He was picking his teeth with a toothpick staring intently at Laura.

The color drained from Laura's face and she quickly turned and pushed into the kitchen. Kristy and Maureen followed her and found her in Carl's office where she was looking through the one-way mirror. Carl liked to keep tabs on what is happening in his diner while he is doing paperwork or on the phone. "Oh, my God," Laura said sitting down in Carl's chair. Her hands were shaking and she felt like she was going to vomit.

"Do you know him?" Kristy asked looking hard through the mirror.

"Do you see the name on his cap?" Laura asked.

"Yeah. It's says Bender's," Maureen answered.

"That's Jason's favorite honkytonk and that guy out there is one of his drinking buddies. I only met him once for like a minute or two," Laura said rubbing the top of her thighs.

"That must be why he asked me what your name was," Maureen said looking concerned.

"Did you tell him?" Laura stood up in a panic

"I didn't like the look of him so I told him your name was Marcy. He then asked where you were from and I told him you were born and raised right here in Guthrie. He then asked how long you worked here and I said about three years," Maureen replied.

"Thank you, Maureen," Laura was relieved, "Your gut was right. He is no good. I hope to God that he doesn't say anything to Jason."

"Really, you don't look anything like you did when you got here in July," Kristy tried to reassure her everything was all right, "Your hair is a different color, you have a fuller, healthier look to you."

"Hey what's with the meeting? Shouldn't you two be out with my customers?" Carl asked pointing to Maureen and Kristy.

"He's right Maureen, we better get back out there," Kristy said pushing Maureen out of the office door, "I should let Roxy know to call Laura, Marcy until that guy leaves. Laura, fill Carl in on what's happening."

"It's a good thing you told me about that guy in booth five," Roxy said to Kristy as she was entering an order into the new computer system.

"Why?" asked Kristy.

"He stopped me and asked me the same questions that he asked Maureen," she told her, "He asked if Marcy was married and I then I told him grease monkeys weren't her type. He said he was a roughneck not a mechanic and he's was heading down to southern Oklahoma to work on a drilling rig for about six weeks."

"That's good," Kristy said putting her hand on Roxy's back, "That means he may forget about Marcy by the time he gets back to Kansas. He must still be suspicious if he asked you about her too."

"Where is Marcy now?" Roxie asked.

"Carl snuck her out the back and took her home. When he got back he said she was pretty upset. Freddie is off today so I phoned him and asked him to go and stay with her," Kristy said.

"She must have gone through hell with that bastard to shake her up like this," Roxy said spitting out the words, "If I see that guy again, I may just spike his coffee with something."

"You wouldn't?" Kristy said surprised.

"No. But I'd like to all the same. We just have to keep our eyes open for him six weeks from now," Roxy watched as he got up and threw money on the table. He nodded to Maureen as he walked out of the diner. He didn't realize there were many pairs of eyes glaring at him as he got into his beat-up truck and drove away.

Chapter 25

"Momma!" Milo yelled as he came running in through the back door.

Laura was just taking bread out of the oven so she set the hot pan down on the stovetop. She didn't have time to take off her oven mitts before two tiny arms wrapped themselves around her legs.

"How was your day?" She asked and squatted down to give him a hug.

"The movie was so good and Kristy let us have popcorn and pop!" He said, excitedly.

"Hey buster, you need to help with the groceries next time," Kristy said carrying four bags of groceries with Logan behind her carrying one.

"Sorry Kristy," Milo ran over to take one from her, "I was too excited to tell Momma about the popcorn."

Laura took the bag from her son, "She's right Boo. Just because you are smaller than all of us, doesn't mean you get out of the heavy work," she smiled down at him. "Who won at dominoes today?"

"We didn't play," Logan said handing her his bag, "Ozzie is sick."

Milo added, "Yeah. He has bronc ice and is clementine."

Laura looked at Kristy with a questioning look on her face.

"No," Logan corrected him, "He has bronc ice and is quarmteem."

"That still doesn't help," Laura laughed.

"Let me translate," Kristy said opening the refrigerator door to put the milk away, "They think Ozzie has bronchitis and have quarantined him until he is better. They don't want it turning into pneumonia which is common for seniors."

"We should make him get well cards and take him his favorite thumbprint cookies," Laura said looking at the boys, "Dinner will be ready in about 20 minutes so why don't you guys get started on the cards now."

"Yeah! We can use the construction paper I got for Christmas," Milo said.

"Let's use the smelly markers I got," Logan replied as they headed for their room.

"Remember to put the lids on your markers!" Kristy yelled after them, "Oh, I almost forgot. Mom got some of our mail today. She ran it over while we were pulling into the garage," grabbing the mail from her purse, she handed Laura one of them, "This one is for you. It's from you grandfather's nursing home. I hope everything is okay."

"Oh yeah," Laura said not too worried, "I asked them to send me a quick note letting me know that Granddad got his Christmas presents," opening up the envelope, she pulled out the paper and began to read out loud, "Dear Laura. Your grandfather was thrilled to receive your presents. He loves the cardigan and wears it all the time. It has been pretty chilly here in Montana. He started crying when he tasted the ginger snap cookies. He said they tasted just like his sweet Carmen's cookies," Laura stopped reading and looked at Kristy, "When I was going through my grandmomma's recipes, I saw her ginger snap cookie recipe. She had made a note at the top saying 'Caleb's favorite'."

"That must have triggered some memories for him," Kristy said.

Laura continued reading, "I'm sorry to say that he didn't remember you when I told him who they were from," Laura frowned to herself, "On a side note. A few days ago, Caleb had a visitor. He said he was family so we let him in to see Caleb. Your grandfather didn't know him (but he doesn't know a lot of people). I overheard him ask Caleb if he had seen you and your son. Of course, Caleb didn't know who he was talking about. I think he said his name was Jason."

Laura stopped reading and leaned against the counter. Looking at the paper, she said, "I knew he would go there looking for me. I almost sent Milo's school picture and a picture of the two of us to him. Something told me not to and I'm so glad I listened. He would have seen them and maybe questioned the staff about us."

"Does the letter say anything more?" Kristy asked.

Laura read the rest to herself, "No. Just best wishes and Happy New Year. This is the second close call in weeks. I'm getting nervous that he will find us."

"We will have to be more careful then. I don't think he is any closer to finding you than he was before. Eventually, he will stop," Kristy said trying to reassure her.

"Not him. He will want his revenge," Laura said.

Kristy asked, "What would he do if he found you?"

"He would take Milo away after he beat me to death," Laura said coldly.

"Should we get a restraining order?" Kristy asked.

"He wouldn't care about it. Guys like that never do," letting out a sigh, Laura continued, "I can't let him ruin my new life. It has taken me months to stop looking over my shoulder. I am so happy now thanks to all of you guys."

"We are a close knit group," Kristy said hugging Laura, "We will continue to look out for you and Milo. We had such a great Christmas and the New Year is a couple of days away."

Smiling at Kristy, Laura said, "That's right. I have so much to look forward to next year. I'll be careful but I won't let the possibility that he may find me control my life."

Kristy ran over to the table and started to write on a piece of paper, "Here is your New Year's resolution, 'I will be in control of my life and my happiness!' Put this some place where you see it every day."

Laura took the 'L' magnet off the bottom of the refrigerator where the boys practice their alphabet and words. She placed her resolution at eye-level on the upper part of the fridge. She found an a, u r and another a, "There. I will see my name every time I go to the refrigerator. I will be reminded to read my resolution and never forget it."

"Are you sure you don't want to join us for the New Year's party downtown? There's going to be fireworks," Laura asked Kristy as she put on Milo's second mitten.

"My New Year's date is at the nursing home. We are going to strap Robby into his chair so I can push him outside to see the fireworks," Kristy said, "Thank you for taking Logan with you. Is Freddie going to meet you there?"

"He will be there already," Laura, replied, "He is technically working because they needed a few of the firefighters to go and supervise the fireworks. They are there just in case something goes haywire and a fire starts. He will be able to meet up with us during the party."

"I can't wait to eat hot dogs and cotton candy!" Milo chirped in.

"All of our friends are going to be there," Logan said walking into the room, "Wow, Mommy. You look so pretty."

"Thanks sweetie. This is your dad's favorite dress. I don't have many occasions to wear it so I thought I would tonight."

"Do you have the party hat I got for him?" asked Logan.

"Yup. Right here," Kristy held up a headband with 'Happy New Year' stretching across the top, "And here is my tiara you got for me when you went shopping with Grammy. It will go perfectly with my outfit," Logan ran and wrapped his arms around Kristy's knees.

"Do you have the goodies I made to take the residents there?" asked Laura.

"They are already in the car. You know Laura, some residents are complaining they are getting fat because you keep sending yummy baking over." Kristy laughed.

"They don't know this, and you can't tell them," Laura held her hand to the side of her mouth like she was telling a secret, "I use them as guinea pigs for new recipes. Those old people are probably the toughest critics in the city so if they like it, I will probably use it at the diner."

"Fair enough," said Kristy. She wished everyone a Happy New Year, "Have fun tonight! We will see you next year."

"Happy New Year Mommy," Logan said giving her a kiss. He kissed her again, "This is for Dad. Wish him a Happy New Year too."

"And Ozzie if he's feeling better," Milo added.

"And this is from your son," Kristy said kissing Robby on his cheek. He already had his 'Happy New Year' headband on. The nursing home staff had Robby dressed and already sitting in his chair when Kristy got there. *He is still so handsome*, Kristy thought to herself when she saw him.

The nursing home was having an early New Year's party so Kristy pushed Robby into the dining room. She was disappointed that she didn't see Ozzie out there.

"He is still pretty sick," Gail, one of the nurses, said to her, "I'll tell him you were looking for him."

"Thanks, Gail. Wish him Happy New Year from all of us and a speedy recovery please," Kristy smiled.

Kristy sat next to Robby holding his hand while a band played a Glenn Miller song. She thought back to the past New Year's Eve parties they had gone to. Robby would look so handsome in his suit and Kristy would wear a new dress that she bought in Oklahoma City during the after Christmas sales. They would drink, (except the year she was pregnant with Logan) eat and dance until midnight. Robby would always stand behind her and put his arms around her as they counted down to the New Year. At the stroke of midnight, he would whisper in her ear "I love you so much." She would turn around and kiss him so passionately as if no one else was in the room with them.

She kissed his hand and whispered into his ear, "If I'd known that last New Year's was going to be our last together, then I wouldn't have stopped kissing you." She thought to herself, *It was a month and a half after that that you had your accident and we thought you were dead.* Still whispering in Robby's ear, "I'm so grateful that I still have you in my life. I am still going to kiss you so hard at midnight, under the fireworks, so hold on to your chair."

Chapter 26

"Then after the delicious dinner he made, he gave me two dozen pink roses with the most wonderful card," Laura said gushing over her Valentine's evening with Freddie.

"Those quiet ones are always the most romantic," Roxy said putting her arm around Laura, "Honey, I'm glad you had such a wonderful Valentine's," looking at Kristy as she wiped down the counter, "Can you beat Laura's night?"

"Well, as a matter of fact, yes," Kristy put the rag and disinfectant spray under the counter, "I was juggling three Valentine dates." Kristy said with a sly smile.

"Oooo. Do tell," Maureen came and sat at the counter. The diner was empty giving the friends time to gossip.

"Well, of course there is my gorgeous husband. We went to visit him and my other two dates gave him a heart shaped balloon and a picture," leaning on the counter, Kristy continued, "I did get a kiss on the cheek from Ozzie Becks who wanted to be my Valentine too but I told him three is all could handle."

Laughing, Laura said, "I heard from one of your dates that you made heart shaped pancakes and put chocolate chips in them."

"Traitor!" Kristy tried to sound mad, "I told him that if we put chocolate chips in instead of blueberries, he wasn't to tell anyone especially his mother."

"What's a little extra chocolate at dinner. I do it all the time, as you can see," Roxy said slapping her bottom.

"Then what did you do with your little men?" Maureen asked.

"We then spent a good hour going through all of the Valentine cards they got at school. I read them out loud and then they would line them up on the floor with their favorites on the left," Kristy said swooping her hand from left to right, "It's funny. Their favorite Valentine cards were from the boys and least favorite from the girls."

"Really?" Laura said laughing, "I guess that will eventually change when they start liking girls."

"That wasn't important to them at all," Kristy said, "They picked their favorite cards based on what was on them not who gave it to them. All the girls gave out princessy, cutesy cards. The boys gave them superheroes, cars and ninjas."

The door opened and a few customers came in, "Well ladies, we'd better get back to work. The lunch rush is about to begin," Roxy said as she walked over to greet the new diners.

Laura looked out of the front window and saw two more customers walking up to the diner. She gasped which made Kristy look over at her. Laura fell onto her hands and knees and was trying to catch her breath. Kristy ran to her, "Laura, are you okay?" she asked putting her arms around her shoulders. She could feel Laura shaking.

Laura laid down on her side and pulled her knees to her chest. She was crying and shaking. She tried to tell Kristy what was wrong, but all she could do is hiccup.

"Laura, take deep breaths," Kristy started to breath with Laura to help her slow her breathing down, "Good. Now. Tell me what's wrong?" Kristy was getting very concerned.

Still crying softly, Laura whispered to Kristy, "Jason's here."

Kristy's eye grew wide with the news, "Where is he?"

"He was," Laura was still taking deep breaths, "W-was in the parking lot, with, with that guy from before," grabbing on to Kristy, she said, "He's here. He's found me."

Trying to help her up, Kristy said, "Let's get you into the back. You will be safe in Carl's office."

Just as she stood up to help Laura, she heard, "Hey. Can we have some coffee here?"

Kristy looked in the direction of the voice and saw two men sitting at the counter about five feet from her. "Yeah, just give me a minute. I'm cleaning up a spill here." Kristy answered. She looked and saw Laura begin to panic. Kristy knew that she couldn't move her without them seeing her. She grabbed a tablecloth that was under the counter and began to cover Laura up. Before she covered her head, Kristy whispered in her ear, "Keep this over you and whatever you do, don't move or make a sound," Kristy looked into Laura's eyes, "Do you understand me?" Laura nodded her head, yes. Kristy covered up Laura's head and stood up.

As Kristy washed her hands, she studied the two men. The guy who was here before was wearing the same dirty jean's jacket and cap. He had a green t-shirt on with stains down the front. His hair was pulled back into a small ponytail and he now had a full beard. Next to him was a shorter, younger guy with brown hair parted in the middle and grey eyes. She could tell that at one time he was quite nice looking but now had scars on his face and hollow eyes. *Probably from too much drinking and bar fights*, Kristy thought to herself. He had taken his hoodie off and she could see a small beer belly under his collared shirt. Kristy grabbed the coffee pot and turned over Jason's coffee cup and filled it. As she turned over his friend's cup, he asked her, "Hey. Where's that Marcy at?"

Kristy just caught herself before she over filled his coffee, "She's not here. Why do you want to know?"

"I thought she was real pretty and wanted to say hi." he said with a sick smile on his face. Jason chuckled at his friend.

Kristy wanted to smash the coffee pot into his face but, luckily, Roxy came by. "Well if it isn't the grease monkey?" she said looking around for Laura. Kristy caught her eye and looked down at the floor trying to tell her where Laura was.

Not impressed, Jason's friend said, "Roughneck sweetheart. There's a big difference."

"Ya'll smell the same to me," Roxy sniffed at him as she walked around to where Kristy was.

Jason slapped his friend on his back, "She has a point their Eddie."

Kristy whispered to Roxy as she walked by, "Watch them. I'm going to talk to Carl."

Kristy ran into the kitchen. She saw Carl in his office. "Carl. We have a problem," getting his attention, she continued, "See those two guys at the counter? The one on the left is Laura's ex-husband Jason."

"Where's Laura?" he asked as he stood up to get a closer look.

Pointing to the floor under the counter, she said, "That lump on the floor under the tablecloth," Kristy said pointing to Laura, "I couldn't get her to move fast enough to get back here. She is in full panic mode."

Carl started to head out of his office when Kristy caught his arm and said to him, "I need you to stay back here and watch. We don't want them to think that we know who they are. I told them that Marcy wasn't here when the creep on the right asked."

"I can't just sit here and watch. I'm going to throw those guys out," Carl said staring out the window.

"For what reason? Besides, we don't know if those guys are armed. Laura told me Jason has a gun. The guy in the cap is probably high on something. He is real jittery," Kristy noticed.

"I'm going to call the cops and tell them that there may be a potential problem here," Carl said.

"Good idea. Even have them come in for coffee. They might not try anything if the cops are in sight," Kristy agreed, "I'd better get back out there. Please keep an eye on things in case something goes wrong. I'm worried Laura might panic and stand up."

As Kristy walked out of the kitchen, she noticed Laura was in the same spot. She dropped her pen beside her so when she bent down to pick it up, she whispered, "Carl has called the cops. They will come in and have coffee and make sure nothing happens. We will be safe."

"Okay," Kristy heard from under the tablecloth.

Kristy stood up. She saw her favorite trucker, Boris walk in. Thinking she needed more reinforcements she walked over to him and said, "Hi Boris. We haven't seen you for a while," pulling him towards the counter, she said, "Here's your regular seat. Can I get you some coffee?"

"Kristy, you know I like to sit in that booth over there," he said using his head to point to the booth.

"Just today. Let this seat be your regular one," Kristy said through gritted teeth.

Catching the seriousness of her face, Boris said while sitting two seats from Eddie, "I'll have my regular I-35 meal."

"And what would that be?" asked Jason as he looked over at Boris.

"Sweet ice tea, chicken fried steak and apple pie. The best you will find within 100 miles," Boris said looking at Jason.

"Sounds good to me," said Jason smiling at Kristy.

"Me too," Eddie agreed.

Chicken fried steak took a little longer to cook than most meals. She needed those two out as quickly as possible. Kristy shook her head and said, "Sorry guys. We are all out of chicken fried steak. How about the famous I-35 cheeseburger and fries? Ice teas are on the house."

"Can I get mashed potatoes and gravy with that instead of fries?" Boris asked.

"Of course, sweetie," Kristy smiled at him. The smile disappeared from her face when she looked at Jason and Eddie, "How about you two? What would you like?"

"I'll have the cheeseburger and fries. Instead of ice tea, I'll take a free beer," Jason said thinking he was clever. Kristy noticed that he had the same smirk on his face that she has seen on Milo so many times.

"We don't serve alcohol here," Kristy responded.

Eddie piped in, "What kind of restaurant don't serve beer?"

"The kind that serves a lot of truckers. Do you want drunk truckers out on the highway with you?" Kristy said defensively.

Boris could tell by Kristy's body language that she didn't like these guys. He had never seen her talk to customers like this before. *Maybe that is why she wanted me to sit here,* he thought to himself.

Boris got up to go to the bathroom. He made a detour to where Kristy was standing putting the order into the computer, "What's going on Kristy?" he asked.

"Long story short Boris, the guy on the left is Laura's ex-husband and he is looking for her. The other one saw her here a few months back and must have told him. We told him her name is Marcy and she is from Guthrie," Kristy informed him.

"Where is she?" he asked looking around for her.

"She is huddled on the floor right under their noses. I've got to figure out some way to distract them to get her up and in the back," she said biting her lip.

"No guy can resist a tour of my truck cab. Leave it to me," he said as he walked back to his seat.

Kristy walked over to the counter just as the three of them stood up, "Yeah man," Eddie said, "I've always wanted to check one of those trucks out. I hear there are good places to hide your weed in those things."

Two policemen held the door open for them as they left the diner. Carl came running out from the kitchen, "Get her in the back," he yelled, while pointing to Laura. Carl intercepted the cops and was talking to them while showing them to a booth close to the counter.

Kristy and Roxy ran behind the counter and grabbed Laura. She was pretty reluctant to get up. Roxy said, "Come on honey. That jackass is outside with Boris. We can sneak you into Carl's office now."

Laura was shaky when she got up. "I've got her," Carl said as he took her from Kristy and Roxy, "You two stay out here and get those guys out of here as fast as you can," he nodded at the two policemen and gently walked Laura into the back.

"Thank God she is away from here," Kristy said putting three ice teas down, "I thought for sure she would give herself away."

"She's stronger than we give her credit for," Roxy said looking towards the door, "Here comes Boris and the jerks."

As they sat down, Kristy said, "Good timing. Your lunch is ready."

She went into the kitchen and carried three cheeseburger platters out. Kristy set down two with fries in front of Eddie and Jason and then walked over and gave Boris his, "You get an extra big piece of pie for what you just did," Kristy whispered.

"Is everything okay?" he asked.

"Yup. We have extra protection too," Kristy said looking over his shoulder.

"Just so you know. They asked about if I knew the pretty blonde that works here." Boris said just before taking a sip of his sweet tea, "I told them her name was Marcy," he said with a wink.

"So, you guys get a lot of buses that stop here?" asked Jason.

"Buses, truckers, families on road trips," answered Roxy. Kristy walked up and stood next to her.

Dipping three fries into ketchup he continued, "Do any buses come from Kansas?"

"Hell, I don't know," Roxy said throwing up her hands, "A bus drives into our parking lot, a shit load of people get off. We spend the next hour running our asses off to feed them and they leave lousy tips. So really, I don't care where these buses are from. They are all the same to me."

"Wow. Bitter, are we?" Eddie looked at Jason.

"Do you guys remember a woman, mousy brown hair, about your height?" Pointing to Roxy," she would have a four year old boy with her? I think it was last July," Jason persisted.

Roxy gave him a dirty look, "Do you have cotton in your head?" Roxy said placing both hands on the counter and sticking her face close to his, "I just told you that we get thousands of people in here and you ask if I remember one person?"

"I remember her," Maureen said walking behind the counter. Kristy gave her a dirty look trying to tell her to shut up, "Is she your sister or something?"

"She's my wife," Jason said with a cold look in his eyes, "Or was. She kidnapped my son and is on the run," trying to look the victim, he continued, "I just want my son back. I miss him so much," looking at Maureen, he asked, "You said you remembered her? Did you talk to her?"

"Yes. She said she was heading to Louisiana. New Orleans I think," Maureen said staying calm.

"Makes sense dude," Eddie said, "A person can get lost down there."

Shaking his head, he looked back at Maureen, "Did she say anything else?"

Maureen said, "No. It didn't seem like she was kidnapping your son. She was very loving with him. She did look like she was freshly beaten and was probably trying to get him away from a terrible situation."

Jason stood up. Kristy saw that his hands were clenched into fists. She stepped in front of Maureen and asked, "Would you like something else?"

He unclenched his fists and reached into his pocket. He threw money on the counter and said, "No. We're done here." Eddie got up as well putting the last of his fries in his mouth. He threw a 20-dollar bill on the counter and walked over to Boris, "Hey trucker? How do we get to Louisiana?"

Boris got up and walked to the cash register counter. He grabbed a road map and opened it up. Showing him the route he said, "Well, it's about 10 hours by car. Take I-35 south. Follow the signs to Dallas then go east to Shreveport. South to New Orleans."

Eddie grabbed the map and gave a salute to Boris. Boris heard him yell to Jason as Eddie waved the map in the air, "Let's go gator huntin."

Kristy gave Maureen a hug and said, "That was brilliant. I thought you were asking for trouble when you said you remembered her."

"I wanted to get them as far away as possible," Maureen said.

The two policemen came over to the counter just as Carl came out from the back. One of them said, "We wrote down the license plate, make and model of the truck and have a detailed description of those two. I will contact the highway patrol in Oklahoma, Texas and Louisiana. I want to keep tabs on them. You didn't happen to get their names?"

"The one driving is Jason Dixon and the other guy is Eddie. We didn't get his last name," Kristy responded.

"Hold on. I'll ask Laura," Carl said running to the back. He came back and said, "His name is Edward Dean and he lives in Park City, Kansas too."

"I have a feeling when I run these names, we will learn some interesting things about them," said the officer whose badge had Sgt. Anderson on it, "Tell the young lady not to worry. If he is heading back this way, we will know."

Chapter 27

"Here you go sweetie," Laura said to Freddie placing a plate down in front of him, "These sticky buns are still warm. Tell me what you think?"

Freddie Mapp took a huge bite leaving brown sugar stuck to his top lip. When he swallowed, he closed his eyes and said, "Laura. You have the best sticky buns in the world."

Kristy was walking by when she stopped and said, "Okay you two. None of that here. We are a respectable diner."

The innocent Freddie blushed, realizing what he just said. Laura laughed, held his chin in her hand and kissed him. She gave his top lip a little lick to clean it up. "Do you think they are good enough to serve here?" she asked.

"No. I think I had better take all of them home," he said, taking another bite.

Kristy and Laura walked into the kitchen together. Laura had a second sticky bun with her and said, "I just have to get Carl to give me the okay on these then we should be able to sell them to the customers as a coffee, sticky bun special today. I remember my grandmomma making these when I was a kid. Here try a bite," she ripped a little piece of Carl's sample and gave it to Kristy.

"Mmmm. They are perfect. I have gained 10 pounds since you started baking here. Everything you make is so good," Kristy said, wiping her hands on her uniform apron, "So how long is Freddie staying today?"

"Probably until I go home again," Laura said, "I feel bad that he thinks he has to be here to protect me in case Jason comes back. What a waste of his two days off."

"I don't blame him," Kristy said walking with her to Carl's empty office, "He's seen you upset on two different occasions. It probably drives him crazy that he wasn't there for you."

"I think you're right," Laura put the plate down wrote out instructions for Carl to try it, "I do find it comforting that he's here but how boring it must be for him."

Pointing to the shipment of food just being unloaded in the back, Kristy said, "Why don't you get him to help you haul your supplies to the baking area?"

"Great idea. He would love being useful like that," Laura walked out of the kitchen and came back dragging Freddie behind her.

"Hey Laura and Freddie, get your butts out here," Roxy yelled through the door she held open, "Find Carl. The police are here with some news."

The three came out from the kitchen to find Kristy pouring coffee for the two officers. Sgt. Anderson looked at the small crowd that had gathered at the counter, "We have gotten reports the two men in question, were spotted driving through Ardmore. They've found themselves in a little trouble in Denton, Texas."

"Where's Denton?" Laura asked.

"It's just north of Dallas," said the other officer, "They weren't too popular with the folks there at Bailey's Bar and Grill."

Laura leaned back against Freddie, "Oh no." she groaned.

"What happened?" Asked Carl.

Sgt. Anderson looked at the other officer and asked, "Hey Joey, hand me that paper?" Unfolding the printout, he began to read it, "Let's see. Drunken and disorderly conduct as well as harassment. I think they tried to pick up a married woman with her husband sitting right next to her."

"Yeah. That sounds like them," Laura shook her head.

Sgt. Anderson continued, "Oh yeah. Assault and our friend Eddie was found with a bag of marijuana on him. With his priors, he will be in a little bit of trouble. I was surprised that Jason didn't have a record."

"That's because he was a local football hero in Wichita," Laura told the officers, "He would get caught drinking and driving all the time but would just get off with a warning once the cops found out who he was. We were even in a car accident because he was drunk and he didn't get charged. He knew he could get away with anything so he didn't care what he did. When I threatened to call the police after he beat me, he would laugh and say 'Go ahead. They aren't going to do nothing.'" She shrugged her shoulders and continued, "He was right. He was buddies with the police in Park City too so when they would see him drinking and driving, they would pull him over and take his keys. He would just sleep it off in his truck then in the morning he would walk to the station and get them back. Even if he was guilty of drinking and driving, they wouldn't charge him."

"He must have slept in his truck every night from what you've told me," Kristy commented.

"No. He would drink and drive almost every night but they would catch him about every two months or so," Laura said.

"That's messed up," Freddie shook his head, "It's lucky he didn't hit anyone or anything."

"He must have," answered Laura, "He'd come home with new dents in his truck all the time."

"What will happen to them now?" asked Carl.

"They will spend a few nights in jail until they can make bail," replied Sgt. Anderson, "They will have to go back down to Denton for a hearing but who knows when that will be."

Roxy walked over and placed a sticky bun in front of them and said, "Can I top your coffee up?" Both nodded.

"We appreciate the update fellas," said Carl, "It's nice to know that those two won't be bothering us for a couple of days anyway," slapping Freddie on the shoulder, he laughed, "I guess you can go back to work without worrying about your sweetie here."

"I kind of like it around here. I get served great food and I get to see Laura all day," Freddie said smiling.

"Guthrie needs you back fighting fires and saving lives instead of being my taste tester," giving him a quick peck on the lips Laura whispered, "But it has been great having you here with me."

"We'll keep you updated if we learn anything more," Sgt. Anderson said.

Handing the officer his business card, Carl said, "Just e-mail me so you don't have to drive all the way out here. I'll let everyone know what's going on."

Joey said with his mouth full of sticky bun and smiled "No, no. I think it's pretty important we deliver the information in person."

"Hey boys, your lunch is ready!" Kristy yelled up the stairs. As the two came bounding down the stairs towards her, she said, "You need to eat quickly and get ready for Noah's birthday party."

"Do you have his presents wrapped?" asked Logan.

"Yes, and they are at the back door with your sleeping bags," Kristy said.

As they walked into the kitchen, Laura was setting two glasses of milk down on the table, "I can't imagine having a sleep over with eight, five-year-old boys. Half of them will probably will be homesick and want to leave."

"Not us, right Logan?" Milo said acting brave, "This is going to be so much fun and we are going to play hide-n-go-seek with flashlights."

"Don't expect a sleep over for your next birthday party," Kristy said putting a piece of sliced apple in her mouth. She set the rest of the apple slices down between the boys. She heard Laura's phone buzz indicating she had a text.

They had been anxiously waiting for more news on Jason and Eddie. Laura walked into the living room so Kristy followed, "Is that from Sgt. Anderson?" Kristy asked.

Laura had finished reading it and said, "They got out of jail two days ago."

"What?! How come we are just learning about it now?" Kristy asked concerned.

"It says here that they were spotted driving south of Dallas heading to the Louisiana border," Laura let out her breath.

"At least they are still driving away from us," Kristy said giving Laura a reassuring hug.

They walked back into the kitchen and saw Milo drinking the last of his milk and Logan getting up taking his dishes to the counter. Laura said, "Wow. Good job guys. It usually takes you two a while to get lunch finished."

Putting his dishes on the counter Milo said, "We don't want to be late for the party, Momma. We didn't play or talk like we always do."

"Let's get you changed and cleaned up so we can go!" Kristy said racing them up the stairs.

Kristy and Laura dropped the boys off at their party and decided to go by the grocery store to buy a variety of cheese, grapes, French bread, olives and a bottle of red wine. They were going to have an adult party of their own. As they turned the corner to their street, they could see a police car sitting in front of their house. Sgt. Anderson, Joey and Carl were standing on their front lawn talking. Kristy quickly pulled into the garage. Grabbing the groceries, they ran into house. Laura walked straight to the front door and pulled it open, "Hi?" was all she said.

The three men came in looking very serious, "We have some news that needs to be delivered in person," said Sgt. Anderson.

Kristy grabbed Laura and helped her over to the couch. Kristy sat next to her and took her hand. Before the officer could say anything, Freddie came through the front door. Laura looked at Carl and he said, "I called over to the station and asked that he be here."

Freddie sat down on the other side of Laura and she looked at the police officer, "He's heading back here isn't he?" she asked.

"No, um. Hell. I'm just going to get to the point," Sgt. Anderson let out a big breath, "Jason and his friend Eddie were killed in a car accident last night in Shreveport."

Laura didn't react the way Kristy thought she would. She calmly stared straight ahead and then after a few seconds she said, "Good."

Not knowing what to do next, the men standing just looked at each other. Laura looked at Sgt. Anderson and asked, "Was he drunk?"

Sgt. Anderson shook his head and said, "Yes. It was reported by a bouncer that they left the bar at around 11:00 pm clearly intoxicated. He tried to stop them from driving when one of them hit him in the side of the head, knocking him out. When he came to, they were gone. The police were called. At 11:14, a 9-1-1 call came in saying a blue pickup truck was swerving all over the road and had side swiped a few parked cars. The police caught up with them and the pickup truck would not pull over. This started a two-minute police chase ending in the pick-up truck driving on the wrong side of the road in a construction zone. They lost control and slammed into a parked cement truck. Both occu- pants died at the scene."

"Thank you, Sgt. Anderson, for coming here and telling me," Laura said standing up.

"Well, that's not all," Joey, the other officer said.

"Because you are next of kin, we need you to identify the body," Sgt. Anderson told her, "They will ship his body to the Oklahoma City morgue. It should be here in a couple of days. If you would like, I'll drive you there myself."

"I would really appreciate it. I think his body should go back to his parents in Wichita. They would probably like to handle the funeral arrangements since I don't want to," Laura said coldly.

"We'll worry about those arrangements after you've ID'd him. Do you know how to contact Edward Dean's family?" the Sargent asked.

"No. I didn't really know him. Jason would tell me about their drinking binges," Laura replied.

"I'll go with you too," offered Freddie unsure if she was in shock or not.

"Do you think we should get Milo and tell him?" asked Kristy.

"No. Let him have his fun," Laura smiled at her, "I won't tell him until it has been confirmed that he is actually dead."

Seeing that Laura seemed to be fine and knowing Kristy was here with her, Carl said, "Well, I'd better get back to the diner," looking at Laura, he continued, "let me know if you need anything. Take as much time off as you need."

"Thanks Carl. I will only need to take part of a day to go into Oklahoma City. That's all," Laura walked him to the door.

"I'll be in touch," waved Sgt. Anderson.

Freddie looked into Laura's eyes. He had his hands on her shoulders and said, "Are you okay?" she smiled and nodded her head yes, "Okay then. I'm going back to the station. I get off 10:00. I'll come by after to check on you."

"Well, I may be pretty drunk by then. Kristy and I are going to be drinking red wine and eating grown up stuff," she kissed him, "thanks for being here for me. I am fine and very relieved that this nightmare is over. I did picture his death a little differently. I always knew it would be because of his drinking."

Chapter 28

Freddie had just filled two cups with tea. He was hungry so he grabbed some cookies from the cookie jar and put them on a plate. He put everything on a tray and carried them into the living room.

"What do you mean? He beat me. I left because he was about to hit Milo," Laura was trying not to yell into the phone. She decided to phone Jason's parents while Kristy and the boys were still at the nursing home. This was something she dreaded because Jason could do no wrong in the eyes of his parents. The police had called his parents once Laura had identified the body in the Oklahoma City morgue. Laura thought it was only the right thing to do to call them and let them know that she and Milo would not be at the funeral. "I'm sorry you don't believe me. I have many scars to prove it. His drinking was out of control and that's what killed him," she stopped talking to hear what was being said on the other end of their conversation. Shaking her head, she said, "I don't know when I can come up to Wichita with Milo. I know you haven't seen him in a few years, but that wasn't my fault. You could have come to Park City. It's only 15 minutes away," listening, she rolled her eyes to Freddie, "I know. I hated living in that trailer. Jason was the one telling you not to come, not me," letting out a sigh, she finished the conversation, "Okay. We'll see. Goodbye."

"Is everything okay?" Freddie asked handing her tea.

"I'm glad that's over," she said taking a sip of tea, "They were trying to make me feel guilty about leaving Jason. They think that if he hadn't been looking for me, then he would have never gotten into the accident."

"It would have been a matter of time." Freddie said rubbing her back. "Drinking and driving is a death wish. Unfortunately, innocent people get hurt or killed because jerks like Jason don't care about what might happen."

"You are so right," Laura agreed, "I can't believe that his parents don't believe me when I said he beat me. They haven't seen him actually hit me but he has shoved and criticized me in front of them."

"Well, I'm proud of you for standing up to them," Freddie said giving her a kiss on the head, "You have come a long way since the summer."

"I have, haven't I?" Laura chuckled, "A year ago, I would have burst into tears if someone talked to me like that. I probably wouldn't have argued and done what I was told." she leaned back on the couch and looked at Freddie, "Do you think I've been too cold about Jason's death?"

"Not after the stories you've told me," Freddie answered.

"Jason's mom called me cold-hearted," she said, looking at Freddie, "People don't realize what I went through being married to that monster. He would put me down constantly and told me I was worthless. He said, the only reason he married me was because I was dumb enough to get pregnant."

"He blamed you?" Freddie was shocked, "Didn't he know how these things worked?"

"Ha, ha. You'd think that," getting serious again, she said, "He blamed everything on me. His excuse for drinking was because I ruined his life. He always told me that he could have done so much better. He would throw it in my face that all these women threw themselves at him at the bars. I told him to go ahead and divorce me so he could be with them. I'm pretty sure he cheated on me anyway."

"What would he say to that?" Freddie asked.

"He would backhand me and tell me to shut up," Laura said rubbing the right side of her face.

"What a coward," Freddie couldn't believe a man could do that to a woman.

"I've never hated someone like I've hated him," she said holding back tears, "That is why I was happy that he died. The world is better without him."

"Come here," Freddie said pulling her over to him. He just held on to her while she finally let go of all her emotions and cried into his shoulder.

Laura and Freddie had just finished their second cup of tea. Laura had made the starving Freddie a sandwich, which he ate in four bites. They were enjoying their time together when two little boys came running in through the back door and interrupted it. Kristy followed and everyone met in the kitchen.

"How was school today?" Laura asked as she gave Milo a welcoming hug.

"It was so much fun!" Milo yelled, "Jackson and his dad brought in their pet snake. His name is Snok."

"That's a strange name," Kristy commented.

"It is Swedish for snake," Logan told her, "It's a Milk Snake."

"Yeah. It has red, black and yellow stripes," Milo said, "Jackson's dad taught us a little rhyme about how you can tell this snake from the bad   one.

Logan, with his photographic memory explained. "The Milk Snake is the one that doesn't hurt you and can be a pet. It has three colors like the Coral Snake. That's the one that can kill you. Mr. Dill said that if you see one in the wild, think of this rhyme." Logan paused to think of it, "Red on Black, friend of Jack. Red on yellow kills a fellow."

"If the red is between black stripes, it's a nice snake," Milo explained, "If the red is between yellow, it's a bad snake."

"Well, I will remember that," said Kristy, "Just so you know, if I see any kind of snake I will run away from it."

"Me too," agreed Laura. Looking at Milo she said, "Hey Boo. Can you come up to my room? I need to tell you something."

Kristy and Freddie looked at each other. They knew that Laura was not looking forward to telling Milo that his father was dead. She told them that she was only going to tell him that he was in a car accident; not that he was drinking and running away from the police.

"I'm glad Milo took it so well," Laura said sitting in the passenger seat of Robby's jeep. The police had given Laura Jason's personal items that included his wallet, keys, clothes and his handgun. Laura told them to keep the gun and send the clothes up to his parents with the body. Kristy and Laura were driving up to Park City to clear out the trailer. Laura still had some things there that she wanted.

"Logan was the one with all the questions," Kristy rolled her eyes.

"He really is super smart Kristy," Laura was impressed how advanced he was.

Kristy looked over at Laura, "Milo is doing so well. He has caught up to everyone in the class and, I think, he's doing better than most of them."

Laura clapped her hands together and said, "I'm so happy to hear that. I was so worried that he would never catch up. I feel so guilty when I saw how behind he was for his age. I was a teenage mom and didn't know babies and little kids could learn like that. I really didn't think about teaching him. Besides, we didn't have the money for books and educational toys."

Laura changed the subject. She gave Kristy a look of concern. "I hope the boys will be fine apart. I just couldn't see your in-laws looking after both. I'm happy Maureen wanted to take Milo." Laura continued, "It should only take us a couple of days to get things cleaned up. Most everything in there will be either thrown away or donated. I have called the landlord and he will meet us after it's cleaned up. It would be nice to get the damage deposit back."

"I told Mom and Dad that we should be home on Sunday night. She told us to come for dinner, by the way," Kristy said, "Since the boys are now in kindergarten all day, Dad said he would pick both up from school and take them to their house. When Maureen gets off from the diner, she can pick up Milo. "

Laura leaned back in her seat and put her feet up on the dashboard, "I like how the boys have been in kindergarten all day since after Christmas. I agree with the school that it gets them ready for grade one. It also worked out well since Rita had her baby in January. There is no way she could have looked after a preemie and four kids."

"Yeah. She needed to spend a lot of time at the hospital until little Fern came home," Kristy agreed.

It was an easy two-hour drive from Guthrie to Park City. The trailer was 10 more minutes outside of Park City, "Turn here," Laura instructed. Kristy stopped in front of the gate that Jason had installed to keep Laura from leaving the trailer. Laura just sat looking at her daily nightmare. Her face was pale and was glistening from the sweat that broke out all over her body. She almost told Kristy to turn around and head home but found the courage to get out of the car and unlock the gate with the keys the police gave her. As Kristy drove down the small driveway to the trailer, Laura yelled, "Stop. I think I'm going to throw up," she quickly opened the car door, ran out and leaned over a tree trunk and vomited.

Kristy grabbed some napkins and Laura's water bottle. She went over and handed them to her when she was finished. With tears in her eyes, Laura started to laugh, "I will probably be doing that a few more times. This is bringing back all those bad memories."

"Do you want to go back into town and have lunch? Maybe you just need to get used to being back here," Kristy said very concerned for her friend.

Shaking her head, Laura said, "Any lunch will come right back up. No. I think we should get started. The faster it's cleaned up, the faster we can leave this hell hole."

Chapter 29

Laura's hands shook as she unlocked the door to the trailer. She took a few steps in and Kristy followed. Looking around, Kristy covered her mouth with her hand. She said, "I don't think you're going to get your damage deposit back."

Laura's mouth dropped open while she surveyed the inside of the trailer. It smelled of stale beer and garbage. She could see beer cans and rotting food laying everywhere. There was cardboard duct taped over the window across from her. She saw holes in the inside wall where a family picture of the three of them once hung. Laura walked over and found the picture shattered on the floor. Looking closer at it, she realized bullet holes in the picture matched those in the wall.

She walked into the bedroom. She shook her head when she saw that there were no sheets on the bed and the pillowcase had a streak of dirt across it. Dirty clothes were piled everywhere with more empty beer cans littering the bedside table and floor.

She headed towards the bathroom and dry heaved when she first smelled and then saw the mess. The shower curtain was ripped and hung down by three rings. The once cream-colored bathtub was now black with dirt and grime. Mold and mildew crept around the bathtub and up the tile. She opened the small window to let some of the stench out. Urine and vomit surrounded the toilet. She thought to herself, *he couldn't hit the toilet sober either.* She saw a large crack in the mirror. The last time she looked in this mirror, she was a broken down, weak woman. She liked what she saw now. Laura walked out of the bathroom and shut the door. "I'll deal with that later if at all," Laura whispered to herself.

Kristy was in Milo's room. She heard Laura come in and said, "This is the only room in the house that hasn't been destroyed."

Laura looked around thinking of the last night they were here. Jason was in one of his rages and had hit her a few times. He grabbed her and threw her out of the front door of the trailer. She landed on the ground and the side of her head hit a rock. Milo had latched onto his dad as Jason started down the steps. He grabbed Milo and pulled him off. He set him down and pushed him away. Milo got back up and tried to grab him again. That's when Jason turned and lifted his left hand. Laura saw the rage in his face and knew he was about to back-hand Milo. She jumped up as fast as she could and ran towards Jason. Laura screamed at him while trying to pull his arm down, "Don't touch him! Leave him alone!"

Jason took his other hand and grabbed her hair. He pulled back her head he looked her in the face and said, "He's just like you. He hasn't learned that he needs to obey me. You can't get it through your thick skull so I don't expect he will." letting go of her hair, "You look like shit. Get yourself cleaned up by the time I get back," with that he got into his pickup and drove to some bar to drink his sorrows away.

That night, Laura had been in her bathroom trying to stop the bleeding. She felt she was looking at a coward and probably deserved it. She knew she was a good mother and that was all she had going for her. She heard a whimper behind her and saw her son standing at the bathroom door crying, "Why does Daddy do that to you? He is so mean to us," she squatted down and took him into her arms, "I don't like him hurting you. You are the nicest momma ever."

She started crying too. She buried her face into his small shoulder and carried him into her bedroom. They just sat on the bed and held onto each other until they stopped crying. She wiped her tears from her face and notice Jason's bankcard on his bedside stand. An escape plan started forming in her head. She looked at Milo and said, "He won't hurt either of us anymore Boo. I think we will have to leave until Daddy can get help with his anger," he nodded his head and understood what she was saying, "We will pack some things in your backpack and I have a suitcase already packed just for a time just like this. We can't take much because we will have to walk into town. Do you think you can do it?"

"Yeah," Milo sniffed, "Can I take my toys?" he asked.

"Maybe one or two small ones," Laura said ruffling up his hair, "Okay Sweetie, we better make it fast. We don't want Daddy to come home and find us packing. He would get really mad." *He would probably kill me,* she thought.

Fifteen minutes later, mother and son climbed over the fence that kept them in their prison. Laura got down first then helped Milo. They walked along the road towards town in the dark. Every time they saw headlights coming towards them, they would duck down and hide in the culvert. Laura made a game of it and Milo thought it was a lot of fun. She didn't want to take the chance that Jason or even one of his friends would see them walking along the road. After 45 minutes of walking, Laura and Milo made it into town. Laura had put on her long sleeve jacket and scarf to hide the bruises on her arms and the cut on the side of her head. Their first stop was to the bank to use the bank machine. Jason sent her to the bank a few times when he needed money for the bar. She would show him the bank statement to prove that she hadn't taken anymore out for herself.

Laura entered his pin number and saw that there was only $66 in his account. "Pathetic," she quietly said to herself, "We hardly have enough money to eat and he goes out and drinks every night." She took out $60 and put it into her purse. She decided she didn't need his bank-card anymore. It would be one way he could find her if she ever used it again. Laura bent the card back and forth until it snapped in two. She threw it away in the garbage can outside the bank.

They got to the bus depot and looked up on the board. She realized that she didn't know where they were going. The next bus leaving was going to Dallas in an hour. Dallas it was. The tickets cost $48. She had $12 left plus a little bit of money she had packed away in her suitcase.

She would find loose change lying around the house or sometimes money would fall out of Jason's pants when she washed them. Laura would tuck it away just in case she needed it to buy groceries. A few times she used it when Jason spent the rest of his paycheck on booze or gambling.

Laura figured that one day she and Milo would leave so she packed an old suitcase with some clothes for both of them and the picture of her mother and Milo. She hid the suitcase behind the washer, knowing Jason avoided doing laundry. In his small mind, cleaning and cooking was a woman's job.

After buying their bus tickets, Milo announced he was hungry. Trying to conserve the money, she bought him chocolate milk and a granola bar from the vending machine in the depot lobby. She and Milo waited in the lady's bathroom until the announcement for them to board. She didn't want to risk Jason seeing them if he came in looking for them.

Laura finally relaxed a little when the bus they were on left Park City and started on its' way to Dallas. Milo had fallen asleep with his head on her lap. She brushed the hair from his face. Panic started to rise in her when she realized what they had done. *What am I going to do when we reach Dallas? I have under $20 and nowhere to stay.* She thought to herself. She stared out into the darkness praying an idea would come to her.

The bus route to Dallas made many stops in small towns, to pick up passengers. At one stop, she woke Milo up because she had to go to the bathroom. As they were walking out of the station, she noticed something on the bulletin board. It was a poster for a women's shelter. There was a toll free emergency phone number on it. She pulled the poster down and folded it and put it in her purse. This may be the answer she was looking for. When she got to Dallas she would call this number and hopefully, someone would help them find shelter and food.

They got back on the bus and took their seats. She felt a huge weight was lifted. At least now she had a plan.

"I'm tired Momma," Milo said snuggling back onto her lap.

"Me too Boo," Laura, yawned, closing her eyes.

"I just got off the phone with the landlord." Laura said sitting back down at the fast food restaurant in town. They decided the cleanup was overwhelming and they needed to step back and make a plan. Kristy was hungry so they drove back to Park City to have lunch, "He will meet us at the trailer in 45 minutes. He wasn't too happy when I told him that the trailer was pretty much trashed."

"At least you are being honest," Kristy, told her while dipping a chicken finger in barbeque sauce, "He may just haul it away and dump it. If he does that, then maybe he can just take everything in it that you don't want. That would save us many trips to the dump."

"I would be willing to pay him," Laura said crossing her arms, "I'm afraid that I may be on the hook anyway for the repairs. He will have the damage deposit but I'm sure it's not enough to cover it."

"Why don't you tell him that he can have any of the furniture and household items he would like?" Kristy said, "Do you want to keep any of that stuff?"

"We really didn't have anything nice. We bought most of it from garage sales or second hand stores," chuckling, she continued, "I even went dumpster diving when the money ran out. I found the kitchen table in a dumpster. The leg was broken but I duct-taped it back together and hid it by putting it against the wall. The three chairs were from another dumpster. They were in perfect shape so I don't know why they were there."

Kristy said, "I bet the fourth one was broken so it was easier to throw away the three and buy four new ones. I think people do that all the time."

Shaking her head, Laura said, "What a waste. I'm happy I was able to recycle them."

"What else did you find?" Kristy asked while cleaning up after their lunch.

"I found that suitcase I used when I left here. Once again, a little duct tape made it practically new," Laura smiled and held the garbage can open for Kristy to dump their trash. Laura looked at her phone and said, "We have just enough time to stop at the hardware store and get garbage bags and work gloves. There is a lot of stuff there I don't want to be touching with my bare hands."

As Kristy and Laura drove up the driveway, they could see that the landlord was already there. Laura got out and waved at him. He came over to the car and said, "Laura? I didn't recognize you. You look so different from the last time I saw you."

Understanding what he meant, she laughed. "Hi Juan. Thank you. I am a different woman. It's amazing how a person can change when they stop getting abused."

Kristy's eyes flew open and she looked at Laura in amazement. Laura saw her reaction and said, "Don't worry Kristy. Juan here stopped by to fix something during one of Jason's rages. He saw what kind of person Jason really was."

"That's right," Juan said, "I was afraid he was going to kill you that night."

"That was nothing compared to some of his other blow-ups," Laura said waving her hand.

"You wouldn't let me call the police," he shook his head.

"I shouldn't have talked you out of it," Laura said knowing better now, "He was so embarrassed that you saw him. He kept that side of himself hidden from almost everyone else. So many people thought he was so much fun."

"I would make up excuses to come out here and check on you," he said, "A few times I saw your fresh bruises or that you had been crying."

"Well, that is all over now. I am now a strong, independent woman and that bastard is dead so I can move on," Laura gave Juan a hug, "Oh. Sorry. Juan this is my best friend Kristy. She literally saved Milo and me. She took us in and helped me onto a better path."

"Nice to meet you," Juan said shaking her hand, "How is Mr. Milo doing?"

Lighting up, Laura said, "He has grown two inches and is in kindergarten. Kristy has a son the same age and they are best friends. He is happy now. And, you know what? So am I. Or I will be when this mess gets cleaned up. Did you see inside?"

"I certainly did," rolling his eyes, "It didn't look like that when you lived here. You always kept it clean and so nice looking."

"Can it be fixed?" Laura asked.

"Well, it wasn't in the best shape when I rented it to you over four years ago. That's why I gave you a deal on the rent," Juan said, "I think there is a mice infestation in there. There are a lot of droppings and I'm sure there will be a few nests too."

Both Kristy and Laura groaned. They hadn't really started looking through things so they hadn't seen the mice droppings.

He continued, "Yup. I think this baby's toast."

Laura leaned up against the car, "I don't think I will be salvaging too much if the mice are in there."

"I'll just have it all hauled away. That trailer is old so it won't be too much of a loss. Even the appliances were old and not worth keeping," Juan said crossing his arms, "Why don't you go through everything and leave anything you don't want. I may just donate the trailer to the police-training program. They can use it for training their rookies. It's a good way to teach them to break through a locked door and how to use tear gas."

"Then the fire department can haul it to a field and set it on fire. It is good to work on a real building not just simulated ones," Kristy added.

"Kristy's husband and my new boyfriend are firefighters," Laura informed Juan with a shy smile.

Kristy was going to correct her but she decided Juan didn't need to know the details of her life.

"I'll get in touch with them too. Good idea," Juan said. Looking at Laura he continued, "Good for you. I'm glad you have found a decent guy. No wonder you look so good. There is a sparkle in your eye that I have never seen before."

Chapter 30

Kristy was carrying another full garbage bag out of the trailer and set it by all the others. "This makes 25," she said to Laura who just hung up the phone.

"We can fill 25 more I bet," Laura, said shaking her head, "That was Maureen. Everything's fine with Milo. He is having a great time with them. Isaac is teaching him to throw a football. Hopefully, he doesn't turn out to be a quarterback like his dad."

They started to head back into the trailer when they heard a truck coming down the driveway. They stopped and saw Juan followed by two more trucks. They walked out to greet them.

"I've brought reinforcement," Juan said waving his arm showing five people getting out of the other trucks. He made the introductions and said, "They are from the Thrift Store in town and heard that you were getting rid of clothes and furniture."

"It's all really gross," Laura, said, "He didn't know how to use the washer. Everything is so dirty. The furniture is in pretty bad shape too."

Rachel, the owner of the Thrift Store said, "Juan told us that it was pretty bad in there. If you don't mind, we would like to look at it. We can wash the clothes and Buck over there is pretty good at repairing furniture and appliances. We would be happy to take it off your hands if you don't want it. We will sell some of it and some we will donate."

"I'd love it if ya'll could use it," Laura said, "I'd rather it be re-used than end up in the dump. Kristy and I have gone through everything and I've taken what I've wanted. The rest is yours."

Kristy said pointing to the pile of garbage bags, "We have put a lot of the clothes in garbage bags already. There are some bags with just garbage in them so you will have to weed those out."

"Why don't we just take all of it with us," Buck said, "We can go through it at the shop. We do dump runs practically every other day for the donated stuff we don't want."

Rachel added, "It's the least we can do for ya'll since we're getting everything."

Stunned that anyone would want what was in the trailer, Laura threw up her arms and said, "Deal. We all win I guess. Let's start loading up your trucks."

"Hey, I've got some stuff in my storage shed over there that I don't want," Juan said pointing to a small garage that was on the other side of the yard. "I'd be happy to donate that."

Juan had gotten one of the Thrift Shop workers to come help him. They had backed Juan's truck up to the shed and started loading. They stopped loading the truck and both came over to the trailer each carrying a box. "Hey Laura!" Juan yelled. When she looked up, he continued, "I almost forgot. These boxes are yours."

"Mine?" she said puzzled. "I didn't have any boxes like that."

"About four months ago I was out here rooting around in the shed when this old Ford truck drove up. Jason wasn't home so the guy came and talked to me," Juan said putting the box down in front of Laura, "This guy said he was your dad."

"What?" Laura said shocked.

"He was looking for you because he had some stuff of your Mother's that he thought you should have. He said he was moving to Florida." Juan said.

Laura quickly opened one of the boxes. She unwrapped a ceramic Arabian horse. Tears started rolling down her cheeks. "This was hers. She had a collection of horse figurines," hugging it to her chest she said, "She started collecting them when she was little and growing up on the ranch. She loved her horses and riding." Laura said putting the Arabian horse back in the box. She unwrapped another horse. It was a beautiful bay horse. "She would show me her collection and tell me stories. A lot of the horses looked like the ones she had as a child. This one she called Misty after her first horse."

Laura carefully rewrapped the horses and put them in the box. She closed the lid and asked Juan to help her carry them to the Jeep. "Thank you so much for bringing me these. I have a piece of my mother back," closing the back of the jeep, she asked, "Did he say anything else?"

"Your dad?" Juan confirmed, "He just asked about you and I told him that you and the boy left Jason. He asked where you were and I told him I didn't know and that Jason didn't know. He did say that he regretted making you marry him. He looked at the trailer and said that Jason was a good for nothing piece of shit that couldn't support a family. Then he got into his truck and drove away. He was a bit cranky, I'd say."

"He's always like that. Thanks Juan," she said. After Juan left, she stood by the Jeep in shock. She thought to herself. *I can't believe he said he regretted making me marry Jason. He always said regretting things showed weakness.*

"Penny for your thoughts?" Kristy asked walking up to Laura.

"I'm stunned Dad brought Momma's stuff. He thought it was a waste of shelf space," Laura said, "I can't wait to get home and go through everything."

"We had better stock up on tissues because I don't know how you will control yourself once you see what's in there," Kristy laughed putting her arm around Laura's shoulders. This made Laura laugh too. Kristy continued, "I was talking to Juan. He said there isn't any reason for us to stick around. The thrift store people will make a few trips and we don't have to do any cleaning. Why don't we leave now, check out of the motel and head home. We will get home by 7:00 and since we aren't expected home until tomorrow, you can go through those boxes without interruption. I'll go over to Mom and Dad's to leave you alone. You can pick Milo up in the morning."

Nodding her head, Laura said, "Good idea. I think I'd better be alone when I go through these. I will pretty much be a mess. I saw some photo albums in there from when I was a kid."

"We can unload everything from the car onto the back porch," Kristy said pulling into the garage.

"All except my Momma's boxes. Those I will take to my room with a box of tissues," Laura said.

After getting everything unloaded, Kristy helped Laura carry the boxes upstairs. Kristy said as she set one down on Laura's bed, "I'm just going to take a shower and wash this smell off me. Then I'll go over and see Logan and my in-laws. We may go and visit Robby since I haven't seen him in a few days."

"I'm glad I took a quick shower at the motel," Laura said with a shiver, "I felt so gross and all I could smell in my hair and clothes was rotting food, stale beer and mouse droppings."

Kristy knocked on Laura's door after a half an hour to say good-bye, "Come in," Laura said with a sniffle. Kristy opened the door and saw Laura with a red puffy face and tear filled eyes, "You were right about me being a mess. I have only gone through half of the first box.

Look what I have found," Laura held up a birthday card from her Aunt Melba for her 13th birthday. "It still has the $50 bill in it and she wrote, 'With Love for such an important birthday. Uncle Jess and I would love for you to come visit us. We miss and love you very much. Aunt Melba and Uncle Jess.' Look." Laura held up a pile of letters and cards that her father had hidden from her. She truly loved her aunt and uncle and missed visiting them in Tulsa, "All of these are from my Aunt Melba. I bet there is more money in them that she had sent. I can't believe my father wouldn't give them to me. At 13, I would have loved to have my own money to shop with. He never gave me any to just go and spend how I liked."

"Luckily money doesn't really spoil," said Kristy, "You can go shopping now with it now."

"I think I will take the money and open a bank account for Milo," said Laura.

"That's a great idea. Robby and I did that when Logan was born. We put $75 into it every month," stopping to calculate the balance in her head, Kristy continued, "He should have about $3000 in there."

"Are you going to use it for University?" Laura asked thinking that is what she would use the money for.

"No, a trust fund was set up for him from my parent's inheritance. That's what we will use for University," said Kristy, "This $3000 will be for him to spend. One day he may want a fancy bike or a game system. He can use this money for things like that."

"Maybe I'll use part of it and set up an Education plan and then put the other into a bank account for him to spend on things like that too," Laura liked that idea. Just a little every month from her paycheck will add up like Logan's account.

"Well, I thought I'd just stop by and see how you are doing," looking at Laura's dresser she said, "I see you have unwrapped all of the horses. They are beautiful."

"Seeing them makes me so happy. I can't wait to tell Milo the stories that my momma told me about them," Laura said looking lovingly at the figurines.

"Okay. I'll leave you alone now. I'll be next door. I don't think we'll visit Robby tonight. I am feeling pretty tired," Kristy said walking to the door.

"I know. We've had three pretty busy days cleaning and lifting stuff," Laura agreed, yawning. "I bet you will come home and find me sound asleep. See ya," Laura waved to her as she turned to go down the hall.

Kristy, Logan and her in-laws, were sitting in Bobby and Vicki's family room watching a movie and eating popcorn. Kristy had dozed off but woke up suddenly when they heard a knock on the back door. Bobby paused the movie and got up to answer it. "Well, it's good to see you darlin'. Come on in," He said escorting the visitor into the room with the others. Once he stepped aside, they saw Laura walk in behind him. Kristy noticed she was pale and had a very serious look on her face.

Kristy picked up Logan's head that had been using her lap for a pillow and got up. She ran to Laura. "You look like you are about to faint," helping her to a chair, "Sit down. Can I get you a glass of water?" Kristy asked.

Laura nodded and just stared at the paper in her lap. She took a sip of water when Kristy got back. She softly said, holding up the paper, "I, um, I found this in my mother's things."

Kristy took it from her and saw that the letter was on very official looking letterhead. Looking at her father-in-law, she asked, "Do you know a company called Williams, Kiefer and Jackson?"

"Yes," Bobby answered, "It's a law firm with offices in Tulsa and Oklahoma City."

Kristy read the letter to herself. She looked at Laura who was still in shock. "I'm so sorry honey," Kristy said to her. Looking at everyone else, she said, "This is a letter from her aunt's lawyer. It's dated about a year ago saying that her Aunt Melba had passed away. They need her to get in touch with them as soon as possible. Laura is her aunt's sole heir and it looks like she has inherited everything of her aunt and uncle's.

Looking at Laura, Bobby said, "You can't do anything until Monday so why don't I come over then and we can call this lawyer. We will see what she has to say."

Laura gave him a grateful look and stood up to leave. Vicki got up and came over to give her a hug. "I'm so sorry about your auntie honey. It will be good for you just to take some time tomorrow and mourn her. Would you like to go to church with us to say a little prayer for her?"

Laura hugged her back and whispered, "That'd be nice. I'll pick Milo up and then we can go," tears filled her eyes, "Thank you all for your help. Why don't we go to brunch at the I-35 after?" Nobody said any- thing so Laura said a little confused, "Well, isn't that what you do after church? I've seen all those people come into the diner all dressed up talking about what happened at church. "

"I think that's a great idea," Kristy said taking her hand, "We haven't been to church since Robby's accident. It's about time we go back and the boys can go to Sunday school."

"Brunch will be my treat," Bobby volunteered, "Can you call for reservations?"

"I think we have connections to get a table reserved," Kristy laughed.

Kristy, Logan and Laura all left to go back home. Bobby and Vicki watched from the kitchen window. They could see Kristy walking with her arm around Laura as she rested her head-on Kristy's shoulder.

Logan was on the other side of Laura holding her hand.

Chapter 31

Laura woke up Monday morning with a sense of dread. She tried to eat some dry toast but it just got stuck in her throat. Even the coffee tasted off. She was all alone sitting in the kitchen when she heard a knock at the back door. She opened it and said, "Good Morning Bobby. I'm so glad you are here to help me."

"After the stories you told us about your aunt and uncle yesterday, I'm happy to help," Bobby said, "Your Aunt Melba was quite the spit-fire."

Smiling, she said pouring Bobby a cup of coffee, "She sure was. I'm surprised that she didn't drive to Wichita and get Momma and me. She would have stood up to my dad in all of her four-foot-ten glory."

"Why do you think she didn't come to get you?" Asked Bobby.

"I really think my mother stopped her," Laura said, "No one wanted Momma to marry Daddy because they could see that he wasn't good enough for her. She fell in love with him and thought she saw a different side to him. She told me that he was so sweet and nice to her while they were courting. It wasn't until after they got married that his true personality came out. By then, Momma's pride took over. I think she didn't want to hear 'I told you so' from everyone. Either that or Daddy threatened to hurt us if we left."

"Too bad," Bobby shook his head, "Did your mother approve of Jason?"

"At first," Laura rolled her eyes, "He was the big catch at high school. Dating the varsity quarterback made me very popular. She thought I was way too young to get married and she could see what kind of person Jason was. Daddy insisted but then she was happy I was leaving."

"You were escaping the hell hole she was living in," Bobby said.

"Yeah, to go live in one of my own," Laura added looking down at her coffee cup.

Breaking up the awkward silence, Bobby said, "It's sure quiet around here. Are the boys at school already?"

"Yup. I knew you were coming over at 8:30 so I took them a little early," Laura got up and grabbed the letter from the lawyer that was on the counter by the phone, "They were very excited to play soccer before school started."

Taking the letter from her, Bobby said, "Well, let's get this done. Why don't we move into the dining room?"

Laura paced from the dining room to the living room the whole time Bobby was on the phone with the lawyer. The call lasted about eight minutes and Laura had no idea what was being said. The only thing she knew was that they were meeting tomorrow. Bobby had asked her if that was convenient and she said yes.

"Okay. We'll see you then," Bobby hung up the phone. Laura had stopped pacing and put her hands on the table waiting for Bobby to fill her in on the conversation. He said, "Your Aunt Melba's lawyer's name is Catherine Mason from the Tulsa office. She will fly into Oklahoma

City tomorrow morning. We will meet at the Oklahoma City office at 2:00."

Laura sat down and asked, "What else did she say? When did my aunt and uncle pass away?"

Looking at the notes he took, he said, "Your Uncle Jess passed away three years ago from pulmonary fibrosis. She said that it is basically scarring of the lung tissue. Your Aunt Melba was a diabetic and she died of complications from that." Looking up from the paper he added, "My sister has diabetes and it affects your organs. I suspect her organs just started shutting down."

This made Laura very sad. She asked, "Did Catherine say when she died?"

"She died on April 1st of last year. This letter is dated April 11th," Bobby held up the paper.

Chuckling, Laura said, "That would be just like Aunt Melba to die on April Fool's Day," getting serious, she continued, "I'm sorry she spent two years alone after Uncle Jess died. I wish I could have been there for her."

"Well, according to the lawyer, she thought of you as a granddaughter. Catherine was getting quite concerned that no one had responded to her letter. She was very happy to hear from us. She was about to hire a private detective to find you," he stood up and walked around to where Laura was sitting. He put his hand on her shoulder and said, "Your aunt left almost everything to you. She did leave money to about six charities. From what the lawyer was saying, I think you have just inherited a lot of money including a mansion in Tulsa. We will get all the details tomorrow when we drive to Oklahoma City for the meeting."

When Laura heard what Bobby had told her, an overwhelming feeling came over her. She remembered the huge, beautiful house her aunt and uncle lived in. She thought it was a castle and she pretended she was a princess when she was there. There was a large koi pond in the backyard. She and her aunt would sit on the side and feed them. Laura loved to put her pinky tip in. The koi would think it was food and come up and grab it. Koi fish don't have teeth so they would just suck on it, which tickled.

Laura put her head down on the back of her hands and started to breathe deeply. She could feel she was going to hyperventilate. This was all too much for her to handle.

Kristy looked at the mantle clock. It was 5:00 and no sign of Laura and Bobby. She paced around the living room and looked out the front window. Then she walked to the back porch to look for any sign of them. When she came back into the living room, her mother-in-law said, "Good gracious honey. You're going to wear a path into the carpet."

Realizing what she was doing, Kristy smiled at Vicki and sat down next to her on the couch. She said, "You're right. I'm just anxious to hear about the meeting. I was hoping they would be home before I left to pick up the boys from their tennis lesson."

"Remember, they were stopping by Peggy's to pick up something for me. I bet they were filling her in on the meeting," Vicki said.

They could hear footsteps on the back porch. Kristy jumped up to greet them. As Kristy, Laura and Bobby walked into the living room, Kristy said, "I was getting worried. How long did the meeting take?"

Laura sat down in the chair by the window and answered, "It took about an hour and a half. I had to sign all sorts of things. It was pretty exhausting."

"I could see you were pretty emotional during the meeting," Bobby said sitting next to his wife, "I don't blame you. Your whole life is about to change."

"What does that mean?" Kristy said, with a hint of concern, "What's going to change?"

Laura burst into tears. She pulled out a tissue from her pocket and wiped her eyes and nose, "Bobby, could you please tell them?"

"Well," he started saying calmly, "This little lady is now a very wealthy woman. Because her aunt and uncle had no children, her aunt left everything to Laura. She has inherited a mansion and everything in it. There was a list of what they had acquired over the years. Laura is now the proud owner of some pretty expensive art work and antique furniture."

Laura laughed through her tears and said, "I'm picturing my little bull in a china shop running around those valuable things."

"If you show Milo these things and explain why they are so valuable, I bet he will be very aware around them," Vicki said, "That's what I did with my kids and with Logan. Nothing was ever broken. Logan would ask me to show him these things over and over again. We used to make up stories about them."

"I'll try," Laura smiled, "Milo is very different than Logan. He reacts and then thinks."

Kristy was getting a little impatient with the change of conversation, "What else did you learn?"

"Now let's see," Bobby said remembering where he left off, "Oh yeah. She and Milo belong to the most exclusive private country club in the state. The only way to get in these days is to inherit the membership."

"Can she sell the membership since she won't be living there?" asked Kristy.

"Well, here's the thing," Bobby said looking up at her, "There was a stipulation in the will. For Laura to receive the inheritance, she must move to Tulsa and live there for five years before she can sell anything. She has enough money to live off of for a very long time."

"What?" Kristy looked at Laura who was already crying. They both got up and wrapped their arms around each other and sobbed into each other's shoulder. Finally, Kristy looked up and said, "You can't go."

Pulling away from her, Laura told her, "I don't want to go. Milo and I are so happy here, but I have to. I will lose my inheritance if I don't. I think my aunt was thinking she would help me get away from such a horrible life by putting this condition into her will. She also made it clear that the only one to inherit anything of hers after I die will be my children. There was no way she wanted my dad or Jason to get their hands on anything."

"So, are you going to move to Tulsa?" Kristy asked stunned.

"I think I have to," Laura replied squeezing the tears from her eyes, "I have to think of Milo's future."

Kristy shook her head indicating that she understood, "When will you be going?" She asked.

"Not until after school is finished," Laura answered.

Bobby interrupted, "Catherine said it would take about that long to get everything settled. So, you still have a few months together," he tried to sound positive.

Laura looked at Kristy and took both hands into hers, "Please say you'll come with us? We can keep the boys together and not have to worry about working."

"You know I can't," Kristy said, "This is my home and Robby is here. I can't leave him."

"We'll move him too. I bet there is a really nice home that we can put him in," Laura said.

"Oh, please no," Vicki cried out, "Please don't take our boy away from us again."

Laura didn't even consider Robby's parents, "Oh, I'm so sorry Vicki. I wasn't thinking very clearly. That is really selfish of me."

"It's understandable sweetheart," Bobby said putting his arm around his wife, "You have had a bit of a shock today I think."

Kristy looked back to Laura and asked, "Have you told Freddie?"

"Not yet," she said looking at the floor, "He has a day off tomorrow. We are going to spend tomorrow morning together before I go to the diner. I will ask him if he wants to move with us. I'm sure he can get on with the Fire Department in Tulsa."

"Why don't we tell the boys after dinner," Kristy suggested, "Everyone at the diner will be sad to see you go."

"Luckily, Maureen has been helping me bake. She is pretty good at it too so I think she can take over when I leave," Laura said. She turned to Kristy with a pleading look in her eyes. "Will you and Logan will come and visit a lot? Bobby told me that it is only about an hour and 40-minute drive there. We will come back here too."

Smiling, Kristy said, "Of course. You have to come back for the boy's joint birthday party."

"Everyone can drive over for Thanksgiving," Laura was feeling excited for the first time since she found out. "I remember that my aunt has a huge dining room table. We'll come back here for Christmas. It's only right that we are here with Robby and I know Freddie will want to be close to his family too."

"You two are just like sisters," Vicki laughed.

Chapter 32

Kristy walked into the country club banquet room and looked around. The tables were elegantly set with beautiful wild flower centerpieces. The catering staff had set up the buffet tables and bar. She was hoping to spot Laura. Kristy heard from behind her, "Hey. Did you get off work early?" Laura said carrying a centerpiece and setting it down on a table.

"Carl knew I wanted to get here to help out," Kristy said. She waved her arm around, "It looks like everything is practically done."

"The staff here is really good," Laura, said, "They do this all the time and have some really good ideas. I feel like I'm getting in the way."

"Well, if you don't need me, I think I'll go home and change," Kristy said. She looked around for two little boys, "Where are Milo and Logan?"

Laura answered, "Those two boys were in the way so Freddie volunteered to take them to the park," looking at her watch she said, "They have been gone for almost two hours. I wonder where they are?"

Kristy smiled, "They're in good hands. He will have them here in time for the start of the party. It won't take me longer than 45 minutes. I should get back before the first guest arrives."

"Thanks. I'm a little nervous," Laura, said surveying the room, "It's the first time I've thrown a party like this."

"Everything will be great," Kristy reassured her, "What was the last count?"

"About 52 adults and 25 kids," Laura answered, "I'm really excited to see everyone. It will be so hard to say good-bye."

"You have made a lot of friends here," Kristy said, "I can't believe you are throwing your own farewell party. Carl and I said we would do it for you."

"I know, but I wanted to do it to thank everyone in Guthrie for doing so much for me. Besides, I have a lot of money now so this is my way of showing my appreciation to everyone," Laura said, "Every time I had a problem, which seemed like a lot, the people here didn't think twice to help me out. I felt so protected when Jason decided to show his face here. Everyone at the I-35 made sure I was safe and I was surprised how ya'll stood up to him."

Kristy laughed, "I thought Roxy was going to take him by his ear and throw him out. She was so disgusted with him."

Two little boys burst into the room, "Momma!" Milo yelled, "We had so much fun at the park. Freddie taught us how to play grounders."

"Yeah," agreed Logan, "He won almost every time because he's so tall."

"What is grounders?" Laura asked kissing Freddie.

"It's a game you play on the play set at the park," Freddie said sitting down, "It's like tag but you can't touch the ground. You have to move around the jungle gym by swinging, climbing and jumping."

Milo interrupted, "If you touch the ground, everyone yells grounders and you are out."

"If you get touched by the person who is it, then you're out too," Logan added.

"They have worn me out," said an exhausted Freddie, "We had about 10 kids join in."

"You played the whole time?" Kristy asked him.

"Of course. It was my favorite game as a kid," Freddie smiled.

"You are such a big kid," Laura laughed rubbing his blonde brush-cut, "Thank you so much for looking after them. Why don't you go take a shower and get back here as fast as you can? This party is for you too."

When Kristy got back to the country club, there were already a few guests there. She saw someone she had to go over and give a hug to, "Ozzie! I'm so glad you made it after your fall. How is that collar bone?"

"Well darlin', I wouldn't miss this," Ozzie Becks said, "I had to make a deal with the nurses that I will stay in my wheel chair. They don't want me using my walker and putting weight on it. It's almost healed but I don't have any strength so I could fall again."

"Good for them for making you stay in your chair," Kristy said patting his hand, "It would be horrible if you fell again. You got pretty banged up last time."

"There you are Kristy," Laura yelled from across the room, "Logan wants to know if you brought his swim trunks."

"I've got them right here," Kristy said pulling his green and purple bathing suit out of her bag, "Where is he?"

"They are in the kid's party room with those three brave high school students I hired to run the kid's party," Laura said.

"You are paying them pretty well, so I think they are happy to supervise." Kristy said.

"They do have some great games planned in the pool and after," Laura said happy she didn't have to worry about where the boys were and what they were doing. She really wanted a chance to talk to everyone and say thank you and good-bye.

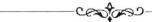

"Wow Laura. That was a great party," Kristy said carrying in her sleeping son, "There were more than 80 people there."

Following Kristy with Milo in her arms, "I know. I can't believe all those people came by to say good-bye to Freddie and me. Some could only stay for a few minutes but it was touching that they made the effort to come."

Freddie came crashing through the door with his arms loaded with farewell presents that some people gave them. The guys at the fire station gave Freddie a quilt that Fire Chief Hunter's wife made. In the center was a fireman's helmet with the station's logo on it. Surrounding it were pictures of the Freddie and all the guys joking around and some pictures of them on the job. He was really going to miss everyone at the station.

It was 9:00 on the morning of the move. They had wanted to get away the hour before but Roxy and Maureen came by to say good-bye before their shift started. Bobby and Vicki Garrison brought goodies for the boys for their trip to Tulsa. Kristy was driving the Jeep with Laura riding shotgun. The boys were in car seats in the back already digging into goodie bags. The Jeep was loaded with suitcases and the boxes repacked with Laura's mother's keepsakes. Freddie was following with his truck that had his stuff packed into plastic bins. He also carried Milo's toys and the bike that everyone at the diner had bought for Milo as a good-bye gift.

"Well, here we go," Laura sniffled, "I'm really going to miss this place and everyone here."

"You'll be back in a few months for the boys' birthday party," Kristy said with a lump in her throat.

Laura smiled at Kristy through her tears, "I will probably be here before that. I am already getting home sick," thinking of the gifts

Kristy gave them, she said, "Thank you again for the picture. I just love the one you gave Milo. It is so perfect with them sitting on the back step sharing their popsicles. It just shows what good friends they are."

"I love that picture too. I gave one to Logan so he will always remember his good buddy," Kristy said.

"The big picture of the everyone at the barbeque is going in my room," Laura laughed, "That picture will remind me how wonderful everyone in Guthrie is. I can't believe you got it enlarged and framed it."

"Are we there yet?" a voice from the back seat asked.

Laura rolled her eyes and said to Kristy, "Are you kidding me? I only thought they say that in the movies. It's going to be a long car ride."

Chapter 33

Three months later

"Are they here yet?" Logan yelled from the kitchen table. Kristy said he had to finish his lunch before he could go out and wait for Laura, Milo and Freddie on the front porch. They had decided to come back for the weekend to plan the boy's joint birthday party.

"Not yet sweetie," Kristy said glancing out the front window. She was just as excited as Logan to see her friend, "Hold on. I see Freddie's truck pulling up in front of the house."

Before she could stand up, a blur came running from the kitchen and out the front door. She chased after him and greeted Freddie. She looked around him expecting to see Laura and Milo coming out of the truck.

"They're not here," Freddie, said.

"Didn't they come?" Logan said looking in the passenger side window.

"We better go in. I have to get you up to speed on things," Freddie said looking at the ground.

They walked into the house. Kristy went into the kitchen and poured Freddie an iced tea and brought it back out to him, "What's going on?" she said concerned.

"Well, I think we just broke up," said Freddie taking a sip, "I told her that I didn't like living in Tulsa with all of her rich, fake friends. I feel like such an outsider with the guys at the fire station there. I think the last straw was when she told me that she was too busy to come here this weekend. She's involved with charity fund-raisers that all the rich people there like to go to and flaunt their money and status. Even Milo has started acting like a spoiled brat like all those kids at the country club. He started throwing tantrums when Laura wouldn't buy him things that the other kids had. I think Laura is trying way too hard to fit in and live like everybody there."

Kristy didn't really know what to say. She just gave him a hug and whispered, "I'm so sorry Freddie."

"I told her I was really unhappy," his eyes filled with tears, "She got mad and told me that I didn't appreciate everything. She told me that I should go home. So that's what I've done. I have all my stuff in my truck and I will move back in with my parents until I can find a place to live. I called Chief Hunter and he said that there was a job for me at the station."

"You are welcome to live here if you'd like," Kristy felt so bad for him, "We have plenty of room and I'll only charge you $200 a month to pay for utilities.

He smiled at her and said, "That'd be great. You like to take in strays, don't you?"

She looked over at Logan who had been quiet through all of this. She could see he was very disappointed that his friend didn't come. She went over and picked him up and just held him while Freddie went out to unload his truck. She whispered, "He is trying to get used to his new life. It is very different from ours here."

Logan didn't say anything. He just buried his face into Kristy's shoulder.

Freddie came in and said, "Here buddy," he handed him a brightly wrapped present, "This is from Laura and Milo. This is for your birthday next week."

Logan took the present and walked upstairs. Kristy heard his bedroom door close. She waited a few minutes and went up. She could hear him crying so she opened his door. She saw that he had moved his chair to his closet. On the top shelf was the present from Milo. "Aren't you going to open it?" she asked.

He shook his head and ran to her. She picked him up and sat on his bed. Kristy started crying too. She felt the same disappointment that her son did. She knew too that Laura was living a different life with much more exciting people in Tulsa. Kristy knew, like Freddie, she had lost her too.

Part 3

In order to discover your true self, you must first unconditionally fall in love with your imperfect life.

—Edmond Mbiaka

Chapter 34

Eight Years Later

"Mom! Do you know where Dad's varsity jacket is?" Yelled the almost 14-year-old Logan as he was throwing clothes out of his closet, "Mom!"

"I'm right here son," Kristy said as she walked into Logan's room. Looking around with a disgusted expression on her face, she continued, "It's a wonder you can find anything in here," she climbed over piles of clothes to get to the closet, "I'm going through everything after you leave. Some of this stuff is from when you were eight or nine."

Logan's aqua-blue eyes flew open. Panicking, he cried out, "No, you can't! Some of this is very sentimental and a lot of this stuff reminds me of Dad."

This tugged on Kristy's heart. It had been three years since Robby passed away and she, like Logan, missed him every day. Robby had contracted pneumonia after a super bug had gone through the nursing home. His body had weakened so much that he just couldn't fight it off. He was surrounded by his parents, sister and of course, Logan and Kristy.

The guys from the fire station volunteered to be with him around the clock so the family could get some rest. Freddie Mapp was with him when the doctor suggested he call Kristy and have the family gather.

Hundreds of people and firefighters came to his funeral. He was considered for a full military-style honors funeral as the result of his accident while fighting the barn fire. Kristy and Robby's family were very honored by this. Logan walked in the precession with the firefighters from Robby's station wearing Robby's formal cap. Robby's helmet was set on his casket, with his jacket and boots below it.

Kristy had written to Laura and sent a copy of the death announcement. She hoped that maybe she and Milo would drive over for the funeral. Kristy was disappointed that she didn't hear anything from her. After they moved, they saw Laura and Milo only once when they came for Christmas. All Laura talked about were her new wealthy friends and all the things she was involved in. Kristy thought that Laura was working too hard to fit in with this new lifestyle. Even Milo had changed. He bragged to Logan about all the new things he had gotten and how much better it was living in Tulsa in their great big house.

Kristy did make the effort to stay in touch and tried to make plans to drive to Tulsa for a visit. Laura was always busy with committees and charity events. The timing was never right for Laura and Milo spent his weekends going to fancy birthday parties for his new friends. Kristy sadly gave up trying and continued living her simple, but happy life in Guthrie.

"Okay then," Kristy huffed, "We will just have to organize it better." Kristy noticed a wrapped present sitting on the top shelf of the closet. She pulled it down and read the tag. 'To: Logan. From: Your best buddy Milo'. "When did you get this?" she asked.

Logan saw what she was holding. He immediately looked down at the shirt he was holding and mumbled, "That was for my sixth birthday. Remember? Freddie brought it to me when he moved back from Tulsa."

Stunned, Kristy said, "I can't believe you've had it all this time. I've been in your closet a million times and didn't see it."

"That's cause it was shoved to the back. I moved it when I was looking for Dad's jacket," Logan said sadly.

"Why didn't you open it?" asked Kristy.

Logan shrugged his shoulders and looked away, "I don't know."

"I think you were pretty disappointed when Milo didn't come back," said Kristy, "I remember how hard you took it when Milo moved away and he didn't even want to come back for your joint birthday party."

"I thought we would still be best friends even after they moved," Logan got up and took the present from his mom. He put it back on the shelf.

"Why are you keeping it?" Kristy asked.

"This reminds me that life can be full of disappointments and people come and go in your life. I have to be strong and only trust what I know for sure," Logan said sternly.

Kristy saw the pain in her son's eyes and walked over and hugged him. Even though he was almost 14, he still liked the comfort of his mom's arms. Logan was a little taller than Kristy so he rested his forehead on her shoulder and started to cry, "I'm so sorry you feel you have to be strong all the time my boy. I know how hard it was losing your father and your best friend. He was like a brother to you."

Logan starting to sob and Kristy held him tighter. She continued, "You were always so mature for your age. You were very sensitive to everyone's feelings. I love you more because of it. I think after Dad died, you thought you had to look after me because I was hurting. Did you keep your feelings hidden from me?"

Logan pulled away and looked at his mother and nodded his head, "You are the strongest person I know Mom. I didn't know what to do when I saw you were so sad and crying all the time. I told you I was fine because I didn't want to make you sadder."

"I didn't believe for a minute that you were fine," she said wiping the tears off his cheeks. Tears started to fall from Kristy's eyes. "You got so mad when anyone tried to comfort you. I'm so sorry that I didn't insist that you get help."

Wiping the tears off his mom's cheek he said, "I'm glad that Freddie was living here. He took me to play basketball or to the park when everything got crazy. I hated when all those people came over with food and stuff."

"I know. It was very nice at first but then it got crazy. Everyone in the town brought food over. We ran out of space to put it here so we had to take it over to Grammy and Poppy's," Kristy laughed.

"Do you remember how many Jell-O salads we had in the fridge?" Logan chuckled and sat down on his bed, "Freddie and I would eat some and then try to make the other laugh. We had Jell-O coming out of our noses. That made us laugh harder."

"What?" Kristy was startled at the news, "Yuck. I wondered how Jell-O got all over the kitchen walls." She started laughing with Logan, "You two sure would find some, um, creative things to do."

Shaking his head, Logan added, "Freddie was the one to think of these things. He is like an older brother to me."

"Is he ever!" Kristy agreed, "I am so glad he moved in with us too. He filled the emptiness that we had when Laura and Milo moved out. I'm sorry things didn't work out between him and Laura. I'm sure they would be married now if she hadn't moved."

"When I was young, I thought you and Freddie would get married if anything happened to Dad," Logan said laughing at his mom's surprised face.

"No, No," Kristy said shaking her head, "He is way too young for me. It really was like having another child here. He was great to fix things around the house and he always volunteered to look after you. That's why I couldn't take any rent from him after he moved in."

"Is it weird that my best friend is 30 years old?" Logan asked.

"Yes," answered Kristy laughing, "It makes sense though. You have always been what people call an old soul." Logan looked at her quizzically, "It just means you are mature for your age and relate better to older people. Freddie in a way took the place of your father. He respected that you still had a dad but a dad who couldn't do dad things with you. He was hurting from the break up with Laura so you helped him too by doing fun things with him and being a distraction."

"Yeah. I can see that. I was upset when he moved out," Logan crinkled his nose, "Why did he have to go and buy his own house?"

"It's a good thing when you're 27. He saved enough money living here that he could buy his own place," Kristy said, "He made sure it had a bedroom for you, so you shouldn't complain. I think you spend more time there than here anyway." Looking around Logan's room Kristy huffed, "I hope you keep that room cleaner than this one."

"Of course, Mom," Logan found a half-eaten chocolate bar in his desk drawer. He took a bite and said. "This is where I store everything and take just what I need to Freddie's. Besides, my laundry gets done here and the food is way better. Freddie can barbeque and open a can of pork and beans and that's pretty much it."

"Well, no laundry is going to get done unless it's taken down to the laundry room and sorted into piles," Kristy said handing her son the empty laundry basket, "I am going to teach you to do laundry because no one else will do it when you go away to boarding school."

"There's plenty of time," Logan said.

"Are you kidding?" Kristy threw a smelly pair of basketball shorts at him, "You are leaving in two weeks."

"I've started packing," Logan said with a sly smile.

"Really?" Kristy knew better, "What have you packed?"

Knowing that he couldn't get anything past his mom, he said, "I've been looking for Dad's varsity jacket. You know I want to take that with me," changing the subject, he said, "Why do I have to pack now anyway? Like you said, I don't leave for another two weeks."

Crossing her arms, she asked, "What do have planned in the next two weeks?"

"Um," Logan stopped to think of his schedule, "Well, on Thursday, Freddie is taking Luke, Eric and me camping for a pre-birthday celebration. Then, I turn 14 and of course, you are planning a big family party. I have two more days left to complete my Junior Fire Fighting diploma and then Carl is having a big going away party for Eric and me."

"Right. When were you going to fit packing in to that busy schedule?" Kristy shook her head.

"But Mom," Logan whined, "We can pack in a day. The guys are playing basketball today and then they are going to the club for a swim."

"A day? You are pretty optimistic," Kristy was getting frustrated with Logan, "I tell you what. If you get all these dirty clothes down to the laundry, I will show you what to do. The rest of this stuff has to be picked up, hung up and put away. Stuff that is not sentimental and you don't use can be donated. I will get you a box or two to use. I have plastic bins for you to put the things in you want to take with you to school. If you get this room cleaned, organized and laundry done, then you can go to the club and swim."

"Mom!" Logan thought this wasn't fair, "It will take me hours to do this."

"Well, you better get started," Kristy said as she was leaving the room, "I only have two days off, so I would like everything you are taking to school, packed and on the back porch by tomorrow. Then on Wednesday, you can pack for your camping trip."

"Fine," Logan said glaring at his mother as she left the room.

Chapter 35

Kristy had just labeled one of the bins 'bedding' when Logan came in with another plastic bin. He set it down in front of Kristy, "Here's the last one."

"See? You were able to condense two bins into one," Kristy said kissing his head.

"It was hard Mom," Logan said looking at his phone.

"You really didn't need to take all those books. They have quite a large library. Now you can bring more memorabilia for your shelves," Kristy smiled.

"Is it stupid that I want to bring the 'Casey the Fireman' book that Dad gave me when I was three?" Logan asked, "I like to look at the note he had written in the front. It cheers me up and I can still hear Dad's voice reading it to me."

"I would have mailed it to you if you hadn't taken it. I know how much it means to you," Kristy smiled at her tall son.

They heard the back gate open. Luke Campbell, Logan's very blonde, curly haired friend walked through pushing his bike. He waved when he saw them on the back porch, "Hey Mrs. Garrison. Hey dude."

Kristy opened the back door and let him in, "Hi Lucas. How did you know Logan just finished packing and is now free to go out?" He was a few inches shorter than her and smelled like chlorine. He volunteered part time, with Logan, as a junior lifeguard at the city pool.

"He texted me," he answered.

"Dude you live five blocks away and I texted you about a minute ago," Logan laughed, "How'd you get over here so fast?"

"I knew you'd be finished soon so I decided to ride my bike over here. I saw that hot girl Sherry who lives at the other end of the Egg, so I stopped and talked to her," he said running a hand through his thick blonde curls, "I think I may have a date with her."

"Ha. Like hell," Logan laughed.

Kristy joined in, "You do know she is 16 and is dating that trouble maker Collin Smith?"

"Yeah, but I think she was really into me," his white smile was amplified by his tan.

"Collin will beat the crap out of you if he finds out," Logan shook his head, "He will probably beat the crap out of me because I'm your friend. He has hated me ever since I got him in trouble for lighting our garbage can on fire when I was five."

"I feel sorry for his parents," said Kristy, "They are really nice people and have tried everything to keep him out of trouble. I think the next step will be military school."

"When he goes," said the confident blue-eyed Lucas, "Sherry will be mine."

"It's been nice knowing you man," Logan said faking a punch to Luke's jaw.

Luke surveyed the scene in the back porch. He saw the bins piled up and knew Logan was taking them to South Eastern Academy in less than two weeks," So you haven't changed your mind about going to that snobby private school, have ya?"

Logan had applied for and was granted a scholarship to South Eastern Academy, one of the nation's top high schools. 80% of the 350 students that go to SEA can get into practically any Ivy League school or International University.

South Eastern Academy is roughly six and a half miles west of Durant, Oklahoma and 14 miles from the Oklahoma–Texas border. Texoma Lake is just a few miles from the school and is on the Choctaw nation land. The school leases the land from the Choctaw Nation and has agreed to provide two, four-year scholarships to incoming freshmen of the Choctaw community. The school and a few members of the Choctaw Tribal Council choose a male and a female recipient. The student must first pass the Academy's grueling four-hour entrance exam. The committee will then look at academics, athletics, extra-curricular activity and the volunteerism of each applicant. A recipient must be involved in three out of the four areas and must be in good standing with the Choctaw tribe.

Logan's great-grandfather and Kristy's maternal grandfather was full blood Choctaw. Growing up, Kristy's family would drive down to Durant, Oklahoma and attend the many Choctaw cultural events. She continued that tradition with Logan so he could learn and appreciate his heritage. On one of those trips, they found out about the scholarship and toured South Eastern Academy. They both saw the many advantages Logan would have if he could attend. Of course, Kristy couldn't afford the expensive yearly tuition, so Logan applied for the scholarship. He won the male scholarship by a unanimous vote. After they looked at Logan's application, he was the clear winner. Logan's GPA has never been lower than 4.0, he was captain of the Middle School Varsity State Champions in basketball and was on the Guthrie Country Club swim and tennis teams. He golfed, was a junior lifeguard volunteer and was completing the Junior Firefighter program at the Guthrie Fire Station. If there was a perfect candidate for this scholarship, it was Logan Garrison.

Logan replied, "It's not snobby. Well, I don't think it is. Eric is going too, remember."

"Yeah. His family's loaded and his brother's already going there," Luke responded, "He's a big ass now."

"Lucas!" Kristy exclaimed.

"Well he is," defended Luke, "I don't know how else to describe him."

"He's right," agreed Logan, "He was kind of nice before he went and after two years there, he thinks he's better than everyone else."

"Well, that's not going to happen to my boy," Kristy said stroking his cheek.

An embarrassed Logan tried to avoid her hand. "Mom," he whispered. Looking at Luke he asked, "Do you know where the other guys are? I'm finished packing and as per our agreement," he looked at Kristy, "I get to hang out until it gets dark."

"Yes, and here is the $20 I promised you for pizza," Kristy reached into her back pocket and handed it to him, "Make sure you text me and let me know where you are. If you don't, I will send Freddie to find you."

Luke started to laugh, "Oh yeah dude. That was embarrassing when that fire truck pulled up and blasted the siren. They kept calling your name over the loud speaker until you came out."

Logan blushed at the memory. He gave his smiling mother a dirty look then said, "I will. See ya later alligator."

Grabbing his head, she kissed it then messed up his hair with her hand, "See ya soon baboons."

"Peace out Mrs. Garrison," Luke yelled as they walked through the screen door.

Chapter 36

"Is that blanket going to be warm enough?" a concerned Vicki Garrison asked her grandson, "Bobby, why don't you go and get that blue and yellow afghan that I crocheted two years ago. It will keep you really warm, dear, especially in that drafty dorm room."

"It's okay Gram. Mom also gave me the one you made for Dad when he was in the hospital," he bent down and gave her a hug. Vicki had developed arthritis in her ankles, shoulders and knees. It was very hard for her to walk, so she rode around town on a bright green scooter, "I remember snuggling up with Dad in the hospital bed and mom would cover us with it."

"Oh yes. That's the perfect one to take to school with you," she agreed and gave him a kiss on his cheek.

Bobby Garrison held his arms out to his only grandson, "Come here son." They wrapped their arms around each other, "I am going to miss you so much. It will be strange not to just walk across the alley and see you any time I want. Have I told you how proud we are of you?"

"At least a billion times," Logan said a little embarrassed.

"Well, here is a billion and one," said Bobby, "We are so proud of you. We knew that when you were very young, you were special. Children don't normally talk full sentences when they are a year old."

Vicki added, "Do you remember how he had books memorized when he was two? Everyone thought you knew how to read but you just knew when to turn the pages."

"E-mail us how you are doing and don't forget to include the game schedule for basketball. Your grandmother and I will drive anywhere in the state to see you play," Bobby smiled at him. He loved looking into Logan's aqua-blue eyes because they reminded him of Robby.

"I need to make the team first Poppy," Logan said shyly.

"You will son. You're a Garrison," Bobby puffed out his chest, "You come from a long line of basketball players. It wouldn't surprise me if you made Varsity."

Shaking his head, he responded, "I don't think so. They recruit players from all over Oklahoma, Texas and Missouri. I think I would be happy just to play freshmen ball this year. I'll have enough on my plate with school."

The back door opened and Kristy held up Robby's high school varsity jacket, "Are you forgetting something?" She asked.

Logan's mouth opened and he let out a gasp. He ran up the back stairs and grabbed the jacket from his mom and hugged it, "Oh my god. I can't believe you found it! Thanks Mom."

Kristy looked tenderly at her son, "I know how important this is to you and I also know I don't have to tell you to take care of it. I found it tucked safely beside Dad's firefighter jacket in the cedar closet," closing and locking the door behind her, she said, "I think that's all."

"It better be," said Bobby, "I don't think you can get any more into Freddie's truck."

"I know," laughed Kristy, "It's a third of a small dorm room." Looking into the covered bed of the truck she continued, "You'd think we were moving him into an apartment or something. I'm very grateful that Freddie loaned us his truck. I could only get half of this into my car."

"Well, honey," Vicki, said to her giving her a hug, "Drive carefully and we will see you when you get back."

"I will. We'll let you know when we arrive," hugging her father-in-law, she said, "Thanks for looking after things here. I should be home in about four days."

Mother and son got into the cab of the truck. Vicki blew them a kiss as Kristy put it into drive. Logan waved and blew a kiss back. He had butterflies in his stomach and tears in his eyes as they drove away from the only home he knew.

Kristy turned the car and drove through the beautiful brick gates of South Eastern Academy. Lining the driveway on each side were 20 magnolia trees. The school's three-story brick administration building was sitting behind a circular driveway with a small grassy area in the middle of the driveway. There was a large bronze statue of a Choctaw pony with a young 1850's Choctaw child, sitting in a bone style saddle, holding leather reins. The child and pony were facing the driveway watching and welcoming those who drove up to the school. At the base of the statue is a plaque that quotes missionary Henry C. Benson (1860), "They were all equestrians, men, women and children; each had his pony and saddle, and to ride on horseback was the first lesson ever learned."

This statue was a gift from the Choctaw nation to the school to celebrate the opening of the school and of their mutual goal to educate the youth of the day.

There were school employees stopping each car and checking names off their lists they had attached to clip boards. Each car was given a map of the grounds and instructions to get to their designated parking lot.

The school was spread out on 50 acres that included an administration building, classrooms, dorm buildings, a dining hall, three gymnasiums, two greenhouses, track and football field, a soccer field, outdoor pool, tennis courts and a 400-seat theatre. There were many green spaces with benches and tables for the students to eat, play chess or study. The beauty of the campus was very appealing to potential students and their parents.

Texoma Lake was only a few miles from the school. The lower classmen, the freshmen and sophomores were not allowed to go to the lake on their own. Every weekend, students who wanted to go could sign up with the campus concierge and go on a supervised four-hour excursion. Picnics would be provided by the dining room and a bus would take them to and from the lake. Junior and seniors had the choice of going with the excursion bus or get there on their own. A lot had cars so most drove themselves. Any time a student wanted to leave campus, they had to check out with the concierge office and check back in. All students had to check back by 5:00 on the weekdays and the lower classmen had to check in by 8:00 on the weekends. The upper classmen could stay out until 10:00 on the weekends. The school would also arrange weekend shuttles to and from Durant so students could go to movies or shop. A lot would go and get fast food since the meals at the school were all healthy and nutritious. The majority of the students came from very wealthy families who would give their children pretty large allowances.

Kristy was given directions to the parking lot that was closest to Logan's dorm building. Before they could unload, they had to check in with the resident manager to get their room assignment and keys. The dorms were segregated male and female. The male dorm was close to the gyms and the female dorm was by the dining hall. Anyone from the opposite sex caught in the others' dorm building after 6:00 were severely punished. They were each four-story brick buildings with the freshmen on the first floor, sophomore on the second, juniors on third and seniors on the fourth. The seniors had access to the roof where they had a large lounge. It was strictly enforced that only senior students were allowed in the lounge. Anyone not a senior caught sneaking in or a senior sneaking someone from another class would be banned from using the lounge for life. Since no one wanted to be banned from the lounge, this rule was respected and followed.

The school did not tolerate hazing, drinking or smoking. Students, staff and visitors were forbidden to smoke on school grounds. All the students were underage so if caught drinking, those students would be suspended until a consequence could be worked out by the parents (who would be requested to be present), the student, and the head master. This usually resulted in privileges being revoked and some horrible volunteer work.

The school believes that a healthy body and mind produces the best students. Most of the students were academically and athletically driven, so they would tend to follow the rules. There were always a few seniors and juniors that would get caught partying at the lake by the security. Those students would do volunteer hours at the lake as well as at the school.

After check-in, Logan and Kristy unloaded Freddie's truck. They provided dollies and carts to help with the move-in. Luckily, Logan was on the first floor so it took no time at all to unload. The building was a large square with the student's rooms on the outside (each room had a large window for natural light) and the showers and bathrooms in the middle. At the west end of the building, by the entrance, there was a very comfortable lounge for the students on that floor to relax and socialize in. It was furnished with big leather sofas, tables and chairs, a fireplace, flat screen TV, and a small refrigerator stocked with filtered water bottles. There was a small counter with a sink and microwave where students could heat up water for tea or hot chocolate and pop microwave popcorn. One corner had shelves that held books and games because television was limited to weekends only. The school was 38 years old and pictures of successful alumni and their accomplishments hung on each wall of the lounges. This was to inspire and motive South Eastern Academy students to get their pictures up on the walls and be forever idolized.

The rooms in three of the corners were larger. Unlike the other rooms on the floor that housed two students per room, these rooms held three. Logan was assigned to a three-person room and he wasn't very happy about it. "Great, instead of worrying about getting one jerk for a roommate, I have to worry that I might get two. Why couldn't Eric and I be roommates?"

Kristy rolled her eyes, "Why do you have to look at everything so negatively. You might get two best friends instead of jerks," finishing the last touches to Logan's bed, she continued, "They said that the payoff is that you have more personal space in a three bedroom than you would a two bedroom."

Looking around at Logan's bins, they both said at the same time, "You/I need it."

Each student had a double bed with drawers built in for their clothes. Next to the bed was a large desk and a wardrobe to hang clothes. Bookshelves hung above the bed for personal items like books, pictures and trophies. The rooms were quite nice with mahogany furniture and luxurious dark mocha colored carpet. The walls were painted a gingerbread color with mocha curtains covering the two large windows. Logan was amazed at how clean and undamaged the room was said, "I thought the rooms would be pretty gross."

"Well we had to put a very large deposit down for any damage that you may cause," Kristy pointed at Logan and said through gritted teeth, "Listen buster, you better take care of your little area so I can get my damage deposit back." Kristy then smiled and said, "I'll make you a deal, if I get the full amount back, I will reward you with half the money."

Logan smiled at his mother and put out his hand, "Deal. It might get messy in here but I promise I won't trash the place."

Kristy shook his hand and laughed. She pointed to the curtains, "I think those are new and I bet this is new carpet too. It smells like a fresh coat of paint was put on the walls. Hmmm. My guess is that this room was in bad shape after last year and those boys didn't get their damage deposit back."

There was a light knock at the slightly opened door. Kristy and Logan turned around and saw a well-dressed man and his over-jeweled wife come in. Behind them was a tall brunette boy who was pulling a suitcase and had a basketball tucked under his right arm.

"Howdy, y'all," said the boy's mother, "We're the Rose family. This is my husband Wesley and my son Georgie."

"George," her son interrupted.

"Oh dear, ever since Georgie turned 14, he thinks he is too old to be called Georgie," she waved her hands back and forth as she talked with a thick Texan accent, "And I'm Pauline but everyone calls me Polly."

Logan walked over and shook Mr. Rose's hand, "Nice to meet you sir, I'm Logan Garrison and this is my mother Kristy," he then shook Polly's hand, "Ma'am."

She got a little flustered, "Lordy be. It's so nice to see such a polite boy. I hope you can teach Georgie a few lessons."

George blushed and walked over to Kristy to shake her hand "Hi." Was all he said.

The two boys then shook each other's hand. George was about two inches taller. Logan pointed to the basketball still tucked under George's arm, "I'm a basketball player too. Are you trying out for the team?"

"Yeah. I play center," George gave him a smile, "You?"

"Point guard," Logan smiled back, "Do you think our other room-mate is a basketball player?"

Mr. Rose said, "I think he is. I heard that they like to put roommates together based on similar interests. It cuts down on the roommate conflicts."

"That makes sense," Kristy said.

Realizing she wasn't the center of attention, Mrs. Rose piped up, "We're from Midland, Texas. Where y'all from?"

"We're from Guthrie, Oklahoma," Kristy answered noticing a quizzical look on her face. She added, "It's about 30 minutes north of Oklahoma City."

"Oh, isn't that sweet. Is Mr. Garrison here as well?" she said looking around as if he was hiding somewhere.

"My dad passed away about three years ago. It's just Mom and me now," Logan said putting his arm around his mother. She was very grateful that he stepped in and answered. She found it hard to say her husband was gone.

"Sorry to hear that dearie. Wha..." was all Polly could get out when the door opened again.

In walked an African American boy with short curly hair, "Hey. I'm Andrew Ward."

He was balancing a box on his right shoulder and was carrying a large duffle bag in his left hand. Logan ran over and took the box off his shoulder, "I'm Logan and that's George," George just waved to him.

"It looks like I'm the last one. I guess I'll take this bed," he said as he tossed his duffle bag down, "We would've been here sooner but the fancy bus that brought the rich kids from Tulsa got in before we did. We had to wait in line a while to check in."

Just as he finished, a boy about 6'2", and looked like Andrew came in. He pointed to the box on Andrew's bed, "Andrew. I think you got my box. This is yours."

"This must be your brother," Polly stated.

"Yup. That's Nathan. He's a junior," Andrew replied.

Nathan waved to everyone as he took the box out of Logan's hands, "Thanks buddy," he studied Logan's face, "Hey, you're from Guthrie."

Logan was surprised he knew who he was, "Yeah. How did you know?"

"We're from Oklahoma City and I would drive up to Guthrie and ref your games sometimes. I refereed the game that you won to go to state. You scored around 16 points I think." Nathan said, clearly impressed.

"Sorry. I don't make it a point to remember the refs unless they are bad," smiling, Logan said, "I guess that makes you a good one."

"I heard this year's male ship was from Guthrie. Good for you," Nathan said.

"Ship?" Kristy asked.

"Yeah. That's what we call the kids that come here on scholarship. They are the smartest kids here. There are usually about 12 ships going to school here," looking at his brother, he said, "Come and get the rest of your stuff. I have to drive Hannah's stuff over to her dorm."

"Oh yeah. We have a sister going here too. She's Nathan's twin sister. You may have heard of her, Hannah Ward, tennis star," Andrew told everyone sarcastically.

"I have, actually," said Kristy, "I coach tennis in Guthrie and we would see her at tournaments. She is really good. She is fast and has good hands."

"No one has said that about my basketball skills," said Andrew shaking his head, "My specialty is rebounding. I've got amazing vertical." he jumped up and touched the roof above the door.

Mr. Rose said, "Okay son, let's grabbed a dolly and bring the rest of your stuffin."

Logan jumped up from where he was sitting on his bed, "I'm done with my stuff so I'll come and help you."

Polly Rose gushed, "Look at that. They're besties already."

Chapter 37

One of the first things the freshmen students had to do after they moved in was to see a counselor and make sure their paper work and class schedule was correct. Logan was already waiting outside his counselor's office when his mother walked into the waiting area, "Have you been waiting long?" she asked him.

"About 10 minutes. I got here a little early. I was afraid I might get lost," Logan smiled at her, "I only made one wrong turn."

"That's better than me. I made at least three and had to ask a student for help," Kristy laughed, "How was your first night in the dorm?"

"Awesome," Logan responded, "I really like George and Andrew. George is pretty laid back and Andrew is sarcastic and funny. We hung out the whole time."

"Great! Getting along with roommates can be checked off my worry list," Kristy said making a check mark in the air, "Now, there are only 19 more things to check off. What did you guys do last night?"

"They had a barbeque for the students. There is only like a third of the students here," Logan said, "After dinner we went to the theatre and some of the upper classmen did a skit about the school rules. They introduced all the teachers and staff and the headmaster said a few words. They are going to do it all over again when the rest of the students get here. After that, we met some of the other basketball players and played a little basketball."

"Of course. What else would you guys do for fun?" Kristy teased, "I wonder why only a third of the school is here?"

"Because we thought it would be better for the freshmen to settle and adjust to the school before the rest of the student body got here," a 30 something, dark haired man entered the waiting room, "It's overwhelming enough being away from home for the first time and starting a new school. We just felt they didn't need the extra stress of having the sophomores, juniors and seniors here. They tend to treat the freshmen like they are contagious," he smiled, "Hi. I'm Sam McKinney." He held out his hand to Kristy, "And you must be the Garrisons."

Logan shook his hand and said. "Yes. I'm Logan and this is my mom, Kristy. Why are the freshmen treated like this?" he asked a little concerned.

"It's all part of the right-of-passage at this school," Mr. McKinney told him, "It's like being the youngest sibling in a family. The older ones have more privileges and are looked up to by the younger ones. The youngest kids are less mature and can be annoying so the older kids really don't want anything to do with them. They are also more fun to tease."

"Are there a lot of bullying issues that happen because of this?" Kristy asked.

"There used to be. We have it under control now. The freshmen expect some teasing as a group and they have fun with it," he answered, "Just to let you know, we have zero tolerance with bullying now. That's why there is a strict no hazing rule. If anyone is caught they will be suspended and possibly kicked out. Parents pay a lot of money to send their kids here so they drill it into their children that they need to abide by school rules. The students who come here want to be here and know the importance of doing well."

"And some of us have scholarships to maintain," Logan said looking at his mom.

"I've read your file and I don't think you will have any problems keeping your scholarship," Mr. McKinney said. "I was the Choctaw scholarship recipient here 18 years ago. It really opened doors for me and I was able to get a doctorate in child psychology. I was happy to come back to SEA and work as a counselor. I also have a small practice in Durant and sit on the child development board of the Choctaw Nation. I grew up here and am happy to give back to the community that raised me. Shall we?" Mr. McKinney said as he held the door to his office open.

"Okay boys, it looks like you are all settled here," Kristy said looking around her son's dorm room, "You certainly can tell basketball player's live here with all the posters and pictures of your favorite players."

"Wait until we start fitness training in a couple of days," Andrew laughed, "It will smell like basketball players live here."

"At least we don't smell as bad as the football players," George added, "They haven't even started practice and their end of the hall smells bad."

They all laughed and Kristy just shook her head, "Better here than in my house," she gave George and Andrew a hug and reminded them to "be good".

Logan put his arm around his mom and said, "I'll walk you to the truck Mom."

They walked in silence to Freddie's truck, arm in arm. Both were trying to hold back tears. Unfortunately for Kristy, she couldn't hold them any longer. When she reached the car, she let out a sob and covered her face with her hands. Logan wrapped his arms around his mom and tears streamed down his face. They just held each other and couldn't care less who saw. They had gone through so much together.

Kristy calmed down, pulled away and looked at her son, "I'm so proud of you and you know your father would be too," Logan wiped the tears from his face with the back of his hand, "You have been the perfect son and I'm going to miss you so much. Remember. This is your time. I just know you are going to shine here so enjoy every minute of it. We are only a few hours away and you will be home for the long weekend in October."

"I know. It still doesn't mean that I'm not going to miss you," Logan looked at his feet, "I'm worried about you in that house all alone."

Laughing, she joked, "You mean the very clean house. At least I will be able to find the remote."

"Yeah. I have the tendency to carry it with me and leave it in obscure places," Logan smiled.

"I think my favorite place you left it was at Grammy's and Poppy's," Kristy shook her head. Now that the tears had stopped, Kristy gave Logan another tight hug, "Please e-mail, Skype or text to let me know how you're doing. You know I will want to hear about your classes, teachers, basketball … just everything."

"Okay. Keep me updated about what is happening around Guthrie. Promise me you will come to some of my games," Logan squeezed her back.

"Wouldn't miss them," Kristy said, "I will be around here for the next few days visiting family so if you need anything I can be here in 20 minutes," tears started to well up in her eyes again, "I love you so much son."

"I love you too Mom" he gave her a reassuring smile, "Don't worry about me, I will be fine. You raised me well."

Chapter 38

The three roommates came into their room and each threw their sports bag on their bed. George followed his bag and flopped down beside it with his arms covering his head. He whined, "I can't believe coach is making us do this. I hated drama class and performing in front of a live audience."

Andrew laughed and slapped George's leg, "Chill out man. You won't be up there by yourself. Besides, everyone will be mesmerized by my awesomeness." he flexed his arms and smiled widely. All the different freshmen clubs had to write and act in a 10-minute skit. It's to be performed on the first night the full student body is present.

Logan grabbed his tennis racket and tennis ball and sat down on his desk chair. Laughing, he asked, "Does your awesomeness have any ideas of what we can do for the Fall Revue?"

They heard a knock at the door and the rest of the freshmen basketball team walked in. Some sat down on the beds while a few others leaned up against the walls and doors. Craig, a forward from Missouri said, "Hey Garrison. Why don't you Google 10 minute skits for 10 guys."

With Richard looking over his shoulder Logan looked concerned, "There's not a lot here. They have skits listed that we can buy but no good ideas."

"Yeah, we unfortunately have to write and star in our own skit," moaned the other team's point guard, Dwight.

Mark, a tall blonde, said to Andrew, "Hey dude. What did your brother do his freshmen year?"

Andrew had to think for a moment, "Oh yeah, they re-enacted movie trailers like Pirates of the Caribbean, Castaway, stuff like that. They put a basketball spin on it so Wilson from Castaway was a basketball not a volleyball. I saw the video of it. It wasn't bad."

"It sounds lame," Dave shook his head.

"No not really," Andrew defended his brother, "What was lame was the football team's skit that year. It was set up like an episode of Hee Haw."

"Hee Haw?" The collective question came from all corners of the room.

"Yeah. It was a show from the 70's I think. They dressed and talked like hicks. They told bad jokes and one guy played the banjo. I heard they made jokes about the basketball team. They even tried to sing some country songs. My brother said it was awful."

Logan picked up his tennis racket and ball. He started bouncing the ball on the floor. He liked to do this at home when he needed to concentrate. The room was silent except for the sound of the bouncing ball.

"Who died?" Asked Andrew's sister Hannah as she walked in with sophomore, Sadie Hudson. Both girls played on the school's tennis team. Hannah was wearing a peach tennis skirt with a white and peach sleeveless shirt. The color was perfect against her dark caramel African American skin. She had a peach colored headband holding back her dark curly hair. She was carrying a garment bag.

They guys looked at the door and all thoughts of the skit left their heads. All they could register was the fact that two gorgeous girls were standing in front of them. Sadie had her straw colored long blonde hair pulled back into a ponytail. Her golden tanned skin looked darker with her pale pink tennis dress and white shoes. Sadie's denim blue eyes surveyed the room full of boys and she rolled them when she saw that they were looking at her like love struck teenagers. All her life she has been told how beautiful she was and boys would constantly hit on her or ask her to go out with them. Since turning 13, she had grown into a striking athletic looking young lady standing at five feet ten inches. At 15, the attention had gotten worse and particularly annoying.

Sadie's passion has been tennis since she was eight years old. Her wealthy Tulsa parents had built a tennis court with a backboard in their back yard. Sadie would spend hours and hours a day hitting against the backboard or with the ball machine. She joined the team at her Country Club and had won many tournaments in her age group.

"What do you want?" Andrew said not aware of how pretty his sister looked.

"Nice," she threw the garment bag at Andrew, "Here's your uniform. Mom wasn't impressed that you left it at home after she told you to pack it in the car, like, a million times. It's a good thing she went into your room because it was hanging on your closet door," standing with her hands on her hips. She continued, "Luckily, Lily's family hadn't left yet and was able to bring it down," she shook her head as she could hear the rest of the guys snicker at him.

Logan started to bounce the tennis ball again. Hearing a familiar sound, Sadie looked in his direction. Her mouth dropped open and she ran over to him, "Is that the new Wilson racket that just came out, like, a month ago?"

Logan stopped, caught the ball and held up the racket, "Yeah. I just got it for my birthday."

Sadie took it out of his hand and turned it over a few times. She gripped it like she was about to take a shot. After shaking up and down to feel the weight, she wacked the palm of her hand to feel the string tension, "I thought these were only out as demos. They aren't going to release them for purchase for another couple of weeks."

"They are only out as demos. My mom was able to talk the pro shop at our club out of one because they had two. I haven't had a chance to play a game with it yet," Logan said looking up at Sadie, "You can borrow it, if you'd like?"

"Really?!" Sadie said hugging the racket to her chest. She smiled and looked down at Logan. She caught her breath when she saw his aqua-blue eyes, "Wow. You really have beautiful eyes."

Logan blushed and looked down at the floor. He heard the rest of the team burst into laughter. Sadie looked at all of them and said, "Well he does you numbnuts," she looked back at him and continued, "I'm sorry if I embarrassed you. Things just come out of my mouth without a second thought."

Hannah, seeing the awkward situation changed the subject, "What are all of you doing in here anyway?"

George stood up and stretched, "We are trying to figure out what to do for the Fall Revue. I hate this stuff."

"Oh yeah," Hannah said back, "Don't worry. Most of the stuff is pretty stupid."

"I heard that a couple girlfriends of the football players are teaching them different dances," Sadie walked over to Hannah, "I think they will do be doing the Gangnam style dance and maybe Beyoncé's single ladies.

Shooting guard, Charley snorted, "I'd like to see them in those tights she wore in the video. They would make ugly girls."

Hannah looked at red haired Charley who was sitting in the middle of blonde Mark and dark haired Andrew, "You three look like you could be in the Spice Girls."

"That's it." Dave said standing up, "We could dress up like the Spice Girls and lip sync to their music."

George groaned and sat back down on his bed. "Aren't there five Spice Girls? We have 10 guys."

"We could do a battle of the bands," Craig said very excited, "We could do Spice Girls against, um, what's another group with five people?"

"How about One Direction?" Sadie suggested.

"Yeah," Logan said, "We can take lines from their songs and act out a skit. We can go to the Thrift Store and get costumes and wigs to look like them."

"Wait a minute," Charley said putting his hands up, "Just because I'm a Ginger doesn't automatically make me Ginger Spice. I'd rather be Liam."

"Your right," Logan said reaching for paper and a pen, "We will put each of their names in a hat and draw our part."

Dwight took off his hat and handed it to Logan so he could put the names into it. He said, "Whoa just a minute here. I couldn't live with myself if Mark here picked Scary Spice. I volunteer to be Scary Spice. A sister needs to be represented by a brother just to keep things right. Andrew, why don't you be Zayn? His skin is dark enough but you have to do something with that fro. You know what I'm talking about?"

"What about me?" Richard, the third and last African American asked.

"Your light enough to play a white guy or maybe girl," Dwight laughed.

Logan put the names minus two into the hat. He walked over to brown haired, grey eyed Craig, "You first," he said.

Craig picked a paper and let out his breath. He saw a guy's name on the paper, "Who's Louis?"

Charley slapped him on his back and then took his turn picking. He looked at the paper and groaned. He held up the paper and everyone burst into laughter. He had picked Ginger Spice.

As the last name came out of the hat, Logan looked around the room. Some of the guys were shaking their heads in disgust and others were laughing with relief. As it turned out, the Spice Girls were, Dwight-Scary Spice, Charley-Ginger Spice, Logan-Baby Spice, Mike-Sporty Spice and Dave-Posh Spice. One Direction were, Andrew-Zayn, Craig-Louis, George-Harry, Mark-Liam and Richard-Niall.

"Okay. This is what we have to do," said Dave taking charge, "Research your name and listen to their music to pick out possible lines we can use for telling a story. Write them down and we can meet at the picnic tables by the greenhouses tomorrow after training. That way we have all afternoon to work on it."

"All afternoon?" Mark said, "What if I've got things to do?"

"School hasn't started. All we've done since we've been here is fitness training and play pick-up basketball," George pointed out, "What could you possibly have to do?"

"Well," Mark looked at Hannah, "I need to get a date to the school dance and I was hoping to maybe get a tennis lesson."

"Whoa," Hannah held up her hands, "I don't date freshmen. The only reason I'm here is because of my dumb brother and I stayed to see how things played out after my great idea."

"It really wasn't your idea," her brother Andrew said. Looking at Mark, he said, "I can guarantee you don't want to date her. She is a card carrying witch."

Hannah shot Andrew a dirty look. Logan interrupted by saying, "Come on guys. We only have four days before the show on Wednesday. The dance is two days after that so there should be plenty of time to get a date."

"It will take Mark a lot longer than that," Charley laughed, "I'm sure every girl in school will be washing her hair."

"Listen, I'm tired of smelling myself. If there isn't anything else Posh Spice," Dwight winked at Dave, "I'm going to take a shower. See ya'll at dinner."

With that, all but the three who lived in the room and the two girls stayed.

Sadie looked at Logan, "Are you a good tennis player?"

"Pretty good," he replied, "I played competitive tennis at our club. Why?"

"I was looking for someone to play with me on Friday," Sadie said. Then she looked at Hannah and squinted her eyes at her, "Some people are going to be busy getting ready for the dance."

"Sue me for wanting to look nice," Hannah playfully stuck out her tongue, "Just because you decided you're not going."

George, who was lying on his bed tossing a basketball in the air, stopped and sat up. "What? How come? I was going to ask you to the dance. You are the only girls I've talked to since I've gotten here."

"I've got a date, thanks," Hannah said quickly.

Sadie looked at the racket she was holding and just louder than a whisper said. "I'm a really bad dancer."

Logan leaned back in his chair and scoffed, "I can't believe that. Aren't all girls good dancers?"

"Yeah," Andrew said, "You guys are always dancing at sleep overs and stuff. I know because Nathan and I would spy on Hannah and her friends."

Hannah punched him in the arm, "You perverted jerks."

"Ow," Andrew said laughing.

Hannah looked at Sadie, "I can testify to that. I saw her try to dance last year and she is awful. It's a bit of a problem when every guy in school asks you to dance cause you're so pretty."

Sadie shook her head, "It is so embarrassing," looking at Andrew she said, "I was invited to sleepovers but I had to say no because I was usually travelling to some tennis tournament. Last year was the first time I went to a dance at all."

"Why can't you just tell them you don't want to dance?" George asked her.

"It's really hard to say no when they ask. I feel awful doing it." Sadie said, "Don't get me wrong. I do want to go but I just want to hang out with my friends and watch other people dance."

"We want you there," Hannah looked at her with sympathy, "All you need is someone to be your date to the dance and then maybe you will be left alone," Sadie shook her head in agreement and Hannah continued, "Ya know. Someone who could just stand there with you while you hang out with us so no one asks you to dance."

"Yeah," Sadie said, "But who could we get?"

George stood up and raised his hand, "I'm available."

Both girls ignored him and turned to Logan. Logan saw them looking at him and panicked. "Me? No, no, no. I don't like dances."

"Perfect," both girls said.

"I think I'm perfect for the job," George pointed out. Andrew just shook his head at his friend's desperation.

Sadie walked over to Logan and pulled him up from his chair. She looked him in the eyes pleading with him, "Please do this for me? I will be forever grateful and will return the favor."

"Oh man," George said slapping the basketball.

"This will keep your stalker away from you for sure," Hannah said to her.

"Stalker?" all three boys asked.

"Yeah. Some kid from my club in Tulsa thinks I'm in love with him," Sadie said rolling her eyes, "I think he wanted to come here because I'm here. He's not too bright," shaking her head she continued, "He didn't get it when I point blank told him I didn't want anything to do with him."

Laughing, Hannah added, "He thinks she is playing hard to get. If he sees you with someone else, he should get the hint."

Looking at Sadie, Logan said, "I'm sure you can find a hundred other guys that would be your pretend date."

She looked at him with thoughtful eyes, "They would all expect something from me. I think you are different. You seem like a pretty respectful guy."

"And, Sadie says you have beautiful eyes," Hannah said laughing.

"Okay, I guess," Logan, said reluctantly and blushing, "I'm only doing this because you aren't going to make me dance."

"Yay! Thank you," Sadie jumped up and down waving the racket over her head, "Do you want to play tennis with me on Friday?"

"No way," Hannah grabbed her and pushed her towards the door, "We have a lot to do to get ready for the dance. Your roommate said that all your clothes are tennis clothes or yoga pants. We have to go shopping."

They walked through the door and Sadie yelled, "Bye Date. Thanks for letting me use the racket."

Logan got up and closed the door then leaned on it. He put his hand over his face and mumbled, "What did I just get myself into?"

"You're kidding, right?" George said stunned, "You have a date with the prettiest girl in the school, maybe the whole state."

Looking at his friends, Logan said, "It's not a real date. Will you guys stay with me? I have no idea what to do or how to act. I don't even know what to say to her."

"Yeah man. I'll stay with you until the babes start wanting all of this on the dance floor." Andrew said moving his hand up and down his body. He jumped up and twirled around thinking he looked like Michael Jackson.

"She said she wanted to hang out with her friends," George said, thinking about the situation, "Maybe, I'll get a few introductions if I'm hanging out with you hanging out with her."

"Thanks guys," Logan said relieved, "Georgie boy. I guarantee you will get some introductions. I will make sure of it."

He laughed when he saw George's big grin.

Chapter 39

Logan was sitting at his desk, typing on his computer when there was a knock at his door. Without missing a keystroke, he yelled, "Come in!"

His friend, Eric from Guthrie, opened the door, "Hey Logan. I haven't seen much of you since we got here. How you doing?"

"Good," Logan replied still concentrating on his typing.

"Sorry dude," Eric said, "I didn't know you were so busy. Don't tell me you have homework all ready?"

Logan stopped typing and smiled at Eric, "I'm almost finished, have a seat."

Eric sat at the end of Logan's unmade bed. He noticed his class schedule sitting on it. He read it and gave a whistle, "Man, this is a crazy schedule. These are all advanced classes. When are you going to have any fun? Oh here," pointing to the paper, "You have gym class once a day."

"And print," Logan clicked his mouse and sat back and looked at Eric, "Math is fun doofus," he grabbed the schedule from Eric's hands, "What are you taking?"

"Well, I have math, English, science, history, wood-working and gym," Eric smiled, "I don't know how you are going to get any sleep with school, homework and basketball."

"You sound like my mother," Logan laughed, "She would like to see me have some down time to socialize."

There was a knock at the door. This time Logan got up and opened it, "Oh h-hi," he said a little flustered.

Sadie walked in holding his racket. Eric saw her and stood up with his mouth open. She smiled at him and looked back at Logan, "Thanks for letting me use your racket. I loved the control it gave me."

"Um. Um. Y-yeah. No problem. Um. Good," Logan was a little tongue-tied.

Eric stuck out his hand and said, "Hi. I'm Sadie." Both gave him a puzzled look. He realized what he said and tried to fix it, "No. I mean you're Sadie and I'm dumb, no Eric."

Sadie laughed and took his hand and said, "Nice to meet you dumb Eric."

Eric blushed and took his hand away. He looked at Logan to help him.

"Ah. Yeah. You can use the racket anytime," Logan said to Sadie.

"Really? Thanks. I might use it for a mini-tournament the school is having in a week," Sadie smiled. Her eyes were really blue against her purple tank top. She was wearing grey yoga pants that stopped just below her knees and flip-flops. Her hair was done in two braids, with one braid in front and the other going down her back. She wore very little make-up. Logan thought his knees were going to give way after she smiled at him. He decided he better sit down before he crumpled to the ground.

"So, Eric, where are you from?" Sadie turned from Logan to Eric. "Um," Eric's mind went blank. Just like Logan, Eric wasn't experienced talking to pretty girls.

"He's from Guthrie, just like me," Logan stepped in seeing that Eric was paralyzed, "He's on the swim team. He's a swimmer." Logan couldn't believe he just said that.

Laughing, Sadie said, "It's a good thing you're a swimmer on the swim team. It makes it a little awkward if, let's say, you were a golfer on the swim team."

"I swim not golf. But I can golf." Eric had to sit down now. "My brother's a golfer. You might know him. He's a junior here. Christian Prather?"

The smile left Sadie's face. "Ugh. Your brother is Christian?" Eric nodded his head, "You poor guy. I'm sorry to say he is a horse's ass."

Eric looked a little hurt. Logan jumped in, "Don't mind her. Things come out of her mouth before she thinks about it."

"Oh man. I'm sorry. Did I hurt your feelings?" Sadie asked sincerely, "He's right, I don't have a filter."

Eric looked at her, "Yeah, no. It's okay. He is an ass. He struts around Guthrie bragging about all the girls he's made out with from here. That's how I knew your name."

Anger crossed Sadie's face, "You mean to tell me he is going around saying we've made out?" Eric nodded his head, yes. "He better stay out of my way or else he might get a kick in the nuts."

Logan started laughing. He couldn't believe that this beautiful girl had so much spunk. He thought to himself that he had better watch what he said around her or else he could be singing soprano.

She looked at him and tried not to smile, "Not funny. I'd better be going. Thanks again for the loaner."

When she closed the door, both boys let out a breath as if they had been holding it the whole time. They both slumped down in their seats.

Eric looked at Logan, "I can't believe you know her. Christian and his friends are always talking about how no one can get a date with her."

Logan smiled and leaned back in his chair putting his hands behind his head. "I did. We are going to the dance together."

Eric's mouth fell open, "What cha do? Bribe her. Told her she could use your racket if she would go to the dance with you."

"Nope," a smug Logan said, "As a matter of fact, she asked me."

"Liar!" Eric couldn't believe what he heard.

The door suddenly opened and Sadie ran in, closing it behind her. Logan said, "Ask her yourself."

"Ask me what?" Sadie leaned against the door just in case someone tried to open it.

"Did you ask this dink to the dance?" Eric pointed to him with his thumb.

"Yeah, yeah, I did," she was panting as if she was running.

"Are you okay?" Asked Logan.

"Not really. I almost ran into my stalker. Luckily, I saw him before he saw me and I was able to turn around and run back here," Sadie slid down the door to sit on the floor.

"Where did you see him?" asked Eric.

"I was at the end of this hall heading towards the door when he turned the corner from the other side. He was busy talking to his friends so he didn't see me." Sadie said picking at her pants.

"Your stalker is a freshman?" Logan was stunned. Eric sat up interested in this story.

"Ya. He's a kid from my club in Tulsa," Sadie said looking at Eric, "For the last few years he has followed me around our club and has even shown up at my house. I told him that I wasn't interested and he just said that I should stop playing hard to get and realize we are meant for each other." She let out an exasperated breath, "He's on the freshmen football team. I think he plays quarter back."

Logan and Eric both shook their heads. Eric said, "Those guys think they are Gods that rule everything."

"Dix has the biggest ego of them all, I think," Sadie said, "He actually showed up at the tennis courts yesterday during practice. He and his buddies stood there whistling and calling my name. Luckily, Coach walked over to them and told them to get lost or else they would have to pick up balls."

"What are you going to do if he becomes a problem for you?" Logan asked concerned for her.

"I've already talked to Mr. McKinney about it. It makes me feel better that they know about him," Sadie sighed.

An alarm on Logan's computer went off. He shut it off and looked at the other two, "Sorry guys. I've got to leave in about five minutes for rehearsal."

"How's that going?" chuckled Sadie.

"Not bad. I don't think we are going to suck," said Logan, "Craig's sister is in the DJ club and has been able to splice together different lines from the One Direction and Spice Girls songs. We actually have a storyline and everything. We just have to work on our lip syncing," he looked at Eric and asked, "What are you guys doing?"

"We are doing a Cirque du Soleil thing. The divers are all like acrobats and the swimmers are strong so we can do lifts," Eric told them, "I just don't like the make-up and costumes we have to wear. They are a little skimpy."

Sadie laughed, "And your speedos aren't?"

Logan stood up and grabbed the pages of script he had printed out earlier, "At least you don't have to dress up as Baby Spice."

Eric looked at him and laughed, "Nice. Can't wait to see that."

Eric and Sadie stood up. Eric volunteered to go and see if the hall was free from football players. Sadie stood behind the door as Logan watched him turn the corner. He came back and signaled them that the way was clear, "Looks like you are safe. Just stay behind me just in case they show up."

Sadie nodded her head and followed Logan out. He locked his door and they were able to make it to the front door without incident. She patted him on the back and said, "Thanks for letting me hide-out in your room. Good luck at the show tomorrow night," she smiled and waved.

"Bye," Logan stood in one spot and waved back. He watched her run towards girl's dorm.

"Hey Garrison!" Logan turned and saw Mike and Dwight walking towards him. Dwight saw the papers in his hand. "Is that the script?"

"Yeah. Did Craig's sister finish the CD?" he asked them.

Mike answered, "Yup. All we have to do is to rehearse and tomorrow go into to town and get our costumes."

Logan said, "I heard that the drama department will let us borrow some of their wigs and things."

"I think we have the best skit," Dwight said, "Ha ha. Charley saw the football players rehearsing their dance and he said they were awful. At least we are making fun of ourselves dressing up like girls not dancing like one."

Chapter 40

"Hey Andrew. Come on wake up!" Logan shook his roommate, "We have to be at our first class in 15 minutes."

"Leave me alone," Andrew said as he rolled onto his other side, "I want to sleep."

The door opened and George walked in carrying muffins, apples and chocolate milk. "Any luck?" he asked Logan.

"Well at least he's talking to me even though he's telling me off," he continued, "It took 15 minutes for him to do that. I thought he was dead but his snoring told me he wasn't."

George put the food down and walked over to the bed, "On three, let's roll him out of bed. Maybe the fall will jerk him awake."

The plan worked. Andrew sat straight up after he hit the floor. He yelled, "Dudes? What the hell?"

"We've been trying to get you up for the last 15 minutes," Logan explained, "Today is orientation and we have to be at our first class in," he looked at his phone, "13 minutes."

George had already grabbed Andrew's polo shirt from his closet and his jeans from the floor, "Just wear the underwear you have on," he found two dirty socks on the bed and threw it at him, "These will have to do. It's a good thing we don't have to wear our uniforms. It would take us forever to get him ready."

Logan had handed his friends each a pen and notebook plus their class schedules. They grabbed a muffin, chocolate milk and apple and ran out the door eating as they made their way to the main building where the classrooms were. Logan had advanced math on the third floor. George and Andrew were in the same English class on the second floor. Logan waved and ran up the stairs two by two. He just made it into the room when the first class bell rang.

Orientation day was a dry run for the students, especially the new ones, to find their classrooms. They got to meet the teacher and the teachers discussed rules and expectations with them. The classes were 20 minutes long with seven minutes to get to their next class.

Logan was very happy with all his classes and especially liked his science teacher, Ms. King. She thought the kids would learn more and retain more by doing hands-on activities. Standing at the front of the class lecturing or reading from the text book was boring for her and she knew from experience that the students would be bored too.

Logan was running a little late getting to the gym for his last class of the day. The science lab was probably the furthest classroom from the gym. He started to run when he got to the open field and reached the gym doors out of breath. He accidently bumped into a large boy who was talking to his friends. Logan knocked his papers out of his hands. The kid turned around to see what hit him.

Logan put his hands up and said, "Sorry man. It was a total accident," he started to bend down to help pick up the papers when the kid grabbed him with one hand by the buttons on his golf shirt.

"You better be sorry, ass wipe," he looked Logan in the eye and said, "Don't let it happen again or.."

"Or what?" asked Dwight as he, Craig and George walked up to them, "Buddy, I suggest you let go of my friend or you will have to deal the rest of us."

He let go of Logan who then stepped back to stand beside his friends. More of the kid's friends came up and stood beside him. Logan noticed all the guys were on the freshmen football team and had the reputation of being bullies at the school. The football players had kept to themselves because their season was about to start. They had full days of practice and studying their playbooks. They would be up and out on the field by 8:00 and would come back in around 4:00. The last few days it was later because they had skit practice for the Fall Revue.

The two groups stood in silence giving each other dirty looks. Logan looked from one to the other. He stopped at the shortest guy. There was something familiar about him. The short guy made eye contact with Logan and looked away. Logan could see that the kid recognized him too. It was driving Logan crazy that he couldn't think of who he was.

"Oh look. The basketball players and football players are making friends," Mr. McKinney said while walking between the two groups, "Don't think that rivalry will be tolerated in my class." He walked to the front of the gym and waved his hands over the floor, "Have a seat and stop looking at me that way. Yes, I am a school councilor but I also teach one gym class and you guys won the lottery and have me as your teacher."

Logan and his teammates were discussing their classes as they walked back to the dorms. They heard behind them. "Oh look. It's the Spice Girls ugly sisters." They turned around and saw the football players making obscene gestures.

"Well at least we were voted best skit," yelled Craig, "I remember you guys getting booed off the stage."

"Wasn't that you doing the booing?" Whispered George to Craig.

"Ha ha. Yeah, I started it but then everyone else joined in," Craig smiled.

"Hey guys?" Logan interrupted their laughing, "Do any of you know who that short guy is?"

They all stopped and looked at him. Dwight said, "Yeah. That guy's in my multi-media class. I heard him trying to impress some chick by bragging that he was the freshmen quarterback. I think they call him Dix."

"Dix? I think he's Sadie's stalker," Logan said recalling that she mentioned him, "Do you know his first name?"

Everyone shook their heads no. Logan made a mental note to ask Sadie the next time he saw her.

Friday was the first dance of the year. It was also the final day of summer holidays since classes started the following Monday. There was a sense of excitement in the air, with most of it coming from the girl's dormitory. All the teams and clubs where given the day off from practice so the girls used the time to get ready. The boys used the time to sleep until noon and hang out in their dorm rooms. It only took them 20 minutes to shower and get ready so most of the day was theirs to have fun.

George came into their room from the shower wearing a towel around his waist. He was drying his hair with another one. He saw that Logan was already dressed and was sitting down tying his shoes. Logan stood up and adjusted his tie making sure it was straight.

"Why are you wearing a tie?" asked George throwing his wet towel on his bed. The one around his waist he let drop to the floor where it would stay until he needed it again.

"I don't know," Logan said brushing his dark hair one last time. He continued as he put gel in to hold it into place, "I just wanted to."

"You want to impress Sadie don't ya?" George started laughing.

"Who wants to impress Sadie?" Andrew walked into the room in his towel and looked at Logan, "Don't answer that," he said pointing to Logan, "It's obvious. You're looking pretty good for a, what cha call it, a mercy date?"

Logan quickly grabbed something from his desk. He hid it from the sight of his roommates and headed to the door. He laughed and said, "Mercy date, real date. At least I have one. You losers just have each other," he saw that Andrew was taking off his wet towel to throw at him. He quickly opened the door and stepped through. He got the door closed just as the towel hit it.

Logan was behind the gym where the dance was being held. Through texts, he and Sadie planned to meet there and then walk into the dance together. She wanted to make sure everyone saw she had a date. Logan was sitting at a bench in the shade. He was grateful that he decided not to wear the sports jacket that his mom bought him for his birthday. It was a hot and muggy Oklahoma day. He was sweating profusely from the heat and from nerves. He wished that she would come soon because his shirt was about to be saturated in sweat. He heard laughing from behind him and when he turned, he saw Sadie walking with Hannah and a few other girls. He started to walk up to her as the others kept walking to the gym. He was speechless at how stunningly beautiful she looked. Her wheat colored hair was down and had been curled into soft ringlets. She was wearing a satin strapless coral dress that was tight around the bust and loose and flowy on the bottom. Her gold sandals had just a small heel, and they complimented her gold bracelet and earrings. Her friends wanted her to get a tight, curve hugging dress and high heels, but she refused. She threatened not to go to the dance if they didn't shut up. Logan could tell that she was feeling very uncomfortable because she kept pulling up the front of her dress or kept her arms crossed in front of her it.

It was the first time he saw her with this much makeup on and thought that it looked very nice. He couldn't stand the girls that wore too much eye stuff and lip-gloss. He thought those girls where trying too hard to look older, but it just made them look tired and sloppy. He mouthed the word "Wow" to her. When they came together he said, "You look really pretty."

Sadie smiled widely and looked down at the ground to try to hide the fact she was blushing. She was way out of her comfort zone in this dress. She was used to tennis skirts, yoga pants, tank tops, hoodies, tennis shoes and flip-flops. She usually just threw her hair back into braids or a ponytail and rarely wore make-up. Hannah had to do her hair and her friend Jackie did her make-up. They had gone into Durant the day before so she could buy her dress and shoes. When she felt the heat had disappeared, she looked up at Logan and said, "Thanks," looking Logan up and down she continued, "You clean up pretty good yourself. You look very dashing with your tie on. I actually like this better than your Baby Spice outfit even though you looked pretty hot in that too, I have to say"

He shook his head and smiled at her and then awkwardly pushed something in front of her, "Here," he said.

She took it from him, "A corsage? You didn't have to do that." She took it out of the container and Logan helped her tie it on her wrist. She held up her arm slightly so she could get a better look at it. The ribbon was pale pink with three small pink roses on the top. Sprigs of baby's breath surrounded the roses. She knew that it was a little corny, but she was thrilled to get it. Since Sadie was afraid of dancing, she didn't go to any of her proms. She made sure she played in a tennis tournament on the same weekend. This was the first corsage she has ever received, "It's so pretty, thank you."

"Um, yeah it was my mom's idea," Logan looked at his feet. His blue shirt matched his eyes. He wore black slacks and black shoes. His tie was multi colored with a diamond pattern in it. He continued, "She got really excited when I told her that I was going to the dance and that I had a date."

Sadie interrupted, "You mean a mercy date."

"I told her that but she still insisted that I get you a corsage and that I should wear a tie." Logan gave her a crooked smile, "Her argument was that it would look more realistic if I gave you a corsage," he paused for a second, "Oh yeah." He looked up at the sky a little embarrassed, "She wants me to text her a picture of us if it's alright. This is my first dance and really my first date," smiling down at her he continued, "Even though it's just a fake one. My mom and I are really close since my dad was in an accident and has since died."

Sadie made eye contact with him and sincerely said, "I'm so sorry to hear that. Of course, we will send her a picture and," she gave a little smirk, "I have to send my parents a picture too. They wanted proof that I was actually going to a dance with a boy and wearing a dress."

They both laughed and Logan shook his head, "Parents," he stuck his arm out, "Shall we?"

Sadie put her arm through his making sure her beautiful corsage was front and center. She looked up at him and smiled, "Let's do this."

Chapter 41

Logan and Sadie turned the corner of the gym to see the majority of the student body milling around outside the front door. Someone from the dance committee announced that the doors would be opening in approximately 10 minutes. The students didn't mind. It gave them the chance to check out what everyone else was wearing and who was going to the dance with whom. Kids were taking pictures of each other and there was a buzz of laughter and constant chatter.

Both Logan and Sadie stopped when they saw all the people. Both were quite nervous and didn't anticipate they would have to face everyone all at once. Sadie took a deep breath and looked at Logan, "We can always pop some popcorn and watch a movie on my computer."

Logan shook his head. He was tempted to take her up on her idea, "No. We need to do this. If we don't, then the guys won't leave you alone and besides, I think we would really regret it," a smiled crossed his face, "Oh yeah, my mom would kill me if I chickened out."

Sadie cringed a little. She didn't like being called a chicken, "Yeah. I guess you're right. My parents were pretty stoked about me going."

Sadie heard her name and looked out into the crowd. She saw Hannah waving at her. She smiled at Logan, "It's too late. We've been spotted."

Logan took a deep breath, "This will be easier than playing in the finals at state."

"I'd rather be doing that then this," she replied through her teeth, "I am really out of my element right now. "

Logan started walking towards the crowd and had to give Sadie a little tug. She relented and started walking with him. She could see people turning and staring at the two of them. She could hear comments like, "Who's that?" and "Isn't he a freshman?"

Logan could hear, "How did Garrison get a date with her?" "I didn't even know he knew her," and "Isn't that the guy who played Baby Spice?" he groaned out loud to that one.

They reached Hannah and her group of friends. Hannah said, "Don't you two look cute together," Sadie gave her a dirty look. Laughing, Hannah continued, "You look so bright and colorful in your coral and blue."

Sadie went around the group and introduced Logan to everyone. A couple of the guys knew him from basketball. Andrew's older brother, Nathan was there with his date. He walked up to him and slapped him on the back. He whispered into Logan's ear, "Dude. No one has gotten a date with Sadie. How'd you do it?"

Logan laughed. "I just so happen to have in my possession, her dream tennis racket. I told her that she could use it if she would go to the dance with me."

Nathan just gave him a bright wide smile and said, "Classic. Nice going."

After quite a few pictures, the doors of the gym finally opened. They could hear music coming from inside the gym. The students started moving towards the door in mass. Sadie took Logan's arm again and felt relieved they were going in. She was tired of everyone staring and scrutinizing them.

As they were walking in, George and Andrew ran up to them.

Andrew said, "Well, well. You guys are the talk of the SEA town."

"Yeah. So many of the upper classmen are wondering what you have that they don't, to score the hottest chick in school," George said. Logan gave him a dirty look knowing that Sadie probably wouldn't appreciate it. George got the hint and looked at Sadie, "Oh man. I'm sorry. I guess I shouldn't have said that out loud, in front of you."

"That's okay," Sadie laughed, "I don't have a filter either, remember." The couple finally made it to the front door of the gym. As they walked in a few pairs of eyes were shooting daggers at Logan. Standing behind a magnolia tree to the left of the doors were a group of freshmen football players. They were passing around a flask when one of the guys noticed Logan and Sadie. He turned his friend around and pointed towards the doors. Anger crossed the freshmen quarterback's face and he said, "What is she doing with him? He better watch himself. Come on."

Groups were forming around the gym with no one dancing yet. Many of the juniors and seniors had already claimed one corner of the gym. Other cliques claimed their spots too. There was a table where teachers and dance committee members passed out bottles of water, granola and fruit bars. Years earlier, kids started fainting from dehydration or low glucose levels. They started charging five dollars for the tickets to cover the cost of the water & bars. The teachers chaperoned the dance making sure everyone's behavior was appropriate and that they had a good time.

The gym was decorated in the school colors of blue, orange and gold. There was a large banner hanging at one end of the gym saying, 'Welcome to South Eastern Academy'.

Logan and Sadie were talking to her friends when George, Andrew and a few of the freshmen basketball players came over. George nudged Logan. Logan just ignored him. George did it again. Logan turned around and annoyingly asked, "Dude, what do you want?"

George leaned over and whispered in his ear, "You said you'd introduce us."

"I hardly know any of them yet," he said a little louder than he wanted.

Sade overheard and asked, "Know who?"

Logan shifted back and forth on his feet, "Um. No one."

She could tell that he was trying to hide something. Then she looked at his friends and put two and two together, "You guys want to meet some girls?"

They tried to play it cool and Andrew said, "Oh, what are you talking about? We know plenty of girls."

George didn't want this chance to slip by, "But if you have some friends that are single and would maybe dance with us, that would be nice for them."

Sadie and Logan laughed. She pointed to the group of girls in the corner, "See that group? I play tennis with some of them. I'm sure they would appreciate it if you asked them to dance. Come on," she grabbed Logan's hand and his friends followed them over for the introductions.

Finally, the DJ played a song that kids wanted to dance to. Couples started to form on the dance floor including the basketball players and their new friends. Logan and Sadie decided to walk around and see who they could talk to.

Mr. McKinney came up to them and shook Logan's hand. He said, "How are things going Mr. Garrison? Are you settling in?"

"Yes sir," remembering his manners he said, "Mr. McKinney, do you know Sadie Hudson?"

"Hi Mr. McKinney," Sadie shook his hand, "It's nice to see you again."

He smiled at her and asked, "Miss Hudson, have you had any problems with what we discussed on Monday?"

Since Sadie had filled Logan in on her stalker situation, he assumed that was what he was talking about. She replied, "No problems at all sir. Everything is fine so far."

"Good to hear," he nodded to Logan. "I see you have made friends with one of our scholarship winners here."

Logan blushed. He didn't broadcast that information out. His mother taught him to be humble and appreciate his gifts. Sadie looked amazed and said, "No. I didn't know that sir."

"Yes. He is one of the brightest Choctaw Scholarship recipients that South Eastern Academy has had," Mr. McKinney winked at him, "Well, since I received the scholarship. We'll see if he can live up to my reputation."

"I'll try sir," Logan said and they said good-bye.

As they walked away Sadie looked at him and said, "Wow. I didn't know you were a ship. You must be pretty smart, huh?"

He didn't answer her question but started guiding her towards the refreshment table. "Do you want something from here?" he asked pointing at the table.

"Sure, I'll take a water," she said while walking with him to the table. She was too afraid to leave any distance between the two of them. She felt very safe with Logan around. Deep down she knew that the vultures would swoop in and ask her to dance if she was by herself.

He handed her a bottle of water and stuck a granola bar into his back pocket for later. He had forgotten to eat dinner so he knew he would be hungry soon. They continued walking in silence when he heard Sadie gasp. He looked down at her and she grabbed his arm and turned in the other direction.

"Sadie! What's wrong?" he asked with concern.

They got to the side of the gym and hid behind some decorative balloons. She pointed to a group of boys waiting close to the bathrooms, "See those guys?"

Logan looked around the balloons and recognized the freshmen football players, "Yeah. They're on the football team."

"The guy who is talking to the girl in the white dress is my stalker," she told him still holding on to his arm.

Logan saw that it was the same guy from his gym class. It reminded him that he wanted to ask Sadie his name because he recognized him from somewhere. "What's his name?" he asked.

"That's Dix. He has been haunting me for the last two years," she said, "Last year was nice cause I was here but he still stalked me on social media even though I deleted him from my contacts."

"No. What's his real name?" Logan already knew is nickname.

She looked at him with curiosity, "It's Milo Dixon."

Logan felt himself sway. He grabbed the balloons they were hiding behind but they didn't steady him. He fell sideways and Sadie was there to catch him, "Are you okay?"

"I know him," Logan said, "He and his mom lived with us in Guthrie for about a year. We were like in kindergarten," feeling an ache in his heart he said, "He used to be my best friend."

"Are you sure it's the same guy?" she asked, "He told us his family owned a large cattle ranch in Montana but sold it after his dad died and moved to Tulsa. He didn't mention anything about Guthrie."

"That's interesting," Logan looked at her, "I know that his great-grandparents did own a ranch in Montana, but he never lived there. He was born in Kansas and him and his mom ended up in Guthrie when my mom invited them to live with us."

"What a liar!" Sadie said, "I can't believe the bullshit he fed everyone. Is his dad dead or is that a lie too? Milo told everyone that his dad died in a horse accident on their ranch in Montana."

Logan shook his head, "Well, one thing that is true in his story." Sadie raised an eyebrow, "His dad is dead but not how he described," he looked at her with concern, "Please keep this to yourself. I really don't think this needs to get out."

"I promise I won't tell anyone. I'm really good at keeping secrets," she said.

Logan decided he could trust her with this information. "Just between you and me, please," he paused and she crossed her heart, "Milo is the result of a teenage pregnancy. His grandfather forced them to get married. My mom told me that they lived in a run-down trailer and Milo's dad was an alcoholic. He used to beat Milo's mom up and she finally left him. They ended up in Guthrie and walked into the diner that my mom worked at. Since my dad was in a vegetative state, that's another story I'll tell you later, she needed help around the house. Milo and his mom didn't have a place to go so my mom offered them to live with us if Laura looked after me while mom was at work. They lived with us for almost a year." Turning away from her, he said just loud enough for Sadie to hear him, "He was my best friend. We were like brothers."

Sadie saw that there was some pain there. She put her hand on his arm. The warmth resonated up his arm and he turned to her. He saw softness in her eyes that told him that he could trust her. She asked him, "What happened. When did you two stop being friends?"

"Her rich Aunt had died and left everything to her. That was just before first grade," he turned and looked at Milo, "That was pretty much the last time I saw or talked to him," he looked down at her, "How did you guys meet?"

"We belonged to the same Country Club. We actually took tennis lessons together. He wasn't quite the ass then that he is now." Sadie shook her head. "He just got in with the snobby rich kids. I'm sure he made up those stories to fit in. There is no way those jerks would have accepted him if they knew he lived in a trailer."

"That's really too bad." Logan said. "We really had a lot of fun together. I'm surprised that his mom would let him act like that. She was always telling us to use manners. Milo did get into trouble more than I did and she made sure he was punished."

"It seemed like she was really busy with different charities and stuff. My mom was on a few committees with her," Sadie told him, "She was always trying to please everyone and I think it was really hard for her to say no."

"There you two are," Hannah was marching up to them, "What are you doing hiding behind these balloons?"

"I wanted to get away from Dix over there," Sadie pointed to him leaning against the wall.

"Makes sense," Hannah said, "Are you guys having any fun at least?"

Logan nodded his head and Sadie said, "We are. It's been cool watching everyone dance. I may pick up a few moves."

"The DJ is pretty decent," Logan said, "I like the music."

"Good," Hannah smiled, "I'm going out to dance some more," she looked sternly at Logan, "Take care of my girl."

Hannah walked away and joined her friends. They were all dancing in a group and having a lot of fun. Sadie turned to Logan, "She's always looking out for me. I think because she's a year older, she thinks she has to protect me. I really am grateful she's my friend."

"My mom says she is an awesome tennis player," Logan added.

"How does your mom know?" Sadie was confused.

"Mom is one of the tennis coaches at our club in Guthrie and has travelled with the team to state tournaments. She met Hannah on move in day and she remembered her," Logan told her.

"No wonder she could get you the new Wilson racket. I wonder if I've met her then?" Sadie said trying to remember the Guthrie Tennis Team.

"She didn't remember you when I told her all about you," Logan said.

Sadie smiled and asked, "You told her about me?"

Logan realized how that sounded, "I had no choice. When I told her about going to the dance she drilled me for details. I explained that I was just going with you on a mercy date but she still wanted me to tell her about you. I bet when we stopped Skyping, she looked up your stats on the Oklahoma tennis website."

Sadie started laughing, "Your mom sounds like mine," she stopped laughing when she realized that the picture of her on the website was horrible. She had just finished a two-hour tennis game in 100-degree heat. Her ponytail was off to one side and she was sweaty and blotchy.

The tempo of the music changed. They looked out and saw that the DJ was playing the first slow song of the evening. Most of the people dancing left and couples took their place. As they turned to each other, the guys put their hands on their partner's hips and the girls put their hands on the guy's shoulders. The couples that were actually boyfriend and girlfriend were a little more intimate. The boy would have his arms wrapped totally around the girl's waist and the girl would be hugging the boy around his shoulders. No matter what way they held each other the footwork was the same? The kids would sway back and forth turning in a clockwise direction.

Logan had been studying this. He looked at Sadie and said, "Whatcha think? This looks pretty easy."

Sadie looked out and watched the dancers. She looked up at him and said, "I guess this mercy date would look real if we actually danced. I think we could handle this, but I can't guarantee I won't step on your feet."

"I'll take that risk," he smiled. They walked out to the edge of the dance floor. It took them a few times but they figured out where to put their hands. They were trying not to laugh too hard at how awkward they felt and most likely looked.

On the other side of the gym, Milo was watching them. Anger started piercing his gut. He took a drink from his flask and started walking towards the couple. He was going to stop this right now. As he pushed his way through the crowd, he felt a strong hand grab the back of his left shoulder. He turned to take a swing at whoever was stopping him from completing his mission. Milo released his fist when he saw Mr. McKinney standing there with his other hand out, "I'll take it Mr. Dixon," Mr. McKinney said.

"Take what?" Milo was confused.

"The flask that is in your back pocket. I saw you take a drink from it," he replied.

Milo pulled the flask from his back pocket and gave it to him. Mr. McKinney unscrewed the top and took a smell of the contents. He made a face, "Is cheap brandy the drink of all the kids now a days or just the 14 year olds?"

Mr. McKinney wasn't too impressed, "You have broken a major school rule Mr. Dixon. I think we should go to my office and have a little discussion while I write this up on your record. You will be suspended from any school activities until we talk to the Head Master on Monday. That includes football practice."

"But Mr. McKinney," Milo started to object.

Mr. McKinney held up his hands, "Next time Mr. Dixon. Respect the school rules. There are reasons we have them. As a matter of fact, why don't you come to my office tomorrow at 9:00 in the morning with your student handbook? I think you need to review the rules. If you're late, then I'll find more fun things for you to do."

Milo caught his meaning. As he turned to leave the gym, he glanced over his shoulder at Sadie and Logan. He thought to himself, *this is*

Logan's lucky day. He came within a few seconds of getting his bell rung. I will have to get even with him some other way.

Chapter 42

The day after the dance was a free day for the students. Most took the chance to sleep in after the late night before. The dance had ended at 11:00 and the kids slowly made it back to their dorms. If they were in their rooms by midnight, they were fine to con- tinue socializing.

There was one student who didn't get the luxury of sleeping in. Milo Dixon arrived at the councilor's office 10 minutes before nine. In his hand, was the student's handbook he was told to bring. He took a seat outside Mr. McKinney's office since Mr. McKinney wasn't there yet. Milo was upset that he wasn't more careful when he took that last drink. *I wasn't thinking straight*, he thought to himself, of *all the guys Sadie could have gone to the dance with, she went with him. Some best friend he turned out to be*, Milo sat back in his chair and put his hands over his face. *I've been asking her out for two years and this guy walks in and flashes those blue eyes. Girls can be so dumb. She doesn't know what's good for her.* He took his hands away from his face and put them behind his head, *I'm the quarterback. So many other girls want to be with me, why not her?* he became distracted by his bicep, *I am putting on weight and getting ripped even if I'm not getting taller*, his thoughts came back to Sadie and Logan,

I've got to get rid of him. Once he's out of my hair, Sadie will come to her senses. Milo devised a plan. He has gotten other guys in trouble before so it should be pretty easy to get Logan kicked out of school.

Most of the students were up and in the cafeteria for their first meal of the day. Milo came in and looked around for his roommates Keith and Les. They had gone to school with him in Tulsa and played on the freshman football team. When he saw them he sauntered to their table. Keith said to Milo, "Well, look who broke out of McKinney prison."

Milo sat down next to him, "Didn't have to break out. He has given me 45 minutes for lunch. I have to go back and help Mrs. Whats-her-name in the library this afternoon."

The group got up and joined the cafeteria line to get the special of the day. Today it was chipotle fish tacos with coleslaw and lemon meringue pie for dessert. Milo was reaching for an iced tea when he saw the freshman basketball team walk into the room. Second from the front was Logan dressed in swim shorts and t-shirt. He had a beach towel around his neck just like the others. They were obviously catching the one o'clock bus to Texoma Lake that afternoon. He saw Logan wave at someone. Milo followed his gaze and there was Sadie waving back at him. Milo shook his head and turned around to his two buddies, Keith and Les. He whispered to them, "Guys, hurry up and eat. I have to talk to you two before I have to go back."

The three inhaled their lunch. After they cleaned up their dishes, they went outside and started walking towards the dorm building. Milo said, "I need you guys to do something for me. I have to get that Logan kid eliminated from the scene if I have a chance with Sadie," both shook their heads showing Milo they understood his dilemma, "Why don't you guys get a few more people and go to the lake this afternoon. Take a football and start throwing it around on the beach. When

Logan goes into the water, throw the ball next to his stuff. I want you to grab his phone and room key and bring it to me."

"What if we get caught?" Les asked concerned they were taking too much of a risk.

"Just make it look like you accidently messed up his things when you were trying to catch the football. Then put things back and straighten up his towel. I know you guys can do this without being seen. We did stuff like this all the time in Tulsa," Milo reassured them.

"What are you going to do with them?" asked Keith.

"I have plans tomorrow when everyone will be at the pep rally. Since I can't go, I will be a little busy framing that asshole," Milo snickered.

The friends said goodbye with a three-way chest bump. Milo had less than 10 minutes to get to the library. He was not happy that he wasn't going to the lake with the rest of them. Instead, he was condemned to spend the afternoon in his least favorite place.

It was just after four o'clock and Milo was walking back across campus to the boy's dormitory. He felt a slap on his back. He turned quickly to see who it was. Keith and Les had run up behind him and Keith said, "Well, buddy. This was way easier than I thought it would be. They spent all their time in the water and we spent our time playing football on the beach. He stuck his phone and keys into his shoe right there out in the open."

"Small town people are so trusting," smiled Milo, "Do you have his stuff?"

"Right here," Les said as he pulled the phone and keys from his backpack. He handed them to Milo, "He doesn't even have a passcode so we did a little snooping. He had Sadie's contact info on there so we deleted it." He was pretty proud of himself.

Milo shook his head, "Doofus. Sadie can still call him so it really didn't do a whole lot and besides, it's pretty easy to get her contact info again."

Keith changed the subject to avoid more backlash from Milo, "Sadie was there too. She and her friends spent a lot of time with the basketball players. She and Logan were wrestling in the water trying to get a ball. It looked like they were getting real cozy you know what I'm saying?"

Milo stopped walking and slapped the closest tree. That was the last thing he wanted to hear. His anger was starting to build. He pushed past his friends and kicked the front door to the dorm open. He went into their room and slammed the door. He paced around the room finalizing his revenge plans against Logan.

The last Saturday before classes start, the school had a tradition of having two bonfires for the student body. The juniors and seniors had their bonfire going in the football stadium parking lot. The lower classmen had their bonfire going in the faculty parking lot. Logan and his friends were on their way to meet up with Sadie and her friends when they walked by Milo's group. Les called out to them, "Hey idiots. You're going the wrong way. The bonfire is the other way."

Andrew and George turned and walked up to them. Logan wanted to ignore them, but his friends felt they needed to straighten them out. Andrew walked up to Les, "We know cement head. We have dates we're meeting," looking around he continued, "What? You guys don't have dates? Not surprising."

Keith snarled at them, "We can get any girls we want. They like football players better than scrawny basketball players."

George looked down on them, "Any girls, huh? Sadie Hudson has made it perfectly clear she doesn't want anything to do with football players," George nodded to Milo, "Especially, a certain creepy one that won't leave her alone."

Milo clenched his hands and charged after George. Luckily, his friends held him back. Keith smiled at Logan, "Yeah, we hear she is slumming with this hick from Guthrie. He can only get into this school on grades because his mother can't make enough money at that diner she works at." Logan gritted his teeth and squinted his eyes. Keith knew he hit a nerve so he continued, "Yeah. That's right, we know all about you and your white trash life. I bet you even live in a trailer park."

Logan's eyes shot in Milo's direction. It was as if Milo could read Logan's mind. He knew that Logan was the only guy around who knew his real background. Before Logan could tell them Milo had actually lived in a trailer with his alcoholic, abusive father and teenage mom, he grabbed his friend's arms and pulled them away. "Let's not waste our time with these ass wipes. I don't need to get into any more trouble." Milo said good-bye to his friends and started walking back to the dorm. He could see Logan and Sadie meeting up. Sadie saw him glaring at them so she gave Logan a hug. Milo was motivated more than ever to carry out his plan.

Milo was in his room when he heard a knock. He opened the door and saw Mr. Flynn the junior History teacher. He was also the floor leader. Every floor in the dorm has a faculty member who lives and supervises that floor. Once school starts, they oversee enforcing the curfew and making sure there are no school rules broken. If any student is sick, they report to him/her and he/she determines if they should stay in bed, go to the infirmary or go to class. The floor leader would report any absences to the attendance supervisor. Every morning, the teachers would get e-mailed the class list showing who would not be attending for that day. It was easy to catch kids skipping class. Because of the small student body, the up to date technology and the fact they were at a boarding school, made it easy to monitor the students where abouts.

Mr. Flynn saw Milo and said to him. "Mr. McKinney has told me that you are not allowed to go to the bonfire tonight and the pep rally tomorrow, is that correct?"

"Yup." Milo said trying to look remorseful.

"You are to stay in your room tonight and report back to the library tomorrow." Milo nodded his head showing he understood, "I will be checking up on you periodically tonight so don't think of leaving this room. Understood?"

Milo said, "Yes sir. I'm just going to watch some movies on my computer."

Milos shut his door and waited a few seconds before he opened it a crack. He could hear Mr. Flynn say, "Come on you guys. You're the last ones here so let's get going." Milo quietly shut his door and went to the window, facing the front of the dorm building. He watched Mr. Flynn and the two boys walk towards the bonfire.

He started his movie and had everything set up just in case he had to run back in. If Mr. Flynn came back early for some reason, then he would see that the movie had been playing. Milo looked out into the hall and listened. He heard nothing so he quietly came out into the hall. He left his door ajar, but not opened. Logan's room was in the opposite corner of the building. Milo had two long hallways to get down without being seen. He had Logan's room key with him and started down the first hall. He stopped when he got to the end and carefully peered around the corner. Clear. He turned right and ran to the end. He knew no one was there, but didn't want to take any chances so he peered around the last corner. Seeing that it was also clear, he put the key in the lock and opened the door. He swiftly went in and closed it. It was still light enough that he didn't have to turn on a light. He surveyed the room and shook his head. These guys are bigger slobs than we are.

He shuffled through things on each desk to determine whose area it was. On one shelf, he saw a Guthrie Blue Jays cap. He knew right away that it was Logan's. He lifted it off the shelf and put it on his head. "This will come in handy," he said to himself. He opened Logan's closet door and saw an old and worn lettermen's jacket. He ran his fingers over the name. 'Robbie' on the sleeve. Milo had a flashback of the two of them putting this jacket on when they were about five. Milo had his right arm in the right sleeve and Logan had his left arm in the left sleeve. Working together, they zipped up the coat. They walked into the family room where their mothers were watching a TV show.

He remembered his mom had burst out laughing and Kristy had said, "Oh look. The Siamese twins are home." He and Logan didn't know what Siamese twins were, but their moms were laughing very hard. His mom had gotten up and asked for a hug. They wrapped their arms around her legs and he could see tears streaming down her face from laughing. Milo smiled to himself from this memory. He realized it had been a very long time since he had seen his mom that happy.

He decided he needed the coat as well. The next step to his plan was to make sure these guys woke up late tomorrow. He changed the time on all their clocks so they were behind the real time. He knew that Logan would have to use his alarm clock since he had lost his cell phone at the lake. The other two probably used the alarm on their phones. Like every teenager with a phone, they had it on all day, draining the battery and would charge it at night. He found the chargers plugged in beside their nightstands. He unplugged them and put a piece of clothing over it so they couldn't see that it wasn't plugged in. They would come home tonight and put the plug into the phone thinking it was recharging, but really the phones would be dead by morning.

Milo grabbed Logan's hat and jacket and walked to the door. He looked around to make sure he hadn't forgotten something. He congratulated himself on being an evil genius. He pulled stuff like this off at home and it was getting easier. He carefully opened the door and looked both ways down the halls. Empty. He made sure the door was locked and stealthily made his way back to his room. He hid the jacket and hat under his bed and saw Mr. Flynn making his way across the lawn. He climbed into his bed and put his earphones on and propped his computer on his lap. *They really don't trust us, do they?* he thought to himself, Well, *they shouldn't*, he smiled.

Chapter 43

The next day, the campus was busy getting ready for the pep rally. The band and cheer squad had been up early doing last minute practices. The athletic teams were trying to sort out jerseys and shirts to wear. The teams starting their season in September were soccer, tennis, swim/diving, and football. Those teams and athletes were going to be highlighted and introduced. That is, except for Milo Dixon.

He skipped breakfast with his teammates since it was too painful to see their excitement. He thought it was bullshit that he couldn't at least participate. He was the quarterback after all. Instead, he went over each step in his head of what he had to do that day. He only had a small window to get things done so it was important he didn't leave anything out. He looked at his watch and saw that Logan's alarm would be going off in about two minutes. Everyone else on the floor had gotten up, showered and were either eating breakfast or at the pep rally. He locked the door to his room and ran to the end of the hall He listened intently for the chaos that was about to unfold.

When he reached the end of the hall he heard the door at the other end fly open. He peeked around the corner and saw Logan and George pushing Andrew towards the shower. They were all wearing their towels and yelling at each other to hurry up. He ran down the other hall and looked around the corner. He saw the door to the shower room close. Conveniently, there was a lock on the outside of the shower door to keep students out in case they had to shut it down for repairs. Milo quietly slid the lock across. He walked quickly towards the front door. The next step in his plan was to develop an alibi. He decided to stop by the cafeteria and see who was still there. He walked through the door and the only people inside where the cafeteria workers. The students had already made their way to the football stadium for the pep rally. He grabbed a muffin and an apple.

"Aren't you going to be late for the pep rally?" Mrs. Jones had asked him.

"I kind of got into trouble Friday and I'm not allowed to go," Milo said sadly trying to get some sympathy, "I'm just grabbing something to eat then I have to go to the library and help sort books."

Mrs. Jones just shook her head and handed him a warm cinnamon roll. His little act seemed to work.

Milo entered the library and saw the librarian standing there with her hands on her hips. "No food allowed in the library," she said sternly.

Milo took the last bite of his apple and threw it away. He had already eaten the cinnamon roll and really wanted to drink the milk he had in his hoodie pocket. He decided that could wait a few more minutes.

"Do you have your discipline slip that I have to sign?" she asked.

Milo faked looking surprised, "No ma'am. I forgot it in my room." Looking concerned, "Please, may I go back quickly and get it. I would hate to get into more trouble," he looked at her with pleading brown eyes. This was his plan from the start. He needed an excuse to go back to the dorm.

She stood there and thought about it. Then she said, "Fine. You can go back and get it but you have to be back here in 10 minutes."

"I don't think I can do it in 10," Milo hoped his act would work. He needed time to carry out his plan, "It takes about 10 minutes to walk just one way."

She looked at her watch and rolled her eyes. She thought to herself, I *have better things to do than babysit unruly kids. Well, this will give me a chance to get a cup of coffee before we start organizing this new shipment.* She looked at him and squinted her eyes, "I want you back here at 9:35 and no later."

"Don't worry ma'am," Milo said walking through the library door. He quickly took his chocolate milk out of his hoodie pocket and opened it. He drank it quickly and threw the empty carton on the grass. He was about to run when he saw out of the corner of his eye, the librarian watching him from the window. He thought to himself, *I hope she didn't see me litter.* He kept walking until he knew she couldn't see him anymore. He took off running as fast as he could. He knew he was fast. He had the track and field trophies to prove it. If he hadn't wanted to be a quarterback like his dad, he knew he could be a running back. He was small, but he had powerful legs. Milo was at his dorm room in no time. He looked at his watch. He had secretly set the stopwatch when he left. He had to keep track of the time so he wasn't late. His mom had gotten him this expensive watch for his birthday. He was still getting used to the large size but loved all the functions it could do. He was the only one in his group with such a fancy watch. The others were jealous and he felt superior to them.

Milo grabbed Logan's jacket and cap from under his bed. He put on the jacket and raised the collar. He then put on the cap and pulled it down low on his head. He needed to cover his face. He looked out his door and was about to leave when he heard voices down the hall. He peeked out and saw Logan, George and Andrew running out the front door. Obviously, they got out and were running late for the pep rally. Milo closed his door and started laughing, "Ha. My plan is going so well." He looked out his window and saw them running across the grass towards the football stadium.

He looked out again and listened. He only heard the vacuum of one of the housekeep staff. *I bet that's how they got out,* he thought, one *of them must have gone to clean the bathroom and found those three-whiny bastards.* Milo slipped out of his room and headed for the stairs next to the front entrance. He wasn't as careful about who saw him. He actually hoped that someone would see him. He ran up the stairs. He was out of breath by the time he reached the top floor. Milo saw the door to the senior's lounge. This was the senior boy's exclusive lounge and patio area. There was a keypad on the door with a combination pad. Only the senior boys and their floor supervisor knew the combination. The seniors wanted to make sure their penthouse lounge stayed exclusive so they changed the code every two-weeks. Milo happened to be in the locker room two days before when he overheard one senior tell another the new code. Milo groaned when he saw a housekeeper with his cart blocking it. *Crap!* he thought. *I'll walk around the other way and hopefully the cart will be moved by the time I get there.* He looked at his watch. He was behind schedule now. He had only 10 minutes before he had to be back at the library.

Milo quickly turned right and ran around the hall. He slowed down when he reached the last hall. He turned the corner and saw the housekeeper slowly moving the cart down the hall. He walked up to the keypad and saw the housekeeper look at him. Milo put his head down and quickly keyed in the number he had memorized, praying that it would work. He heard the click of the lock release. He threw the door open and ran up the stairs to the rooftop. He got to the top and was stunned at how nice the room was. He quickly surveyed the area. There was a large screen TV mounted above an electric fireplace. It was extremely clean with large black leather sofas and chairs. There was a heavy wooden desk in one corner and large bookshelf covering half the walls. Hard cover books and keepsakes lined the shelves. On the main wall was a large trophy case. It was filled with years of achievements and recognitions. Milo quickly browsed the trophies and decided he was going to have his name on at least one of the athletic trophies. If they had one for 'Evil Genius', his name would be on it. He quickly circled the room, knocking over plants, scattering papers and tilting pictures. He looked at his watch and saw that three minutes had gone by. He took Logan's phone out of his pocket and planted it in a spot that wasn't too obvious but would be seen eventually.

He wanted to steal something so he looked around the room. A glint of something caught his eye. He walked over to the bookshelf where the item was sitting. Inside a small silver frame was a stamp that had a sunrise behind the Oklahoma plains and a river. Milo picked it up and read the inscription engraved in the frame. 'This 100th Anniversary of Oklahoma Statehood stamp is presented to the 2007 senior class of South Eastern Academy. It is a reminder that the youth of the state of Oklahoma have been and will be the leaders, teachers and innovators shaping and moving this great state forward into the next century. Proudly presented by The Durant Rotary Club.' Milo thought this was perfect so he slid it into Logan's jacket pocket.

Milo looked around the room and was satisfied with his handy work. He decided he better be on his way so he ran down the stairs and out through the locked door. He saw that the housekeeper was still in the hall. He pushed past him and down the main stairs to the bottom floor. Instead of turning left to go to his room, he turned right and ran down to Logan's room. He unlocked it with the Logan's key. He quickly took the lettermen's jacket off and hung it back up. He placed the ball cap back on the shelf and threw Logan's keys just under his bed. Milo then opened the door and looked down the hall. It was all clear. He didn't care about locking the door again. He figured they were in such a hurry leaving it would not be a surprise to them that they had forgotten to lock the door.

Milo checked his back pocket and pulled out the discipline slip that had been there the whole time. He made sure he had it so he didn't waste time going back to his room to get it. He ran down the hall, out the front door and sprinted across campus to the spot he knew the librarian could see him. He could hear the roar of the pep rally. He angrily thought, those *cheers should be for me*. He looked at his watch. One minute to go. He walked quickly to the library building and made it to her desk with 20 seconds to spare.

South Eastern Academy Mustangs' first Pep Rally of the year had already started. The varsity and junior varsity cheerleaders performed many cheers and a dance routine. They also formed a tunnel of waving pom-poms for the athletes to run through as their names were called. The band was playing the school song and voices were proudly singing along.

The students had dressed up in the school colors of orange, blue and gold. Many of them had war paint on their faces. The school spirit was already on high when Logan, George and Andrew arrived at the stadium. They stood at one entrance scanning the packed stadium for seats.

"Well, well, well," Mr. McKinney said as he walked up to them, "Thank you gentlemen for volunteering."

"Volunteering for what sir?" Andrew asked.

Mr. McKinney just smiled and waved at them to follow him. They went down the stairs to field level. He held the gate open that lead from the stadium to the field. He continued walking until they reached a garbage can holding three shovels. He picked up two shovels and handed one to Logan and another to Andrew. He put the third shovel on the ground and handed George the garbage can. He said to them,

"This is what happens when you're late for a pep rally. You volunteer for clean-up duty."

"What are we cleaning up?" George was almost afraid to ask.

He got his answer right away. They quickly turned around when they heard thundering hooves behind them. Two seniors dressed as Choctaw Native Americans riding horses came rushing past them. The crowd exploded to their feet and started cheering. The horses raced around the perimeter of the stadium with the seniors whooping it up. The school started chanting, "Go Mustangs go".

Mr. McKinney pointed out something to the boys, "That, gentlemen, is called a horse plop. Now, before someone steps in it, you three must run out and scoop up the horse plop with the shovel and put it in the garbage can. This has to be done very carefully so you don't get in the horses' way," he saw the disgust on the boy's face. He started to laugh, "Next time, don't be late. It is very rude."

"But Mr. McKinney. We got." George started to protest.

Mr. McKinney held up his hands, "No buts. You were late and now you are falling behind on the job," he pointed across the field to another brown pile, "There's another horse plop. You better get going."

The boys started to run towards the first pile. The crowd stopped chanting and started laughing. Most knew what was happening. George, Logan and Andrew where so humiliated. They heard some people yelling, "Look! It's the horse plop patrol. Ha, Ha."

Over the microphone, Mr. McKinney said, "This is a little reminder to the returning students and for those new students," he pointed in the direction of the boys, "This is what happens when you are late to a school event. We will find some kind of job for you to do. We take punctuality here at South Eastern Academy very seriously."

Someone yelled from the crowd, "What happens if no one is late?"

Mr. McKinney smiled, "Good question. If every single one of you are on time, which would be a miracle, I will personally be the horse plop patrol," laughing he continued, "If that's not incentive enough for you students to get here on time, then I don't know what would be. Congratulations Mustangs! Let's have a great year!"

Chapter 44

The students of South Eastern Academy were still buzzing when they reached the cafeteria for lunch. Milo walked in and joined his friends. He was in a good mood even though he had missed the pep rally and had spent the morning unpacking books and magazines with the grumpy librarian Ms. Churchwood. His mood got even better when he heard how Logan and his roommates where humiliated in front of the whole school. He smiled to his friends, "It shouldn't be long before the shit hits the fan. I hope I'm around when they drag his ass off to the office."

Logan, Andrew and George had decided they didn't need lunch even though they were starving. They were done being ridiculed for cleaning up after the horses at the rally. The three were in their room complaining to each other about how unfair it was that they were late because they got locked in the bathroom when they heard a knock at their door.

Andrew jumped up and opened it. He said, "Oh hi. Are you here to tell me how mom and dad are going to flip out when they hear what I had to do today?"

Andrew's sister Hannah pushed past him with Sadie following. Logan, who was lying down in his bed, stood up and waved to Sadie. Hannah said, "They won't flip out. They'll think it's funny. Ha, Ha. Nathan predicted this would happen because you're late to everything."

"We didn't see you in the cafeteria and figured you were skipping lunch," Sadie said, giving Logan an empathetic look, "We grabbed some sandwiches, grapes and cookies for you." She handed them to Logan.

"Here's some milk to wash it down," Hannah said holding up her bag.

George jumped up and grabbed the bag from Logan. He quickly set it down on his bed and opened it up. He threw Logan and Andrew wrapped sandwiches and unwrapped his own. He was so hungry that he didn't care what kind he ate. He took a big bite and said to the girls with his mouth full, "Thanks so much. I didn't think I would make it to dinner," he swallowed, "Granola bars just won't cut it."

"Why were you guys late?" Sadie asked.

Logan shook his head, "I really don't know. My alarm went off and when we were trying to get Andrew up, we saw everyone already outside heading to the Pep Rally. I set my alarm for 8:00 and that should have given us an hour to get there. Then we got locked in the bathroom and had to wait for the cleaning staff to unlock it."

They looked at Logan's digital clock and it read 11:15. Hannah took her phone out and held it up, "No wonder. It's actually 12:30. Your clock is wrong," she looked at Andrew, "Didn't you set the alarm on your phone? That is the only thing that wakes you up."

George looked down at his phone still plugged into the charger, "Mine is dead."

Andrew grabbed his phone, "So is mine and I made sure I plugged it in last night."

Hannah walked over to Andrew. She followed the charger cord and held up the end that plugs into the wall, "Maybe you should think about plugging it into a power source. It charges better that way," she said sarcastically.

George leaned over and held his up, "Mines unplugged too. That's weird. I never unplug it."

The boys finished all the food that Sadie and Hannah brought. Logan smiled at Sadie and said, "Thanks for bringing us lunch," she returned his smile.

They were interrupted by another loud knock on the door. Logan walked over and opened it. Standing outside was Mr. McKinney, Brody Stewart, the student body president, Mr. Flynn, the floor leader and Mrs. LaSalle, Assistant Principal in charge of school enforcement and discipline. "Mr. Garrison. May we please come in?" Mrs. LaSalle asked.

"Yeah sure," Logan said a little confused.

The four walked into the room and Mrs. LaSalle looked at Sadie and Hannah, "Miss Ward and Miss Hudson. Would you mind leaving us alone with these three?"

"S-sure," Hannah said looking at her brother. Sadie nodded.

As they left the room, Mr. McKinney shut the door and turned around crossing his arms. Logan, George and Andrew saw the serious looks on all four of their faces. Logan knew that there was something a little more serious than being late for the pep rally they wanted to talk to them about.

Mrs. LaSalle held up a phone and asked, "Do any of you know who this phone belongs to?"

Logan held up his hand and said, "It's mine. Where'd you find it?"

No one answered his question. Mr. McKinney turned around and opened the door, "Gentlemen, we need you to wait in the lounge with Mr. Flynn. We need to search your room."

Andrew held up his hands and said, "Hold on here. I'm pretty sure that's an invasion of our privacy."

Mrs. LaSalle shook her head, "Yes, it is. Under the School's Code of Conduct, if there is evidence of a crime, we have every right to conduct a search of personal property. You were to read the rules and regulations of the school before you arrived. We have on file the document signed by your parents and yourselves stating that you read everything and agree to it."

Logan said, "I remember reading and signing it."

"You actually read it?" George asked.

"Yes, I did," Logan, answered. He looked at Mrs. LaSalle and asked, "What crime has been committed?"

"All I can tell you is your phone was found where it shouldn't have been," Mrs. LaSalle said, "Now, if you wouldn't mind leaving, we can get on with this."

The boys left with regret and followed Mr. Flynn to the freshmen boys lounge. As they were entering the lounge, Logan looked up and saw Milo leaning against the doorframe of his room with a satisfying smirk on his face. Logan asked himself, could *this day get any worse?*

Logan was escorted into Mrs. LaSalle's office by one of the school secretaries. Andrew was asked to go with Mr. McKinney and George was in the boardroom by himself. Logan knew that they were in serious trouble. He couldn't imagine what they had done to be here. He knew his phone was involved so he sat in the chair across from Mrs. LaSalle's desk, trying to recall when he last saw his phone and when he noticed it was gone. The door opened quickly and the voices behind him broke his train of thought. He stood up and turned around to see Mrs. LaSalle, Mr. McKinney and Brody Stewart come in. Brody was carrying a large bag that he carefully laid on Mrs. LaSalle's desk. She walked around and took a seat and pointing to Logan's chair and said. "Have a seat Mr. Garrison." He took his seat at the same time Mr. McKinney sat in the chair next to him. Brody stood behind Mrs. LaSalle and leaned against her filing cabinet. They were all very serious.

Mrs. LaSalle was the first to speak, "Do you have any idea why you are here, Mr. Garrison?" He shook his head, no. She continued, "So you can't think of any reason why we may have your phone or what we may have found in your room?"

Logan's voice cracked, "No ma'am. I'm very confused about everything."

Mr. McKinney was the next to talk, "We are going to ask you some questions and just so you know, we will ask your roommates the same questions. We want to see if your stories match each other. We will be recording this. Do you understand?"

Logan nodded his head telling them he understood. Mr. McKinney opened his tablet and pushed a few buttons. He then gave the date, time and who was present in the room. "For the record, that was yes. First question," he paused and looked at the sheet of paper in front of him. Logan could see several handwritten questions on it, "Mr. Garrison. Please tell us why you were late for the pep rally this morning?"

He looked at Mrs. LaSalle and Brody. Then he looked at Mr. McKinney and grimly started talking, "Um. We woke up late and when we ran to the showers, we got locked in the bathroom from the outside."

Mrs. LaSalle sat back in her chair and asked, "You are telling me that between the three of you, you don't have an alarm clock?"

"Well, ma'am. We all do." Logan looked at her, "I set my alarm on my bedside clock last night for 7:00 this morning."

"Did it not go off?" Mr. McKinney asked.

"Yes, it did but we just discovered that the time on my clock was wrong," Logan could feel sweat starting to bead on his back.

Brody stood up and said, "I actually saw that it was about one hour and 15 minutes behind when we were searching their room," he asked Logan, "How have you been able to make it to breakfast the last few days? I know I've seen you in the cafeteria."

"I don't know what happened," Logan looked at Brody, "I set my clock with the time on my phone when I moved in and it has been right until this morning."

"Really?" Mr. McKinney said as he wrote something on a writing tablet, "Don't your roommates have an alarm?"

"Yes," Logan said. He explained, "We all use the alarms on our cell phones but since I lost mine, I set my alarm clock. I remember watching both George and Andrew set their alarms on their phones."

"And why didn't their alarms go off?" asked Mrs. LaSalle.

"Both of their phones were dead," Logan answered.

"Both?" Mr. McKinney exclaimed, "That's very convenient."

Logan wasn't sure what he meant by that. He added, "Yeah. We usually charge our phones at night because by the end of the day, we are down to one bar. Both George and Andrew had plugged their phones into their chargers but didn't realize that they weren't plugged into the wall."

Mrs. LaSalle looked confused, "I really don't understand what this means."

Brody held up his hand, "Let me explain. If you look at the kids around here, most have their cell phones are in their hands or pockets. Our phones are always on and we are using them to check social media and texting our friends. This drains our phones pretty quickly so at night we plug our phones in, usually next to our beds in case we get a text or a notification. I know from my own experience, it's just easier to leave the phone charger plugged in the wall so all we have to do is plug the phone in and it's charging. I can see how the phones would be dead by morning if they weren't plugged in."

Mrs. LaSalle smiled at Brody and said. "Thank you for the clarification Mr. Stewart."

"Okay," Mr. McKinney said, "You three woke up late. Then what happened?"

"We decided we needed showers so we quickly got into the shower room," Logan said, "When we finished, we went to leave and the door was locked."

Mr. McKinney mumbled. "Umm. Interesting."

Logan continued, "We yelled and pounded on the door for like, five minutes before one of the cleaning staff unlocked it. Then we got dressed and ran to the football stadium."

"You didn't make any other stops between your room and the stadium?" Mrs. LaSalle asked.

Logan knew there was something more to this question. He just shook his head, no.

Mr. McKinney stood up and stretched his back. He walked around the desk and stood on the other side of Mrs. LaSalle. He looked at Logan, "You said you lost your phone. Do you remember when and where you lost it?"

"The last time I saw it was yesterday afternoon when we went to the lake. I put my phone and room keys in my shoe and put my towel over it. When we came back from swimming in the lake, I dried myself off. I was going to check the time and that's when I noticed my phone was gone. I couldn't find my keys either"

Brody interrupted, "Your keys are under your bed. I saw them there."

Logan couldn't imagine why they were there.

"Did you see anyone suspicious around your things?" Mrs. LaSalle asked.

"No. There were a lot of people on the beach. Most of the students from the school put their stuff in that area," Logan added.

Mrs. LaSalle picked up her desk phone and punched a button on it, "Hello Millie. Could you please bring me a copy of the list of students who went to Lake Texoma yesterday? Thank you."

Mrs. LaSalle looked at Brody and Mr. McKinney, "Are there any more questions regarding the phone or the where about, this morning, of the three students in question?" Both said no. She stood up and began to open the bag that was on her desk. Logan saw her take out his dad's Guthrie High School Blue Jays cap. Then she took out a familiar jacket. Logan sat up and said, "Hey! That's my dad's lettermen's jacket."

"So, you admit this belongs to you," Mr. McKinney asked.

"Yes. And that's my dad's ball cap from home," Logan was a little angry seeing they had taken his prize possessions. Mr. McKinney nodded to Brody. He nodded back and walked to the door. He opened the door and signaled for someone to come in. Logan noticed the man who walked in was around 40 and was wearing a 'Nice N' Clean' green shirt that all the cleaning staff wore. He didn't recognize this housekeeper.

Mrs. LaSalle smiled at the man, "Hi Monty. Please look at these articles of clothing." She gave him a few seconds to look them over, "Do you recognize them?"

"Yes ma'am," he said, "He was wearing them when he went up to lounge."

Logan stood up, "What? Who was wearing them?"

"Calm down Mr. Garrison," Mr. McKinney said putting his hand on his shoulder. He looked at Monty, "Do you recognize this student Monty?"

Monty looked up at him and shook his head, "I'm not sure. I didn't really see his face," he looked closer at Logan, "This guy seems taller than the guy I saw but I'm really not sure."

"Thank you, Monty. We may have some other questions to ask you so please don't go too far," Mrs. LaSalle said.

Mrs. LaSalle looked sternly at Logan, "Please take a seat Mr. Garrison," she reached into the pocket of the jacket. Logan saw that she pulled out something silver. She handed it to him, "Do you know what this is?"

Logan took it from her and saw that it was a silver frame surrounding something. He looked closer at it a saw that it was a stamp. He looked at her and said, "Yeah. This is the Centenary Stamp. My school in Guthrie got one of these to celebrate the state's centennial."

Mr. McKinney took the frame away from him, "Do you think they are valuable?"

"Yes probably," Logan was getting overwhelmed with everything that was happening to him, "Why do you have my stuff?"

"That will be all Mr. Garrison," Mrs. LaSalle said, "Mr. Flynn will escort you back to your room where you will stay. The only time you can leave your room is to take a bathroom break but you are not to talk to anyone. Do you understand?" Logan nodded his head, yes, "We will have your dinner delivered to you."

Logan started to figure out what was going on, "How long do I have to be under house arrest?"

Mr. McKinney said, "We have to interview Mr. Rose and Mr. Ward first. It might not be until tomorrow morning that we talk to you again."

Logan was angry now. He was starting to put two and two together but decided not to say anything until he could think more about it. He followed Mr. Flynn out of the office without looking at anyone.

Chapter 45

Logan was typing on his computer when George came in. He walked over to his bed and threw himself on it. "This has got to be the single worst day of my life. I can't believe we got grilled for being late to a stupid pep rally," George pulled the covers on his unmade bed up to his armpits. He closed his eyes and said, "I'm sleeping until school starts."

"There is more to this than just being late to the pep rally," Logan said reading the e-mail he just typed.

George opened his eyes, "What are you talking about?"

"Let's wait until Andrew gets here. I'm curious to hear what you guys said to them. I have a theory," Logan said.

George rolled over and said, "Wake me when he gets here."

Andrew walked in at the same time the boys' dinner arrived. He grabbed a breadstick from the tray and took a big bite. He said with his mouth full, "That was bullshit. What did they say to you?"

George woke up when he heard Andrew's voice. He sat up in bed and rubbed his eyes. George said, "They asked me why we were late this morning and were very interested in why our alarms didn't go off."

They sat at their desk each with a tray of food. George, who was always hungry, dove into his food. They spent a few minutes eating and then Logan sat back in his chair. He had finished his salad and picked up one of his two pizza slices. He took a bite and waved the slice in the air. "I have a theory about what happened. I don't have all the details but I have enough to figure out that we, well actually I, am being framed."

His roommates stopped eating. Andrew exclaimed, "Framed! Why do you think that?"

George piped in, "Yeah. Remember Mrs. LaSalle said that Logan's phone, which went missing at the lake, was in a place it shouldn't have been."

"That's right," Logan said, "What you guys don't know is my dad's lettermen jacket and ball cap were used to steal this valuable stamp from somewhere."

"Uh?" they both said in unison.

Logan explained further, "They brought one of the housekeepers in and he said that he saw a guy wearing my dad's jacket and ball cap going up to some lounge."

Andrew sat up and said, "The only lounge around here that you go up to is the senior's penthouse."

"What d'ya mean?" George asked.

"The senior's lounge is on the roof. You have to go through a door with a combination lock and then up some stairs," Andrew sat back.

"How do ya know that?" George wasn't sure if he believed him.

"My brother and his friends were dared to go there when they were freshmen. They didn't know there was a lock on it," Andrew smiled, "They got caught on the senior's floor and they made them clean the senior's bathrooms."

Logan was half listening to the banter between his two roommates. He said, "Whoever had the jacket on went there and must have had the combination to the door. I think he stole a framed Centenary Stamp from the lounge and put it in the pocket of my jacket." Logan turned to his computer and started typing.

"They must have planted your phone in there so it would be obvious who was in there," Andrew stood up.

"So, your phone and keys were obviously taken at the lake." George said to Logan.

Logan stopped typing and said, "My keys showed up under my bed. Of course, whoever had taken them needed to get into our room to use my clothes to make it look like I was the one going into the lounge. They took the stamp and left it in the pocket of the jacket. It was back hanging up in my closet when our room was searched." He ran his fingers through his dark hair, "So all of this must have happened while we were at the pep rally."

"Bet I can guess who changed your clock and unplugged our chargers," Andrew said.

"The same guy who locked us in the bathroom," George said picking up his basketball and hugging it.

They heard a knock. They all looked at the door but the knock didn't sound like it came from there. They sat quietly and listened. There was a second knock that came from behind them. George pointed at the window and said, "There. It came from there."

All three got up and looked out the window. Logan opened the window and saw Sadie and Hannah crouched between the window and a bush. Logan said, "What are you girls doing here? We're off limits so you better go before you get in trouble too."

Sadie whispered, "We were going crazy. What is going on?"

"Yeah. When we didn't see you at dinner, we knew something bad happened to you," Hannah added.

The boys gave them the condensed version of what happened and then told them their theories. Sadie stood up and anger crossed her face. She said. "I know exactly who it is."

"Who?" All of them asked.

"It was Dix," Sadie said, "He has done this before in Tulsa. He got a guy on our tennis team kicked off because we had been flirting with each other. He framed him too."

"He wasn't at the lake and that's when Logan's phone went missing," George said.

"He wasn't, but his goon friends were," Hannah said, "I saw them playing football on the beach and they were messing up everyone's towels and stuff."

"I'm going to Mr. McKinney," said Sadie.

Logan's blue eyes opened wide, "You can't. Not right now."

"Why not?" Sadie asked.

"I'm writing an e-mail to him presenting evidence that we couldn't have done it," Logan said, "I don't want to get you involved if I don't have to."

"He's got to know," Sadie almost shouted at him, "Dix can't get away with this one like he did with the other guy. He was pretty smart to cover his tracks but we all knew who was behind it."

"All they have to do is look at the security footage," Hannah pointed out.

"They have cameras?" Andrew looked worried.

"Yeah," Hannah answered, "Those little black ball things in the corners on the ceiling monitor all the hallways. When I was a freshman, there were things like computers and stuff that went missing. People even complained that someone was stealing their food. The school secretly installed those cameras and caught the guy right away."

"Who was it?" asked Andrew.

"I can't remember his name, but he had insomnia," explained Hannah, " He would wander the halls at night. He would go up and down on all floors and check to see which room doors were unlocked. He would walk in and take things while people were sleeping."

"That's pretty ballsy to steal things right under people's noses," George said shaking his head.

Hannah continued, "When they searched his room, they found all sorts of stuff. He was even stealing utensils from the cafeteria. He was a, what do you call those people who steal things all the time?

"A Kleptomaniac," both Logan and Sadie answered.

"That's why they are drilling it into us to lock our doors and to leave valuable things at home," Andrew said.

"Makes sense," Logan said. He had been very quiet during the conversation. He got a big smile on his face and said, "We have nothing to worry about boys. They will have on tape the guy locking us in the bathroom and who ever came into our rooms." he looked at Sadie, "See. You don't have to tell Mr. McKinney. I'm sure he has figured it out already."

Chapter 46

Sunday, the last day before the first day of school, started out slowly. All of the student body had been up late the night before watching a double feature out on the lawn. Everyone, that is, except four freshmen boys. Milo was still banned from participating in the school's welcome week activities and the three roommates were confined to their room for the night. The students brought blankets, towels and pillows to put down on the lawn to watch the movie on the outdoor inflatable screen. Popcorn, soda and ice cream bars where provided for the students to snack on.

Students were making their way to the cafeteria for Sunday brunch. Those who liked to sleep in could get food anytime between 8:00 and 1:00 on Sundays. Usually they had to have breakfast eaten by 9:00 on Saturday and 7:00 on school days. School started at 8:00 a.m. and lunch was served between 11:50 to 12:50. School continued in the afternoon at 1:00 and went until 3:20. After school snacks were provided for those who had activities starting at 4:00. Dinner was served from 6:00 to 7:00. Students were then let back into the cafeteria at 7:30 to study or work on group projects. Campus curfew was 9:00 p.m. and all students were to be in their rooms for a head count at 9:15. The floor leader and two student leaders would go room to room to make sure everyone was accounted for. The only time students could leave their rooms after curfew would be to use the bathroom facilities.

The last day of welcome week was South Eastern Academy's Mini House Olympics. In a small ceremony, each student would find out which of the six houses they would be in for that year. At the end of the previous school year, the students research and submit potential house names for the next year. They are given a topic, predetermined by the Headmaster, and have a week to submit one name and reasons why their choice is a good house name. A committee made up of the Headmaster, staff and students would read each submission and debate the top six names. Nothing would be revealed until just before the Mini-Olympics. Each student would be placed in a house, given a t-shirt with their house colors and as a group, vote a senior student as house president. A house logo would be quickly designed to go on their banner.

The topic for the houses was 'Influential People in Science and Technology.' They had numerous submissions making the top six a very hard decision.

From 2:00–4:00, the students would participate in 16 fun, competitive activities like an obstacle course, scavenger hunt, trivia, watermelon eating contest and the popular raft race. Each student on the team would have to compete in at least two activities. The house with the most points at the end of the day would be treated to a barbeque rib dinner while everyone else would have hot dogs and hamburgers. The house banner would then be displayed in the cafeteria. Competitions like this happened throughout the school year and winners of each competition would have their banner hanging from the roof of the cafeteria for the year. At the end of the year, the house that had the most banners hung, would win the house trophy. This was to promote friendly competition amongst the students and give an opportunity for the students to meet and interact with students from other grades.

Logan woke up at 8:00 and was showered and dressed by the time his roommates started waking up. While he was in the shower, two of his basketball buddies had started questioning him about why they had missed dinner and the movie. They hadn't seen the sign on their door stating that their room was under in-house detention and no one was to bother them. Logan just told them that there was some kind of misunderstanding that they were working out.

At 9:00 Mr. Flynn came in with one breakfast tray. George was awake so Logan went over and woke Andrew up. Mr. Flynn explained that Logan was still under investigation but George and Andrew where cleared of any wrongdoing. They were free to go to the cafeteria and have breakfast. They were also allowed to participate in the Mini House Olympics. Mr. Flynn looked at Logan and said. "Eat up Mr. Garrison. Someone will be here in about 20 minutes to escort you to the headmaster's office."

Logan lost his appetite when he heard the headmaster was getting involved. He just drank the juice that was on the tray.

"Do you want those eggs?" George asked. He had noticed Logan pushing the tray away.

Logan took the tray over to George and said, "Eat anything you want. I don't want to throw up on the headmaster when he tells me I'm kicked out of school."

"They're not going to kick you out," Andrew tried to reassure his friend.

"Then why didn't I get cleared too?" Logan pointed out, "They must think I had something to do with this."

The door opened and Mr. McKinney came in, "Let's get going Mr. Garrison please."

Logan put his hands in his pockets and shook his head. He turned to his friends and said. "Bye guys," like he was never going to see them again.

Logan and Mr. McKinney walked quickly but silently to the administration building. As they walked in, Mr. McKinney said, "I read your e-mail and you made some pretty substantial points. I appreciate that you took it upon yourself to defend yourself and particularly your friends. That is the reason they are exonerated."

They were walking down to the end of the hall when someone called out from behind them. "Mr. McKinney!" both stopped and saw Sadie running after them. She was panting when she reached them. She said, "I just saw George and he told me that you were going to the headmaster's office. Please, may I talk to you Mr. McKinney before you go in?"

"What is this about Miss Hudson?" he asked her. Logan was shaking his head telling her to stop. He didn't want her to get involved.

"Logan is innocent and I am pretty sure I know who did it," she said.

"Come with us, please Miss Hudson," Mr. McKinney said.

Logan rolled his eyes but Sadie just ignored him.

They got to headmaster Woodward's office. His secretary said that he was just with someone and asked the students to take a seat. Mr. McKinney excused himself and said he just needed to get things set up.

After he left, Logan looked at Sadie, "What are you doing? I don't want you to get involved. You may have something happen to you for being an informant."

Sadie started to chuckle, "Informant? You make it sound like we are dealing with the mob."

Logan gave her a half smile and said, "You know what I mean. It's not that I don't appreciate it."

Sadie looked at him sternly and said, "Look. If I hadn't asked you to take me to the dance, then Dix wouldn't have gotten jealous and wanted to frame you."

"True. It's all your fault," was all Logan said smiling.

Sadie's mouth opened and she shoved him with her shoulder. That was not the answer she expected to get from him. She was about to say something when the door to headmaster Woodward's office opened. Both kids stood and Logan wiped his sweaty hands on his pants. Coming out of the office first was Kristy with the headmaster following. Logan moaned and Sadie looked at him. Logan knew he was going home because his mother was here to take him. The headmaster went over to talk to his secretary. Kristy smiled at her son and said, "I didn't think I would be visiting so soon."

"Sorry Mom. I didn't know you were coming," was all Logan could think of saying.

"Mom?" Sadie knew now why he moaned.

"Yup," he pointed at Sadie and said, "Mom, this is Sadie Hudson," he then pointed to his mother, "Sadie, this is my mom, Kristy Garrison."

"Sadie?" His mother realized this was Logan's date to the dance, "Well, it's very nice to meet you."

"Hi Mrs. Garrison," Sadie replied, "It's nice to meet you too."

"I should tell you that you looked so lovely the night of the dance. Logan sent me pictures of the two of you," she started to go on but Logan saw that headmaster Woodward was walking over.

"Mom!" Logan said under his breath. He was so embarrassed she had said those things to Sadie. He looked behind his mom and said, "Hello sir."

The headmaster held out his hand and Logan shook it. Headmaster Woodward then held his hand out to Sadie, "Miss Hudson," she smiled and took his hand. He then continued, "Mr. McKinney would like for us to come to the board room if you don't mind. That includes you Miss Hudson."

They all walked out in silence. They followed the headmaster to the boardroom and saw Mr. McKinney, Mrs. LaSalle and Brody Stewart already sitting at the table. There was a large projection screen set up with a recording device sitting in the middle of the table.

Mr. McKinney stood up and pushed the record button. He stated the date, time and named each person in the room. After a brief pause, he began speaking. He said, "At this time, Miss Sadie Hudson has come to me stating that Mr. Garrison is innocent," he looked at Sadie, "Miss Hudson, please stand up and tell us your thoughts."

Sadie stood up and in a confident voice said, "Thank you for giving me a chance to speak. I know for a fact that Logan Garrison is innocent. I've only known him for a few days but I am a good judge of character and I think he is someone who would not do something like this."

Mrs. LaSalle interrupted, "Other than your opinion of Mr. Garrison's character, do you have any proof that he is innocent Miss Hudson?"

This rattled Sadie a little bit, "No but I think I know who did do it," she saw Mrs. LaSalle's eyebrows go up, "I believe that Dix, I mean Milo Dixon did this to frame Logan."

Kristy turned to Logan when she recognized the name. Logan just nodded his head like he was reading her mind.

"That is a pretty serious accusation Miss Hudson. Please continue," Mrs. LaSalle said.

"Milo belongs to the same country club as my family. He has made it very clear that he has had a crush on me for the last two years. He has done this before to a boy who was interested in me. He got him kicked off the tennis team," Sadie said sadly.

"How do you know it was him?" Mrs. LaSalle asked.

Sadie was beginning to get annoyed by Mrs. LaSalle's remarks. She took a breath and calmed herself down, "He bragged about it to a friend of mine. My friend told me but there is no proof that he did it."

Mrs. LaSalle started to sound like a courthouse Judge, "That is just hear-say Miss Hudson. That really isn't proof enough."

"Maybe not, but I think Logan was targeted by Milo when I asked Logan to take me to the dance. He has even gone so far as stalk me back in Tulsa," Sadie told everyone.

Before Mrs. LaSalle could speak, Mr. McKinney piped in, "I can attest to that. Mr. and Mrs. Hudson came to me when they brought Sadie down, and told me of the situation with Mr. Dixon. They were concerned that it would continue here at South Eastern."

"Is that the freshman quarterback?" Brody asked.

"Yes," Sadie answered.

"I've heard him talking about a girl in the locker room and it was pretty disrespectful. I assume it's you?" Brody said.

"He was upset that I wouldn't go to the dance with him when he asked. I told him to stay away from me and my friends," Sadie looked at her hands.

"Thank you, Miss Hudson. Please take a seat. Now Mr. Garrison just so you know, your mother got here about 45 minutes ago. I called her last night and asked her to drive down. We have brought her up to speed at what has transpired here over the last 24 hours," Mr. McKinney said, "Now, we have a few more people that need to join us before we continue."

Headmaster Woodward had been sitting quietly listening to what Sadie had to say and to the questions being asked. He looked at Logan and said, "Mr. Garrison. You have a pretty good friend here," he pointed to Sadie, "Miss Hudson has taken a risk coming to us with really no proof but a gut feeling."

"Yes, sir I know," Logan responded.

Headmaster Woodward continued, "This is the first time I have met you but I know of you and of your reputation. The scholarship you have won is very prestigious and the person who wins it must show incredible character. You have absolutely no motive to do the things you are accused of and I will go on record and say that I believe you are innocent."

"Thank you, sir," Logan let out a breath of relief.

"But," Logan didn't like the sound of this, "The proof we have so far still makes you look guilty, unless we can prove otherwise."

There was a knock at the door. Brody, who was sitting closest to it, got up and opened it. Mrs. Hunter, the school secretary was there with two other people. She smiled at them and stepped aside so they could go in. Kristy stood up when she saw who it was. She said out loud, "Laura!"

Laura Dixon came in and stopped when she heard her name. She was a little confused, "Kristy? What are you doing here?" She then looked at the boy sitting next to her. She recognized those aqua-blue eyes, "Logan?"

Kristy could tell that Laura had been crying. She went over to her and gave her a hug. Laura held on to her tightly and with tears running down her cheeks. Kristy looked behind her and thought she was looking at Jason Dixon. Milo was the spitting image of his father. Milo was a few inches shorter than her but he was stocky.

Laura pulled away and wiped her tears with the tissue she was holding. She wiped her nose and tried to smile at the headmaster, "I'm so sorry sir. I haven't been able to stop crying since I got called last night from Mr. McKinney." She looked at Milo and squinted her eyes at him, "I thought those calls would be over once he got here. He promised me he would be on his best behavior." She started to cry again, "School hasn't even started and I have to come down and hear about trouble you are causing."

"Momma. I told you I was innocent," he said with defiance.

"Mrs. Dixon, please take a seat over here," Mr. McKinney said pulling out a chair next to him, "Mr. Dixon, please take a seat beside your mother."

Laura sat down and saw Sadie sitting across from her and whispered, "Is he harassing you again?"

Mr. McKinney stood up before she could answer and said, "Mr. Dixon, do you know why you are here?"

"No. I don't," he snarled.

"It has been brought to our attention that you may have tried to frame Mr. Garrison and make it look like he ransacked the senior boy's lounge and stole something from there," Mr. McKinney said to him.

"I don't know what you are talking about," Milo sat up straight. He looked at Sadie and said, "Did she say I did it? I think she has a grudge against me."

Mr. McKinney ignored this accusation, "Let me tell you what happened. Mr. Garrison is a suspect. A witness saw someone wearing a letterman's jacket belonging to Mr. Garrison as well as a Guthrie High School ball cap. This person, wearing the cap and jacket, went up to the senior's lounge. The witness did not see his face but identified the jacket we found in Mr. Garrison's closet. Inside the jacket pocket was the missing item from the lounge. Mr. Garrison's phone was conveniently found in the lounge," Mr. McKinney paused to see if Milo gave any kind of reaction. Of course, Milo didn't flinch, "Mr. Garrison was late for the pep rally making it look like he had the time to commit the crime he is accused of. Of course, Mr. Garrison says he is innocent and has made some very good points to back up his statement of innocence. For one, he has witnesses, including Miss Hudson, stating he lost his cell phone and room keys at the lake. Also, he and his roommates were locked in the shower room causing them to be late for the pep rally."

Milo interrupted, "Well, right there I couldn't have done it. I was working off another punishment in the library on Friday. Instead of being at the pep rally, I was again in the library. Mrs. Churchwood is my witness."

"We are very aware of this Mr. Dixon," Mr. McKinney held up his hands, "We do know that some of your friends were at the lake and had the opportunity to assist you in this."

"There's no proof Mr. McKinney," Milo said through his gritted teeth.

"Milo!" Laura turned to her son, "Stop being disrespectful."

"They are accusing me of something I didn't do!" Milo almost yelled at his mother.

"Enough of this," Mrs. LaSalle said, "Mr. McKinney, please just show the security tape."

Mr. McKinney pushed some keys on his computer and a picture came up on the projector screen. Brody got up and turned out the lights. Mr. McKinney said to Milo. "Mr. Dixon. Are you aware that there are security cameras all over the campus including the dorm hallways?"

Milo shook his head, no. He didn't even think that there were cameras on the school grounds. He now realized he might be busted unless he can dispute what the cameras showed. Sometimes, the pictures on security tapes are poor.

On screen was the security tape from the day before. Brody, who was in the multi-media club, was up most of the night splicing together the different security footage from the different security cameras around campus. The footage they were watching shows Milo leaving his room sneaking around the hall. Next, Andrew, Logan and George rushed out of their room in bath towels, heading towards the shower. Logan slumped in his chair embarrassed by this scene. He knew Mrs. LaSalle, Laura, his mother and most importantly, Sadie saw him in his bath towel barely covering his privates.

Milo ran down the hall and around the corner. It clearly showed Milo as the person locking the bathroom door where the boys were showering. Milo walked quickly out of the front door. The next shot was taken from the cafeteria camera. The cafeteria was empty of students except for Milo. He talked with the cafeteria staff and was given food, which he started to eat as he walked out the door. He checked his watch as he ate a cinnamon bun and walked up the library steps and through the doors. The next scene shows Milo walking back out of the library approximately three minutes later. Mr. McKinney, the school's environmentalist cringed when he saw Milo throw his milk container on the ground. Next, the footage showed Milo running, very quickly to the boy's dorm. The three roommates were then seen running down the hall towards the exit with George stopping to lock their room door. Milo immediately emerged from his room wearing a letterman's jacket and ball cap. Laura turned and gave Milo a scorching look.

Milo held up his hand and Mr. McKinney paused the footage. Milo said, "You can't tell that's me. It could be anyone coming out in that jacket. It could be one of my roommates."

Brody got up and walked over to the projection screen. He pointed to the person's left wrist. He said, "I believe that is your watch Milo," the picture showed a very large round watch with a leather strap.

Laura didn't say a word but reached over and grabbed Milo's left hand. She lifted it up and pointed to the watch.

Mr. McKinney clicked the play button. Milo walked toward the front door but instead of going out the front door he turned and headed up the main stairs. Another camera switch showed Milo arriving on the fourth floor. The camera also showed the housekeeper who was a witness, cleaning the hallway. Milo walked in the opposite direction from the housekeeper. He emerged from the other side and went straight to the locked door. The housekeeper looked in his direction but Milo had pulled the cap down low and stood with his back to the housekeeper. Milo punched a code in the combination and was able to open the door on the first try. There are no security cameras in the senior's lounge but the time on the next footage showed Milo emerging from the lounge three minutes and 24 seconds later with his hand in the pocket. He walked quickly down to the stairs.

Back in the south hallway, Milo is seen entering Logan's room with a room key. Thirty-six seconds later, he came out of the room. He was not wearing the jacket or ball cap. Milo checked his watch and smiled as he ran down the hall and out the door. Brody decided he didn't need to include the footage of Milo going back into the library. The lights came on and everyone looked at Milo. Milo looked down at his hands with an angry look on his face. He would have had the perfect plan if there weren't security cameras.

Headmaster Woodward stood up. He walked over to Logan who stood up as well, "Mr. Garrison. On behalf of everyone here, we would like to apologize for what you have had to go through the past 24 hours. Please know that we take these things very seriously."

"I understand sir," Logan smiled relieved he was proven innocent.

"Now," Headmaster Woodward said, "This is your last day before classes start. Please go out and enjoy it. Good luck in the Mini House Olympics this afternoon," he looked at Sadie, "You too Miss Hudson."

"Thank you, sir," they said together.

Mrs. LaSalle stood up as well, "We appreciate that you drove down here Mrs. Garrison. If Mr. McKinney and Mr. Stewart had told me about the security footage, I would have not asked you to come," she looked at Mr. McKinney and raised her left eyebrow.

He chuckled, "We wanted to make sure the timeline was accurate before we told anyone about our findings. Unfortunately, we didn't finish until after you starting driving down here. My apologies Mrs. Garrison."

"Please don't worry," Kristy smiled at him, "It's only a two hour drive and I have been missing my son. It's nice to see him."

"We hope you can stay for the Mini House Olympics as our guest," Headmaster Woodward said, "I promise we won't make you eat hot dogs. I hope the two of you will join me at the barbeque rib dinner?"

"We would be happy to. I appreciate all that you have done for my son," Kristy said. Brody held the door open and Kristy, Sadie and Logan began to walk out.

"Kristy!" Laura got up and ran over to her, "Can I talk to you after please?"

"Of course, Laura," Kristy could see the anguish in her eyes, "Do you still have my cell phone number?"

"Yes. I'll phone you and maybe we can meet somewhere," Laura said. She turned to Logan and continued, "Logan, I'm so sorry this happened to you." She looked over her shoulder at Milo who caught her gaze, "You two used to be such good friends."

Logan looked at his feet and mumbled, "Yeah we were," he looked back up at her and could see fresh tears in her eyes.

Laura looked at Kristy, "We should never have moved to Tulsa. It changed both of us for the worse. I have never been happy there. Not like I was in Guthrie."

Kristy smiled at her and rubbed her arm, "We'll talk about this later."

Chapter 47

Kristy was sitting in the stands of the football stadium watching, with great interest, the announcement of the house names. Sitting next to her were Logan and Sadie. The house ceremony had just begun when they arrived and seating was limited. The six most voted on Science and Technology innovators were Steve Jobs, Benjamin Franklin, Mary Anderson, Henry Ford, Elizabeth Blackwell and Thomas Edison. So, the six house names were Anderson, Blackwell, Edison, Ford, Franklin and Jobs.

Six teachers had volunteered to be the staff representative for each house. They each got up and read the names of the students in each house. As each student's name was called, they gathered in a designated spot on the field. Sadie heard her name called and stood in the Blackwell House area. That made her happy because she had submitted Elizabeth Blackwell's name. She admired her because she was the first woman to receive a PhD in America. *What a wonderful role model*, Sadie thought to herself.

Andrew was also called to the Blackwell House. Logan secretly wished he was called to Blackwell too. "Sadie is very pretty. Is she as nice as she seems?" Kristy whispered to her son. She saw him watching her go down to the field.

Startled, Logan said, "What?" Kristy's eyebrows went up and Logan knew she read his mind, "Yeah. She isn't like a lot of girls. You know the kind that giggle a lot and look at you weird. She is not fake and is very honest."

George came over and sat with Logan and Kristy, "What happened dude?" He asked Logan. He then saw Kristy and said, "Hey Mrs. Garrison. Is this guy in trouble?" He gave Logan a slap on the back.

"Hi George," Kristy chuckled at him, "Everything's good. Logan can fill you in later. By the way, we missed the first part of the ceremony. Can you tell me who Mary Anderson is?"

"Yeah sure," George said, "She invented something very insignificant but very important," George paused to see if they would guess.

"Just tell us," Logan laughed.

"She invented the windshield wiper," George smiled at his friend, "Can you imagine what it would be like to drive without one?"

They were announcing the members of the Franklin House when Logan heard his name. He gave his mom a hug and said, "Thanks Mom. I'll see you later, okay?"

She squeezed back, "It's so nice to see you sweetheart. I will be here all day so just text me when you have a chance. Let me know what events you are in so I can come and watch."

Logan quickly said, "I'll have to use George's phone. They didn't give me back my phone," he waved and turned. Kristy watched as her tall, handsome son ran out on to the field.

More names were announced followed by "George Rose." He jumped and said, "Cool. We're both in Franklin House. See ya Mrs. G," Kristy shook her head and waved as George ran out on the field. She saw Logan and George give each other a high five.

After the last name was called, each house and its members left to spend the next hour designing and creating their banner. House colors were pre-determined so t-shirts could be made up. They were also voting on a senior student to be the house rep. The Mini-Olympics were starting in an hour and a half so each house had to make sure each member participated in at least two events.

Logan and three other Franklin House members were on the Trivia team. Logan knew a lot about Sports and Science and the others knew Pop Culture, Literature and History. He also was on the rafting team. They had to inflate a raft and then get it across the pool without paddles using as many people as possible. Those students who weighed less where asked to be on the team. Logan was skinny and had long arms so he was perfect. George, who liked to eat, was tall and stocky so he was going to be a cheerleader on the sidelines. George did volunteer to shoot at the basketball basket from designated spots around it. They had two chances to make a basket and if they made it, points were awarded. The further away they shot, the higher the points. The top three houses with the most accumulated points received house points towards their total score. The other event George volunteered for was the watermelon-eating contest. He loved watermelon so it was a no brainer. George would do the eating and another house member would stand behind him, blindfolded, feeding him. They would have two minutes and the team that had the most eaten watermelon with the cleanest rinds, would win.

After each House had left the stadium, Kristy decided to take a walk around campus. She wanted to digest what had happened since she arrived only a few hours ago. The hardest thing to wrap her head around was seeing Laura and Milo again. Laura was not in good shape. That beaten down state reminded Kristy of the first day she met Laura. Laura was literally beaten physically as well as mentally. This time, Kristy didn't see any bruising but could tell that Laura was very unhappy and probably at her breaking point. This wasn't the person she knew eight years ago. Neither was Milo. She couldn't believe his arrogance and disrespectful treatment of his mother. As a five year old, he was so outgoing and loving towards everyone. He was very funny and could bring out the kid in her very serious son. Kristy couldn't imagine what had happened to them in the last eight years to bring on so many negative changes.

Kristy was able to get a cup of coffee from the staff lounge and was about to walk out towards the library building. She heard her phone chime indicating she had a text. She looked at the new text and saw it was from Laura.

Laura: "Can we talk please!"

Kristy: "Meet me on the front steps of the library building in five minutes."

Laura: "Thanks"

Kristy turned around and got another cup of coffee. She remembered that Laura liked one sugar and two creams in her coffee. She was walking up to the library with the two cups when she saw Laura sitting on the top step. Her head was in her hands undoubtedly crying. Kristy shouted up at her, "You look like you could use a cup of coffee."

Laura took her hands away and looked down at Kristy. She got up and ran down the stairs and wrapped her arms around Kristy's neck. Kristy almost dropped one of the cups. Kristy cooed in Laura's ear, "Shhh. You're going to be fine sweetie."

Laura released her hug and stepped back. Laura wiped the tears from her eyes and said, "How did you know I needed coffee?" sniffling, she said, "You don't know what I've gone through in the last eight years."

Kristy handed Laura her coffee, "I don't know what you've been through but I have seen you in worse shape. I know what a strong person you are and what you are capable of." Kristy pointed to a bench in the shade to the right of the building, "Why don't we sit down and you can tell me what happened."

Laura felt better just having Kristy around. Kristy was always so calm and knew what to do in bad situations. Laura said, "Well, to start with, Milo is no longer welcome at South Eastern Academy. I don't know what I'm going to do with him. He caused a lot of trouble at his middle school, even his elementary school." She looked remorsefully at Kristy, "I'm so sorry this happened to Logan. They used to be so close."

"Inseparable," Kristy added.

"Do you know that the year we lived with you was the best year of our lives? Both of us were so happy," Laura smiled at the memory.

"We were happy too," said Kristy, "You really helped me out at just the right time."

"You saved my life," Laura looked down at her coffee, "I'm so sorry I ditched you like that."

"You had your hands tied," said Kristy remembering Laura's Aunt's will, "It was overwhelming for you to live such a different life."

"Was it ever," Laura took a deep drink of coffee, "Mmmm," she closed her eyes, "I haven't had sugar or cream in my coffee for years." she opened her eyes and shook her head, "I drink black coffee because I'm so worried about gaining weight. Those women, who I thought were my friends, criticized me for drinking it with cream and sugar. They were all about looking skinny and perfect. Plastic surgery is very popular amongst them. They almost had me convinced that I needed it."

"What?" Kristy exclaimed, "That is so ridiculous."

"Luckily, I figured that out," Laura took another drink of her coffee finding comfort in it, "They thought I needed Botox because of the worry lines on my forehead and I should get rid of the bags and dark circles under my eyes. They were part of the reason I had bags and dark circles. Oh yeah, they though I needed to get my boobs done because clothes would look a lot better on me if I had curves in the right places," she shook her head, "I'm not even 31 yet."

Kristy started laughing, "That is the silliest thing I've heard of. I can't imagine what they would say about me."

"They can't hold a candle to you," Laura smiled, "You are the prettiest woman I've ever seen with your dark eyes and hair. You are a natural beauty, not a plastic one."

Kristy was a little embarrassed but said, "That's nice of you to say. My dad used to say how much I looked like my mother. She was so beautiful. My mom was half-blood Choctaw."

Laura let out a big sigh, "I think I've calmed down a little bit. Thanks," Kristy smiled at her. Laura continued, "Oh yeah, Milo tested positive for steroids."

"No?" Kristy was stunned, "When did you find out about that?"

"After you left, the football coach came in and told us," Laura looked up to the sky, "He would have been kicked out of school for that too."

"What did Milo say about that?" Kristy asked.

"He didn't say anything to the coach but when we were alone, he told me he started taking them in May to bulk up. He is shorter than the other guys on the team so he thought he needed the extra help," Laura said.

"He must have known that they were going to drug test him at the beginning of the season?" Kristy said.

"He did and he stopped using them two weeks before. Apparently, steroids can stay in your blood stream up to four weeks," Laura was holding back fresh tears, "It explains his aggressive attitude all summer. He was just plain mean at times and I didn't know what to do."

"Where is he now?" Kristy asked looking around.

"He is packing his stuff. I'm going over there soon to make sure it gets done," Laura sniffled, "I just needed to talk to you."

Kristy gave her a hug and Laura released the tears. Laura softly wailed, "I don't know what I'm going to do with him. I'm sure the news will get to Tulsa before we do." she sat back and pulled a tissue from her pocket, "I am humiliated enough as it is, but it will be like standing in front of a firing squad when we get back."

"That seems a little dramatic," Kristy told her honestly.

"You don't know those people" Laura shook her head, "They judge everything you do. If there is any sign of disgrace, they turn their back on you. I spent eight years trying to fit in and never really found my spot."

"It sounded to me you had a lot of friends after you moved," Kristy thought back to that time, "You were always being invited to dinners and lunches. You were on all sorts of committees."

"I was new blood and my Aunt and Uncle had a lot of money. They knew I was rich and wanted me in their exclusive club," Laura rolled her eyes, "I thought I had to go to every function and lunch that I was invited to. I didn't want to rub anyone the wrong way. Then they saw a sucker and roped me into being on all these charity planning committees. That is really hard work."

"I think that is what upset Freddie so much. He felt he didn't fit in with those people and hated being around them," Kristy said.

Laura's frowned, "Oh poor Freddie," she said sympathetically, "I did force him into going to some posh dinners. He saw that we weren't like those people, but I refused to believe it."

"So, you chose your new friends over Freddie," Kristy added.

"Yeah," Laura felt bad, "I see now that he was so right. Those people are such snobs. There isn't one person I would call my friend. Not like my friends in Guthrie. Instead of turning their backs on me if I was in trouble, my Guthrie friends helped with no questions asked. In Tulsa, they loved it when someone else found themselves in trouble. They loved to gossip and you know what?" She looked away, ashamed, "I fell right in with them. It made me feel better to gossip about other people because it took any negative attention away from me. I even lied about my background. I was so afraid of being rejected by them that there was no way I would tell them I actually lived in a trailer and had no money. They thought we owned a ranch in Montana and my husband died in a horse accident. They made me feel so ashamed of even living in Guthrie."

"It sounds like you went through a lot after you moved. I can see why we lost touch," Kristy said patting Laura's hand.

"You must think I am an awful person. You helped me so much and then I turned my back on you. I did to you exactly what I was trying to avoid happening to me," she put her hand over Kristy's, "I am so sorry. You didn't deserve that."

Kristy smiled, "Don't beat yourself up about it please. I'm surprised you didn't move away from Tulsa after the five years was up."

"I thought about it. I was so stressed out all the time. I mentioned something to Milo but he got very upset. He had made a lot of friends and he turned out to be a bigger snob than the rest," Laura looked at her coffee cup, "He always had the best and most expensive things. They impressed each other with material things. I just gave them to him because I felt so guilty."

"Why did you feel guilty?" Kristy asked.

"Well, I was so busy being on these committees that everyone told me I had to have a nanny. So, I hired one, then another one and they were the ones to raise my son not me. I was always gone and he started to rebel. I would bribe him with things just so he would stay out of trouble because I didn't have time to deal with it. Then everyone told me that I should send him to boarding school because a lot of the Tulsa kids came here. I thought it was a wonderful idea so I wouldn't have to worry about him," Laura snorted, putting down her finished coffee, "Hhmm. He almost didn't make it in. He barely past the entrance exam and when he was denied, I flew down here and begged them to take him. I even tried to buy his way in with a large donation but they didn't fall for that. I then gave them a sob story about how his father was killed when he was five and that he would be devastated being away from his friends. I made it sound like having another bond taken away from him would be horrible and crushing his dreams of being a quarterback like his father."

Kristy looked at her puzzled, "Really? You actually told them that?"

Laura twisted the large diamond and ruby ring that was on her right hand, "I was desperate. I couldn't deal with him anymore. They did say they needed a freshman quarterback so they said they would take him this year and review his academic standing to see if he would be welcomed back next year. Besides, how was I to face everyone back home when they heard Milo was not accepted?" Laura groaned when she realized that she would have to face them after this latest fiasco.

"What's wrong?" Kristy asked after she heard Laura groan.

Laura shook her head, "Oh God. I just realized how horrible it will be going home and facing everyone after they find out that Milo was kicked out and was using steroids. I will be shunned."

"From the sounds of it, they will do you a favor," Kristy tried to look on the bright side. "If no one talks to you, then you don't have to keep playing their little games."

Laura started laughing, "I didn't think of it that way. But, I still don't know what to do with Milo. I am so angry at him."

"I think you are angry at yourself too," Kristy was again being brutally honest, "You realize that you put him second behind all of your charities and now you are regretting it."

That was hard for Laura to hear, "You're right. I was being so selfish thinking we needed to fit in with the upper class snobs that I pushed Freddie away, pushed you and Logan away and totally ignored Milo. I can't believe I had other women raise my son."

Kristy put her hands on Laura's shoulders and turned her to face her. She looked her in the eyes and said, "The Laura I knew was an amazing mother. Milo was your world and your first priority was your son. You saved yourself because you saw the danger he was in and you didn't want him to grow up abused and without his mother. I don't know what has happened in the last eight years but I don't recognize you and that boy I saw with you was not the Milo Dixon I knew," Laura started to cry. Kristy continued, "Look at me," she demanded softly. Laura looked back at Kristy, "How did you get down here?"

Laura responded, "I flew down and took a taxi here."

"How are you going to get Milo's stuff home?" Kristy asked.

"The school said they would help me ship it home." Laura said.

Still holding onto Laura's shoulders, Kristy said sternly, "This is what is going to happen. You and your son will pack his things up and you will put them in my SUV. Tonight, after dinner, you and Milo will drive back to Guthrie with me and you will stay until you feel you can go back to Tulsa."

"But," Laura tried to say.

"No buts," Kristy was firm, "You are right. You are in no shape to go back to Tulsa and face that firing squad."

"But Milo won't want to go there," she sobbed.

"So what," Kristy almost yelled at her, "It's not about him. He has lost all privileges and needs to be disciplined. You are the one that will have to do that and you can't if you don't have support. Where have you had the most support?"

Laura sniffled, "Guthrie."

"Guthrie," Kristy confirmed, "Come home with me, stay a few days or however long it takes and we can work things out together. I know Roxy and Maureen would love to see you again. We talk about you all the time."

"Oh, how I would love to see them," Laura said with excitement. She paused thinking about Kristy's plan. She looked at her and said, "The last time you talked to me like this, I almost didn't listen. Thank God I did because you saved me."

"This is me saving you again. So, what do you say?" Kristy asked.

Laura wrapped her arms around Kristy's neck and said into her ear, "Thank you so much Kristy. I know I can work this out with your help," she pulled away from her and continued, "I would love to go back with you and you're right, Milo will have to do as I say and he needs to learn that he can no longer manipulate me."

Kristy pulled Laura back in for another hug, "Now that's the Laura I know."

Chapter 48

"Okay, now son. Call me tomorrow and let me know how your first day of school went," Kristy gave Logan one more tight hug.

"I will Mom," Logan squeezed back, "Drive carefully and let me know when you get home," he held the car door open so Kristy could get in. After he shut it, he looked at Laura in the passenger seat and said, "Bye Laura."

"Bye Logan. Good luck in school," she replied.

Logan didn't even glance into the back seat. Laura made Milo apiol- ogize but Logan knew he wasn't sincere. Milo had made his life hell and he wasn't ready to forgive that.

Kristy decided to watch the Mini-Olympics but not stay for dinner. Milo and Laura had finished packing up the car and were anxious to leave. It had been a long day and Kristy was feeling tired. She was thankful that the two-hour drive was an easy one. She checked to see if her passengers where buckled up and put the car into drive. She blew a kiss to her son and headed down the long magnolia lined driveway.

The first 10 minutes of the drive was silent. Finally, Laura broke that and said, "Thanks again for letting us go home with you. I am really excited to see Guthrie again. Do you think some of my old friends would want to see me again?"

Kristy laughed, "Yes. Of course, they do. Roxy still talks about you and people always ask how you are doing."

"Really?" Laura thought she was forgotten, "Tell me about them? You know Maureen, Carl, Roxy, Robby."

"Well, Robby died a few years ago," Kristy looked straight ahead at the road.

"I'm so sorry to hear that," Laura said feeling heartache for her friend.

"Yes. His body was just getting weaker and finally couldn't fight off a serious case of pneumonia. I mailed you the notice but I guess you didn't get it," Kristy said.

"No I didn't," Laura said, "I would have phoned for sure if I had."

"I know," Kristy smiled at her, "And our favorite domino player Ozzie Becks didn't even make it eight months after you left."

She saw Milo in her rearview mirror turn his head to hear what she was saying. He and Logan loved Ozzie like their own grandfather. She thought Milo was sleeping in the back but obviously, he was listening to their conversation.

"Oh, sweet Ozzie!" Laura exclaimed, "He told the best stories and loved those little boys so much."

"We were his only family," Kristy added, "He actually left some money to Logan, Freddie and me. He donated a big chunk of his estate to the veterans since he was one."

"How nice of him. What did you do with your money?" Laura asked.

"Logan's money went into his education fund and I renovated the kitchen, dining room and living room. Freddie put a down payment on a house two blocks from the Egg," Kristy laughed, "It was a real fixer-upper. It took Freddie a few years to get it refinished but it looks so good now."

"Oh, how is Freddie," Laura asked shyly. She was embarrassed by the way she treated him.

"He's great! He has moved up ranks in the fire-station and is in charge of training the new recruits," Kristy saw Laura frown and look out the window. She continued, "He was a godsend to me. After he came back from Tulsa, he lived with Logan and me for quite a few years. He and Logan are like brothers. He really helped me out by looking after Logan and I gave him free rent."

Looking down at her hands, Laura asked, "Does he have a wife or girlfriend?"

"No," Kristy smiled at her, "To be honest, the break up with you was really hard on him. He tried to keep himself busy to forget you but I really don't think he has. A few girls have shown interest in him and he did take a few out but nothing came of it."

Laura was secretly happy about that, "What about Maureen? Are they still in Guthrie?"

"Oh, my yes," Kristy chuckled, "Isaac is the head football coach of the varsity Guthrie Blue Jays. Maureen is a little bit busy right now," Laura looked at her wondering why Kristy was laughing. She continued, "She and Isaac had twin boys about four years ago." "Really!" Laura exclaimed, happy to hear the news.

"That's not the best part," Kristy smiled, "They just had their second set of twins two months ago. A boy and a girl."

Laura was stunned, "You're kidding. Four, kids under the age of five. Wow. The two of us had our hands full with two, five year olds not to mention adding two more babies to the mix."

"Roxy and I try to help out as much as possible," Kristy said, "It's so nice to be around babies again. They are all really sweet. Isaac kind of runs the house like a football team."

"It is a football team," Laura laughed. Kristy saw Milo smile in the back seat.

"How is the I-35?" Laura asked.

"About the same," Kristy answered, "Carl has done some minor renovations again and it looks really good. Roxy is still there and I pick up a couple of shifts a week just because I love everyone there. Carl is such a good boss."

"He was so nice to us and really looked out for everyone," Laura paused. She realized that Kristy said she only worked a couple of shifts, "What else are you doing if you only work a few shifts?"

"Well, I have been going to nursing school," Kristy said, "I used the insurance money after Robby passed, and enrolled. I will be finished next spring."

"Good for you," Laura was very proud of her, "You were always such a good care giver to Robby."

"That's why I specialized in brain trauma," Kristy told her, "I am doing a practicum right now in a hospital in Oklahoma City. We see a lot of head trauma and concussions there. It's pretty interesting but sad at the same time."

The two ladies continued talking and catching up for the two-hour car ride. Milo sat quietly in the backseat and fell asleep for the last 40 minutes of it.

"I've got an idea," Kristy said turning to Laura, "Why don't we get something to eat at the I-35. Carl would love to see you guys."

Laura panicked, "I'm not sure if I want to see anyone. I don't want to have to explain how horrible my life is."

"They won't care," Kristy reassured her, "They will be excited about seeing you. Remember this is Guthrie, not Tulsa."

"Maybe a quick bite," Laura was still not sure if she was ready to see people.

They drove up to the I-35 Diner, "Wow. It looks so good. Carl re-painted and did some nice stonework on the outside. I really like the new windows too."

"Wait until you see the inside," Kristy looked at her watch. They walked up to the door and Kristy opened it, "After you guys."

"Yay!!" Laura heard a big cheer as she walked in. At the counter she saw Roxy, Carl and Kristy's in-laws, Bobby and Vicki. Two little African American boys came running up to Kristy and she picked them up. Laura figured they were Maureen and Isaac's twin boys. She then looked over and saw both Maureen and Isaac each holding a baby. Maureen looked so good for having two sets of twins. Laura waved at Becky and Charlie who were talking to Mary-Sue and her husband, Alex. Laura walked over to the crowd and Roxy grabbed her and gave her a big hug.

Roxy said, "It is so good to see ya' darling. You look so fancy," Roxy looked at the boy behind her and squealed, "This can't be Milo?" Laura nodded her head yes. "Come here son and give old Roxy a hug," Milo really didn't know what to do. He remembered Roxy but he felt awkward hugging her. Roxy grabbed him and said, "You look a lot like your daddy."

Bobby and Vicki came over to him, "Look at you sweetheart," Vicki said, "It is so nice to see you again." Milo smiled at them. He actually thought of them as his grandparents when he lived here.

He mumbled, "It's nice to see you too."

"What is everyone doing here?" Laura said as she gave Carl a hug.

He answered, "Your friend here," Carl pointed to Kristy, "called me and told us you were coming. I told a few friends and they told a few friends and here we are," he held out his hands.

Laura looked at Kristy, "You planned this before we left?"

"Yup," she said smiling, "I just thought you needed to have the support of your old friends."

"Here he is," Bobby said pointing to the door. Everyone turned and saw a tall, good looking blonde walk through the door. Freddie was wearing his uniform. He didn't take his eyes off of Laura when he walked over.

"Hi," Laura waved at him.

Freddie blushed and smiled shyly, "Hi," He looked around at everyone. He stammered,"Um. I um I just got off work. That's why I'm a little late."

Laura smiled, "I'm happy you're here," she looked at everyone, "I don't know what to say. I can't believe ya'll came here to see us."

Roxy put her arm around her, "Darlin'. It's been a long time and we couldn't wait to see you so we decided to throw you a party. Now come on over here and eat some of this great food Carl has put out for us. Dig in everyone!"

"Oh, my goodness," Laura snorted. She was laughing at all the funny stories Roxy, Kristy, Maureen and Carl were telling. They had reminiscing about all the strange and funny customers that have walked into the I-35 Diner. She continued, "I haven't laughed this hard in a long time" she looked at Milo who wasn't saying much but was enjoying the stories.

Bobby and Vicki were sitting at the counter when Vicki said, "I think you should write a book about life here at the diner. Those stories are wonderful." She looked at her husband, "We are going to miss living here."

"What?" Laura asked. She walked over to them and continued, "Are you moving away?"

"We sure are honey," Bobby said, "We decided it's time to move into a seniors' residence. It's getting hard for us to look after the house and yard. We love being so close to Kristy and Logan but we aren't going that far."

"Where are you going?" Milo spoke for the first time.

"Well, son," Bobby smiled at him, "We bought a nice condo in a brand new seniors' residence in Oklahoma City. It is so beautiful and only a few minutes away from Peggy and her family. See, not too far from Guthrie."

"Are you putting your house on the market?" Maureen asked.

"We are meeting with a realtor on Tuesday. It's been so long since we sold a house that I don't even know what the market is like," Bobby responded.

Kristy's childhood friend, Becky, piped up, "You shouldn't have any problem selling your house. The Egg is in a very desirable place to live."

Kristy looked at the time, "It's 8:30 already. I think we better get you home and settled in. I am going to bed early tonight."

Everyone gave another round of warm hugs. Roxy held Laura by the shoulders and said, "It is so good to see you again darling. Let's get together before you leave. I'd love to hear what you have been up to."

Laura wrapped her arms around Roxy's neck and said into her ear, "I would love that."

Freddie was talking to Kristy when Laura came up. Freddie smiled shyly at her and then said to Kristy, "So, I'm off tomorrow. Why don't I come by and fix that gate?"

Kristy started to say, "I thought you fixed it last week," she then realized he was looking for an excuse to come over to see Laura. She gave him a wink and said, "Would you mind looking at a few other things for me. I might as well take advantage of you while you are there."

"Sure. How about I come by about 10:00," Freddie stood up straighter. He waved to everyone and almost ran out the door.

"He is still as sweet as ever," Laura gushed a little bit.

Kristy could see what was happening and was thrilled. She remembered how happy they were together.

They pulled into the garage and Kristy said to them, "Why don't we unload Milo's stuff and put it in that corner," she pointed to an empty corner of the garage.

"Milo can do that himself." Laura looked sternly at him. He knew that he was in no position to argue with his mother. He just nodded his head. Laura stopped, "I just realized that I only have enough clothes for a day."

"You can borrow some of mine or we can do a little shopping tomorrow," Kristy said opening the door and walked into the back yard.

Laura walked through and said, "It looks so nice here. I see you still have the patio furniture that the neighbors gave you.

"It's looking a little worse for wear but it still works for me," Kristy said. She unlocked the back door they walked into the house.

Kristy was giving Laura a tour of the new main level when Milo walked into the screened porch. He looked up and saw stars on the ceiling. Kristy walked over and put her arm around him, "Do you remember those?" He smiled and nodded his head. Kristy waved her arm showing him that the whole ceiling was covered in stars and planets, "We've added a few more since you were here. When Logan learned about the universe and the Milky Way, we put up planets and constellations. That's the big dipper right there." She pointed to the group of stars above the door.

She had taken Laura and Milo upstairs, "Laura, why don't you take your old room and Milo can have the room next to you," she had promised Logan that he wouldn't sleep in his room. He wasn't very happy that Milo was going to be in his house. He didn't trust him and worried he would take or wreck some of his stuff.

Milo stopped as he walked past the room he used to share with Logan. It was very different without the toys and bunk bed. He did notice that the wallpaper and curtains were the same. Kristy took his arm and pulled him into the room. She took a framed poster of Oklahoma City, Thunder's point guard, Russell Westbrook off Logan's wall. The poster was covering about five baseball-sized holes. She looked at Milo and said, "Do you remember how these got here?"

She heard Laura gasped. Milo laughed and nodded his head, "Logan and I decided we needed to play baseball on a rainy day. Those are our homeruns."

Laura and Kristy started laughing. Laura said, "I remember that I told you boys that you had to fix those holes."

"Oh, they did," Kristy added, "They stuffed the holes with tissues." They all laughed, "We decided to just cover the holes with a picture until we re-painted the room. As you can see, we haven't. Logan won't let me because he loves his cowboy wall-paper," she walked over to the closet door and opened it, "That reminds me. I think you left something here that we were going to give back to you the next time you visited," Kristy pulled out a ratty stuffed tiger, "Do you remember this guy?"

Milo walked over and took the tiger from her, "Timba," he said looking into his face.

Laura walked over and took Timba from Milo, "We got him for you so Logan's stuffed polar bear had a friend. What was that bear's name?"

"Bumper," Milo responded. He looked around the room to see if Logan still had him. He spotted Bumper on the bed.

Kristy went over and picked up Bumper, "He has lost an eye and all his stuffing has seemed to gather into his butt. He is one well-loved bear."

Milo looked back at the closet. Something on the top shelf caught his eye. He walked into the closet and saw a present wrapped in little boy paper. He saw a tag that was written by a kid. It said. *Happy Birthday Logan. Your buddy MILO.* The "y's" were backwards and Milo was in all caps. He always wrote his name that way until his second grade teacher refused to accept his work unless he had written it with a capital "M" and lower case "ilo".

Kristy saw him looking at it. She said, "He was so disappointed that you didn't come and give it to him yourself. It has been sitting up there all these years," she pulled down a framed picture that was sitting next to it on the shelf, "Do you remember this picture?"

Milo tucked Timba under his arm and took the picture from her and nodded. Laura said, "I have always loved that picture. It is so cute of the two of you sharing your popsicles. You have this picture, don't you?"

"Yeah," Milo answered, "I don't know where it is."

Kristy took it from him and put it back on the shelf and closed the closet door, "Well guys, it's been a long, busy day. If you don't mind, I think I'll head to bed."

"I'm exhausted too," Laura said, "I think we should all hit the sack. What do you say Boo?"

He hadn't heard her call him that in a long time. He smirked, "Yeah. Getting kicked out of school takes a lot out of you," Laura and Kristy chuckled. He saw a book sitting on Logan's book self. He walked over and picked it up. He looked at Kristy and asked her, "Do you mind if I read this?" It was a kid's book that Logan got for his fifth birthday. "Logan was reading this to me when we moved. I never did hear the ending."

"Of course, Milo. Good night all," Kristy said as they walked out of the room.

"Good night," the Dixons said back.

The next morning, Kristy woke up to the smell of coffee and bacon. It took her a few minutes to realize that it must be Laura making breakfast. She looked at her clock and saw that it was 9:30. She sat up and pulled the cover off her. As she was running to the bathroom, she thought to herself. *I must have been extremely tired. I haven't slept past 7:30 in years.*

As Kristy was walking down the stairs, she heard voices and laughter coming from the kitchen. She walked into the kitchen and saw her in-laws sitting at the table and Freddie standing next to Laura who was pulling muffins out of the oven.

"Well good morning sleepy head," Vicki said as she poured Kristy a cup of coffee.

She took the cup and said, "If I'd gotten the invite for this breakfast party, I would have been up a while ago."

"I didn't get one either," Milo said standing behind her rubbing the sleep out of his eyes.

"I haven't slept that good since I moved from here," Laura said walking over and kissing her son's head, "I have forgotten how comfortable that bed is. I was up at 7:00 and full of energy. I decided I wanted to make breakfast but you didn't have any eggs. I saw that Bobby was in his backyard so I went over and asked for some. That's when I asked both of them to come for breakfast. I then sent a text to Freddie and told him to come a little early and join us too."

Milo sat down at the kitchen table and poured himself some coffee. Laura put the hot muffins on the table and Freddie brought the bacon. They both sat down. Laura was really excited about something. She looked at Kristy and said, "Bobby, Vicki and I have been talking. I can't believe how much I've missed Guthrie. Last night reminded me of that. I have been so unhappy with that life-style in Tulsa and it just doesn't suit me. I have decided that Milo and I are going to move back here and I am buying your in-law's house."

Kristy was shocked. She looked at the smiling Bobby and Vicki. Freddie stopped chewing and said, "Really? You're moving back?"

Milo was the only one not smiling, "What? You decided this without asking me?"

Laura looked at him and said sternly, "Yes I have. After what you have put me through the last few years, I feel this is the best thing for us."

He crossed his arms and said, "What I've put you through. It would have been nice if you were around and not going off to your charity things. I hated most of my nannies and I just wanted you to come and watch me play sports. Do you know that kiss you just gave me was the first one in a long time?"

Laura softened her eyes. She said to him, "I'm so sorry son. You are so right... I haven't been there for you," she put her hand out towards him, "Don't you see why it's so important we move back to Guthrie? We have so many wonderful memories in Guthrie and I know I will be back to the mother I should've been all along."

Milo turned his head away from her, "My friends are in Tulsa."

"Your friends are as fake as mine," she said, "They only liked us because we have money. I doubt their parents will want them hanging out with someone who got kicked out of school and is a steroid user."

"Do you know how many of those kids use steroids? Where do you think I got the idea and the drugs?" He snarled at her, "A lot of them do other drugs as well."

Laura raised her voice a little, "I know their kids use drugs and their parents probably know too. The disgrace is on those that get caught and then the gossip starts," she looked at the others, "That is how screwed up that rich lifestyle is. It has changed the both of us and I can't take it anymore."

Kristy, saw how frosty the room had gotten, spoke first, "I think that is a wonderful idea. Milo can go to Guthrie High and I know Isaac said he was looking for a good running back. One that is steroid free of course."

"I'm a quarterback, like my dad," Milo snapped at her.

"Your dad was a loser," Laura blurted out. Milo got up to leave the room but Laura blocked his way, "I hate to say that I can see a lot of his bad traits in you and I want to stop it now."

Milo started to push his Mother out of his way when Freddie stood up and put his hand on Milo's chest, "Why don't we go outside and have a little chat," Freddie said. Milo looked from Freddie to Laura and decided he better go. As they walked out, Laura grabbed the back of the chair and let out a sob.

Kristy got up and put her arm around her. She said to Laura, "You are doing the right thing. This is your chance to just concentrate on your son and living your life on your own terms."

Laura sat down and wiped her nose with the back of her hand. Vicki said to her, "You can make a nice little home and give that boy some structure. His was probably acting out just to get your attention."

Laura smiled at her and said. "I think you're right. One of the first things I will do when we get settled here is to find a good family therapist to help both of us," she started chuckling, "Not to be pushy or anything. When are you guys moving? I can't wait to move back here."

They all laughed. Bobby said, "The movers will be here in three weeks. We are having a great big garage sale next week. We have 28 years of stuff in that house and of course we can only take a quarter of it."

Kristy could see that Laura was disappointed, "You two can live with me until the house is ready. Why don't you call a contractor and take this opportunity to do some renovations?"

Laura's mood changed. "You're right. I think I will do reno's if it's okay with you?" She looked at Vicki.

Vicki started laughing, "It's your house now darlin'. One of the reasons we decided to move was because it needed a lot of fixing up. I say, have at it."

Laura put her arm around Vicki, "You know what else I'd like to do? I want to open my own bakery."

"Won't that be a lot of work? What about Milo?" Vicki pointed out.

"I wouldn't do it until we are settled and getting along," Laura said, "Milo can come and work at the bakery and learn how to earn money; not just stand there with his hand out."

Kristy said, "I think that's a great idea. Everyone around here really misses your baking. You can start small and work your way up. It would be less complicated that way. What are you going to do with the Tulsa house?"

"I will sell it. It shouldn't be too hard because I have had a few people asking if I would sell," Laura continued, "There are some very valuable antiques and artwork in it so I think I will have an auction. It will be sad to see it go because my Aunt Melba worked so hard building up her collection. I just don't appreciate it like she did so hopefully, people who do know and appreciate those pieces will buy them," she paused for a few moments then said, "I think I will use the money made from the sale of the house and the auction to build safe houses for abused women and their families. I want to name them *The Stella Mason Women's Crisis Center* after my mother." Everyone liked her idea. Laura continued, "These shelters will be in small towns around the mid-west. I probably would have left Jason sooner if I knew I had somewhere to go. The first one I will build will be in Park City, Kansas."

Freddie and Milo walked through the back door. Laura stood up and tried to read the mood on their faces. Freddie gave her a crooked smile and she could she Milo had tears in his eyes. He walked over to his Mom and wrapped his arms around her. He buried his face into her shoulder. She pulled him in, resting her tear stained cheek on his head. He looked at her and said, "Mom, I'm so sorry for being such a jerk. Freddie and I had a good talk and I think it would be great to be back here. It will be different, but at least you will be my mom again."

Laura kissed the top of his head, "I'm so happy to hear you say that," she looked at Freddie and gave him a grateful smile, "After breakfast, let's go for a walk and we can discuss things. I think we need to make a lot of plans for our new life."

Epilogue

One year later

"Okay everyone!" Kristy shouted over the loud chatter in the backyard, "I just got a text from Sadie and they should be here in about five minutes. He will come in through the house so let's try to be quiet now please."

There was a hushed whisper of anticipation. Kristy, with the help of Logan's girlfriend Sadie, Laura, Freddie and Milo, had planned a surprise party for his 15th birthday. Logan's grandparents were there along with his Aunt Peggy and her family. Peggy was sitting with Laura looking at Freddie and Laura's wedding photos. Peggy whispered, "I can't believe you surprised everyone like that. They showed up thinking you were throwing a New Year's Eve Party and they walked right into a wedding. How did you pull that off?"

"Easy. I only told my Maid of Honor, Kristy, Milo, Logan, Carl, who officiated and of course my fiancé Freddie. They were sworn to secrecy and really it was a New Year's Eve party with our, "I dos", as the entertainment," Laura said standing up. She stretched out her back and rubbed her protruding stomach, "Our first wedding anniversary may be spent in the hospital welcoming this little girl into our lives."

Kristy came running over to her and asked with concern, "Are you okay? Do you need a more comfortable chair?"

Laura laughed, "Would you stop playing nurse for one second. I know you are her Godmother but you can't be so bossy. I just have to stretch out once in a while. Having a baby at 32 is a lot different than having a baby at 18," Kristy put her arm around her friend. Laura put her head on Kristy's shoulder and continued, "I'm glad the second Crisis Center will be open and running before little Stella is born. I'll be a little busy for a while," Laura smiled and rubbed her stomach. She and Freddie were so excited about their growing family.

They heard a car door slam and then Logan say, "Thanks for the ride Freddie. Just think, this time next year I may have my driver's license and I won't need you to chauffeur me around."

Everyone sat quietly. A few of Logan's friends started giggling. Kristy put her finger to her mouth and shh'd them. They put their hands over their mouths because they couldn't stop. From inside the house, they heard, "Mom! Hey Mom where are you."

Sadie said, "Maybe she's in the back?"

Logan opened the back door and everyone shouted, "Surprise! Happy birthday!" Logan almost lost his footing on the steps. Sadie grabbed his shirt and steadied him.

She then hugged him from behind and whispered in his ear, "Happy Birthday blue eyes."

He looked around at the yard full of his family and friends. Of course, Roxy and Carl were there. Along with Maureen and Isaac and their four adorable, rambunctious kids. He saw his best friends from Guthrie Eric and Lucas. Lucas had his arm draped around his new girl- friend. Andrew and his sister Hannah drove up from Oklahoma City. He nodded to Mark and Dwight from the school basketball team. In the back, he saw Milo standing there with a big cheesy grin on his face.

Next to him was his girlfriend Beth, whose mother Rita looked after them when they were in kindergarten. It was Milo's idea to throw him a surprise birthday party.

The summer had been a good one for the two boys. Milo had a wonderful school year at Guthrie High School and learned the meaning of true friends. He loved having a mother again even though she was pretty strict. But the best part for him was having a father too. Freddie didn't put up with any of his crap and wouldn't let Laura either. The therapist really helped them become a family again and he was so excited to become a big brother.

When Logan got home for the summer, things had been a little tense between them. Freddie kept bringing them together by going camping with them or having them help him with chores. Milo sincerely apologized to both Logan and Sadie. He was over her and only had eyes for his old daycare friend, Beth. She was a little shorter than Milo and had long brown hair. She had just gotten her braces off and he was mesmerized by her beautiful smile. He finally got the nerve up to ask her to the Spring Dance and they have dated ever since.

While Logan went around hugging his family, Laura and Freddie slipped out the back gate to get the birthday cake Laura made. A few minutes later, they came back through the gate and Freddie was carrying a very large cake that looked like a basketball. Everyone started singing and when they had finished, Logan said, "Gee thanks for coming everyone. That was a great surprise. I'm not sure what to wish for," he found his mother and smiled, "I have everything I could ask for."

"How about a basketball team that makes it past the first round of playoffs," Dwight yelled. Everyone laughed and Logan closed his eyes. He blew out the candles but made sure to leave one lit.

"Good thing you only have one girlfriend." Sadie teased. "It's hard enough for you to keep up with me, let alone two or three more."

"What do you mean?" he retorted, "Are you a little sore that I beat you in tennis today?"

Sadie just smiled at him like she was keeping a secret. He read her mind, "Do you mean you let me win?" She tried to look innocent. Logan continued with a smile. "Well, that was the best birthday present you could have given me," he grabbed her and gave her a kiss.

"Okay everyone! Dinner is served! Kristy yelled and everyone immediately stood up and walked over to the food.

Logan went up to Laura and gave her a hug for making the cake. She was baking part-time. When she did the renovations to the house, she put in an industrial kitchen with three ovens. She was back baking for Carl again as well as other coffee shops in and around Guthrie. She even made her own, four-tiered, gold and cream wedding cake as well as a firehouse groom's cake for Freddie.

After dinner, everyone gathered around Logan as he opened his birthday presents. Some of the boys were on their second helping of cake and ice cream. After Logan opened the last present, he stood up and said, "Thanks everyone for the wonderful gifts. I am still stunned that you are all here and that you kept this a secret from me," he looked at Andrew, "Especially you big mouth."

"Hold on," someone yelled from behind. Logan turned around and saw Milo coming out the back door with his hands behind his back. Milo continued, "You have one more gift to open," Milo pulled a brightly colored gift out from behind his back and held it out to him. Logan recognized the gift that had sat on his closet shelf for so many years. Milo said, "To Logan. From your buddy, MILO."

Logan took it from him and gave him a side hug. He asked Milo, "Do you remember what it is?"

"No clue," Milo answered, laughing, "I'm dying to find out."

Logan ripped into the paper and said, "Me too." After the paper was off, he saw that it was a remote control Red 1972 Corvette Stingray. They saw one at the I-35 Diner one time and they both fell in love with it. Logan just stared at the picture and said, "Awesome," Logan looked at Milo and smiled and Milo shook his head. They both took off into the house.

About 10 minutes later, Kristy walked up to Laura and asked, "Have you seen Logan? His Grandparents are about to leave and they want to say good-bye."

"Last I saw of him, he and Milo ran into the house," Laura answered. Both Laura and Kristy went in to the house to look for them.

From out in front, they heard, "Whoa. That was awesome,"

The two women looked out the front window and saw the boys taking turns driving the Stingray. They walked out onto the front porch and watched them. Logan was trying to do a donut with it but it kept flipping. Luckily, it was made of durable metal and only the paint job was scratched.

The friends started laughing at their sons. Laura said, "It's like they were five again."

Kristy came up behind her and wrapped her arms around Laura's shoulders. She said, "It's so wonderful to have you guys back. It's like you have never left."

"I know," Laura agreed. She smiled thoughtfully, "This is where we need to be. I appreciate now what true unconditional love and friend-ship really is."

Marilyn, the youngest of four, was born in Casper, Wyoming. Having lived in Denver then Oklahoma City, at four years old, her family moved to Calgary, Alberta, Canada. She grew up in Calgary but did move to Spokane, Washington to pursue a career teaching high school and middle school special education. The love of Calgary and the beautiful Canadian Rockies brought her back to her home.

Marilyn loves to travel, play tennis, badminton, curl, ski and hike. She is an avid sports fan, loves going to movies and reading.

Her biggest passion is her family and is very proud to be the mother of her daughter, Charlotte.

Acknowledgements

I came up with the idea for this book 15 years ago. I told my mother about it and said to her, "I want it to take place in your childhood home of Guthrie, Oklahoma". We visited Guthrie in 1991 and I fell in love with the town, her stories and her memories. My mom, Sanjean Remund, grew up on the "egg" and my grandfather; Milo Remund is "Baldy Mike." I just wish she and my father, William Oakley, were still alive to see the finished book.

Dad grew up in Barnsdall, Oklahoma and they met at the University of Oklahoma. To this day, the Oakley's are still Sooner fans. I am so grateful they shared their childhood stories with us. These stories were inspirational and helped me understand what it was like to grow up in Oklahoma.

My sweet, wonderful daughter, Charlotte Tetley encouraged me to write. She had put reminders all over the house in the form of yellow sticky notes with "write your book" on them… I still have one on my mirror. She was very helpful with editing and bouncing ideas off of and I loved sharing this experience with her.

I am so grateful to Susan Kingsley for reading, editing, pushing and encouraging me to finish this book. Like Milo and Logan, we were best friends at five. I still have memories of us holding hands as we entered the school heading to first grade, trick-or-treating and how she rode to my house and got my mom when I wiped out on my bike. I'm sure we shared popsicles too.

I have so many cheerleaders that I would like to thank. Your support over the years has helped so me get through this process. Cathy Schneider, Wendy Lambert and my sweet sister, Susan King... thank you.

I must acknowledge my constant companion during the writing of this book. My English springer spaniel, Casey was either under my feet or lying beside me during the writing of this story. You have been gone for a year now but I can still feel you right next to me where you were for 14 wonderful years.

A big thank you goes to Sandy Oakley of Sandy Oakley Photography. Your talent came in handy with the cover photo and my bio picture. I have had this book cover pictured in my mind for many years and you were able to bring it to reality.

It was so much fun shooting the cover pictures with my great-nephew Hayden Oakley and his best friend Joey Meier. You did a wonderful job boys and ate a lot of popsicles in the process!

I would like to thank someone who I have only talked to briefly. I was at a spring bazaar in Spokane, Washington when I heard beautiful music coming from two rows over. I followed the instrumental music and found Brian Crane selling his CD. I bought it and still play it constantly after 20 years. It is so calming and I play it during bad times as well as good. It has gotten me over some rough spots in life and helped me through writing the emotional passages of this book. "Morning Light" is my favorite.

I am so blessed to have the family I do. I would like to thank my brothers, Bill and Mike as well as my brother-in-law Fred. You made growing up very interesting. I have unconditional love for my nieces, nephews and great-nephews. Sara, Matt, Reese, Erica, Pete, Tyler,

Sandy, Wendy, Chris, Todd, Kimberly, Hayle, Quinn, Hayden, Brycen, Kai and Nixon.

I would also like to thank Gary Cochrane, Sean, Jamie, Carissa, Jennie Hunt, Christine Oakley, Susan Watkins and all my wonderful friends who will be so surprised I have written this book.

Last but not least...my sweet wonderful sister Sue. You are the best sister in the world. We have never fought because you are so patient and full of love. You have shown me so many things. Unconditional love, beauty, grace, strength and what living "Life Unconditionally" really looks like. You are my hero and rock star. I love you.

Crisis Websites and Hotlines

Dear Readers,

The message in this story is to expect life to change for the good or for the bad. There are many things we can't control in our lives. When times are bad, this can lead to feelings of hopelessness, depression and suicide. The actions of others who rob us of our dignity and health can be so hard for anyone to deal with. Mental health is another factor that is so hard to predict and control. If you are dealing with mental health issues yourself or know someone who is, understand this can be so lonely and isolating.

As you have read in this story, life can hit rock bottom but there is a happy ending to your story if you have faith and take that first step to getting there. You can't do this alone and you shouldn't have to. Listed below are numerous resources in the form of websites, support groups and hotlines that can be called if you find yourself down and out. What I have listed just skims the surface of what's out there. Remember, they are in the business to make positive changes in people's lives and give so much love and support to those who desperately need it.

If you or anyone you know are showing signs of being suicidal, abused, bullied, addicted or having a hard time coping with life, please,

please find that happy ending by contacting anyone to help. Calling **911** or talking to someone involved in a church could be a good place to start. Reaching out to an organization listed or online will be life changing.

I, myself, have gone through many ups and downs but luckily, I have a wonderful support system in family and friends. Not everyone has one but there are people out there that want to be that support system. Please contact them as soon as possible. Your life is worth it and happiness is right around the corner.

With much love,

Marilyn E. Oakley

If you are feeling or are victim of the following (this is only a small example) please seek help:

distress	domestic abuse	crisis
crime	dementia	depression
addiction	debt	bullying
veteran affairs	youth crisis	postpartum depression
suicidal	violence	sexuality
family crisis	bereavement	rape
homelessness	single parent	LGBT discrimination
child protection	mental health	eating disorders
child abuse	racial discrimination	cyber violence
	PTSD	

No Problem Is Too Small!

WORLDWIDE

YOUR LIFE COUNTS: www.yourlifecounts.org

WORLD YWCA: www.worldywca.org
Email: worldoffice@worldywca.org

CANADA

DISTRESS CENTRE: www.distresscentre.com
403-266-4357 or for the hearing impaired: 403-543-1967
Call 24/7
Email: help@distresscentre.com

DOMESTIC ABUSE SERVICES: www.domesticabuseservices.ca
1-888-833-7733
Call 24/7
Email: das_olgcs@telus.net

KIDS HELP PHONE: www.kidshelpphone.ca
1-800-668-6868
Call 24/7

NATIONAL YWCA: www.ywcacanada.ca
416-962-8881
Email: national@ywcacanada.ca

USA

NATIONAL SUICIDE PREVENTION LIFELINE: www.suicidepreventionlife-line.org
   1-800-273-8255
   Call 24/7

CRISIS CLINIC: www.crisisclinic.org
   1-866-427-4747

CRISIS TEXT LINE: www.crisistextline.org
   Text to 741-741

THE NATIONAL DOMESTIC VIOLENCE HOTLINE: www.thehotline.org
   1-800-799-7233 (SAFE)

WHEN GEORGIA SMILED (domestic abuse): www.whengeorgiasmiled.org
   Click on the "GET HELP" button on the right side. Listed are even more websites, support groups, resources and phone numbers.

UNITED KINGDOM

RAPE CRISIS CENTRES: www.rapecrisis.org.uk
   0 808 802 9999

SAMARITANS: www.samaritans.org
   116 123 (free call)
   Call 24/7
   Email: jo@samaritans.org

SUPPORTLINE PROBLEMS: www.supportline.org.uk
   Helpline: 01 708 765200
   Calm: 0 800 585858
   Hope line UK: 0 800 0684141
   Email: info@supportline.org.uk

77757010R00219

Made in the USA
Columbia, SC
27 September 2017